SHEE ...ES

The attack ... olf boldness. They ha~~ ... ~~ had taken what they wanted without challenge, and they had grown confident. Now they wanted her sheep.

Now they wanted her.

The pack leader, silver-tipped-black and immense, faced Faia and strode stiff-legged forward; head down, ears flat back, pale, cold eyes gleaming. His lips drew back from yellowed teeth. He rumbled a warning growl as he advanced.

She clutched her staff, and her belly tightened with fear. There was no time to reach for the slingshot and the studded wolfshot. She made a quick thrust at the beast with her walking stick that caught him in the teeth. He danced back, and crouched for a leap, his eyes fixed on her throat.

Lady, help me!

Faia drew the earth's energy, thinking it into her staff, thinking, *Give the staff strength!*

And somehow, she was outside of herself, and staring down at the massive black wolf and the tall, rangy girl who faced him off with nothing but a brass-tipped walking stick.

At the same instant, she was inside herself, and the strength was there—earth-strength, Lady-strength, confidence. Faia, stilled inside, deadly calm, swung the staff up as the wolf lunged and caught him across the chest; the impact of his great weight flung her backward a staggered step. But light flowed from the staff around the wolf, blazing green fire. The wolf screamed, its voice for a moment disconcertingly human. Then he crumpled to the ground and was still—unmarked, stone dead.

At the scream, the other wolves vanished into the forest, disappearing like the memories of shadows.

MAGE IN
SHEPHERD'S CLOTHES

Fire in the Mist

Holly Lisle

FIRE IN THE MIST

This is a work of fiction. All the characters and events portrayed in this book are fictional, and any resemblance to real people or incidents is purely coincidental.

A Baen Books Original

Baen Publishing Enterprises
P.O. Box 1403
Riverdale, NY 10471

ISBN: 0-671-72132-1

Cover art by Stephen Hickman
Map by Ellen Kostyk

First Printing, August 1992
Second Printing, March 1993

Distributed by Simon & Schuster
1230 Avenue of the Americas
New York, NY 10020

Printed in the United States of America

This book is dedicated to my Mom and Dad, who told me I could do anything I wanted—and who meant it.

SOUTHEAST TRILLING

WEN TRIBES
1 Allwater 4 Blackstone
2 Pennfish 5 Firemountain
3 Smoke

ARHEL

DELMUIRIE'S BARRIER

PENNAR CHAIN

AMOTIC ISLE

BÓSÉLEIGH BAY

SAG SEA

PENNAR

Wennish Jungles

Ono Bay

PUNDAK OCEAN

CUMBLEY SEA

Wen. Tribes
Omwimmee Trade
Treaty Line

Little Tam

Big Tam

Gunnit

Maisee
Cliffs

Cumbley Bay

ARISS

FEY PLATEAU

Hak

Dumforst

Otwoch

Swom

Bonwite

BOOAR MTS.

Bright

Willowlake

Sairefe

Belldote

Fey Branch River

Braxille

Punce

Cailte Pass

Chak River

Kéle Bay

KÉLE SEA

LITTLE SOUTH SEA

Hoös Domain

DELMUIRIE'S BARRIER

Stone Teeth

Chapter 1

A Pox on Bright

In front of a fieldstone cottage, on a crisp spring morning, Risse Leyeadote and her leggy, dark-eyed daughter, Faia, hugged each other goodbye.

Faia pulled away first and grinned. "I love you, Mama. I will see you soon."

"Such a hurry. My youngest daughter cannot wait to abandon me for the flocks and the fields."

"Oh, Mama—!"

Risse laughed, then held out a wrapped packet and a necklace. "Take these, Faiachin. I have more than enough jerky here to get you to the first of the stay-stations, and I have finished the work on a special amulet—added protection against wolves. And I am sending my love. You have your *erda*?"

Faia nodded.

"Wolfwards?"

Another nod.

"Knife? Herb bag? Matches? Needles? . . ."

Faia nodded at each item on her mother's list until

1

finally she burst out laughing. "*Mama!* How many years have I been taking the flock upland? I have everything I need. I will be fine, the sheep will be fine, the dogs will be fine, and I will see you in late summer with a nice bunch of healthy lambs and fat ewes."

Her mother smiled wistfully. "I know, love. But it is a mother's job to worry. If I did not, who would? Besides, I miss you when you are not here."

Faia's face grew serious for a minute. "I always miss you, too, Mama—but it will not be forever."

Her mother nodded. "Have you said your goodbyes to Rorin or Baward yet?"

Faia caught the conspiratorial inflection and winked. "To Rorin, yes. Last night. Baward is going to meet me at the Haddar Pass pasture in about a month, and we are going to—ah, graze the flocks together for a few days."

"Are you, now?" Her mother smiled a bit wistfully, remembering long summers in her own youth spent "grazing the flocks" with one young shepherd or another. "Remember to use the alsinthe, then. Well, I'm glad you aren't going to be up there alone the whole time. Really, Faia, there seem more wolves than usual this year. Do not forget to set the wolfwards. Not even once. Remember, Faljon says, 'Wolves need not knock/at the door that's open.'"

Faia hugged her mother again, then whistled for the dogs. "I know, Mama. I know." She hung the brightly colored chain of the silver-and-wolf-tooth amulet around her neck and tucked the jerky into one of the pockets of her heavy green felt *erda.* "Love you, mama."

"Love you, too, Faiachin," she heard her mother call when she was halfway down the slope to the pasture.

Faiachin, Faia thought, and winced. *Sometimes she still thinks I am five years old instead of nineteen.*

Chirp and Huss, black-and-white streaks of barking energy, were under the fence and hard at work before she could even get across the stile. They needed little direction from her to pack the sheep into a nice tight bunch and get them moving to the gate. Diana, the old yellow-eyed lead goat, knew the routine too. She trotted up to Faia and stopped. Faia put the supply harness on her, and checked to make sure the bags on either side were securely attached. The bags held emergency rations for Faia and the dogs and coins for the stay-stations. They also made Faia's pack lighter, and she was grateful for that.

Faia scratched the goat behind the ears and tapped her once on the rump with her staff to hurry her to her place at the front of the flock. That done, the flock, the dogs, and she moved onto the narrow two-rut cart-path that would dwindle to a dent in the grass by the time they got to the highlands.

The sheep, their bellies already starting to swell with lambs, looked oddly naked after the shearing. They trotted after Diana while Chirp and Huss ran vigorously at their heels, nipping and barking and otherwise trying to demonstrate to Faia that they were the only reason the sheep were going anywhere. Faia suspected a fair amount of the show at this point was just because the dogs were so damned glad to be heading for the highlands again.

And as for her—

She started whistling. The tune was "Lady Send the Sunshine," but she thought up some words for the chorus, and switched abruptly from whistling to raucous singing.

> "No damned shearing
> No more carding,
> No more spinning
> And no dyeing!
> No more weaving
> And no sewing—
> Flocks must to the uplands go."

She liked it enough that she trilled it a few more times, getting louder and louder with each rendition, until with her last chorus, she threw in some silly dance steps with her brass-tipped staff as her partner.

The trees that lined the lane arched over her head, blossoming or barely greening; spring smelled fresh and earthy and new; and, *Lady, it is good to be on my way and free!* was the thought foremost in her mind.

At the top of the first hill, the trees were cleared and she turned to look back at Bright nestled below her. At her own house, which lay nearest her point of view, a wisp of smoke rose from the chimney. Further back, the smith's forge was already going at full blast, and she could just catch the steady "clink, clink" of the smith's hammer on the anvil as it drifted across the distance. The littlest children played tag in the cobblestoned street; their older sibs helped mothers and fathers with the serious work of readying the plows and harnesses for ground-breaking and planting. She could see Nesta shoving round loaves of bread into the tall stacks of ovens—an older relative of those loaves rested in her pack, along with some cheese from Nesta's sister Gredla.

She smiled. Home, wonderful, home—where just at the moment, unfortunately, everybody was busy as birds with nestlings. Thank the Lady for giving her the gift of tending; if it were not for that, she'd be home doing the dull labor, like tilling or planting or pulling weeds, and some other lucky soul would be heading for the hills for the summer. For, thanks to her magic with flocks and dogs, ahead for her lay the upland pastures. There she could dally about and play her rede-flute and watch the stars and admire the newborn lambs when they came. And cloudgaze nearly to her heart's content.

The flock trotted onward, and she blew Bright a smug little kiss and hurried after them.

*   *   *

Risse watched her youngest child depart and felt a special pang of maternal longing. Nineteen years old, tall, strong, and beautiful, Faia was everything she could have hoped for in a daughter, and more. In spite of Faia's heated arguments to the contrary, Risse was sure there would be special young men soon; not the current casual lovers, but men Faia would want to have children with. And Faia's life would change, as she had to accept responsibility for babies. She would have less time to wander in the hills, less time to play with her dogs. Risse tired to imagine her daughter with children, and came up with a mental picture of Faia with beautiful babies swaddled on her back as she bounded across an upland pasture after her sheep. The older woman grinned. It was actually the only way she could imagine her youngest with children.

She will be such a boon to the village—when she grows up and gets her father's wayfaring ways out of her system.

There was more to Faia than stubbornness and independence and wanderlust, though, and Risse worried about that, too.

She has more of the Lady's power than I have ever sensed before—even if it has not surfaced yet. She's like a river—deep and quiet and unbelievably strong. I just wish she had more interest in exploring her talent—the Lady does not give gifts in order for them to be wasted.

Risse shrugged her anxieties off. She was having plain old mother-worries compounded by the fact that this was the last of her four children to grow up. Those worries, added to her "wolf-worries," were giving her the worst case of jitters she'd ever had. Still, life was dangerous. She carried memories of packs of wolves, sudden snow-squalls, avalanches, big mountain cats, and crumbling mountain paths from her own summers spent with the sheep. The highlands posed threats even to smart, cautious, experienced shepherds like her daughter. She hoped Faia did not run into more trouble than she could handle.

The amulet should help. I spent enough time and energy on it. If she finds out what it really does, though ... Faia's mother shook her head ruefully. Faia's independence was legendary in Bright. *Faia* asked help from no one—never had, even as a tiny child, and, Risse figured, probably never would. So Risse had done a thing she considered slightly sneaky. She made a link between her and her daughter, which would let her know if Faia needed help without having to wait for Faia to ask.

The amulet would do exactly what she'd told her daughter it would do. It would ward off all but the boldest or most crazed of wolves, two- or four-legged. But it would also carry a distress message from Faia to her mother, who could then summon help. *There's a chance Faia will sense the link*, Risse thought. It wasn't likely. Faia rarely heard—or felt—anything that she didn't want to hear. Besides, it was a chance Risse had to take. Her nerves screamed with the possibilities of disaster—*wolves*, her dreams said—and the signs of wolves were heavier this year than they had been in a decade. She had an uneasy feeling about them.

Risse had learned to trust her feelings.

Half an hour's walking made Faia think that the jerky in her pocket might be getting lonely for the company of her stomach, so she pulled one of the leathery strips of meat out of her mother's packet and began to introduce them. Diana had taken goatish interest in the tender, juicy leaves on the trees and refused to lead the flock along the road, the sheep were already doing their mindless best to wander everywhere but where Faia wanted them, and the dogs acted as if they suddenly remembered that these trips to the uplands were not all play. Faia wanted to laugh, but Huss and Chirp would have thought that she was laughing at them, and they would have acted hurt and betrayed for the rest of the day.

Lady forbid! Faia thought. *They try to make me feel guilty often enough without me giving them a reason.* She decided to help them out a little. After all, Huss had just finished weaning a batch of puppies—*Not a one that went for less than ten-and-a-half*, Faia thought cheerfully—and the girl figured her dogs deserved a break.

She grounded herself and mentally reached into her center. Then she closed her eyes and visualized a tunnel with high, blank walls to either side and a huge pasture of deep, luxuriant clover straight ahead. She drew energy from the earth, and sent the verdant image to Diana and into the lentil-sized minds of the sheep. They abruptly left off their munching and moved down the road, their purpose in life—the filling of their insatiable bellies—given a new direction.

But in the time that her eyes had been closed, a stranger had appeared over the crest of the next hill, riding toward her. His beast was a solid-looking bay with an excellent gait, well-formed and beautiful, but white-footed. Faia spat surreptitiously to one side to avert the bad luck associated with white-footed horses and studied the strange rider from under the brim of her hat.

The ill-fortune was all with the horse, she decided when she got a closer look at the odd pair. That was the only way she could explain to her own satisfaction how such a scabby bit of human flesh could own such an otherwise excellent animal.

For the rider was no match for his horse. The man was pale as skimmed milk, with gaunt cheeks so pimpled Faia's face hurt in sympathy. His jerkin was well cut from expensive cloth, but flapped around his skinny frame as if it were dressing up a stick man.

The man and horse edged along one side of the flock while Faia kept to the other.

"Care you—" he began to shout, but was interrupted

by a fit of coughing. When it passed, he tried again.
"Care you to see the merchandise in my packs?"

Faia considered only an instant. His packs flapped
almost as slackly as his jerkin—there was not likely to
be much of interest in either. "Thanks, no."

"The village—?"

"You have almost arrived."

"My gratitude, then," he said as he drew even with
her.

She stepped up the embankment to be out of the
way of his horse, thinking uncharitably that such
homeliness really ought to stay at home, where innocent bystanders wouldn't have to see it.

She was glad when the dull thudding of horse's
hooves on packed dirt faded into the distance. She
went back to her intervals of whistling and singing and
jerky-munching.

Near twilight, she stopped again to water the flock
and to rest and get a drink for herself. By her best
guess, she still had a torchmark of hard pushing to get
to the first of the stay-stations. She was tired, and sank
gratefully to the grass by the side of the stream. Huss
and Chirp, tongues lolling, flopped at her feet as the
sheep and Diana lined the stream. Both dogs grinned
up at her, grateful for the break. They trotted to her
side and nuzzled her, and she split a piece of her jerky
with them.

"We have gotten soft and lazy from too much sitting
around the cottage during the winter, hey, kids?" she
asked them.

Their eyes seemed to assure her that this was truth.

She knelt on the bank upstream from the flock and
cupped her hands to draw out some of the icy water,
when suddenly a low, mournful howl took up, echoed
and reverberated down from higher ground. It was
followed by another, and yet another.

Wolves! Faia froze and concentrated, trying to

determine their number and location. *Wolves should not be this close in,* she worried.

They were not right around her, she decided after careful listening, but they *were* within half a day-walk—definitely too close for complacency. And there were a lot of them—maybe fifteen. The howls were not their hunting cry—at least, not for the time being. They were merely talking, entertaining themselves, engaging in evening wolfsong. That could easily change if they were hungry, and if they knew there was a flock of sheep within striking distance.

To Faia's animals, it did not matter whether the wolves were presently hunting or not. The sheep were already spooked, and the dogs stood rigid with hackles raised. Faia loosened her sling in her belt and made sure her special spiked shot was ready in its pouch, just in case. She admired wolves, and would not willingly harm one—but if it came to a contest between the wolves and her sheep or her dogs, she would do her best to make sure the wolves were the ones who got hurt.

Mama was right about wolves being plentiful this year, I guess.

It began to seem that the trip would be less cloudgazing and more work than she had hoped.

She whistled the dogs back to work. Making the fork as soon as possible had become suddenly not a matter of personal comfort but a matter of safety for herself and her beasts.

So much for making good time to the first stay-station, Faia grumped. What with the skittish sheep bolting off the main trail into the scrub with every branch-crack and owl-hoot, she and her flock had hiked long past the arrival of full dark before the familiar clearing finally appeared. Muscles whose existence she had forgotten throbbed, and a blister on her right heel reminded her that new boots were best saved for short trips. As she and the flock made their way toward the corral, she noted sadly that the windows of the stay-station were dark, which meant that she would have no human companionship that night—and also that no earlier arrival would have the wolfwards already set. She and Chirp and Huss struggled to get all the sheep packed into the grassy pen. Then, so bone-tired she wished she could drop on the stones to sleep, she began to set the wolfwards.

From her pack she pulled eight wooden circles—already glyph-marked with a drop of wolf urine painted with a wolf-hair brush—and laid these in a circle on the stone altar that sat just outside the fence on the north edge of the circular corral. She set her knife across them, and brought out the round, shallow stone bowl that was kept under the altar. She placed the bowl in the center of the circle, and crumbled a handful of kwilpie leaves and sweet-smelling ress powder into it, then grounded and centered herself, and visualized a circle of blazing blue that grew like a bubble from the altar. Her protective circle stretched to encompass the whole of the corral plus the stay-station that lay at the exact south point of the circle. She rested for a moment, gathering energy from the earth, then lit the leaves and powder with a quicklight. The incense blazed brilliant green.

Softly she chanted:

> "*Lady of the Beasts, Tide Mother Woman,*
> *Lady of the Earth, Virgin, Mother, Crone.*
> *Lady, loan to me your eyes;*
> *Loan to me your faeriefires*
> *To watch and ward us while we sleep,*
> *That flock and folk will safely keep*
> *Until the night is done.*"

Faia finished her chant, and touched the point of the knife to the green fire, then to each round circle in turn. As she did, there appeared above the circles small dots of green light, each no bigger than a robin's egg. They held position two fingers' breadth over the center of the disks.

When each wolfward held its beacon of faeriefire, she bowed her head for a moment.

"Lady, thanks," she said, and the fire in the bowl guttered out. She picked up the wards, and following the path of the Tide Mother around the corral, laid them out in the shape of the Lady's Wheel. Only when this was done did she gather her things and head gratefully for the stay-station. Hot tea, a soft bed, and a late rising; they all sounded awfully inviting.

She left the heavy wooden door unbarred. First, the wolfwards would warn her not only of wolves, but also of the arrival of any other danger. Second, if the wolves were desperate or brazen enough to challenge the wards, she would need to get through the door quickly. With that in mind, she also placed her sling, her staff, and her wolfshot on the stand beside the door.

Huss and Chirp settled themselves on the stone step outside. Faia dug through the stockroom, found the food kept there for shepherds' dogs, and put a bowl out for each of the two exhausted border collies. They grinned at her and wagged their tails and ate like they had never seen food before.

"Poor pups," she snorted. "Faljon says, 'Best is the meal/earned by the brow.' You two should be thankful for the hard work we did today."

Huss glanced up from the bowl and cocked an eyebrow with an expression that seemed to question the sanity of hard work, Faljon, and anyone who would quote such a ridiculous proverb.

Faia laughed and scratched her behind the ears. "Indeed. I wonder myself whether Faljon ever chased idiot sheep across the hills or fought off wolves and mountain lions or tromped for leagues with prickleburrs under his *erda*—or whether perhaps he just sat in his cottage and thought of ways to tell the rest of us how to do it."

"Still," she added, mostly to herself, "he is right about the food."

She rose and stretched and went back into the stay-station. From the storeroom, she took a packet of tea, a small box of soup powder, and two little potatoes. She put a single copper fourth-coin in the box on the storeroom door in exchange. When she had the fire in the fireplace going, and water heating for tea and soup, she sprawled across one of the station's narrow bedframes and stared at the ceiling.

It is good to be on my way again, she thought. *Sore muscles and all. Away from Bright, out from under Mama's roof and Mama's worries, maybe I'll have a chance to think.*

She had a lot to think about. Much as she loved her mother, her brothers and her sister, she had never been so glad to leave Bright as she was this spring. All winter long, her relatives had hinted to her mother that perhaps Risse would like to send her flock with one of their older children, since surely Faia would not be heading into the hills with the sheep *again*. When they asked, Risse had looked hopeful, and Faia sullenly defiant.

Risse alternated between moments of understanding her youngest child's yearning for freedom, and bouts of fury at what she perceived as lightmindedness. In the bad times, mother accused daughter of dithering with her life, of doing what amused her instead of planning for her future, for work that would be to the long-term good of the village. "You can't be a shepherd forever, Faia," she had said. You're a woman, full of woman's magic. You could become a healer, learn with me, and take over for me when I am too old and weak to continue. You could be better than I'll ever hope to be—"

Faia thought that she was quick enough with the healing lays, but she hated the idea of spending her time picking and drying herbs, mixing decoctions and elixirs, and running from house to house to deliver babies or tend the sick, dead, and dying.

Then there was Kasara, her sister, who, with a shuttle in her hand and her babes playing on sheepskin rugs on the packed dirt floor, had offered to apprentice her little sister, and give her a room out from under their mother's roof. But while Risse was gentle and thoughtful, Kasara was shrill and shrewish and wanted an apprentice, Faia suspected, to double her output without significantly increasing her costs. While Kasara had remarked that she liked the workmanship of Faia's keurn cloths, Faia doubted that once in her sister's employ she would ever be judged good enough to earn her own master's shuttles. Kasara would see to that.

The girls in Bright who were Faia's age now had babies and bondmates with whom they worked their dowry fields. And as for unbonded young men—well, there now remained only Rorin and Baward in her own age group. Either would be happy enough to form a public bond with her, but . . .

Faia rolled over on to her stomach and sighed. But *what*?

Faia did not want to be a weaver, nor a healer, nor a bondwife with babies.

When she closed her eyes, she could hear her father's voice as sharp and clear and wistful as the last time she had heard him, talking, as he had loved to do, about far-off places. "Faiachin, my little lambkin," he had said, "there is a world beyond these hills, flat as a table, full of odd folk with odd ways, and magic such as your mind cannot imagine. Flatters have not the need to chase sheep in the hills, so they spend their days playing at music and illusion and pretties for rich men and women." He had stared off toward the unseen wonderland, and sighed. "Someday, littlest, I will take you to the Flatters' lands."

He would have, Faia believed, had he lived long

enough. But her mother had loved an old man, whose body wore out long before his spirit. He had given Faia his wanderlust, but had not survived to slake it.

Faia stared at the ceiling of the stay-station. She had no real wish to see the Flatterlands anymore, she admitted to herself. Her dogs were her friends; her flock, riches; and the wondrous wild beauty of the upland fells was the magic her father had spun for her in his tales of other lands. Her hills would satisfy her— if only she could stay in them.

Though Faia heard the wolfsongs nightly during the week's travel to the high country, she never saw the wolves. They were always a few valleys away, always hunting other game that did not carry the freight of a human guardian. She stayed cautious—but her caution began to seem more a formality than dire necessity.

In the highland pastures, spring flowers poked out of the edges of melting snowfields. The rocky hills were alive with the chirruping squeals of busybody conies; otherwise the meadowland pastures were idyllic. Faia kept the wolfwards replenished nightly, and spent a busy few days as the waxing of the Tide Mother brought the majority of the lambs in a rush. For a while, it seemed she was running from sheep to sheep, working tiny hooves free from a birth canal, calming a first-time mother, making sure that each ewe was willing to nurse her own lamb or lambs, and lastly watching for signs of sickness in mothers or newborns. Lambing went well. She lost only two newborns—and them to deformity—and one mother to old age; and she tricked the mother of the deformed lambs into thinking the dead ewe's baby was hers by rubbing both beasts down with skunkweed until they smelled to high heaven . . . except to each other.

After the peak of the full Tide Mother, the rhythms of her days settled down. She watched the clouds as she had hoped to, sent the eerie melodies of her rede-flute whistling down the valleys by the light of the

stars, and danced in the high meadows for sheer love
of the goodness of life. Her anguished arguments with
her mother receded into her memory, leaving only
ghostly tracks at odd moments—the highlands were
their own balm. Mild weather and an abundance of
small rodents kept the wolves politely at their distance,
and kept her and Huss and Chirp supplied with the
occasional fresh cony or rabbit to supplement their
steady diet of jerky and shepherd's stew.

The Tide Mother, waxing when she left Bright, was
waning when premonitions started.

From a sound sleep she woke, a scream caught in
her throat.

Something is wrong!

Her heart pounded; she was drenched in sweat. She
sat shivering in her bedroll in the gray light of pre-
dawn. She grounded herself and reinforced her
shields, then sent out searching tendrils.

There was nothing nearby. Nothing. But the terror
was as palpable while she was awake as it had been
in her dreams.

Where is this coming from?

Wolves howled in the distance, the echoes ringing
up the valleys from far down into the lowerland.

*Lowerland? Where the village is? Why?! In the
winter, when they have no food, when the cold and
ice force them out of the wilds toward the flocks, of
course they migrate toward the village—but in the
midst of the most abundant spring in years?*

Something *was* wrong.

Faia shivered again.

*Faljon says, "A goose on the grave/means that grain
has grown there." That is all it is—bad dreams, the
wolves hunting an animal that has fled downland,
every bit of it is my nervousness.*

Still, she pulled off the necklace that her mother
had given her and slipped the wolf talisman off it. She
ran the chain through her fingers. The chain was an
old piece, a *kordaus* or scrying cord her mother

had used for years, decorated with thirty-three round, incised beads of varying types of stone, bone, wood, and metal, no two alike. Faia could feel the reassuring tingle of power in it. She closed her eyes and calmed herself, while the beads slipped across her fingertips with soothing steadiness.

One caught, and the comforting rhythm ceased. She opened her eyes and looked at it.

Black iron. Disease.

She winced, then closed her eyes again, centered, breathed deeply, reached inside herself.

Click, click, tick, clack, stop.

Red-stained clay. Death.

Faia's hands began to tremble. One final time, she began her rounds of the beads, begging for the reversing bead, for some sign that things were as they should be.

Click, tick, click, click, tink, click . . . stop.

Polished white shell.

—Home!—

And the wolfsong echoed up from the lowerlands, foreboding, deadly.

Goddess of Life, what am I to do?! The lambs are too young to take all the way back to the village yet— and I could be reading this wrong, or it could mean nothing, even yet, except the reflections of my own fears. That I read disease and death at home could be meaningless. Sometimes, after all, the beads do not work—at least not for me.

Faia shivered, trying to decipher the import of the wolfsong in the valley. Knowing the languages of animals was not among her talents.

Then inspiration struck. Baward had planned to leave Bright a week after she left, moving his flock of goats along a harder, faster route to the Haddar Pass pasture so that they would meet there. She and her flock were only two days from Haddar Pass.

With Baward would come information—and, she hoped, peace of mind.

She held that thought close to her heart and tried to banish her anxieties.

He is three days late. That can only mean he is not coming.

She sat nestled between the two sheltering stones, her wide-brimmed hat covering her neck, her *erda* staked like a tent over her. Both dogs crowded in beside her, understanding that their duty was temporarily suspended. Diana and the sheep and their lambs huddled miserably, their backs to the wind and the blowing, chill rain that gusted and spattered in erratic torrents. As long as the weather held, they would not go anywhere by choice. A tattered gray cloak of mist hid them from view at intervals, then parted to reveal them still in the same stodgy clumps, commiserating with each other. When the fog hid them for too long, Faia Searched to check their positions, drawing the power of the earth into her and linking with the flock. With her eyes closed, she could see the bright glow of each sheep, a glow that meant life.

Faia peered through the early twilight, still praying to the Lady that Baward would arrive. But when she Searched for him and his flock, which should have made a huge glow to her mind's eye if he were anywhere near, there was nothing but darkness.

He has been detained by the birthing of his flocks, or some sickness among the beasts. A wolf attack. Nothing serious. Or he forgot the time we agreed upon.

The excuses didn't ring true.

Come morning, lambs or no lambs, I am going home.

Several lambs died in the forced march, and the ewes dropped weight, fretted, balked. A mountain lion attacked, and won a weary ewe from Faia, at the price of one of his eyes. Her body ached, the dogs complained—and the premonitions never left her.

But if the return trip was bad, her first sight of Bright was worse.

From the hilltop on which she had last stood long weeks ago, she saw the village frozen in the cool, brilliant sunshine—the dark, blank eyes of houses stared vacantly at each other from across lifeless streets. She heard the silence that told of a smithy stilled, children hushed, farmers leaving all the fields for fallow, the market closed.

No smoke, her nose told her. Not from the cottages, not from the baker's ovens, neither from the kilns nor the washers' fires nor the dyeing vats; not from cookfires. But the air *was* scented—the reek was heavy and cloying; sweet, putrid.

Deathstench.

And on the cobblestone streets and in the pastures, Faia's eyes registered still forms. Unrecognizable, they lay scattered in piles of red and gray, bloated, tattered, with gleams of white.

Then the sheep clustered together, bleating terror, and huge dark monsters shot from the edges of the forest, and for a while Faia could not ponder the meaning of the motionless village.

The attack was not wolf madness, but wolf boldness. They had come, had taken what they wanted without challenge, and they had grown confident. Now they wanted her sheep.

Now they wanted her.

The sheep—stupid sheep—scattered in a dozen directions. A few made it to the woods intact; more, as they broke from the flock, were hamstrung or gutted or had their throats ripped out. Diana, poor old goat, stood her ground, horns slashing, and cloven hooves flying, but she was overpowered, too. The dogs darted and blurred, flashes of black and white amid the bulk of gray—and first Faia saw Chirp die, with his neck crushed between one wolf's massive jaws, then Huss screamed, and Faia saw her, her teeth still latched to a big bitch's throat, with her belly opened and her guts dragging in the dirt.

The pack leader, silver-tipped-black and immense, faced Faia and strode stiff-legged forward; head down, ears flat back, pale, cold eyes gleaming. His lips drew back from yellowed teeth. He rumbled a warning growl as he advanced.

She clutched her staff, and her belly tightened with fear. There was no time to reach for the slingshot and the studded wolfshot. She made a quick thrust at the beast with her walking stick that caught him in the teeth. He danced back, and crouched for a leap, his eyes fixed on her throat.

Lady, help me!

Faia drew the earth's energy, thinking it into her staff, thinking, *Give the staff strength!*

And somehow, she was outside of herself, and staring down at the massive black wolf and the tall, rangy girl who faced him off with nothing but a brass-tipped walking stick.

At the same instant, she was inside herself, and the strength was there—earth-strength, Lady-strength, confidence. Faia, stilled inside, deadly calm, swung the staff up as the wolf lunged and caught him across the chest; the impact of his great weight flung her backward a staggered step. But light flowed from the staff around the wolf, blazing green fire. The wolf screamed, its voice for a moment disconcertingly human. Then he crumpled to the ground and was still—unmarked, stone dead.

At the scream, the other wolves vanished into the forest, disappearing like the memories of shadows.

And Faia was left with the remains of her flock—clumps of white and bloody red—and the mangled goat, and the dogs, two motionless bundles with ripped and dirty fur that blew in the chill wind. And below her lay the village.

Her feet moved slower and slower as she approached her cottage. The stench, which had only

blown in suggestive eddies to the top of the hill, was
inescapable in the sheltered valley. Faia took two of
her scarves and wrapped them around her face. The
wolves had been at the village. Carcasses of horses
and cattle lay on the road and in the street, Baward's
goats in their pen, all their bellies ripped and tattered,
the entrails gone, decay well set in. All of them lay
where they had fallen, while vultures glared at her
as she passed and flapped their wings in threat. She
abandoned the idea of making any attempt to clean
the carcasses up. And as she drew closer, she could
see things that had not shown up from the hill. Rats
were everywhere. Doors hung partway open, and flies
roiled out of them—the sound of the village was the
sound of flies.

Faia's own door was closed, and that gave her hope.
She opened it, and inside, things were in order. There
were no flies; the deathstench was muted and obviously not coming from the house. Sunlight filtered
through the oilskin windows onto the table where
Mama's healing bag lay, empty of supplies. There was
no fire in the fireplace, but the wood was laid by the
side, ready to start. And Mama had some weaving
spread out.

"Mama?" Faia called, walking across the main room
toward the weaving. "Mama, are you here?"

Then Faia studied the weaving more closely, and
bit back panic.

*It is the same piece she was working on when I left,
and there is almost nothing done!*

And her eyes admitted to the other details she'd
been denying. Dust coated the tables, the plates that
lay out—every single surface in the two-room cottage.

Her throat ached, and her eyes began to burn.

"Mama?" she whispered, and walked into the
bedroom.

Her mother's bed was neatly made, her clothes lay
stacked in precisely squared piles on the rocking
chair, where her mother *never* left clothes, and on

the clothes pegs, everything was present except for her mother's red celebratory dress. Both her house shoes and her boots were stacked under the pegs.

What do you have on your feet, Mama?

Faia's pulse began to roar in her ears.

She turned and began running, screaming "MAMA!" as loudly as she could. She flew outside and around the house and down toward the shed and her mother's garden. *She has to be in the shed*, Faia told herself. *Mama has to be in the shed.*

But that was not where Faia found her mother.

The earth was still soft, still unsettled over the grave on the hillside, and garlands of flowers, now withered, lay in disarray. Faia studied the wood plaque with blurred eyes, fighting belief.

Those are her symbols. The healer's wand, the weaver's shuttle, the mother's circles.

And though Faia couldn't read the words painted underneath, she knew what they said.

Risse Leyeadote.

"Mama," Faia whispered, and knelt in the soft earth of the grave, and wrapped her arms around herself to fight back the tears. "Oh, Mama—I did not come back in time. I did not get back . . . Mama . . ." And then she collapsed, and lay stretched in the dirt on her mother's grave, as close as she would ever be to her mother again.

It was much later that she was able to pull herself away from the grave to walk through the village. The reek of decay was worse in some places—and finally, timidly, Faia entered her sister's home. The smell was horrible, and flies were so thick she hit scores of them every time she waved her hands to keep them out of her eyes. She pulled the scarves tighter around her nose and mouth.

Inside, the beds held the family—though Faia had a hard time recognizing them. A few days dead and badly bloated, with skin gray and edging into the bruised purple of decay, they bore the marks of agonizing disease. She could make out the mottling of pustules and open sores on each of them—Kasara; her bondmate Sjeffan; Liete, their oldest son; Vaurn, the toddler. The splashed brown of vomited blood stained the floor. All lay clutching their stomachs.

Plague!

Faia fled the cottage, bile burning in her throat. She pulled the scarves away from her mouth and vomited, then leaned weakly against the house. "Dead. All of them—Mama, Kasara, the kids, and surely my brothers, too, or these would have been buried. . . ."

Unbidden, an image rose up in her mind—a pale, gaunt, coughing man with his face covered in red spots—*Not pimples, but Plague!*—the man she had passed the day she left Bright for the highlands.

He killed all of them, she realized, and knew then that her mother would have been one of the first to die. *Mama would have tended to him, even once she knew he had Plague; would have tended to the rest of the village, too, as long as she could have. She probably could have isolated him, too, and prevented most of the deaths—except that the man was a trader, and the winter had been hard and boring and lonely for the villagers; and a little amusement, a little interest, a new face, must have exposed most of Bright to the stranger before it became apparent that he brought disease.*

So Mama, exposed early and a lot, died early. At least she had a grave, Faia thought. *At least she was spared the indignity of rotting in her bed, like the rest of my family.*

Faia shuddered as the eyes of rats studied her with speculative hunger, calculating—waiting. She flinched at the hum and buzz of the flies, at the patient smiles of the vultures. She wanted out of Bright, to be well and far away. But hope had not entirely deserted her.

Has anyone survived? she wondered.

She closed her eyes and Searched, sending desperate

tendrils to the farthest corners of the village. At first, she got nothing but the dim backglow that indicated the rats, insects, cats and birds who had inherited the village. But on the far side of Bright, past the baker's ovens, she finally picked up a solitary glow, unmoving but still blazing yellow with life. And she, who thought her heart had died from despair, felt a final surge of hope.

Do not die! she pleaded with the fragile light she Sensed. She raced through the streets, fighting back tears. *Please, please by-the-Lady, do not die.*

At the house of Sehpura Gennesdote, she stopped. The lifeforce was strongest inside. She shivered and sent a hasty prayer for protection to the Lady, tightened the mask back over her face, and hurried in before her courage could fail her. She knew she was going to see one last wasted, pocked human, dying horribly in bed, but she begged anyway that this would not be the case.

"Hello?" She called into the darkness and silence, and at first got no response. Her heart fell—this would be as bad as she had dreaded. But she called again anyway, noting with dismay the massed presence of flies, the deathstench, the lumps of unmoving shapes in the beds.

"Hello? Is anyone here?"

And a blurred shape suddenly charged her, and grabbed her by her waist, and buried its face in her breasts, sobbing. She hauled the terrified creature out of the house into sunlight, where she could identify—

A boy. Aldar Maylsonne. He was a few years younger than she—perhaps fourteen or fifteen—unmarked by Plague, so far untouched, though he had been curled up in a corner of his own house, with his dead family all around him.

For how long? Faia wondered.

"When did this happen, Aldar?"

"I don't know . . . I don't know . . . I came home today and j-j-j-just found them—"

Aldar clung to her, lost in wordless sobbing, and she held him, her own grief once again overwhelming.

But I will not be alone, she thought. *If they were all dead when he found them, he has not been exposed.* There was a little comfort in that thought.

"We have to leave." She whispered, and felt his head nod against her breast.

"I should bury them," Aldar told her. "Mama and Papa, my sibs—" His voice broke, and he started sobbing again.

"We cannot. There are too many, and only two of us."

He raised his head to stare into her eyes. "No one else is left? *No one?!*"

Faia's fingers clutched at the boy's narrow shoulders. "No one but us."

At last, he let go of her and wiped viciously at his eyes. "My pack is inside the house. It has all I will need."

"Go ahead and get it—and take something to keep the wolves at bay."

She watched him drawing himself together to go back into his family's house.

He is brave. I wish I could help him. Lady, I wish I could help me. We are all that is left of Bright, he and I. Where can we go? I have no one left in the world. Has he?

He stumbled out of the cottage, his pack on one arm, his walking stick in hand, with his *erda* held over his nose and mouth.

"Let's get out of here," he muttered.

They fled along the dirt road that led downward, toward the Flatterlands, hurrying as fast as they dared. When they came to the bend that would take them out of sight of Bright for the last time, Faia stopped. It was no good.

"Wait," she whispered. She gripped Aldar's shoulder, and turned to stare back at the village. Faia's thoughts kept returning to the bodies that lay unburied,

to the rats and the flies and vultures—to Aldar's family
and hers, who had not been returned to their Mother
Earth. She kept thinking of how it would haunt them,
knowing that the people they had known and loved
lay crumbling in open air.

*I cannot—will not—leave Bright this way. I have
to do something. I have to cleanse it—for his memory
and for mine.*

Aldar's eyes questioned her.

"We cannot bury them, but there is something that
I think *I* can do. Give me a minute." Her voice was
terse. She was already beginning to draw in energy.

She had never done anything like this, but something inside of her assured her that she could. She
planted her staff on the road and closed her eyes and
saw herself drawing up the fire from earth's heart. She
raised her left hand and pulled down the heat from
the sun, and the deep red blaze of the Tide Mother.
She brought them together, and with her eyes pressed
tightly closed, she formed the spell that would cleanse
Bright.

She felt enormous energy surge within her. She
became a storm of fire, pulling and drawing until she
could hold no more. Then with a convulsive shudder,
she lifted her staff high over her head and swung it
toward the little cluster of houses and shops,
screaming—

"All death and decay,
All evil, all disease,
Begone!"

There was a tremendous clap of thunder, and green
flame shot from the point of her staff. Bright glowed
with a green light so brilliant the sun dimmed in
comparison. The sky darkened as enraged vultures
launched into the air, suddenly deprived of their
meals; the ground ran black with fleeing rats.

You killed my mother! Faia raged, seeing the skinny

specter of death on his unlucky white-footed horse. Tears streamed down her cheeks. *You killed my family, and my lovers, and my friends, and my world. You took it all away from me. And I should have died, too,* Faia thought bitterly. *I wish I would have.*

Her power grew with her grief and fury. A wind rose as the blazing village drew air to the flames, which leapt higher and brighter. The wind became a storm that gathered force as it moved and drew, until the fierce keening of its galewinds were so great Aldar flung himself on the ground and covered his ears. Clouds streamed from the four corners of the earth to the center of Faia's maelstrom, and the sky grew black and grim.

Still Faia fed her energy and her anger and her grief into the fire, until the winds began to pull leaves and branches off the trees and into the conflagration, and lightning darted from the towering clouds into the fireball.

"*Stop it, Faia!*" Aldar screamed above the roar.

She kept on, burning her emotions as she burned the city.

Aldar started pummeling her with his clenched fists, yelling, "*Stop it, stop it, stop it!*" until the terror in his voice broke through. Stunned and spent, she dropped her staff and crumpled to her knees.

The hellish green blaze dimmed and flickered and died, and Faia shivered. She stared at the place where the village had been. A cold wind blew up and the first fat drops of rain splattered against her cheeks to mix with the tears.

There is nothing left inside of me, she thought.

She pictured her mother, laughing and hugging her, with her beautiful face tipped up to catch the heat of the sun, and Faia felt—nothing. She could not cry for the loss of Chirp and Huss, for Diana, for her brothers and sister, for her nephews or nieces, for her mother's needless death, for her village, of which nothing remained but a blackened circle. She could not cry for Baward, who made her laugh, or for Rorin, who made her lust. She could feel no sympathy anymore for Aldar, who was staring at her as if she were the Goddess Kallee, the bringer of death.

I have become a shell, she thought. *A husk doll with nothing inside but air and darkness. I am dead now. My body just has not realized it yet.*

She sighed, and stared up at Aldar, who was flinching in the torrential rain and pounding wind. She pulled herself out of the mud that the road had suddenly become, and slung her pack across her shoulders. She didn't bother with her *erda*. She couldn't feel the rain any more than she could feel her soul. Besides, the *erda* was something a person wore if she cared what happened to her. Faia didn't care.

"We must go, Aldar," Faia said, voice flat.

He nodded mutely, stared at her with huge, horrified eyes, and fell into place a few steps behind her.

In Ariss, far from the conflagration in the tiny village of Bright, powerful mages and sajes were interrupted in their work, as the magic they were working with was drawn off and abruptly, simply gone. They were thrown to the ground by an overwhelming, unseen force, their bodies drained of energy by some monstrous magical entity, by a screaming psychic rush of pure grief and rage, and by an odd undercurrent of evil elation.

The universal reaction to this was a panicked thought thrown up to the gods and goddesses of the city: *What in the hells was* that?!

Chapter 2

WATCHERS AT THE BRIDGE

"WHERE are we going?" Aldar ventured.

Faia looked around her and actually saw her surroundings for the first time in hours. It was dark, and she supposed that they must have been walking trudging half the day without food or rest through endless rain and tenacious mud.

She thought about the question for a moment.

"I do not know. Does it matter?"

"I guess not—but I am tired. It is getting dark. If we are not going anyplace in particular, I would really like to stop for the night."

Faia shrugged, walked to the side of the road, and dumped her pack beside a tree.

"Would you not prefer to look for a clearing?" Aldar suggested.

She stared at him. "Do you want to stop?"

"Yah."

"Then we will stop here and sleep under the trees."

Aldar did not say anything else—but as Faia knotted

28

the tiecords of her *erda* over the low-hanging branch
of a tree, she noticed his expression as he watched
her. His eyes were wide and scared. She pretended
not to notice. Instead, she continued making her shelter for the night. She tied the hood of the *erda* flat
over the neck hole, then she took her roll of fishing
net out of her pack, and ran cords through the loops
on either end. She hung her makeshift hammock
under the angled tarpaulin. It would keep her as dry
as she cared to be. Aldar began making his own camp
a stone's throw away. He kept his back to her.

Why should he not be scared? she thought bitterly.
*I just made our whole village disappear as if it had
never been. He must wonder what sort of a monster
I am. But then, I wonder what sort of monster I am.*
She bit her lip and hung her head. *I wonder what
Faljon would have to say about me.*

She decided she was glad she would never know.

Aldar shivered and sat under his own staked-out
erda, his face pale and miserable. She watched him
for a moment, and felt stirrings of pity—he had lost
as much as she had. And worse, he was terrified of
her, the only person left who might offer some
comfort.

I suppose I should try to set Aldar's mind at ease,
she thought.

"Aldar, what do you have in your pack that we can
eat?"

His face brightened a little. "Well, ah . . ." He rummaged nervously through his pack and began produc-
ing foods. Once he found them, they continued to
appear in a steady stream. " Akka-bread, dried apples,
gath cheese *and* mebal cheese, chicken, coffee, a bit
of lamb haunch, a few fresh foxberries—not many—"
he added apologetically, "and a few raisin-and-grain
sweetballs. How about you?"

Faia grinned in spite of herself. "All that? I have
some jerky strips, powdered soup base, and tea."

"That is *all?*"

"Mmm-hmm. I usually do a little foraging while I walk. Or stop in the upland stay-stations. I do not like to carry a lot."

He brought his pack under the meager shelter of her *erda*. "I do not mind. I will share."

Her grin twisted lopsidedly. "I will make a bargain with you. If you can get a fire started, I will make us a stew from some of my soup stock and some of the rest of this."

He looked bewildered. "Start a fire?"

"Of course. I can get everything else ready while you get the fire going. I have tinder and quicklights in my pack if you have none—"

He still looked confused. "I have everything. But if you can do—uh, what you did—why do you need me to build a fire?"

Ah, yes. To him, that must seem like the most reasonable question in the world. If I can destroy someone's whole world in a blaze of heavenfire by pointing at it, surely I can also get the cookfire going.

"Because I am never going to do that again, Aldar. Not ever." She cut pine boughs with her camp knife and twisted them into kneeling pads to avoid looking at him while she talked. "Besides," she said, "faeriefire is the wrong kind of fire. No heat. You cannot use it for cooking."

There was no need to mention that successful magic required concentrated emotion—and she did not have enough emotion left to conjure a single tiny faeriefire as a camp ward. He would not understand. She just said, "Please build a fire for us, Aldar." And she turned her back on him.

Aldar struggled with the wet wood but eventually built the fire, and after a few feeble attempts at conversation, lapsed into silence. Faia prepared the meal without seeing what she was doing. Her eyes saw only her mother's grave, her sister and her children lying still and cold, and the tattered fur of Huss and Chirp. It was a grim, dismal meal.

After the two of them cleaned up, Faia crawled into her bedroll. The rain had gone from deluge to steady downpour. Gusts of wind blew cold water across her face and rocked her hammock and soaked the bedroll through to her skin.

In spite of that, the exhaustion of the day overcame her, and she immediately fell into dreamless sleep.

She was awakened by a hand gently shaking her. At first, she could not remember where she was or what had happened. But the blackness of the night and the steady drizzle of rain, and Aldar's hopeless voice begging her to please wake up brought the reality back to her.

"What do you want, Aldar?"

"I cannot sleep. I just want to know what killed them, Faia. What killed my family?"

Faia's eyes flew open. *Oh, Lady, he is just a kid— and I did not tell him . . . . I just thought he would know. Or I did not think. . . . How could he possibly know Plague when he saw it? I would not have recognized it if Mama had not been teaching me the Healer's lays.*

She rolled over to face him. The few glowing embers of the campfire cast dim light that gleamed in the tears on his cheeks. Eyes round as an owl's—he was determined that he would not cry when he asked her.

Lost everything—and trying to be brave.

She sat up and wrapped her arms around him. "It was Racker's Plague, Aldar. I am almost certain a trader brought it with him when he came to town."

"Plague? Are we going to die, too, Faia?"

Reasonable question.

Faia studied his dark, worried eyes. "Not likely. The dead do not give Racker's Plague to the living. Only the living do."

He nestled his head against her shoulder. His wet

hair brushed her skin, and she felt him shiver with chill. "Why did they all die?" he whispered.

Why did they all die? What a question, Aldar. If I knew that, I would be the greatest Healer that ever lived, instead of just an unwilling student of herbs and roots. They all died because anyone who gets Plague dies. They all died because everything dies in its time. They all died because no one knew enough to save them.

"I do not know, Aldar. I do not think anyone knows. They just did, and if we had been there, we would have died too. We could not have helped them."

His shoulders heaved convulsively. "I want my family back, Faia."

She felt her eyes filling with tears—the sweet relief of tears that came just when she was sure her heart had gone dead. "Me too, Aldar. I want my family back, too."

They clung to each other—wet, cold, crying; they wept until they were exhausted. Then Aldar crawled into Faia's hammock, and, curled tightly together, the two drifted back to sleep—survivors with nothing left but each other.

Faia woke first, thinking it was dawn—but the rain was sheeting down again, and what faint light there was came from directly overhead.

Midday?

Aldar, even in his sleep, clutched at her with the strength of desperation.

What am I going to do now?

Yesterday, leaving Bright had been obvious. There was nothing else she and Aldar could have done. But she had no idea where to go. Her life had centered around the village and the highlands. She had never been to a village other than Bright. She rememberd her father's tales of such places, of course; but faced with the sudden prospect of going to one of them—and without her father to guide her, she felt sudden terror. Such places would be full of Flatters—and how human could such folk be, to live without farming or flock-tending, to dally without toiling from day to day? She yearned for the familiar security of Bright.

There is no Bright, Faia, and you are going to have to figure out something to do, because you cannot sleep on the road for the rest of your short, miserable life.

Aldar shifted, and she found herself stroking his hair.

Thank you, Denneina, Lady of Beginning and Ending, that I am not alone. Thank you that there is another with me who remembers Mama and my sibs; who recalls the Floralea Day pole dance, and the Tidelight procession at Sammahen Eve on the village green; who remembers the love that was in Bright. Because I do not think I could live if I had to remember it alone.

Aldar cried out, and flailed around.

Faia tightened her grip on him. "I am here, Aldar. I am right here."

He woke up, and Faia could see the terror still in his eyes.

"It really happened, didn't it? They're all gone."

"Yes. They are all gone."

His shoulders sagged, and the faint remainder of light in his eyes went out.

He needs to think about something else. We both do.

Faia sat up and faced him. "Aldar, we need to make some decisions. Right now, we have no place to go. We have very little food, and no trade goods. I have never been out of Bright except to go to the highlands. Have you been anywhere else?"

He nodded solemnly. "I just got back from Willowlake yesterday. I was there getting merchants to agree to buy our wool."

"Would that be a good place to go?"

"I don't know any other one."

Faia smiled sadly.

*   *   *

For three days, the mages and sajes of Ariss hadn't been able to conjure so much as a warm beer. Ever since the terrifying disappearance of magic, the city of Ariss sat in a silent darkness brought on by the grounding of flying carpets and the snuffing of the ghostlights. At the same time, the naenrids and darklingsprites who had been kept on their best behavior by warding spells ran amok. With their magic weakened, the damage they could do was slight—still, they did their level best to inflict grief where they could. They spilled water on cookfires and peppers into sweets and sugar into fuel, tracked dirt over clean floors and loosed livestock from their pens. When, on the fourth day, the ghostlights flickered dimly back to life, the magicworkers of Ariss cheered, and began cleaning up the mess—and also began Searching in earnest for whoever or whatever had caused it.

In small groups, mages and sages tracked the flow of magic backward, finally narrowing the source to the place where a tiny hamlet called Bright was supposed to be. When they found only a slagged and blackened pit that followed the outlines of a village, the strongest and best of Ariss' magical community girded for war, and sent out scouts to find the cause.

Faia and Aldar ran out of food on the third day; they did not run out of rain at all. But they were thinking and acting as a team, Faia realized, and there were times when, trudging along the road, she could once again think about things other than Bright.

I worry, mostly. Never does any good, but at least I come by it honestly. For a brief instant, she managed a smile. *Yes, I am just like Mama that way.*

"Anything in your snares?" she asked.

Aldar, crouched by a thicket, grinned up at Faia. "A rabbit. Did you have any luck?"

"The rain is wrecking the berries, but I got a

perryfowl—lucky hit with the slingshot. So we eat at least one more day."

"We're only two days away from Willowlake, I figure." Aldar studied the forest. "I think we'll be out of *this* by late tomorrow."

"Good. I like to see where I am going. I am not used to all these trees."

They sat together, their *erdas* overhead hooked together to make a larger covering. Faia had found that their nightmares were not as bad if they slept next to each other. The campfire glowed with friendly warmth as they cleaned the game.

Aldar skinned the rabbit carefully and rolled the hide— "I'll tan this if I get a chance," he told her. "It won't be worth much, but it will get us something."

Faia nodded agreement. "We might be able to get a bit out of these feathers, too. If I had a loom and some yarn, I could make two or three keurn-cloths; perryfowl feathers are better woven into those than almost anything else."

Do the people of Willowlake use keurn-cloths to ensure the fertility of their flocks—or do they do something different? Maybe even if I make these into keurn-cloths, I will not be able to sell them.

Suddenly, she was a little nervous. "What is Willowlake like?"

Aldar flicked an eyebrow—an oddly adult expression on his young face. "Fancy. There is a rooming house there that has running water indoors—you can take a bath that comes hot straight out a trough tap stuck in the wall. I got to stay there one night because the village had me listed as a merchant trader." His voice grew enthusiastic. "They have three full streets of shops, and the main streets are all paved in cobblestones. They've even *named* the streets. The Willowlakers do not allow livestock to be herded on the shop streets, either."

He looked thoughtful. "I have heard that some of the people have their privies indoors, too—though I do not imagine that is true. If you keep livestock off your main street, I reckon you will not stick a privy in your house."

Faia nodded. Willowlake did not sound like a comfortingly familiar place so far; it sounded alien. "I imagine you are right," she mused. "How are the people?"

"They are nice enough. Shopkeepers are all the same, no matter where you find them—they are looking to get something for cheap they can sell for dear. Bakers are about the same, too. If you look hungry enough, sometimes the baker will give you some dough-ends or day-old crusts, just like in Bright." He grinned wolfishly at that. Apparently, like the other village boys, Aldar had made a habit of looking pathetic and starved when in the presence of anyone who might give him something to snack on. "One of Mama's sisters lives there—she took me around and showed me the sights. She told me that almost five hundred people live there."

Faia, who knew her own village had had about eighty people living in it, tried hard to imagine five hundred people all together. "How could they possibly remember everybody's names?" she murmured.

Aldar sighed. "I truly do not know—but I do not think there is anyone there my aunt does not know."

"So you will have family when you get there?" Faia thought about that wistfully. Her whole family had lived in Bright. She had no one left.

"Yes. My aunt Sarral. Mama did not think much of her—her going off to Willowlake and becoming all fancy . . . but I like her. I suppose Sarral will take me in." His eyes darkened with concern. "There will not be anyone there for you, will there?"

Faia shook her head.

Aldar bit his lip. "I am sorry, Faia. But Sarral is really nice. She will let you stay with her; I know she will."

And what place will I have in a big city like

*Willowlake? Will I be able to find work tending some-
one else's flocks? Will they be able to use a half-trained
healer? Or will I just be in the way? Aldar will manage—he already knows the people who buy and sell,
and they know him.*

But there was no sense feeling sorry for herself. She
would manage. Somehow—she wasn't sure how—but
somehow she would find a place for herself in
Willowlake.

In the tenuous morning mist of Ariss, under a dull,
gray, rain-laden sky, soft light reflected off a secluded
bay of the lake next to the campus of Daane University. A transparent, one-sided bubble—a gate of rain-
bow-washed light that opened into nothingness—grew
larger and brighter. Its light flickered off the surface
of the water, and drew the attention of a lean tan-
and-brown cat who had been hunting along the shoreline. The cat crouched beneath a sweet-smelling dzada
bush and waited.

Magic had been returning slowly to Ariss—slowly,
but steadily. The bubble grew with the magic it drew
through the ley-line streams that coursed overhead
and through the earth, and reflected exactly the
amount and quality of the power available there. The
growth of the bubble, too, was steady and slow.

The cat who watched did not wait for an event, as
a human observer surely would have. It did not look
for explanations. It was satisfied simply to observe
the patterns of light the bubble put forth, and later,
the wispy shadows that began to take shape behind the
transparent wall. The cat was not hungry, or perhaps it
would have looked for dinner instead lolling under
the shrub entertaining its curiosity. Perhaps not. The
bubble was outside of its experience, and its experience was broad—for a cat. Its curiosity regarding
magic in any form was acute.

For a very long time, nothing happened except that
the bubble grew larger, and brighter. This was

sufficient for the cat. It rolled a leaf back and forth between stubby fingers, and waited.

The shapes inside of the bubble became more defined and more pronounced. One of the dark shapes began to deform the surface of the bubble, as though pressing against it. The stretching became more and more pronounced, until there was a sudden "pop," and a dark, furred form splashed into the water.

The cat watched this remarkable occurrence without apparent surprise. He had, after all, seen many startling things—had even participated in some of them. He stretched out one lean foreleg and admired the sharp claws and neat, mobile fingers of what had once been a paw, but was now unmistakably a hand.

He waited further, and was rewarded with one repetition, and then another, of the bizarre event. When the bubble had popped seven times, it grew abruptly and painfully bright, and with incredible speed tightened and shrank until without warning it vanished.

Seven large, furred shapes swam along the shoreline. The cat watched them until they disappeared around a bend in the little bay. He waited still longer—hoping, perhaps, for yet another miracle. When finally he yawned and stretched and turned to stalk home, midday bells were ringing in the city, rain lashed the surface of the lake, and the fog was long gone.

Aldar had judged their distances about right. Even in the pouring rain, they still managed to come within sight of Willowlake just after sunup three days later.

The town covered the entire far side of the valley from one bend in the river to the next. It had spread from the river bottom-land to the ridge, and edged along the lake from which it obviously drew its name—her eyes tried to adjust to the size of the place, and could not.

"Oh, gods," Faia whispered, "it is huge. . . . So *big*. Willowlake lay on the other side of a deep, slow-moving river. The road she and Aldar were on led directly to a covered stone bridge that arched across the water. The bridge was wide enough that two wagons could cross it side by side; Faia was in awe. On their side of the river, cultivated fields spread over every tillable inch of land; the rocky fields held sheep and goats and cows. Right across the river, at the edge of Willowlake, there were little fieldstone cottages with thatched roofs that looked very much like the houses in Bright. But beyond them, there were cut-stone buildings that soared two stories high, and buildings with roofs of slate cut and laid in pretty patterns, and houses that looked for all the world as if they were built of *wood*—

"Faia, are you all right?" Aldar's voice cut through her anxious reverie.

"I cannot go there. I could never feel at home in such a place."

Aldar became very grown-up and reassuring. "You will do fine. It is big, but the people there have always been good to me." He gave her a quick, fierce hug. "You are wonderful, Faia. They will be glad to have you there."

Fifteen-year-old eyes looked into hers with a devotion she had not anticipated. She was surprised to find that she actually did feel better.

"Thanks, Aldar. As long as we are together, I guess we will be fine." She hugged him back, and sighed. With a nervous gesture, she pulled the wide brim of her hat lower across her face and wiped the rain from her cheeks. She was sniffling a little; apparently she was going to catch a cold from all her days in the rain.

Her stomach churned.

I just wish I had someplace to wash up before I walked into that big, fancy town. What will they think of me? I am covered in mud and soaking wet and my clothes reek from six straight days of wearing— She clenched her fists until the nails bit into her palms, then squared her shoulders and took a deep breath. *They will just have to understand, I suppose. I have been doing the best I can.*

She gave Aldar another brief hug, then smiled uncertainly. "I am ready," she said.

Aldar became more animated with every step toward Willowlake. Now that it was in sight, he chattered on, all about the wonders in the massive town of five hundred—the elegant horse-drawn carriage he had seen, the fountain that one woman had in her front yard, the stall in the market where a traveling vendor sold animals as pets. Not practical animals like the kittens of good mousers or dogs for herding sheep or guarding property, he remarked—but *pets*. Birds that sang, or talked; gaudy fish that were no good for eating, but that simply swam around in glass bowls to be looked at; even a miniature horse that, as far as Aldar could tell, was no good for anything.

Faia listened with half her attention. The other half was concentrated on the covered bridge, where, she became more and more certain, something was wrong.

Something was wrong—and the prickling hairs on the back of her neck insisted that it concerned her and Aldar.

As they drew closer, she could make out shapes standing under the covering on the bridge, out of the rain. There appeared to be more than a dozen people—and she could feel their eyes on her and Aldar.

"—and Sarral does not cook on a rack in the fireplace. She has a stove—" Aldar was saying.

Faia cut him off. "Are there always that many people waiting on the bridge?"

Aldar peered into the gloom of the covered bridge, and noticed what she was talking about. "Usually there is only the toll-taker." He looked puzzled for a minute, then he smiled. "I guess not everyone wants to walk in the rain like us."

Faia was neither convinced nor reassured. "It has

been raining for days without a break, Aldar. They would not all just stay under that bridge, waiting."

She noticed movement from the crowd, as the people who had been standing in the front moved aside to let several others through. Faia was close enough now that she could make out details.

The ones who had come through the crowd to stand in front were two men and two women dressed unlike any she had seen in her entire life. The men wore gaudy gold-and-green robes that swept in smooth lines to the ground, and rich carmine hoods that fell away from their faces in gracious draping curves. Their hair was long, pulled back and braided, and their beards were worn long, also braided, and adorned with heavy gold rings and wires. The women had their hair cut straight off at their shoulders and worn loose—in fact, had it not been for the revealing tightness of their clothes, she would have thought them to be men as well. They wore leather pants and matching leather jackets—the tall, dark brunette wore red, the tiny redhead, pale blue. Both sported soft, loose black boots that bagged around their calves, and heavy silver rings at neck and wrist and ankle over the boots.

The two men were standing close together, conferring; they were obviously maintaining as much distance from the two women as they could without going out and standing in the muddy, swollen river.

"Lady bless," Aldar whispered. "I have never seen anything like *them* before."

Wonderful. Faia shivered in the cold rain and worried. *There is something off kilter about that mob on the bridge, and about their interest in us—*

"Aldar, stay here," she hissed. "I do not like this, and I do not want you to get hurt. I will go up and talk with them and find out what is going on."

"But what about you?" Aldar worried.

Faia thought of what she had done to the village of Bright, and shook her head grimly. "I can take care of myself if I have to. I want to know that you are safely out of harm's way first, though."

Apparently Aldar was remembering the village, too, because his eyes grew round again. He gripped her hand. "Be careful, sis'ling," he said, using that childish term of endearment for the first time.

She bit her lip. "Just stay put."

She and Aldar had paused several stones' throws from the entryway to the bridge. It was trouble that was waiting for her, and no doubt of it. She took a firmer grip on her staff, and even though she had not intended to, she pulled the energy of earth and sky like a cloak around her and Aldar. Then she strode forward to meet and challenge whatever Fate had in store.

It had been a long and weary wait. The Sensings of the magic that had first been felt when it blasted Bright came at odd intervals. Those Sensings were almost always in the dark of night or the very early morning. They were random fluctuations, undirected—unlike that first horrifying burst that had destroyed the entire village to such a degree that only the etchings of foundation marks melted into the native bedrock remained to show that the village had been there. And though the random power only reappeared in brief, untraceable, and apparently harmless bursts, the talent behind it was still so awesomely strong that Frelle Medwind Song broke out in a nervous sweat just thinking about it. The surges couldn't be pinpointed, but the general areas of their occurrence could be mapped—and whatever was making them, it had been heading directly from Bright to Willowlake.

Medwind and her colleague, sitting in their shared office in Mage-Ariss had figured direction and speed and had determined that whatever it was that was causing the disturbances—and whatever it was that had, not incidentally, leveled Bright—would be arriving in Willowlake fairly early on Terradae morning.

Apparently, in Saje-Ariss, the same calculations had been made and the same conclusions drawn, for along with Medwind and her colleague, Frelle Jann Raxesmotte, there were two sajes on the bridge in the pale, cold, rainy morning, as tense and drawn and worried as the two women.

And now, at just the appropriate time, we have a man and a boy coming down the road, and though both of them appear to be peasants, well—appearances can surely be deceiving.

Medwind leaned over and whispered to Jann, "If either of these is the one we've been waiting for, at least it's going to be their problem, not ours." She indicated the two pale, nervous sajes in their glorious, overdone robes.

Jann nodded slowly. "We could actually leave now, and let them deal with it."

"I know. But suppose Bright's destroyer decides *we* are a problem for *him*, even though we are from the mage side of the city. Suppose he attacks."

Medwind didn't miss the fact that, when the man and the boy stopped to confer about fifty yards off, the two sajes grew even paler and more anxious. She felt a great deal of sympathy for them.

After all, if either of those two had been female, I'd be in the boiling pot now, instead of them.

Suddenly there was an enormous surge of magic, so overwhelming that Medwind felt light-headed. "Bitch-Goddess," she swore, "what in the saje-hells is that?!"

Jann had been watching with Sight, her eyes pressed tightly closed. "The tall one," she whispered from a throat gone suddenly dry and tight. "All of that energy swarmed to the tall one. It doesn't feel male, but it doesn't feel female either. The magic has no gender signatures on it at all. It is drawing from the earth-lines and the sky-lines."

Oh, no, no—I don't want to think about the implications of that. What could possibly use the magic of ground and sky together? How could anyone do that?

"*Wild talent?*" Medwind got very scared, very fast. "Could there be a wild talent that powerful?"

"By bloody Horned Adar, what if you're right?"

The two frelles stared at each other, eyes wide with speculation. "Could what happened in Bright have been an accident?" Medwind croaked.

Stiffly, as paralyzed by the approaching apparition as songbirds transfixed by a deadly snake, the two women watched the tall peasant stalk up to the bridge. Behind her, Medwind was conscious of the villagers, packed together like sheep tucked behind the shepherd when the wolf approaches.

If only they knew how scared their shepherds were, I don't wonder but that they'd be running for the hills right now.

Medwind tried to read the approaching peasant's intent, to no avail. "I can't pull anything through those shields at all. I feel like I'm attacking a seamless stone wall with a thread."

Jann said, "If he goes on the attack, it is going to take all four of us just to contain him."

Medwind gave her a sideways glance. "Tell me something, Jann. Even pooling our strength, do you think the four of us could level a village the way Bright was leveled? Down to a puddle of glass and slag? Hmmm?"

Jann shivered and shook her head slowly.

Medwind nodded, her black hair bobbing. "Right. So what, exactly, do you propose we do if this saje-peasant does attack? Aside from dying bravely, I mean?" The woman in red glanced down at her feet, then tipped her head at an angle. "The only thing we'll be able to accomplish if he attacks is to make enough noise when we die to alert Ariss."

Jann paled and wrapped thin hands around her torso.

The peasant stopped a few paces away from the waiting crowd. He sniffled, and Medwind noticed that he was young, and that he was suffering from a bad cold, and that he looked like he hadn't had enough rest or food in a long time. He was a tall boy, dirty, covered from neck to knee by the heavy shapeless *erda* the peasants all admired so greatly and used for so many things, and wearing a big, hideous, broad-brimmed leather hat that hid his eyes and bulky, mud-covered peasant boots that went at least to the knee, and perhaps higher.

He braced his feet apart and planted his staff vertically in front of him. He sneezed once, then settled into a waiting attitude.

The four magicians looked anxiously at each other. No one, it was obvious, wanted to make the first move.

It isn't actually my problem . . . but thrice returns the good as well as the bad. So I don't suppose it would hurt if I got things rolling. . . . Medwind cleared her throat, hoping against hope that her voice would not crack from nervousness. "Greetings. From where do you hail, stranger?"

The stranger angled his head to one side in a bird-like gesture, seeming to think about the answer. "I was from Bright—but Bright is no more."

Medwind felt icy rain racing down her spine, even though she was under the shelter of the bridge, and dry. "We had heard rumors of Bright. Do you know what happened there?"

She felt, even through the shields, an enveloping wave of grief. "I do."

She waited with the others on the bridge, but the stranger was not forthcoming with any more information.

One of the sajes asked, "What did happen to Bright?"

The stranger ignored the question. "What are all of you people waiting for?"

Medwind closed her eyes and took a deep breath and centered herself, trying to prepare herself for the attack that her response was likely to bring. "Something terrible happened in Bright, and we are waiting for the person who can tell us what something that was."

"Plague." The stranger's response was terse, but Medwind thought that she could hear a sob clipped short in that answer.

One of the sajes was braver than he looked. "I know of no Plague that makes even the stones disappear," he ventured.

"Oh . . . that. *I* did that. It was an accident."

Medwind and Jann and the two sajes threw frantic looks back and forth at each other.

It was an accident? An accident*! By the gods, what sort of a rutting "accident" could someone have that would do melt the very stones?!* Medwind wondered wildly.

"Wh-what kind of accident?" she asked, voice shaking.

The stranger hung his head. "Aldar was here in Willowlake, and I was in the hills with my flock when Plague struck Bright. He and I returned to find no one alive in the village. We both lost everyone. Most were—most were . . . were dead in their beds when we found them." He stopped speaking, and Medwind could see his shoulders shaking.

He's crying.

She felt pity for this poor young man, even through her fear.

The peasant resumed his story. "We could not bury them all. Not just the two of us. And the rats and wolves and flies and vultures—"

As his voice ground to a halt, Medwind shuddered at the picture her mind painted.

The boy resumed talking. "Aldar and I left Bright. We were going to leave it just as we had found it— but they were our families. They deserved better burial than the open air and the rats. I can call the faeriefires. Before we were too far out of Bright, I called them, and set them to clean Bright. I did not know that . . . that . . ."

Emotion, Medwind realized. *Emotion channeled through someone with enormous potential, and sent completely out of control—and, gods, think of the amount of power it took to annihilate a village with peasant magic and—and bloody rutting faeriefires.*

"I did not know it would do that. . . ."

The sajes seemed about as reassured by this tale as she was—perhaps less.

The two sajes conferred for a moment. "We're s-s-sorry about your village," one of the men finally stammered. "But we have a new home for you now. We hope you'll let us give you room and board, and some teaching. We'll take you to Ariss, lad, to get training for your talent, before you have an—" He swallowed, and winced. "—An *accident* that involves the living."

The young man glanced behind him at the boy. "Thank you, but no. I will be doing nothing else with the Lady's Gift."

His lips twitched at the corners. It was the first glimpse of something other than pain that Medwind had seen written on that young face. "And I'm no lad," the peasant continued.

One of the sajes shrugged. "Young man, then."

"Not that, either."

The hair stood up on Medwind's arms, and she stared. The tall boy removed his hat, and cascades of heavy brown hair tumbled below his—her—waist. The cool, pale gray eyes that appraised the group were edged with thick black lashes, under arched black brows. The broad peasant cheekbones and the strong peasant jaw no longer hid the fact that the powerful stranger was, in fact, mage, not saje. Was in fact a woman, and, Medwind thought, rather pretty too, in spite of her brawny size and coarse features. Was, in fact, *Medwind's* problem.

"Aw-w-w—*tsanngas!* . . ." Medwind swore in her native tongue, softly. It was a vile imprecation, but not nearly potent enough to express her feelings.

Jann's breath whistled through her teeth. "Gods—

the most powerful natural wizard in at least a century—and a mage. And she's ours—all ours." Jann looked at Medwind, and her eyes widened. "Ouch. *Lucky* us."

The gaunt, golden-haired saje growled something to his companion, and the two of them, relief etched plainly on their faces, turned away, and vanished in a cloud of viridian smoke.

The peasant girl's eyes widened at the dramatic disappearance of the sajes.

Medwind saw the dark humor of the moment, and grinned. *If we don't get killed dragging her home, what a stroke of luck this will be. Imagine training that much power, that much talent. Of course, she'll probably toast us to charcoal before we even get out of Willowlake—*

She turned to Jann and whispered, "Bring the wingmounts." Then she returned her attention to the young woman.

"What is your name?"

"Faia Rissedote."

"Faia. Well, I'm—happy—to meet you. I'm Medwind Song. I'm an instructor at Daane University, the University of Women's Magic at Mage-Ariss."

Faia nodded acknowledgement at the introduction.

"Faia, the saje was right when he said that a talent such as yours cannot be left loose and untrained. We sensed magic in Bright six days ago, and went there to see what had caused it. You must imagine how worried we were when we found nothing left of Bright at all. And the side effects of that spell are still going on."

Faia looked puzzled.

"Oh, yes. Didn't you think it was odd that, though last Watterdae was clear and beautiful, the storms started after you did your magic with the faeriefires? Haven't you noticed that it has rained constantly since?"

The girl's brows knitted in worry. "Then I have made it rain forever?"

"No—the storm will blow itself out in a few more days. But you changed the weather drastically, and we'll feel that come harvest-time this year. Farmers are already complaining that they are late getting their crops into the fields, and those that were already in have been washed away."

"I did *that*?"

"Sadly, yes. And you used no ward-confinements, and not one single stop-spell. You just let the magic run its course. Your simple faeriefire spell stripped the magic, not only from your own area, but also from ley-lines that stretched as far away as Ariss. You turned loose every contained wizard spell there, and you had no way to call any of them back. In Ariss, we have been the week cleaning up the mess and setting things right. There is no telling what the mages and sajes in outlying areas have had to do. We've found nothing particularly deadly that was set loose—but we were lucky. What will happen the next time your magic runs wild, Faia?"

Faia sighed. "I am not going to use the Lady's Gift again, so it does not matter—not really. Though I am awfully sorry about the rain and your problems."

"You aren't going to use magic again?" Medwind raised an eyebrow in disbelief. "Really?"

"Really."

"Then what did you surround yourself with when you walked to the bridge? What surrounds you even now? The energy that courses through you even at this instant is completely out of control. I don't think you realize how much of the earth's strength and the sky's power you are pulling in—and I've already seen proof that you have no idea of the consequences of using that power."

Faia flinched.

"I'm sorry," Medwind concluded, "but you could be dangerous left untrained and to your own devices. Last

time you were mostly lucky. Next time you might not
be—and more people than you alone could suffer
from your ignorance."

Jann returned and told Medwind, "The wingmounts
are ready."

Medwind nodded. "Good." She turned to Faia, and
said, "We'll offer you the same thing the sajes offered.
Room, board, training—we can't make you come with
us, but we can tell you that, for the good of everyone
around you, you must make yourself see this our way.
Your talent cannot be allowed to continue unschooled;
that way lies certain disaster. You needn't worry about
yourself or your future, though. We'll take care of
you."

Faia looked into the implacable eyes of the two city-
women. She could sense no wavering in their determination to convince her to go with them. She looked
behind them to the villagers of Willowlake, her eyes
pleading with them to show her some sign of welcome.
But the villagers had heard, not only Faia's story, but
Medwind's assessment of the danger Faia and her Gift
posed to them. Her glances were returned with coldness. Faia could see that they wanted nothing to do
with her.

Except for Aldar, then, she would have no support
in Willowlake. Her presence would bring nothing but
resentment. And if she fought the will of the Ariss
mages, she would also make life hard for Aldar.

She turned her back on the bridge and slowly
walked to the waiting boy.

Behind her, she heard the small red-headed Ariss
woman say, "Stop her."

The other one replied, "Let her go. She'll be back."

Aldar had waited patiently in the rain. His eyes were
trusting when he asked her, "What's going on?"

She saw no reason to soften the blow. It would
benefit neither him nor her to pretend that everything
was going to be fine.

"I am going to go with those women to Ariss," she said.

"You cannot. You are all that I have left."

Faia gripped her staff and leaned her cheek against it. *No. You are all that I have left,* she thought. "That is not so," she told him. "You have your aunt here, and you will be accepted. The townspeople here are afraid of me because those Ariss women told them what happened in Bright. The townspeople are afraid that I might do something like that again."

"You would not, Faia." The boy was loyal.

"I do not know." Faia found to her surprise that when she said that, she meant it. She really was not sure if she might not make another stupid mistake with magic—a deadly one. "I did not mean to do what I did the first time," she added.

The wind gusted stinging drops of rain against her face and in her eyes; Aldar moved around so that his back was to the wind.

His expression was hopeless. "Faia, if you go, there will not be anyone with me who *remembers*. You do not want to go, do you?"

"No. But I have to." It was simple truth. More than anything, she wanted to stay—but that choice was not hers to make.

"Goodbye, Aldar. You will be fine." She embraced him and whispered, "I will miss you, brae'ling. Be happy."

His eyes were bright with unshed tears. "I will miss *you*, sis'ling. . . ."

Faia turned her back before he could see that she was crying. It would be hard enough for him if he thought she was resigned to her fate—she could not let him know how miserable she was to be leaving.

She returned to the waiting women, and nodded. "If I must go, then let us leave now."

The woman in blue, the one the other woman had called Jann, wrinkled her nose and ruffled her fingers through her dark red hair. "Like that?! You can't go

to Ariss looking like that! You're dirty, you smell like
a stable, and your clothes are dreadful. We'll get you
a bath and take you to a shop where we can buy you
some clothes that civilized people wear."

Medwind made a surreptitious jab with her elbow
at Jann's ribs. "What Jann means to say is that you
would probably feel better if you got some clean, dry
clothes on before we left," she said, and glared at her
associate.

That is not what Jann meant to say at all, Faia
thought. *Prettified helke! She meant that I look bad, I
smell bad, and I dress funny, and she does not want
anyone to see me with her. Well, too damned bad. Just
for that, I will make sure that everyone sees me with
her, and I hope she dies of embarrassment.*

Faia crossed her arms in front of her chest and
glared at the petite redhead. "I will go as I am, or not
at all."

Jann looked at the other woman in mute appeal.
The other woman shrugged, eyes amused.

Jann whispered, "Gods, Medwind, back me up on
this. We can't take her to the University looking like
she's been wallowing in a pigsty—and you can't even
tell she's female. Looking like that, someone is going
to think she's goddamned saje and throw her off the
campus."

The whisper carried surprisingly well. Faia felt her
face burn. Furious, she moved toward Jann. She
wanted to rearrange that over-pretty face with her fist,
or her walking stick. Medwind gave her a panicked
look that stopped her cold, though. *Gods—she acts
like I am going to turn that redheaded shrew into a
pondworm. Maybe she thinks I can.* Faia thought
about that an instant longer, and her stomach flipped
queasily. *Maybe she is right.*

Medwind, turning back to Jann, shrugged again.
"She'll be fine. She has the right to dress as she
wants—and I'm sure she'll feel more like washing up
when she gets someplace warm and dry."

Medwind turned to Faia. "I know these past few days have been hard for you. It will be up to you, though, to decide whether the next few days will be as hard."

Medwind gave a piercing whistle, and three dappled gray horses broke loose from the man who held their reins, and trotted forward.

At least, they looked like horses to Faia's first glance. At her second glance, though, Faia found herself gawking at the beasts in disbelief. They were far slenderer than regular horses, though as tall, and incredibly dainty, with legs that appeared to have been created of smoke and dreams, they were so fragile. Their muzzles were finely tapered and delicate, with nostrils that flared twice the size of horses' nostrils, on faces only two-thirds the size. The creatures tossed their heads and snorted, and unfurled wings that had been tucked tightly to their lean sides.

Wings— Faia mused. *Huge gossamer wings on horses from my dreams.* She held her breath and stared, almost afraid that they might disappear into clouds of smoke as the Flatter-men had if she blinked. *These are the miracles Papa talked about, then. It was for this he wanted me to see the Flatterlands.*

The wings spread wide, and Faia saw downy gray membranes so thin they let through more light than the oilskin windows in Bright. The black wingtips and the red lines of the blood veins over the bones stood out in high relief. The beasts' wingspreads were tremendous. She inched closer, attracted like metal to a lodestone by the exotic creatures.

"What are they—where did you get them?" she asked Medwind.

Medwind smiled and said, "They're called wingmounts. They're one of the varieties of experimental animal that we are developing at Daane University. Perhaps someday you will make wingmounts, too. Gods know, it would thrill the Mottemage to have someone else studying her specialty. At this point, we haven't managed to get them to breed true—so each one we have has been created magically, over a long period of time, from a normal horse foal. There are very few of them, and we are only permitted to use them for urgent transportation."

Faia's eyebrow raised. *Urgent transportation? Which makes me something of value to these people.*

Medwind read the look. "We were more than politely interested in the force that annihilated Bright. We're less anxious about it now that we know no one was killed when the village was destroyed—but only a little less anxious. We need to make sure you learn control. Quickly."

Medwind's wingmount knelt at her side, and she slipped into the saddle. Jann followed suit.

Faia's mount failed to kneel fast enough to suit her. She shrugged and vaulted on as she would have when riding one of the plowhorses around the pasture when she was younger—and looked up in time to see Jann's pained expression.

To the hells with her. I may be some stupid peasant in her eyes, but I did not volunteer for this, I did not want this, and if she does not care for me the way I am, she can just freeze in the Dark Gods' underworld for a turn of the Wheel or two.

Bravery was all very well, and defiance was wonderful for keeping the courage up—and putting that helke Jann in her place felt fine—but once astride the dainty wingmount, Faia was awash in niggling doubts. The creature had wings for a reason; and sitting on its back, the reason became clear enough, even when one was not thinking clearly. Obviously, the wingmounts were intended to fly—

Faia suddenly decided that she did not wish to go flying. The ground seemed like a much safer place to be. At that moment, however, the two city-women urged their steeds forward, and Faia's, tethered to Medwind's, followed.

They rocked through a jolting, teeth-clattering trot

into a canter, and Faia locked her knees tightly into her mounts' sides. *No climbing off now.* She clenched her fists into the wingmount's mane and looked back helplessly at Aldar, who stood twisting his hat in his hands, with tears streaming down his cheeks. She looked away as fast as she could.

I really do not want to do this, she thought, as the wingmount's smooth gallop shifted to something else, and the ground dropped away from her with a sickening lurch. She clenched her eyes shut.

Sweet Denneina, I really *do not want to do this.*

Chapter 3

IN THE CITY OF
FOGS AND BOGS

HER mount's legs thrust against the air with each wingbeat, and Faia relaxed into the rocking gait. The soothing rhythm and the steady rush of chill wind against her face made her sleepy. The white terrain of solid-looking clouds so close underfoot promised safety, even though she knew that those clouds would not hold her if she fell.

The clouds startled Faia. She had always imagined them as dry and fluffy and warm—while they were, in fact, quite cold and wet. She could not see or feel or taste any difference between them and fog, actually, and she began to wonder if a difference existed. She discovered, too, that the world above the rainstorm was one of cold, brilliant light.

The sun had climbed from its place on the horizon to directly overhead when Medwind gave a signal. Abruptly they began to descend. Faia was once again battered by rain that stung her face and hands.

The travelers broke free of the clouds, and Faia saw

an enormous city crowded onto a monstrous artificial hill built between towering cliffs and a huge bay. Surrounding the city was marsh, running along the base of the cliffs in both directions as far as her eyes could see. This was Ariss. And what an astonishing place it was. Faia had heard the word *city* before, but only at her first sight of the panorama below her did she begin to understand what it meant. Buildings piled on top of buildings to fill every inch of the raised ground; they spread from a massive pile of structures that lay at the city's center outward and downward in concentric circles. Walls defined the circles, and broad, white thoroughfares counterpointed them, running through walls and circles like spokes in a wheel. The whole metropolis was a giant mandala of towering white stone dotted with the green of parks and the blue of lakes and streams. And even though it was immense and terrifying, still Faia thought she had never seen anything more beautiful in her life.

As they drew nearer, she could overlook the walls—and the image of a city of white swiftly altered to that of a city of riotous color. Beneath the white walls and white buildings spread all the colors of imagination. Gaudy tents of red and green, gold and pink, purple and orange and brilliant blue filled the open marketplaces; rainbow pennants with fanciful devices flapped from windows and doorways; and the human occupants, in garb of colors and styles that defied description, scurried like overdressed ants through the broad, curving thoroughfares.

Her mount stiffened his wings into a glide and cruised toward the city's center at a gentle angle, following the lead of the other two wingmounts. The trio passed over line after line of walls; thousands of buildings lay beneath her, and more roads, that twisted and turned and doubled back until Faia doubted that she would ever have the courage to wander through those streets, lest she be lost forever. Unidentifiable and unlikely-seeming vehicles raced on

the streets underneath her and soared through the air
beside her—the drivers of the flying vehicles shouted
and waved and cursed as the three wingmounts flew
through their midst. Faia's stomach tightened from
the tension and the strangeness of it all.

"Hold on tight now!" Medwind bellowed above the
rush of the wind. "Landings can be rough!"

Just when I was beginning to think I liked this,
Faia thought dryly, and wrapped her arms around the
wingmount's neck and locked her legs tightly against
his belly.

The wingmounts began backwinging, bodies lurching wildly. All three came down stiff-legged in a white-
fenced pasture within sight of a single, immense,
gleaming white tower.

They bounced when they hit.

Faia paled as her own mount nearly threw her off
while getting his feet under him. His legs windmilled,
and he careened into the ground at a dead gallop,
lurching twice more into the air before he finally
pulled his wings in to his sides and slowed gradually
to canter, then trot, then gentle walk. He carried Faia
to the gate, and a large, well-kept stone barn.

Faia dismounted quickly, legs shaking. She seriously
considered kissing the earth under her feet.

*Lady of the Beasts—my thanks for safe arrival!
Never, beloved Goddess, never give me reason to do
that again!* she prayed.

The two city-women handed off the three wingmounts to a young stablegirl, who clucked her tongue
at them and led them away to be cooled down and
watered.

Medwind stretched, catlike, and grinned. "When the
breeding program gives us one that can land without
nearly crashing, then I'll believe wingmounts may become something more than a curiosity—or the
Mottemage's personal fetish."

Jann laughed. "I'm sure every time I come in will
be my last."

Medwind turned to Faia, and rubbed her hands together briskly. "So. Welcome to Ariss, known by those of us who aren't from here as 'The City of Fogs and Bogs.' You'll find out why all too soon." She chuckled. "We made it back in time to let you get cleaned up and still pick up midday meal from the Greathall if you hurry. Then we'll show you around campus, and get you lined up for testing tomorrow, and find you a roommate and a room. And we'll need to get your supplies together, too. I'll take a look at what you brought, so we can fill out the papers, and requisition the rest of what you need. I want you started in classes as soon as possible. After all, the sooner you get that power under control, the sooner the rest of us will be able to sleep again at night. But I'm ravenous—so let's stop by the bath house first, then eat."

Faia jammed her hands into the pockets of her breeches because she did not know what else to do with them. She wished that she had her staff with her. She could not have carried it on the wingmount— what would have happened to her had she fouled her mount's wings with it?—but she felt awkward now, standing without it. She shifted the weight of her pack, trying to get comfortable. Then she waited for the two women to lead her where they wanted her to go.

Medwind stood watching her. "Well—is that satisfactory?"

Faia bit her lip. "I did not realize we were pretending that I had a choice in any of this. But since you ask, yes, that is satisfactory."

Medwind looked startled, and an angry gleam lit Jann's eyes.

"The education you'll get here is worth a fortune, you ungrateful peon. Our own people work for years to pay for the training we have offered you for free. You ought to be thankful that we came and pulled you out of that little mud-hole country hamlet," Jann snarled. "That we went to the trouble to bring an

ignorant peasant like you from the back country all
the way to Ariss to teach you and train you—"

Medwind's face was a study in horror. Jann's fanati-
cal loyalty to Daane University and all things related
was legend, but Medwind wouldn't have credited her
colleague with insanity. Not before this outburst, anyway. "Jann—" she whispered as she not-too-surrepti-
tiously stepped on Jann's foot. "Think about this a
minute."

Faia ignored Medwind, and stepped directly in
front of Jann, so that she towered over the dainty red-
haired beauty. Calmly, she crossed her arms in front
of her chest. "Look, you shriveled, dry-dugged milk-
cow, I did not ask to be here. I do not want to be
here. You came and got me and made me come. I
will be happy to return to a little 'mud-hole country
village' any time you decide you do not want me
here—but as long as I am here, let us not pretend
that it is because you are doing me some great favor."

Jann backed up, her face dark and flushed. She
glared at Medwind. "Did you hear what she said?!"
she shrieked.

Medwind looked at her fellow instructor with an
expression that suggested the woman had abruptly
sprouted several extra heads. Finally, she shrugged her
shoulders, and nodded. "Mmm-hmm."

Jann's voice became even shriller. "Aren't you going
to do something about it?!"

Medwind always found Jann funny when she lost
her temper. She arched one eyebrow and bit back a
smile. "No," she said, after giving the matter consider-
able thought. "I don't think I will. Why don't you go
ahead and get midden now, Jann; I'll take Faia over
to the bath house, and meet you at the Greathall when
we're done."

Jann's face was an ugly shade of red when she
stomped away. Medwind watched her leave, wearing
a thoughtful expression.

When she was out of earshot, Medwind sighed.

"There are people I would rather have as enemies, Faia. Still, I can't say that I blame you for choosing to make her one. I just hope that you find you can live with your decision."

Faia looked startled. "I did not choose to make her an enemy!"

"Was what you said to her an accident?"

The young hill woman cocked her head and stared at the Daane instructor. "No. Of course not."

"And what effect did you think your words would have?"

"Well—I was fighting back—"

Medwind crossed her arms and leaned against a fence. "Actions have consequences, Faia. First rule of magic, first rule of life. And the second rule is this—you are the only one responsible for your own actions. Jann chose to be obnoxious. You chose to be obnoxious. The two sets of behavior are in no way related to each other."

"That is nonsense! She started the whole thing—I just treated her the way she deserved to be treated."

"Oh, no. That isn't the way responsibility works. Jann will have to take the blame for treating you badly—but you will have to take your own blame for treating her the same way. If you don't accept responsibility for your own actions, then you are forever chained to a position of defense." Medwind's head lowered, and she moved away from the fence and began to pace back and forth through the tall grass. Her shoulders were hunched and tense, and Faia thought she looked worried.

Finally the instructor stopped her pacing and glanced back up.

"Offense is a better position for a mage," she continued. "It gives power, but in order to take the offensive, you have to admit your own ability to effect change—and consequently, to make mistakes."

The look in Medwind's eyes became fierce. "You are far too powerful to blame somebody else for the things you do. Any action you take could have potentially overwhelming repercussions, not just for yourself, but for all of us. So you must learn to face the fact, always, that you choose to do what you do, and that everything you do affects not only you but others."

Faia snorted. "I did not choose to come here."

"Didn't you? You got on the wingmount of your own free will. We insisted that you come, but really, I don't think we could have forced you. Had you chosen, you could have resisted—leveled us the way you did Bright. You chose to take the path of least resistance, to make things easier for the boy you had with you, to leave the people of Willowlake who, you could see, would not have welcomed you. You chose to admit, if only to yourself, that you needed the training that we could provide."

Medwind flipped the bangs of her fine, black hair back out of her eyes, and tipped her head at an angle to study Faia. "First, actions have consequences," she said. "Second, you are the only one responsible for your actions. Those are your first two lessons as you join us."

Medwind stood an instant longer, staring at Faia as if she were trying to read her mind. Then, with a nearly imperceptible shrug, she turned and marched through the barn, leading Faia across the landscaped green in front to a busy street.

"Enough of that. . . . Let's get you clean and dry and fed. We'll have time to talk later."

Faia stewed along in Medwind's wake, keeping her anger under wraps. It did not seem that anyone was prepared to be sympathetic.

I am being blamed for Jann's nastiness. Just how did Medwind expect me to react when she treated me that way? Actions surely do have consequences, but sometimes you get caught up in the consequences of someone else's actions—then what happens is not your fault, is it? And no matter what Medwind says, I did not choose to have Jann treat me like an ignorant peas-ant. She did that on her own—I am what I am, and if they do not like that, well, Faljon says, "Wool yarn will not/a cotton shirt make."

Her head began to hurt. There was a smell to the city of sweat, heavy perfumes, incense in a dozen ill-matched varieties, and cooking smoke. Spices both unfamiliar and somehow unpleasant mingled with the overwhelming odor of old fish—*Lady, how much fish could these people possibly eat to leave such a reek?* she wondered. And on top of that, there was barnyard stink and the all-pervasive scent of too many people crowded together.

But the smell was not the only thing overpowering about Ariss. Sound, too, assaulted senses used to lonely hills, to the cries of birds and the rush of wind through trees and over rocks. Here, two-wheeled machines whirred and beeped, their riders screamed obscenities at any who failed to move out of the way fast enough; street hawkers shouted nasal, sing-songed lies about their wares; horses clattered, metal-shod, over the stone street, dragging wagons that clanked appallingly; riders of flying beasts and flying rugs and flying crates howled at each other, and evidently beneath it all, every single person in the city talked at the same time.

Medwind caught her wrist at an intersection and suddenly darted across the road, dodging two-wheelers and horse-carriages with reckless abandon. One two-wheeler screeched to a halt a fingers' breadth away from running over Faia, and two others plowed into him. The ensuing tangle-up left irate riders casting imprecations and cursing vigorously behind the two running women. Faia felt herself to have been barely snatched from the fangs of death for the second time in one day.

Medwind was breathing hard from the run. "We shouldn't have done that, but it was another quarter-furlong to a designated crossing, and then the same distance back. The place where we're going is right over there. I didn't want to walk the extra distance."

Faia looked over at the big, single-storied stone hall that stood in front of the tower she'd noticed earlier, then at the street clogged with traffic, then back at Medwind. Her expression mirrored her disbelief.

Medwind grinned, her smile apologetic. "I do it all the time. It's not as dangerous as it seemed."

Faia took a deep breath and said with profound sincerity, "I do not wish to do that ever again. I would rather walk the length of the city."

Medwind laughed. "Oh, you'll get used to it."

Faia stared through the massive wooden doors, down the long stone corridor of the bath house, noting the patterns of light that scattered across the pale floor from the arched windows high overhead.

Medwind Song, standing quietly beside her, noted the look and said, "I'll never forget my first time in here—I came from the eastern plains, and I had never seen an indoor privy before, much less running water. I thought Rakell—she's the Mottemage now, but she was just a primary instructor then—was going to laugh herself into a coma. I didn't understand what the water chair was for, and had no idea the little rope pull made the thing flush. You should have seen me jump. The wall basin was a wonder—but the tub—I thought that had to be for watering livestock. It was a terrible shock for a barbarian kid when hot water came straight out of the wall—I was sure these folks had a direct line tapped into hell."

Faia bit her lip and nodded. "So you are not from the Flatterlands, either?"

"Flatterlands? That's what you call this? It fits." Medwind chuckled and headed down the corridor. "No, the locals would be appalled that you mistook me for one of them. I'm from the wide plains just west of the Stone Teeth fjord, way southeast of here. I'm a warrior of the Huong Hoos tribe. 'Round here, I'm called a barbarian—sometimes a headhunter. There's some truth to both descriptions ... enough, anyway, to keep these bog-loving *makcjeks* from bothering me too much. Well," she stopped and indicated a door that did not have a blue marker hung on the latch, "this one is empty. Go on in, give me your clothes, and I'll get you some clean ones while you wash up."

Faia figured out the workings of the big metal tub by trial and error, and silently thanked Aldar for his description of city bathtubs and Medwind for her own descriptions of her first experience—she had had no intention of admitting to Medwind that she had never seen indoor running water before, but the instructor's tactful remarks around the subject gave her a fairly good idea of what to expect.

When the bath was full, she climbed in and sank into the deep, hot water. The novelty of flying horses had worn off, and she had become numbed to the wonder of soaring through the air like a great falcon. The beauty of Ariss was much less noticeable up close, being obscured by the noises and smells, and in any case, the charm of any city was hard to find without someone to share the wonders with. In the bathroom, she was by herself for the first time since she had walked into Bright and found it desolate.

In the emptiness of the pale stone room, the extent of her isolation settled over her like a gray, suffocating blanket. *I am in a stinking, noisy city, without even Aldar—everyone and everything I ever loved is dead or gone. Oh, Goddess, I wish I were dead too! Nobody here cares about me—their only interest is in the Lady's Gift. They would as soon be rid of me as not, if they could be sure I would not wipe out another village.* She allowed herself, at last, to weep.

How simple it would be if I could drown myself now. I could put an end to this—and why should I not? I have nothing to live for. I would leave if I knew for sure that I would not hurt someone accidentally. But I am dangerous to everyone around me.

It would not be hard to die, Faia decided. There would be one quick moment of pain and fear, and then the waiting Wheel, where her spirit would heal and rest, and perhaps, choose another, better, life to live.

There are no solutions to my problems. I cannot be where I want to be, I am not wanted where I am, and I do not dare leave. I am trapped, I am lonely, I am miserable, I am friendless. I want out.

Drowning was not supposed to be a bad way to die, although, Faia admitted she had not actually talked to anyone who had died that way. There was always speculation in the village, though. The faces of those who drowned always looked peaceful. . . .

Face down in the tub, she thought. *That way my nose will not float to the top by accident.*

She rolled over, sobbing, and braced herself on her hands and knees in the hot water. Tears streamed down her cheeks. Again she saw Kasara, and her mother's grave, and Aldar's face just before she abandoned him.

She forced the air out of her lungs in a slow, hard breath. The fact that she could not stop crying made it difficult to keep all the air out of her lungs.

Lady, please just let this all end!

She held her head under the water and gasped in . . .

. . . And came flying out of the water, coughing and sputtering, her throat and eyes and lungs burning. She lurched to the side of the tub and hung her head over and vomited until nothing was left to come up. Then she retched in painful dry heaves. Every labored breath was agony. The chill air of the stone room made her shiver, and the mess on the floor made her cringe with embarrassment.

I do not want to die, her mind shrieked, as she clung to the side of the tub. *Lady, Lady, what sort of idiot am I?* She shivered and shuddered, and slowly caught her breath, and allowed herself to slump back into the tub.

I do not want to die, she told herself again,

beginning to believe it. *In spite of everything, I still want to live.*

Faia looked at the mess she had made, and felt ashamed—both for her weakness in trying to kill herself, and for the weakness of her body when she failed. Finally she felt strong enough to do something about it. She clambered onto the cold stone floor, grabbed one of the coarse white towels dangling from the rack, and began mopping up the bile.

"How did you know she wouldn't kill herself?" Medwind Song looked slit-eyed at the short, round woman who propped casually against the wall of the bath house.

The Mottemage of Daane University shrugged. "I didn't know. I only knew that if we interfered when we sensed her intent, and stopped her from trying, she would try again later, in some manner perhaps more likely to succeed than by drowning herself in the bathtub."

"She almost did succeed, Rakell."

"*Motte* Rakell, you heathen. And yes, indeed she did. Her will to die was very powerful, and her grief was powerful, and she almost managed to suicide in a manner I would have thought impossible." The Mottemage dropped her voice to a whisper as several students drifted by on their way to the Greathall. "She knows she almost succeeded, though—and that is all to the good. Right at this moment, she is very, very thankful that she didn't. Your feel the emotions she projects as clearly as I do. Now, finally, she is grateful to be alive—and that is something, Med, that we could not have given her, no matter how we talked to her about the wonders of life or the promises of tomorrow."

Faia waited impatiently for Medwind to bring her clothes back. The coldness of the stone room made it impossible to sit outside of the tub, but her skin was as wrinkled as the hide of a hairless cat, and she had already added hot water to her bath twice to keep from freezing.

The discomfiting notions that Medwind might have been delayed, or have forgotten her, or have gotten even hungrier than she had been and abandoned her, naked, in the bath house, flitted through Faia's mind.

The slam of a door echoed through the bath house, and she overheard the chattering voices of two young women coming closer. Neither voice was Medwind's—and Faia didn't want to be joined, even accidentally, by strangers.

She slipped out of the cooling water of the tub and silently locked the door of her bath cubicle.

The words of the girls' conversation became distinct.

"—and I think she got bored with the Magerie's rules and ran off with a man."

"Hah! Hasn't that thought crossed your mind, too, more than once, Layadar?"

"Of course. But then, I'm not Enlee. Enlee was so close to graduation. She was the best adept in her Circle—she could have had almost any open position in the University. And she had all that talent—I can't imagine giving up a lifetime career in the University for a mere man."

The second speaker mumbled something that was drowned out by the sound of water filling a tub.

"Sure, it was strange she left her stuff behind. But maybe she hadn't planned on running off with him. If he was really, you know, exciting, maybe she forgot all about her stuff. I mean, if she'd give up a position in the Magerie, what would a few possessions be? Nothing but things you have to drag around behind you from place to place, that's what." Layadar sounded confident about that.

The second voice held a knowing smirk. "You'd leave your precious stuff behind, hmmm?"

Layadar giggled. "Well, I don't know . . . but maybe for the right man—"

"Sure. If he comes along, let me know. I want your beakers and your athame. Mine are getting really shabby."

Faia heard the two dissolving into peals of laughter. She winced.

I could just sink under the water a bit. Then I would not be eavesdropping.

The first voice took on a conspiratorial tone, and Faia's attention was captured in spite of her intentions.

"By the way, our instructors found the cause of that massive energy drain. Did you hear?"

"No. What made it?"

"Some big, hulking peasant shepherd girl— Lavia saw Frelle Medwind bringing her from the wingmount stables."

"You jest."

"Sworn truth. Covered in mud and wearing men's clothing. I heard she's going to train here."

"Rutting gods!—a hedge-wizard, huh? Who would have guessed?" Layadar began to giggle. "Anchee, you *know* where they're going to have to room her, don't you?"

Anchee thought about that for a moment and apparently came up empty. "No. Where?"

"With her Immaculate and Bitchy Highness, Yaji. She's the only one not sharing quarters right now. Yaji will just die. Can you imagine?"

Anchee apparently could. Faia heard her response— "The Glorious Spoiled Yaji and a stinking peasant!"— and the cruel laughter echoing around her little stone cubicle until finally she lay down under the water and the sound muffled and lost its sting.

Well enough, she thought. *If they want a peasant, by the Lady and Lord, they shall have a peasant— and no compromises. I'll shove peasant down their throats until they never laugh at one of us again. Bitches!*

After the grief, anger felt good.

* * *

Medwind tapped at the cubicle door, and arranged her face to look cheerful. She didn't want Faia to know that she knew about the suicide attempt. That seemed to be the best course of action.

"Faia," she called, "it took me a while to find some student's gear that would fit you, but I have it now. Sorry about the wait." She handed a nice belted jade green robe and some matching undergarments and a pair of calfskin slippers in through the door.

Faia shoved them back out. The hostility in the girl's voice carried clearly. "I will wear *my* clothes. No others."

Ouch! What has set her off like that? I wouldn't have expected her to be angry at me at this point.

"Your clothes will make you stand out among the other students, Faia. You are already very different. If you at least look as they look, they may have an easier time accepting you—and you won't find yourself so lonely."

"My clothes, lady, or none. Either suits me."

Medwind thought about that. There was a certain determination in the girl's voice that made her think Faia might actually choose to tromp around the campus stark naked if she didn't get her own *d'leffik* clothes back. Wouldn't that look good to the Mottemage, who would hold none other than Medwind Song responsible for the breach of etiquette?

It's your life, dear, the instructor thought grimly. *You can make it as lonely and unhappy as you like.*

"I'll get your clothes, then, but we are going to be very late for midden."

"I will not starve."

And that is to be that. I've been put in my place, and as far as she's concerned, I'll stay there. That attitude isn't going to make her one of the great favorites around here.

A thread of the Mottemage's thoughtspeech broke through Medwind's irritable musings. :*She doesn't have to be a great favorite. She has to learn control, and discipline, and responsibility—and the path she is choosing now will take her to that knowledge faster than a path full of air-headed silliness—though I am sure this is not her intent.:*

Two giggling students came out of one of the bath cubicles, rosy-cheeked and with their hair dripping. They nearly bumped into Medwind, so lost were they in their own gossipy conversation—until they recognized her, when they both paled and shut up.

Medwind watched their scurrying forms disappearing down the hall with bemusement.

I guess lonely is less objectionable than dizzy. She sent her own thoughtspoken comment back to the school's head mage. *:Yes, Mottemage, I believe I see what you mean.:*

She couldn't imagine the dour, reserved Faia acting like that—but, well, one never knew.

Yaji Jennedote sat at the far end of the Fourth Circle's trestle table, pretending she didn't notice the seat across from her was the only one empty—again. Her spine was ramrod straight and her chin held high; and she ate her thick, crusty bread and spiced stew as if she were the Mottemage dining on erd glabon and fine sturgeon roe. She told herself she didn't care that the others of Fourth Circle despised her—after all, they were just jealous.

But eating alone every day grew tiresome. And the giggling, whispered conversations that mocked and excluded Yaji hurt more than she would have ever admitted.

So Yaji sulked in her own little world at the far end of the table. She was almost too far gone in her own grim fantasies of personal glory and retribution to notice the astonished hush that fell over the Greathall. Almost . . . but not quite—

She glanced down to the double doors of the Greathall, where the stunned gazes of the rest of the students and instructors were fixed.

By Broeyd's eyes, where did they find her?

Yaji had never seen the like of the woman who stood framed by the ancient stone doors. She was taller than any woman Yaji knew—in truth, she was taller than most men Yaji had seen. She even towered over that barbarian Medwind Song. Her square jaw and high cheekbones gave her a proud, stubborn look; her pale eyes beneath their dark brows missed nothing as she stared across the lines of tables.

Her white cotton tunic draped gracefully from her broad shoulders and cinched at her small waist with a woven belt that held a dagger on her right hip and a magic bag on her left; she'd braided her thigh-length brown hair in a complex pattern and had woven red and blue cords through it. She wore a primitive silver-and-bone necklace, too, which had an aura of Power that made Yaji nervous. Even the woman's worn leather pants and stained leather knee-high boots looked *right* on her somehow, in spite of the setting.

Yaji thought the woman could pass for a heathen goddess easily enough. All she'd need would be a flaming sword—and an army of lusty men behind her.

What a heathen goddess was going to do at midden in the Greathall was a mystery to Yaji, however.

The instructor that stood at the goddess' side said something to her, and Yaji watched, fascinated, as the two fixed their eyes on the empty seat across from *her* and began working their way to the back of the hall.

"That's her," the girl seated beside Yaji whispered to the friend that sat across from her. "That's the one they brought in by wingmount this morning. She's a big thing, isn't she?"

"Gods, Lavia," the friend whispered back. "Is she the mage everyone has been so lathered up about?"

"I guess so."

They fell silent as the tall woman and the instructor neared.

Yaji bit her lip nervously. If this was the mysterious mage, then even Yaji, notoriously insensitive to Power, had felt her surge several days earlier. Yaji had heard the rumors—that the surge she'd felt had made a city and everyone in it disappear, and had flattened trees for ten leagues in every direction, and had raised tornadoes and earthquakes and turned loose the demons of the saje-hells.

Lavia, sitting beside her, elbowed her sharply, and flashed a malicious grin in her face.

"Your new roommate," she whispered.

Yaji's stomach tightened and her appetite vanished. The idea of rooming with a powerful and perhaps temperamental mage who had the look of a goddess would make anyone lose her appetite, she thought.

Medwind Song looked at the peasant and said, "Faia Rissedote, this is Yaji Jennedote. She'll be your roommate."

Faia glanced at her without interest, and nodded to show she had heard.

Medwind raised an eyebrow, but shrugged and said, "I'll leave you to make your own introductions, then."

When she left, the tall girl sat down across from Yaji without making a sound, as haughty and standoffish as if she were the goddess she seemed to be. She ladled a bit of stew from the tureen into her bowl, then fixed her eyes on that bowl, eliminating any chance of introductions.

That, Yaji decided after watching her for a moment, would be just fine.

Because Yaji had come to the conclusion that the peasant girl was not quite so imposing sitting down. The clothes that looked impressive from a distance smelled faintly of sheep from close up. The silver wolf's-head amulet around the girl's neck hung on a silly peasant fortune-telling chain like those Yaji had seen in the local market—cheap, worthless trinkets, those chains. Which meant that the amulet was undoubtedly a cheap trinket, too. And the girl looked younger up close than she had at a distance—and she was simply *covered* with freckles, and her eyes were red from crying. Yaji guessed the stranger was at least several years her junior.

So. Not a goddess, after all. Just another brawny peasant girl—big as an ox and about as attractive. And slated to be my roommate, too.

Yaji dipped delicately into her spiced stew and studied the girl from under her eyelashes.

Not likely that she was responsible for that rush of Power, no matter what the rumors are. She doesn't have the look of a mage. More likely she's someone who might know who was responsible. And they're going to stick her with me until they find out what she does know—which, from the look of her, could take forever.

Yaji wrinkled her nose. She hated the idea of sharing her room with anyone; she'd had roommates, and had managed to, well—"encourage" might be the right word—she'd managed to encourage them to ask for transfers in short order. She supposed if she had to share, a powerful mage, even an untrained one, would have been livable. After all, rooming with a real Power would have reflected some glory on her.

But rooming with a peasant—

Yaji smiled slyly. It shouldn't be any problem to get a timid country mouse to ask for a transfer. A few demonstrations of Yaji's magic would scare her off in a hurry.

Faia tried to count the number of people she saw in front of her in the Greathall, failed, and was reduced to estimating the way she would have estimated the size of another shepherd's flock.

More than eight hundred people! More than in the villages of Willowlake and Bright together. The shepherd with a flock that size, she decided, *would need a pack of sheepdogs, two assistant shepherds, and horses to ride while chasing after the whole mess.*

Every single person in the huge hall was a woman, Faia noticed—and all of them were staring at her.

She straightened, presenting to them the same aura of fearlessness she had presented to the mountain lion that attacked her flock in the highlands. At that moment, not Faljon's words, but her mother's, came back to her. They were the words Faia heard when she made ready to take her mother's flock to the highlands alone for the first time, when she was fourteen years old.

Faia, wolves sense weakness, test for it, watch for it—and if they are not stopped by something stronger than they are, the weakest of your flock will die. With wolves, you have two tasks to perform in order to be a good shepherd. First, you must be stronger than they are. Second, you must make sure that they know you are stronger.

Faia imagined the women before her transformed into a pack of wolves. These were her enemies. She could respect them, as she respected the wolves—they had strength and cunning and courage, perhaps—but she could never forget that they only waited for her weakness to cull her out of their midst. She could see the hunting look in their eyes. The hunger was there. She was not one of them, and that meant that she was either a stronger predator . . . or prey.

She would never let herself become prey.

So she strolled calmly through their midst to the empty seat Medwind pointed out, ignoring them as only a great predator can ignore lesser predators. She took her seat at the end of the table without faltering, and spooned some of the foul-smelling stew into a bowl. Then she forced herself to eat the noxious stuff, even though the spices made her throat burn and her tender eyes water. She ignored the fragile, raven-haired beauty who sat across from her, and the young women who sat to her right. She was not a wolf as they were wolves—but neither was she prey. She was a solitary predator, and greater and more deadly than a pack of wolves.

She kept reminding herself of that.

* * *

A tentative ray of sunlight peeked through the clouds and shone into the study in the Mottemage's private quarters. The light shimmered through half a dozen colored crystals that hung on the windowpane, then fragmented and bounced off of carelessly piled stacks of books and got lost amid hundreds of oddly shaped and colored candles. One of the fragments of light made it far enough to flash off the side of a delicate, fan-tailed goldfish that swam in a miniature fountain in the corner of the room.

The sunlight never reached the tawny, gold-pointed, blue-eyed cat who sat on a gargoyle that adorned Rakell's oak end table, patiently trying to strike a quicklight on the starter·strip on the side of the box. The cat looked out the window as the fragile beam vanished behind the clouds. He gave an enormous sigh and returned his attention to the quicklights.

"Flynn, put the damned firesticks down and go catch some mice or I'll slice you into tidbits and feed you to the fish." The voice was husky, scratchy—and very stern. The cat's tail twitched and his ears flattened back for the briefest of instants before he thought better of it. Then he dropped the matches and arched fluidly off the end table, neatly missing the various books and pieces of magical paraphernalia and art objects that covered the floor.

"Mottemage, I wonder at the wisdom of giving a cat hands—even rudimentary ones."

"As I have wondered at someone else's wisdom in giving humans hands. I assume it will all begin to make sense to me in some far future life." The raspy voice laughed.

Medwind had to search for a moment before locating the owner of the voice. She finally found her—a woman with graying hair that still held a touch of its original auburn, and blue-fire eyes that were, even at that moment, lit by inner amusement. The Mottemage curled deeper into the heavy brocades of the chair and snorted.

Medwind thought the snort sounded more than a little like that of one of the Motte's pet wingmounts, but she shielded that errant impression carefully.

"Your new peasant protégé and her screaming aura must be giving you a headache by this time," the Mottemage observed.

Medwind grinned. "She is a little loud. I just left her at midden, facing off the entire campus as if they were a pack of wolves."

"I *know* that, dear. I could feel the tension from here."

"The amulet she wears amplifies her emotions. She's a very weak empath, if she senses emotions at all—and I don't think she's aware that she's projecting. But even when she was fully shielded at Willowlake, I could pick up her grief, Rakell."

The Mottemage took a long draw on the huge silver stein she held, sighed deeply, then grinned at her favorite. "*Motte* Rakell, Medwind, dear. I don't care if you are a damned barbarian—you can remember the formalities with me . . . or I'll turn you into a neutered wingmount. You'd hate that. So—get the girl to quit wearing the bloody amulet, if it's what's making her emotions scrape across the back of my mind that way. She's grating on my nerves."

Medwind chuckled. "I'll take care of it, *my'etje*."

"Don't give me any of you foreign nicknames, either, you. I could still eat you and a dozen of your ilk for *nondes*." Motte Rakell flipped a page of the mammoth tome that rested on her lap, and focused for a moment on the contents of the page. Her eyebrow flicked with interest, and she glanced up at Medwind.

"Hand me one of those plants, Med."

"Which one?"

"Doesn't matter. This looks interesting, and I want to try it."

Medwind picked a small, sickly looking philos off the windowsill, thinking that there weren't many people in the world who could wreck a philos. The Mottemage could—she put her love and her energy into animals and people; her plants got taken care of on the sly by any of the instructors or students who could slip the poor green martyrs something when she wasn't looking.

Motte Rakell picked up the yellowed plant and rested her fingers on the glossy, heart-shaped leaves. She closed her eyes, and for a moment, nothing happened.

Then Medwind saw the plant's shape change. Its flat leaves curled in on themselves and grew long, shiny spines along their inside surfaces. Its stalk pushed out hairy, dew-covered needles which thickened and darkened.

The spiny stalks began to move up and down on their own, slowly, while the spiny leaves spread open like toothed jaws.

The Mottemage opened her eyes, studied the results of her experiment critically for a moment, then smiled. She handed the potted plant back to Medwind.

"Now the damned thing will feed itself," she growled. "Careful how you pick it up or it may try to make you its next meal."

Medwind gingerly carried the plant over to the windowsill and returned it to its place.

"Now," the Mottemage said from her perch in the brocaded chair, "why are you interrupting my rest?"

Medwind searched for a chair that wasn't occupied by books, papers, paraphernalia, or cats, and gave up. She settled cross-legged on the floor, then nodded. "As a matter of fact, I wanted your opinion on something."

"Your hulking country mage."

Medwind grinned ruefully. "I want to room her with somebody other than Yaji."

"Yaji has the only open room."

"I know. But I think she would be willing to take in someone other than Faia."

The Mottemage's sarcastic snort was not lost on Medwind. "Of course she'd be willing to share with someone other than your big, ignorant peasant. And what would she learn from that?"

"I'm not worried about what Yaji will learn at this point. She isn't living up to her potential because she's lazy and self-indulgent. I am worried about how her hostility will affect Faia—and Faia has suffered so much already."

"Yes, she has. And Faia has already proven that she's a big girl who can take care of herself."

Medwind watched the Mottemage out of the corners of her eyes, studying her thoughtfully. "How do you mean?" she asked.

"Did you think that Jann wouldn't come racing in here looking for blood after her little fight with Faia? That story, in a dozen variations, is making its way around campus right now, by the way. Faia has garnered a bit of support for her attack. Apparently Frelle Jann has been stepping on toes other than ones wearing peasant's boots of late." The Mottemage smiled slowly. "No, Medwind. Your prize pupil may not make rooms full of new friends in the next few days, but I think you'll see that she won't become a stepping mat for Yaji, either. And I think she may be just the medicine that will boost Yaji into living up to her potential."

Medwind sighed. "As you wish, then, Motte Rakell."

Medwind rose and prepared to leave.

"By the way," her superior said, "it's nice to see you without that damned bone thing sticking through your nose. I hope you've gotten rid of it for good."

"Only for today."

The Motte sighed excessively and rolled her eyes in mock-dismay. "Too bad."

As Medwind left her superior's apartment, she heard Rakell shouting again. "Flynn, you infernal beast, if

you strike that quicklight, I'll hang you by your whisk-
ers and rip your tail off with my bare hands!"

Medwind grinned. The Mottemage *deserved* Flynn.

The trees arched overhead, leaving the forest floor
in twilight gloom even at midday. A slender young
woman, dressed in student robes, lay on the ground.
Her wrists and ankles were bound with ropes clumsily
twisted from vines. A wad of cloth torn from her robe
and shoved in her mouth kept her from screaming.
She struggled, and lashed out magically at her captors.
Rocks, leaves, twigs, and other detritus from the forest
floor spun in a miniature tornado that the group clustered about her shielded themselves from, then effec-
tively ignored.

The leader of her captors mindspoke the others.
:*Have you readied her for the ritual?*:

One of those spoken to groveled. :*Oh, yes. Yes—
and is she not lovely? Surely you will find her fair
enough, and young enough, and mighty enough—*:

The first speaker regarded the groveler with disdain,
:*I will find her all of these things if this works. If not,
you will find me someone more suitable.*: The leader
studied the intended victim with sudden displeasure.
:*Why does she fight? Why have you not subdued her?*
Why, you snivellers?!:

:*We have not the strength to control her mind. She
is strong, and we are still weak.*:

:*If this fails, we will be weaker still.*:

:*There is still* mehevar.:

The leader was suddenly thoughtful. :*There is. But
we will try this first.*:

The leader leaned over the student and stared into
her eyes. The aura of wicked magic pervaded the area.
The girl's eyes grew huge, then narrowed with concentration. After an instant, miniature bolts of lightning
erupted from her body and leapt at her captor. The
leader, however, fended them off without apparent
difficulty. The girl appeared to realize she was lost,

and struggled harder, fighting to free herself from her bonds, to rid her mouth of the gag—then abruptly, she lay still, staring up into the eyes of her tormentor. Her color changed to ash-white, and when she failed to blink, the leader backed off, swearing.

:*She's not breathing,*: one of the observers mind-whispered. :*Look at her—she's dead!*:

:*She was defective,*: the leader noted bitterly. :*There was a weakness in her heart—she would have been useless, even for mehevar. Thank the gods the weakness manifested before I took her over. But now I have wasted all of that energy for nothing.*:

The leader snarled at the followers and demanded, :*Nevertheless, some power may linger from her death. Glean off what you can, then use the energy to find me someone more suitable. When you are finished, dispose of her body in the woods. And hurry. I weary of this long wait.*:

Chapter 4

THE SAVAGE, THE HEATHEN, AND EVIL AWAKENED

:*COME here*,: a gentle voice whispered into the minds of the students studying in their dorms and the library. :*Come here*,: it requested, so reasonably, so faintly that mages and students felt only a sudden slight tug, an impulse to go to the lake. :*Come here*,: it crooned into the souls of mages and hedge-wizards scattered throughout Mage-Ariss.

Several University mages looked up from their work, frowned as their concentration was interrupted by a sensation as slight as the whine of a stingfly heard from another room—and then, when the passing strangeness that caught their attention did not recur, turned back to their work. A few students went so far as to look out their windows toward the darkening sheet of water over which the sun set.

The pretty girl who ran the Aelere District herbal supply shop on Five Round Way put down her mortar and pestle and herbs when she heard the call. The fertility decoction she was making for the wealthy young wife of the district banker would wait. She looked at her bondmate, and with a puzzled expression, kissed him. "I'm going out for a little while," she said. "If the baby wakes up, I have some nut-milk already prepared. That will keep him happy until I get back."

Her mate looked at her, surprised. "Where are you going?"

Her expression became troubled, and she averted her eyes. "I don't have something I need," she told him. She knew it was an evasion, but still, it felt like the truth when she said it.

He nodded, not liking the look in her eyes, but not knowing what to say to keep her from going.

Out on the Sookanje periphery, in the little blue cottage beside the Woolcloth Makkenhaus, the neighborhood's new hedge-wizard wrapped her divining cards in the middle of a reading and told her client, "I'm sorry, but something has just happened in the spirit realm that requires my attention. Will you be able to come back—" she looked on her filesheet and made a notation, "about sixth bell tomorrow?"

The client nodded, bewildered. "Well, I suppose so. But couldn't you just tell me now about the man in my future—" She discovered herself talking to an empty room. The pretty young card reader was gone. "Well, I never—" the older woman muttered. Then she shrugged. The ways of the magical folk were frequently beyond explanation. Quietly, she left, locking the door behind her.

A child three weeks away from her adult initiation heard the call, quit floating objects around her room (a newly acquired talent she had not yet announced to her parents, since they were hoping she would take an apprenticeship in the weaver's makkenhaus, and since they had often spoken badly of the city's mages), and slipped out of her bedroom window. She ran through the city streets in her nightrobe.

A delicate ebony-skinned house-bruja, out tending

her plants in the darkness, put down her watercan and followed the rich unspoken promises of the voice without a word to the family and friends who sat laughing and chatting in her house.

And walking from the wingmount stables to an appointment with a friend in the senior students' dorm, one apprentice heard the call, and felt it more clearly than any of the rest of her classmates. To her, it was a soft tickle at the back of her neck, a sudden rush of excitement, the promise of something—well, wonderful—waiting just over there. :*Come here,*: she felt—and having lacked much of anything wonderful in her life for a very long time, she complied. To the voice that beckoned to her soul, Amelenda Tringdotte responded by turning off of the path and drifting across the quad toward the woods surrounding the Kie Lake with a boneless, liquid gait. Her student robe flowed around her ankles, her hair lifted and danced around her face. She looked very young and very beautiful—but only Flynn, the cat with hands, was out on that part of the grounds to notice, and because Flynn was deeply involved in paying court to a round-eyed, jet-black queen, he paid her little attention. No one else noticed her at all her.

So when Ame entered the woods, she did so unremarked.

"Well, this is the room."

Yaji elbowed past Faia and shoved one of fifty identical doors on the long, narrow stone hall open and stomped in. Faia followed behind her in time to see Yaji flick her fingers in the air to set lamps all around the room blazing with cool white light. When she looked startled, the other girl smirked.

"Ghostlights," Yaji said. She didn't need to add *dimskull* to her curt remark. Her tone implied it.

It had been an exhausting day, and Faia felt drained. Medwind Song had grabbed her following midden for a whirlwind tour of the campus, a flurry of introductions, a mountain of paperwork, and then dropped her off in the tender care of her new roommate.

The new roommate was visibly unhappy with the news. The girls in the other room of the bath house had been right. Faia sensed impending trouble.

Medwind had not been willing to listen to any arguments when she went about confirming the rooming assignment for the two young women. Yaji had attempted to bargain a trade, Faia for any other student—an action that left Faia feeling very much like a wormy sheep at market—and when Yaji discovered Medwind was unshakable, accepted her fate with sour humor. And Faia had found herself toted along in the other student's wake as if she were carrion three days dead.

What she had hoped for more than anything was just to be able to drop into bed to sleep without any conversation.

That, obviously, was not to be.

Her new room bore heavy marks of its other occupant. All the walls were covered with papers, parchments, diagrams, and fancy scripts in brightly colored inks; the desks and the "spare" bed were equally inundated by beakers and athames, books, ledgers, odd jewelry, scrying balls and mirrors, candles, chalk, ink and jars of exotic ingredients. Projects in all stages of completion (except, Faia noted, for completion itself) littered the floor, the chairs, and the tops of every article in the room that didn't move. The doors of both of the room's wardrobes were open, displaying overflows of Yaji's brilliantly colored finery. A bell lute lay on Yaji's unmade bed.

Underneath the mess, it was a large, agreeable room. Pale wood paneling over one of the stone walls added warmth, and the desks and beds and wardrobes of the same pale wood were well made, and fancier than any Faia had ever used. The single window was glazed with tiny diamonds of pale rose glass, and was flung open to reveal, in the last shadowed stretches of daylight, a wooded park and the leading edge of the lake that lay across the grounds. There were two pentacles painted side by side on the floor, properly oriented with their leading apexes aimed north. Yes, she decided, it was a very nice room.

Still, Faia had never seen such an abundance of junk in her life. Tactlessly, she admitted as much.

"Do you never clean in here?"

"This is organized the way I want it. I like to have my work spread out and undisturbed."

Faia nodded. "Well, I like to sleep lying down, and unless you move this stuff, I will not be able to." She looked closer at the equipment that littered her bed. "Some of these things of yours are a waste."

Yaji glared at Faia. "Oh, really? You know so much about magic, do you?"

"I know what works. A bowl of water serves as well as one of those pretty crystal globes for scrying, and you can change the water's ingredients to suit your purpose. There is nothing wrong with dried herbs if you cannot get fresh—but this time of year, fresh can be had, and cheaper, too. And what in the Lady's Name do you intend to do with a jar full of butterfly wings?"

"It's a spell I'm developing myself. For beauty."

Faia snorted. "You misuse the Lady's creatures for your own vanity, and you will find the price high indeed."

Faia started shoveling Yaji's things without ceremony into a heap in the middle of the floor.

"Wait a minute!" Yaji yelled. "I didn't tell you you could move my things!"

"No, you did not. And I did not ask." Faia continued excavating through the mess in search of the bed.

"But that's all *mine*!" Yaji wailed.

"You are welcome to help move it."

Faia was not in the mood for any more of Yaji and was not, she thought, going to be able to tolerate any more of anything this day. She found the covers on the bed, pulled them back, then stripped to the skin.

"What are you doing?" Yaji asked.

"Going to bed."

"It's almost time for *nonce*, and afterward, evening studies. You can't go to sleep now. And you can't intend to leave all my belongings on the floor."

Faia crawled between the covers and pulled them over her. "Good night, Yaji."

"Look, you, I have an entire set of lessons I have to do tonight," Yaji mewled, "and I'm in no temper to work them while crawling over and around some slumbering giant."

"Pity. Then work them elsewhere."

Faia closed her eyes and feigned sleep. Yaji's voice nattered on, but the words drifted by without ever connecting. And soon, Faia wasn't feigning at all.

Nightmares crawled through Daane University that night—crept from student to student, slithered from instructor to assistant, until they touched, briefly, every single soul. They were weak and tentative nightmares, new-hatched dragonlets hesitantly breathing flames for the first time. But like new-hatched dragonlets, they held the promise of becoming much bigger.

The first tentative ray of sunlight fell through the rose-tinted window directly on Faia's face. She woke, pushing away the last clinging shreds of an unrecallable bad dream, and thought the sunlight and the breaking day pleasant—until her eye caught her new roommate, dressed in an obnoxiously frilly pink cloud of a nightgown, sprawled on the other bed.

Yecch. Here I am, then, and there she is, and things could only get worse from this point.

Faia rose and pulled her tunic over her head. She crept to the window.

Outside, it was beautiful. The endless rains were

gone, and the sky had cleared, and promised sunshine.
The lake that began on the other side of the campus
greensward beckoned invitingly. In the still morning
air, its surface reflected the silhouettes of the ancient,
gnarled trees that dipped to its edge, and the horsetail
whites of cirrus clouds high overhead. Boulders, worn
smooth and round by near-eternities of passing time,
stretched along the shore like a line of lizards crawling
out of the shadows to sun themselves. Little blue
hovies skimmed and dipped and circled in the pink
dawn, chasing insects.

*I'm sure I'm not supposed to wander around here
without telling someone what I'm doing—but I don't
care. Let the rest of the world find me if it can,* Faia
thought. *I'm going to go see that lake.*

The deed was as simple as the idea. Faia tugged on
the rest of her clothes and her boots, shoved her rede-
flute into her pocket, and sneaked out the door.

At the water's edge, she pulled off boots and socks
and dropped them on the first boulder she passed,
and stepped barefoot into the lake. She laughed as
slippery, chilly clay mud oozed between her toes.

Faia reveled in the crisp bite of the morning air and
the startling heat of the just-risen sun on her cheeks.
It was glorious to wander, free of watching eyes and
whispers and stupid curiosity and stupider bigotry. She
squelched along the muddy lake edge until she was
out of sight of the dorm and the tower. The tiny
splashes of her steps stirred up clouds of clear-winged
dew-flies; each misstep on the moss-covered rocks that
alternated with the mud underfoot sent minnows and
crayfish careening in front of her, disturbed by her
passage.

Ahead, one huge flat rock cut far into the water;
she had seen the point of it from the dorm window,
but had not imagined how much more of it there was.
To Faia, the rock looked like it had once intended to
make itself into a bridge, before it had wearied of the
task and quit partway. She clambered up on it, wary

of snakes, and crawled along its length. From that vantage point, she could see that the lake was longer than it appeared from shore. It curved back on itself, and extended northeast into a wilderness of huge trees and tangled thickets—in the midst of giant metropolitan Ariss, that dark and secluded piece of forest sent a chill shiver down Faia's spine. For an instant, she felt terribly isolated, and imagined herself the prey of some great, deadly beast.

Then the feelings were gone, and she laughed at herself. The "wilderness" could cover no more than a few hundred square *estas*. Her sudden flight of fancy had to be nothing more than her sensing the incongruity of an untended stand of trees in the midst of a city manicured to within a fingers' breadth of hysteria.

She relaxed and enjoyed the solitude. There was no one visible. Not on the lake, not in the woods—nowhere. The noises of the city were still audible, but Faia found she could block them out. She concentrated on the tiny susurration of water against the rock, and the chirp of birds, and the lazy drone of insects.

Sunlight warmed the boulder and slanted across her exposed face. She rolled over to lay on her back, and pulled out the rede-flute. Closing her eyes against the glare, she put the flute to her lips and tried a few notes. They carried softly across the water, and picked up echoes from backwaters of the lake.

She played the "Shepherd's Lullaby"—slow, measured, soothing—and then worked variations on it, liking the harmonies of the echoes the water reflected back to her.

The ball of pain she had carried around inside of herself since Bright shifted, and slightly loosened its grip. She sat up, realizing that she felt good. She wished she could make the feeling last. She centered herself, and brought up the circle of earth-energy, and let it move from the rock through her and back into the rock. She changed her music, into the intricate

instrumental for "Lady Send the Sunshine." She sang
the words in her mind as she played.

On the Wheel of/Life I ride,
Circle round from/Birth to death.
Choose my spoke and/Live my life,
Glad for times of sunshine.

> *Lady shears and*
> *Lady cards;*
> *Lady spins and*
> *Lady dyes.*
> *Lady weaves our*
> *Lives to cloth and*
> *Lady sends the sunshine.*

For the moment/I rejoice,
Whatever the/Moment brings.
Cry for sorrow,/Laugh for joy for—
Sometimes I have sunshine.

> *Lady shears and*
> *Lady cards;*
> *Lady spins and*
> *Lady dyes.*
> *Lady weaves our*
> *Lives to cloth and*
> *Lady sends the sunshine.*

I have known the/Pain of birth;
I will know the/Pain of death.
Days between are/Mine to cherish—
Storm and snow and sunshine.

> *Lady shears and*
> *Lady cards;*
> *Lady spins and*
> *Lady dyes.*
> *Lady weaves our*
> *Lives to cloth and*
> *Lady sends the sunshine.*

When she concluded the music, she sat motionless, eyes closed, letting the energy she'd built flow through her.

I am where I need to be, she told herself. *And I can be miserable here, or contented—but I cannot go back to Bright, and I have nowhere else. So I might as well be happy.*

And indeed, she felt happy. Or, if not exactly happy, then free at last of the dark burden of Bright's annihilation.

The sound of bells drifted across the water—deep, rich peals that signaled this first major event of the campus day. As those bells rang, others from across the city began to clamor, too.

As Medwind Song had explained to her the day before, this was the signal of rising time. In the dorm, the rest of the students would be opening their eyes, dragging out of their beds, and readying themselves for *antis*, and then for morning classes. Faia sighed. The bells meant that in a few more minutes, she would have to leave her tranquil hideaway. She would have to go back and face yesterday's mocking students and yesterday's displeased instructors and the unknown and terrifying ordeals of classes.

So it is, so it must be. When the next bells rang, she would go back. Until then, she had no intention of leaving her protected circle.

She played the rede-flute, eyes closed, until the peculiar sensation of being watched drove her music to a faltering halt. Skin prickling, she opened her eyes—and froze. The music had drawn an audience that rested, almost submerged, in the lake, and stared at her with winsome brown eyes.

Otters?

They appeared to be. Blunt-snouted and whisker-faced, they floated in the shadow of an overhanging willow. She counted seven of them.

They were scattered along the bank, up against huge, gnarled roots and low-hanging branches. She measured them against the monstrous, ancient willow, and rubbed her eyes with confusion. *They must be enormous! But they cannot be as big as they appear. I have misjudged the size of the tree—otherwise the beasts would be as long as a tall man.*

Deceptive, those distances—and that had to mean that the lake was smaller than it seemed, too. *A miniature dark forest—the illusion of untamed wilderness— and I will bet that means that this lake is just like the rest of the campus and the city. Artistically planned to just the right, safe scale, manicured and trained to be a play forest.* She felt somehow betrayed. Ariss had seemed friendlier when she thought that there were a few places uncontrolled by people.

There were still the otters, however. She had loved the antics of the little beasts since she was a tiny child. She watched them watching her. Then, recalling games she had played with the highland otters around Bright, she whistled a few notes, then played a brief trill with the rede-flute. The trill imitated as closely as she could the rolling speech of the creatures. Immediately, one of the otters chirped back, its deep contralto warble an odd mockery of the normal soprano call. The beast swam out of the shadow in her direction, while the other six hung back, watching.

She was forced to upwardly revise the scale of the tree and the lake. The "otter" swimming towards her was exactly as huge as her first seemingly impossible estimates had made it. *Mother of us all! How can that be?* she wondered.

She longed to stay and lure the creature closer— but the bells began to ring for *antis*, and she had missed *nondes* the night before. She was starved.

Maybe they will still be here after classes. I shall come back and look for them then.

With real regret, she grounded her shields and turned her back on the swimming otter to hurry toward the Greathall.

*   *   *

Even before the first bells rang, Medwind Song was up and preparing for the day. She stared at her reflection in the mirror and pulled a gold-and-bone ornament from a rack that rested on her dressing table. She fitted the pin through the hole in her left nostril and surveyed the result.

This morning she only vaguely resembled the Daane University instructor she'd so obviously been the day before. Gone was the bright red instructor's uniform, exchanged for a brilliantly colored and precisely patterned Huong-tribe *staarne*. The tribal costume wrapped at wrists and waist and flowed in sweeping folds to mid-thigh. Under it, blue-dyed leather Huong breeches met curl-toed, quilted boots. Gone was her plain, straight hair style, replaced by myriad braids woven into a midnight-black crest that ran from the top of her head to the nape of her neck. Her deep blue eyes were lined by black *esca*, in the Huong-sacred cat-pattern of the senior magician. And now the curving insignia of the Huong-revered *sslis* dangled from her left nostril.

It was this last item that especially drove the Mottemage crazy. The gold-and-bone nose ornament was the sort of barbaric flourish Rakell tried to suppress in her university. The Mottemage said she was striving for unity among her students and professors; Medwind Song thought she was actually trying to achieve homogeneity. Medwind didn't approve of homogeneity.

The instructor listened to the first bells ring across the city and grinned at herself in the mirror. She decided to sit next to Rakell during *antis* to see if she could give the administrator a bad case of indigestion. If she could, it would be sweet revenge for Rakell's insistence that she wear the idiotic red school suit during her search for Faia.

She padded down the spiraling tower steps three at a time, hoping to get to the Greathall before the call to *antis* rang—there might, after all, be an extra sweetroll for her if she was early—passing other, correctly garbed instructors, who apparently had the same plan in mind. They saw her battle dress and gave her knowing smiles as she sailed by.

"Rakell annoy you again, Med?" one called, and laughed.

"Just a little," Medwind admitted. "If she annoyed me a lot, Thea, I could do much better than this."

"Skyclad at High Nonce?"

The barbarian instructor snorted at the idea. "Nothing of the sort. I'd just teach Flynn to mis-play the violitto. I've heard that cat sing—he's tone-deaf as hell."

"Remind me never to make you angry at me! Still, giving Flynn hands wasn't her best idea, either," the other woman agreed. "If that lunatic cat starts playing bad music, it will be her own fault."

The stairwell filled with chuckles.

Medwind continued her headlong bounding down the steps.

Without warning, a wave of blinding pain caught her between the eyes and sent her staggering against the wall. She missed her footing and fell heavily down several steps before hitting the landing. She was conscious of the frightened, inarticulate cries of her colleagues. From all around her, groans and sobs echoed against the cold stone. Red light pounded through her tightly shut eyes, and the scent of blood and fear assailed her nostrils. She was aware of an alien elation—of sheer delight at the misery she sensed. Medwind's breath came fast and sharp, and her fingernails dug into her palms as she willed the torture to stop.

The horror surrounded her and suspended her inside its timeless, eternal self—*It has always been this way, and will always be*, she thought—and abruptly, the horror and its attendant thought were gone.

Silence roared in on heavy feet to fill Medwind's overloaded consciousness. She opened her eyes, and saw nothing but brilliant, awful white. Scent vanished, and sensation with it. Medwind felt she'd been transmuted into bodiless light, as if she were on the point of vanishing.

Then the absence of sensation disappeared too, and she was aware of the throb of a twisted ankle and the taste of blood from her bitten lip, and of aches from arms and knees and back that had careened against stone. She was back in the stairwell with the rest of the instructors, who were beginning to shake themselves and move around. She met their eyes, and saw only stunned disbelief, and terror, and bewilderment.

Litthea Terasdotte, a city-born, civilized instructor—well-dressed, petite, black-eyed, and blonde—bit her lip and glanced at Medwind. "What happened?"

Medwind sat on the step and rubbed at her throbbing ankle. "Don't have any idea, Thea. Nothing like that where I come from—not ever."

Thea nodded. "Nor here. That was bad."

"Bad—intentionally crazy. Evil."

"Evil. Yes, definitely evil. But it's gone now."

Medwind felt a thrill along her nerves, and in the pit of her stomach something lurched. From the back of her mind, she felt echoes of the thing as it laughed. She shivered involuntarily, and shook her head. "Not gone. Just waiting, I think."

Faia sat in the Greathall, listening to spoons-clicking on bowls and teeth, and the shuffle of leather soles on stone, and the occasional rustle of a cloth-covered rump shifting uncomfortably on a hard wooden trestle. All around her, eyes fixed on plates, fingers stirred food listlessly, voices were mute.

Suddenly, there was a clatter from the front of the hall, and heads lifted dully. Faia turned to look too, and saw a barbarian in exotic attire beating on an empty wooden mug with a spoon. It was not until the barbarian began to speak that she recognized the woman as Medwind Song, the tall, red-garbed instructor who had brought her to the university, then stuck her with Yaji.

Song shifted from one foot to the other, then cleared her throat.

"I know you felt the disturbance this morning before *antis*—I understand that all of you are upset."

Disturbance? Faia wondered. *What sort of disturbance?*

"I just wanted you to know that the Mottemage herself is tracking down the source of the Sending. She feels that the mindscream was a random impulse, and was not directed at us—that it was, most likely, an accidental projection from some young woman who suddenly opened up to her *getlingself*, and was overwhelmed and frightened by the experience. None of us feel that you have anything to worry about—and we think we will be able to find the person responsible and bring her under control so that this won't happen again. Until then, please try not to let this incident disrupt your studies."

Getlingself . . . , Faia thought, *getlingself . . . What by-the-Lady could that be?*

The instructor returned to her seat, and the students resumed eating. The silence had been broken, though, and gradually, they began to talk in whispers. The noise level in the Greathall rose.

Yaji, sitting opposite Faia and determinedly ignoring her, turned to the girl sitting to her left and said, "I don't believe what Song said for an instant. Do you?"

The other girl tried to pretend Yaji was not speaking to her, Faia noticed. Then she changed her mind and shrugged. "I guess I might. I remember when I turned twelve and my *getlingself* woke up one day. I was sick, and wanted water so badly—and I wanted it so hard the water came to me. It scared the life half out of me."

Getlingself . . . Lady's Gifts, Faia decided. *Why couldn't they just say Lady's Gifts?*

"Of course it did," Yaji agreed. "My question is, did

it scare the life half out of everyone else in the city at the same time?"

"Well . . ."

"No," Yaji interrupted. "It didn't, of course. So that story they're giving us to keep us quiet and happy is just that. A story."

Faia could not suppress her curiosity any longer. "What are you talking about? What happened this morning?"

Yaji's eyes riveted on hers, and other girls along the table turned and stared.

"What do you mean, what happened?! Didn't you feel that awful mindscream this morning? That torture?" Yaji's voice was shrill enough that other students down the table and from several other tables turned to see what was going on.

"No," Faia admitted. "I did not feel anything. What was it?"

"Nobody knows, *Faia*," Yaji said, the tone of her voice replacing *Faia* with *stupid* in her answer.

Faia winced. "When did it happen?"

"It happened after the get-up bell, right before the call to *antis*. I can't believe you're supposed to be so talented, and you still missed it."

"Well, I am sorry, but I did not feel anything."

Down the table, Faia heard the whispers.

"Wasn't she supposed to be such a mighty hill-mage?"

"I guess what I heard she did to that village was just a fluke after all, if she couldn't feel *that*."

The students snickered and cast superior glances over her head at each other.

Faia felt the heat of embarrassment in her face and on the back of her neck, and knew that she had blushed for everyone to see. *Gods, but I hate this place*, she thought. She bit the inside of her lip to keep from crying.

She choked down the cold grains and slippery white paste from her bowl, wishing she could simply disappear.

The other students eventually tired of staring at her and shifted to other topics of conversation.

Faia tried to ignore the chatter, but found she could not.

"Did Amelenda decide to sleep this morning instead of eating?" one student asked her seatmate.

The other sounded confused. "I don't have any idea. She's your roommate. Why are you asking me?"

"Didn't she spend the night with you?"

"Of course not. Why would you think she did?"

The first girl wrinkled her forehead in worried concentration. "She didn't come to our room last night, and I knew you two were doing a project for Communications—I just assumed—"

"Ame was supposed to come over last night to work on it, but she never showed up, and I thought that she decided to work on her Divinations—" There was a pause. "She promised she would be over one bell past *nondes*. She was very emphatic about it, because I wasn't there the last time she came over to work on the project. I just thought when she didn't show up that she was getting even."

The absent Amelenda's roommate sighed. "What an awful idea. Amelenda wouldn't do something like that. She's too serious about her work. What do you suppose she's doing?"

"She's pretty discreet. I know she's been studying the Mottemage's wingmounts. Maybe she has some private project she's working on to win her a place on staff when she graduates."

The girls gave each other worried looks and changed the subject.

Friends, Faia thought. *I wish I had one.* She pictured Aldar, and for a moment, regretted leaving him in Willowlake.

He is better off away from me, though. He has family. . . . She shoved that line of thought away before the tears that welled up in her eyes had a chance to run down her cheeks and cause her further embarrassment.

She bit her lip in sudden irritation. *Why do you not just sit and feel sorry for yourself, Faia? I am certain there is no one in the world who has ever hurt before, no one who had ever been lonely—*

Her tears dried up, but her appetite was still gone. She pushed the cold, lumpy mess of food away from her and sat staring at the joints in the ceiling stone-work until the bells began their clamor announcing first class.

Mottemage and barbarian instructor strode across the green toward the classrooms.

"Did they believe it?" Medwind Song glanced over at her superior.

"Of course not. Would you have? On the other hand, they'll at least think that we have some idea of what happened—that, perhaps, we even have matters under control. That fact alone will buy us time and will prevent a panic."

"Was it our missing student?"

"Unknown. It was someone with magical aptitude— otherwise the mindscream would not have carried with anything like that force. But Enlee? Who could say."

Medwind looked at the Mottemage, eyes dark with worry. "Or Amelenda. She was missing at breakfast this morning, and her roommate doesn't know where she is."

Rakell's face went white. "No," she whispered. Amelenda was one of her favorites, and her protégé, and the student most likely to carry on with the work the Mottemage had done with wingmounts.

Medwind said softly, "It may be nothing. It may be Amelenda has a young man . . . or got an emergency call from family—there are a hundred explanations."

"And one of them is horrible."

"Don't think the worst." Song rubbed her temples

and sighed softly. "Meanwhile, what should we be doing?" she asked.

"Gods, Medwind—I wish I had an idea. Any idea."

Medwind closed her eyes and inhaled deeply. "Whatever it was that had her scares me. I've never felt such evil. Such concentrated, purposeful, strong evil."

"Nor have I." The Mottemage glanced at her friend with worried eyes. "Except in my nightmares."

"Funny you should mention—" The barbarian shook her head and looked away.

"Nightmares?"

Medwind shook her head, but said nothing. Rakell knew her protégé well enough to understand that to the Huong Hoos, nightmares meant more than they did to the civilized people of Ariss. She also knew Medwind wouldn't be willing to talk about it. She didn't pry. "You'll have to go on with classes today, you know, Med. Nothing can change. We daren't let the students suspect how bad this is, or how close to home."

Medwind nodded grimly. "Something out there slaughtered one of my most promising students, if not two. You knew Enlee was missing?"

The Mottemage nodded affirmatively.

Medwind's voice grew bitter. "And I'm going to sit in a drafty class discussing Fundamentals of Plant Mutation to flighty First-Circles." She jammed her clenched fists into the pockets of the barbarian tunic. "I'll do what I can," she finally muttered.

"What else is there?" the Mottemage asked.

"You can't read, you can't write, you don't know the standard spell signs, you don't know any of the basic wards or entry-level procedures—and you have access to power that leveled a village. What in the seventy abominable saje-hells am I supposed to do with you?"

"I do not know." Faia stared miserably at her feet.

"It was a rhetorical question." Medwind sighed. "I

know where I'm going to place you. There's going to be a riot when I do it, and you can expect to have most of your classmates furious with you, but you'll be going into the advanced classes."

"Why will that cause problems?"

"Because, dear, you can't read. You can't write. You don't know the basics. You just happen to be a conduit for energies that could run bronzeshod over your classmates. They're struggling to gain power. You are trying to find a way to control more power than they'll ever have. Don't expect them to like you for it."

Faia stared at the instructor with frustration. "I did not ask for this."

"No. But you got it. Stop whining and be an adult, Faia. A lot of us ended up with our lives going in directions we hadn't intended."

Medwind studied a sheaf of papers. "Since you're joining us halfway through the school year, I'm going to do something I usually don't. I'm going to assign you to take all your classes with one person, which will save you from having to learn the schedules and instructors, and will give you someone to study with whose schedule exactly matches yours. I'll put you with Yaji."

"No!" Faia blurted. "She cannot stand me!"

"Nor are you terribly fond of her. I already noticed. However, she's good—perhaps one of the few of your peers who has the potential to keep up with you. She isn't living up to her potential, but your presence may be the goad she needs. And she can easily familiarize you with the basics."

There was a light tap on the door, and Yaji came into the cluttered office. Her eyes fixed with unconcealed loathing on Faia. "I'm sorry," she said to Song. "I'll come back later, when you aren't so busy."

"I wanted you here now," the instructor said. Faia noted the cool control in her voice, the "I'll have no nonsense" tone.

Not a woman to cross, Faia thought. *And not a woman to annoy.*

Yaji, however, seemed impervious to the ice in Song's voice. "I'd rather wait until you finished with her before we talked about whatever it was that you wanted to see me for."

Medwind Song's eyes narrowed, and her face grew a wickedly sweet smile. "Just by sheerest coincidence, what I wanted to talk to you about is Faia. Not only is she your roommate, but now she's going to be your class-partner as well. You'll show her what you know of the basics of our system of magic—and in return she'll show you the things she knows. And the two of you will be in every class together so that you can keep up with each other. I think you'll find this arrangement very stimulating—don't you, Yaji?"

There was a long silence.

Song's smile vanished. "Well?"

Not even Yaji could miss the threat in the instructor's voice that time. "Yes, Frelle Medwind," she muttered.

Yaji stared over at Faia, and Faia had the urge to back away from the raging fury in those eyes. *I would as well throw myself in the lake right now with a stone around my neck. That is where I am no doubt going to find myself anyway, and I shall save Yaji the trouble of mussing one of her outfits dragging me there after she has killed me.*

It is going to be hell to sleep in that room tonight.

Fifth class. Fifth cold, stone-walled, slit-windowed room. Fifth long-winded instructor expounding nonsense words like "Keplef theorem" and "wall of impulse" and "cellular resistance" with the air of a god imparting the secret of fire to freezing primitives. Fifth hour of blank-faced students muttering "Yes, Frelle This," and "No, Frelle That." And this time was the worst. This time it was that pompous little helke bitch Frelle Jann.

Faia squirmed in her seat and resisted the urge to yawn. To her left, Yaji made little scratch-marks on pale green sheets she called drypress. To her right, the high slit window displayed a tantalizing glimpse of hot late-spring sunshine and allowed passage to the faintest suggestion of perfumed almost-summer breezes. Faia's eyes fixed on the slit. She could almost feel herself outside, playing her rede-flute and watching new lambs harassing their mothers and chasing each other over the hillside. She could feel the heavy wool of her *erda* pillowed beneath her head, and hear the whisper of meadow grass under her back as she shifted her position; she could smell clover and wildflowers and mountain air. She relaxed into the dream. It was comforting, familiar, and somehow very real. If she concentrated, she could even bring to mind the ripple of a stream. Carried to her on the breeze, she could hear the soft murmur of laughter from a long way off. . . .

Laughter? . . .

She started, and returned her attention to the class. Every face was turned to her, and every eye watched her with malicious amusement, and a touch of calculating anticipation. And they laughed.

"So she's decided to rejoin us. How nice," Frelle Jann commented. "Perhaps we should each thank her for gracing us with her presence." There was more laughter, which trickled off to nearly nothing. There were a few snickers, but even these died down as the class waited to see what the frelle would do.

"Come up to the front of the class, Faia, and, since you feel you know this material so well that you don't need to pay attention, I'll let you demonstrate some of it for us."

The faces of her classmates glowed with unholy joy.

Wolves, Faia thought, *who have spotted the sick sheep, and are waiting for an easy shot at the kill.*

They had enjoyed her lack of education at every opportunity. All day she heard "You mean you can't

read?" and "How can I teach you if you can't write?"
and "What do you mean, you haven't heard of Loink's
Basic Formula for Circle Cleansing? You can't do a
first-level pentacle without it," and "What do you
mean, what's a first-level pentacle ?"

She had ignored the whispered jokes told just loud
enough that she could hear them, about farm girls too
stupid to move out of the way of running horses, too
foolish to know not to buy kellinks from Ranmeers—
She hadn't said a word. She'd pretended not to hear.

Walking to the front of the class, though, she could
not pretend anymore that she was not hurt. She was.
*So what if I am not one of them? So what if I do not
have their education or their money or their fancy
clothes and fancy manners. I'm somebody. I can do
things, too.*

She was overcome by the urge to show them. She
wanted to prove that she was as good as any of them,
so that they could never laugh behind her back again.

Frelle Jann stared coldly up at the tall farm girl
when she reached the front of the classroom. She
leaned forward and whispered upward, for just Faia
to hear, "I'd like for you to remember this in future,
Faia. We have these classes to teach talented mage
students the elements of magic. Not to provide ignora-
muses with a chance to cloudgaze out the windows.
If you haven't any more attention than that, you can
go work in a kitchen cleaning pots. You'll never be a
mage." She raised her voice so that the rest of the
class could hear. "Take this apple, Faia, and repair it
so that it is edible again. We've been discussing the
formulas in class—since you seem to know so much
about them, you shouldn't have any trouble."

Faia held in her hands the withered, dried remains
of an apple. It was a sorry, wormy red windfall apple,
one of last autumn's. She had, in her young life, seen
more windfall apples than anyone had any business
seeing. *Fix it?* she thought. *Fix it? Surely she's joking.*

Faia repressed a smile of unholy glee. They thought

fixing an apple was some sort of wonderful demonstration of magic? *That* was what all these hot-air formulas and equations and long-winded talks were about? No one had said anything before about apples.

She turned to face the class, and held the apple in her outstretched hand. She centered, pulling energy from the earth below her and from the air above, and visualizing the apple as one of her favorite huge tangy green Highland Susskinds. She could taste it, feel it, hear the crunch when she bit into it, smell the pure autumn smell of it—she could see it sitting pale yellow-green and glossy in her hand. She looked at it from all angles, and when she had it fixed in her mind, she closed her eyes and let the energy she'd drawn into herself feed carefully into the withered brown fruit.

When she heard gasps, she opened her eyes.

A perfect Highland Susskind rested in the palm of her hand.

Her dear instructor's jaw rested on the floor.

So the stupid hick from the highlands can do a few tricks they cannot, in spite of their fancy schooling. That ought to show them. Faia grinned viciously, took a bite of the apple with a cheeky toss of her head, and remarked loudly to no one in particular, "Been doing *that* since I was six."

:*I felt that! Did you feel it too?*:
:*Yes, Sahedre. I feel the song of the magic, too.*:
Sahedre was elated. :*Yes-s-s-s! Gods, yes! A body with the power I crave resides here. I glimpse her only at odd moments, but here she hides. Sooner or later, I shall trail this magic back to its maker, and then I shall have her.*:
:*If she has the power, Sahedre,* the second protested, *perhaps she will resist you.*:
:*Aye, she might. I shall see that she does not want to. First, though, I must find her.*:

* * *

Yaji walked beside Faia after *nondes*. They were heading back to the dorm, and Yaji was uncharacteristically quiet. She had been, Faia noted, ever since Frelle Jann's class. Faia saw no purpose in spoiling a good thing.

Yaji took a deep breath, started to say something, then stopped. Her fair brow furrowed, and she glanced at Faia from under her lashes.

What is this? She looks like she is just dying to ask me some question, Faia decided, *and it galls her lily-soft hide to even think of it.* The hill-girl pretended that she had noticed nothing unusual in her roommate's manner. No sense in making things easier for the detestable Yaji.

Yaji, however, was determined. "How did you do that?" she finally asked.

Faia pretended ignorance. "Do what?"

"With the apple. That's advanced work. I mean, I've been doing magic for years, and I've never been able to rejuvenate an apple."

Faia's response was a mild rebuke. "I have been doing magic for years also, Yaji Jennedote. Has it occurred to you that maybe I am better at it than you are?"

Yaji snorted. "Not a chance. How could you be? You don't *know* anything."

Faia laughed, an explosive belly laugh that brought a flush of deep red to Yaji's cheeks. "Perhaps I do not know anything. But I can do things. That is better, I think."

"I'm sorry I asked."

"You only asked so that you could laugh at me, or tell me that I did not do my magic correctly."

There was a long pause. Then Yaji answered with a gentle rebuke of her own. "I only asked because I have never had any luck with that particular assignment, and I was hoping you could help me."

Faia walked along in silence, feeling suddenly small and petty. "Oh," she said. She walked further, staring

at her feet, at the campus, everywhere but at Yaji.
Finally she added, "I am sorry."

Yaji shrugged. "I suppose you had every right to
think what you thought."

"Yes."

"Look—I'm sorry, too. I admit that I didn't want to
room with you. Don't take it so personally. I didn't
want to room with anyone—"

"I heard about that."

"You did?"

"Mmm-hmm. Two girls in the bath house yesterday
referred to you as 'Her Bitchy and Immaculate Highness.' They thought it very funny that you should be
stuck with me."

Yaji was suddenly incensed. "You think that's funny—
what they said?!"

"Not really. The things they said about me were
equally unkind and also untrue—and they had never
even seen me. I hoped they were wrong about you,
too."

Yaji walked slowly up the steps to the dorm, her
fingers trailing on the stone rail. "They were," she said
slowly. "They didn't know it, I guess, but they were
wrong about me. I took a lot of grief from everyone
when I came here. My mother was expelled from
Daane—expelled because she was pregnant with me.
The story got around, and a lot of my fellow classmates
decided that the fact my mother was a local hedge-
wizard instead of a great university mage made me a
failure, too. I was a lot better at magic than everyone
else, though, so when my roommates mistreated me,
I got even. I did really awful things to them. Pretty
soon, no one would room with me. I liked it that way."

"I see."

"It's hell being an outsider—not having any friends."

Faia raised one eyebrow and looked sidelong at Yaji.
"No!" she said. "I cannot imagine."

"That was a stupid thing to say, wasn't it?"

"Yes."

Yaji, a few steps ahead of Faia, stopped dead at her own doorway and stared at her new roommate. "Gods! You just say whatever you think. That's an awful habit." She touched three spots on the door, and muttered a short string of syllables, and the door opened. Yaji stepped across the threshhold, snapped her fingers, and the ghostlights flickered on. She stared at her roommate in the cool white light. "Why are you really here, Faia?"

Faia paced across the room, avoiding Yaji's mess, and sat down stiffly on her own bed. "I am here because my village was destroyed by Plague, and because I grew angry and created a firestorm that melted the very stones into a puddle on the ground. The fine people here did not think I should have done that, so they sought me out and brought me here to make sure I did not do it again."

"Not really." Yaji's expression indicated that she expected Faia to admit to the joke any second.

Faia stretched out on her bed and stared up at the ceiling. "Really."

Yaji stared at her as if she were trying to see straight into Faia's brain. Then she shrugged, and began pulling books off her shelf. "Whatever you say, Faia. Anyway, we have homework to do. Since you can't read the books, I might as well help you with it."

Faia imitated Yaji's shrug. "Whatever you say, Yaji."

Several frelles stretched out in their private lounge, reading by soft white ghostlight. Four sat at the little wooden table in the far corner, submerged in a tight and vicious game of Three-and-One, played for stakes. Their voices rose at irregular intervals, crosscurrent to the readers, and they received dark stares and dropped their volume again until the passions of the game overrode their caution. Two Idargga players clicked their stones across the board, wordless as statues and nearly as motionless. In the near, offhand corner, one group chatted over tea and hardrolls.

All of that Jann saw as soon as she entered the lounge. None of the frelles in the room that evening ranked her, either. She smiled slowly. *Good,* she thought. *Then I can have peace and quiet and put my day behind me.*

The tea-and-rolls group looked her over, and Tella and Delis grinned and waved. "Bring a book, or come to talk?" Tella called.

"Either." Jann went over to join them. She took a cup and poured herself tea, then curled into one of the stuffed, round-backed chairs. "I just want to ground out—today wasn't one of the good ones."

Delis and two of the very new instructors—both of whom had been Jann's students before being taken on staff—laughed heartily. Delis said, "Yah—the story about your day is already making the rounds. I hear you and the child hill-wizard crossed staffs again, and she rubbed your face in the dirt."

Jann's back stiffened. "Hardly. I asked her to rejuvenate an apple, and she did. It was a classroom assignment."

Delis giggled. "Oh, certainly." The blonde girl grabbed another hardroll and looked around at the other frelles. "From what I heard, Jann here told that brawny heathen that she would never be a mage and took her up to the front of the class to humiliate her. Handed her a rotted red fodder apple and told her to fix it. So the girl takes the apple and stares at it like she's never seen an apple before—like so," Delis held out her hand and widened her eyes in mimickry, "and then she draws in enough power to run every ghostlight in the city. *Then,* does she rejuv the apple? *No!* She transforms it. Red fodder apple becomes gorgeous yellow pedigreed eating apple—and in front of everyone, she takes a *bite* of the damned apple—

"—No, she didn't!—"

"—That's crazy!—"

"—Yes, she did. And then tosses off some impudent remark about doing that when she was a little child."

The group surrounding Jann laughed. "Students are
such an agony to the fundament," one remarked.

Tella chuckled. "I wouldn't have thought the girl
capable of much of anything, no matter what the
rumors said she did up in the hills. She doesn't look
bright enough to find her own shoes in the morning."

Delis agreed. "Evidently she's a bit smarter than
she looks—"

Jann blocked out their cheerful remarks. She heard
only the laughter of her colleagues, and not the empathy. The laughter grated deep into her soul, and cut
her pride to ribbons. *Faia has embarrassed me—
humiliated me,* Jann thought. *Twice now, she has
made me into the butt of jokes that are bantered back
and forth among the other students and my colleagues.
I will extract payment for this. She owes me.*

Chapter 5

NIGHT-BOGANS AND MYTHS REBORN

YAJI took nearly an hour to get ready to do homework. Now, dressed in a black-and-gold robe, with her face hidden deep in the folds of a gold velvet cowl, she was carefully chalking along the circumference of one of the dorm's pentacles. Faia, still wearing her shepherd's clothes instead of the robe Yaji had offered, and seated on her bed, watched curiously.

". . . and for the *first* level pentacle," Yaji was saying, "you have to sketch the *outside* circle first, drawn *sunwise*. You say,

> "*By Ehahe, by Vastee, by Glarinia,*
> *Within the circle, about the circle,*
> *By the Eye above, and the Sun her partner, her lover—*
> *Once, twice, thrice.*
> *Once, Ehahe,*
> *Twice, Vastee,*
> *Thrice, Glarinia.*
> *So be ye within this circle.*

"Close the circle, and start with the southwest point of your pentacle, drawing to the north point. Name each wall of your pentacle, like this:

"This, the wall of sound . . .
This, the wall of the sight . . .
This, the wall of touch . . .
This, the wall of taste . . .
This, the wall of smell . . .
To enclose me . . .

"Then you go back over each of your lines again, and rename them with the spirit lines.

"This, the window to Listening . . .
This, the window to Othersight . . .
This, the window to Bringing . . .
This, the window to Knowing . . .
And this, the window to Remembering . . .
To set me free."

What a total waste of time and energy, Faia thought wonderingly. She asked her roommate, "You go through all of that every time you want to work a spell? My gods, it is a wonder you accomplish anything."

She could see Yaji's back go up instantly. "Setting the circle prevents the intrusion of any unwanted elementals, and controls the spell so that it doesn't get out of hand," the slender girl said in a haughty voice. "If you haven't been setting a circle before you work, it's a wonder there's enough left of you to scrape off the floor."

"And since there obviously is, I must be doing something right," Faia countered. She stood and walked to the center of the other pentacle. "My way works just as well, and does not take so damned long. I close my eyes and see myself reaching down through the earth until I find an energy line. I connect my feet to that. Then I see my head stretching up until

I feel an air energy line, and I connect my head to that. Then I run air energy down to my belly, and earth energy up to my belly, and I let them mix until I have filled with the power—and then I form a white ball out of this with my hands and spread the sphere out until it surrounds me.

"It takes longer to explain it than to do it." She closed her eyes and quickly mimed the making of a ball that grew invisibly until her arms were spread out straight. There was energy within easy reach in the city; it felt good to find it and hold onto it. When she touched the heartbeat of earth and sky, her beloved hills did not seem so far away.

Yaji sniffed. "And which gods do you invoke during this quaint little procedure of yours? Whom do you honor? Your method may be fast, but it's inelegant. There isn't any art to it . . . or any beauty."

"Inelegant?" Faia was hurt. She crossed her arms in front of her chest and glared at her roommate. "If you want art, paint a picture. If you want magic, be practical. It is like that silly outfit you are wearing—"

"My *ceremonial robes*," Yaji corrected in a knife-edged voice, "have the blessing of hundreds of years of tradition. Unlike your outfit, they wouldn't be suitable for wearing while mucking a pigsty—but since I don't plan to muck any pigsties soon, that shouldn't be a problem."

Faia refrained from pounding her roommate into paste with her fists only by sheer willpower. Her face went white and her voice grew strained. "*Mucking pigsties?!* This is *shepherd*'s dress. You *earn* the right to wear it, if you have the gift of Tending. In Bright, a piddling little pretender to magic like you would have ended up digging potatoes and washing squalling babies with the rest of the Talentless. You would have had none of your silly clothes and fancy airs there!"

"*Piddling little pretender to magic!*" Yaji shrieked. "Piddling . . . little . . . pretender—I'll show *you* who's a piddling little pretender, you horse-faced, cow-assed

cretin! Any *gift* that includes chasing sheep around a
field like a dog isn't much of a gift." Inside her circle,
Yaji began drawing symbols in the air.

Faia spread her arms out and closed her eyes. Around
her, the air flickered with bright points of visible energy
that coalesced into a glowing blue half-sphere whose
edge followed the pentacle at her feet.

As the energy accumulated in a visible ball around
Faia, Yaji stopped drawing symbols in the air and
stared. "By Gatho's Balls," she whispered in horror.
She had never actually *seen* a shield before. She had
not realized until she saw the shield that such a feat
was possible. It was not possible for her, she knew. "I
quit," she said, and stepped out of her pentacle without a further word or gesture.

Faia, eyes still closed, felt a jolt as her roommate's
circle shattered, and the ungrounded energy that was
released bounced around the room. At the same
instant, she felt the sudden arrival of a presence—a
curious, somehow dangerous presence. When it
sensed her awareness of it, it vanished without a trace.

That was odd, she thought, and opened her eyes.
The bright blue glow that surrounded her startled her
as much as it had Yaji. She sucked in her breath, and
began to ground her energy. *I could have cooked her,*
Faia realized. *I almost did. When they told me that I
needed to learn control, I did not realize how very
right they were.*

Yaji sulked on her side of the room. Faia regretted
the fight, but did not really want to talk to Yaji in
order to resolve it. So she climbed into her own bed
without a word, and forced relaxation upon herself
until she fell asleep.

Medwind commandeered one of Rakell's chairs for
herself. She removed a stack of texts and manuscripts,
a globe of crystal the size of a morka egg, and Flynn,
who fixed her with the feline version of the evil eye
before he stalked over to Rakell's unoccupied chair

and curled up in it. "We off duty?" she yelled toward the kitchen.

The Mottemage yelled back, "Do wingmounts fly?"

"Thank the gods." Medwind slid into the chair and put her boot-shod feet up on the table next to the gargoyle and the goldfish and leaned back. She wriggled more comfortably into the chair and closed her eyes. "What a *d'leffik* day!"

"I imagine that is the kindest thing that could be said about it." Rakell came out to the sitting room with two giant bowls of crisped corn and two huge tankards of tare-ale. She plunked one of each next to Medwind's feet on her end table, raised her eyebrows, but refrained from comment, and chased Flynn out of her chair. Flynn spat and swore creatively in the ancient tongue of cats and demanded to be let out. "Get the door yourself, you sorry beast," Rakell snarled. "That's why I gave you hands in the first place."

The cat glared at her, then stalked over to the door and jumped up, hung on the door, and twisted. With his hind legs, he pushed against the doorjamb. The door popped open, and the tawny cat dropped to the ground and exited.

Medwind shuddered. "It makes my skin crawl, watching him do that."

Rakell sighed. "Not mine. I just wish that he would close the damned door when he let himself out, and that he could let himself back in."

"He can't get back in?"

"He can work the latch well enough, but the little business with the hind legs only works for pushing. So he can only open doors that swing inward."

"So you still have to tend the door for him."

"Yah." Rakell took a sip of her ale, and chewed with meditative concentration on her crisped corn. "Even if the modifications had worked so well that he opened and closed it for himself every time, I still wouldn't give another cat hands."

Medwind laughed and took a swig of her ale. "Don't tell me the mighty Rakell admits she made an error."

Rakell laughed. "Never. My technique was flawless—my results were exactly what I intended. I simply never realized what firebugs cats were. I cannot keep Flynn out of my quicklights, no matter what I do. If there were more like him, the city would burn to the ground inside of a week."

"It's a stone city."

"I can't imagine that making the slightest difference, somehow." Rakell curled up in her brocaded chair and stretched—a movement Medwind found disconcertingly reminiscent of the absent cat.

The barbarian munched corn chips and asked, around a mouthful of them, "So, what did the Council say?"

"They'll 'look into it.' They say a few of the local junior hedge-wizards went missing last night—they aren't willing to speculate on a connection—but all the missing, including our two, are young, pretty, and magically adept." The Mottemage stared out her window at the brightening stars.

"How, exactly, are they going to 'look into it,' did they say?"

"They're sending over Council Regents tomorrow to interview everyone who knew Enlee or Amelenda. They want to see if they can establish any connections. They're voting on sending out patrols."

"In the meantime, we sit and stare at the four walls and hope for the best? That sounds about as useful as their usual ideas."

Rakell waved her tankard at Medwind. "You lack sufficient respect for the Council."

"The Council—yourself excluded, dear Rakell—is made up of a bunch of doddering, neutered ninnies who insist on sitting on their hands, blocking progress at every turn, and keeping the magic of this city locked into patterns four hundred years old, no matter how insufficient to our needs those patterns have become."

"Med, you insist on thinking of gender-specific magic as aberrent. I assure you, it is highly efficient and functional. Your own distaste for celibacy is all that keeps you from admitting that."

The barbarian grinned around her ale. "My 'distaste for celibacy,' as you so lightly refer to it, is no minor detail. I'll give up men when you give up horses."

Rakell sputtered, "I don't like the parallel you've drawn there, *Frelle* Medwind."

"I was not implying any significant parallel, *Mottemage*." Medwind munched on her corn chips and smirked, though.

"Never mind. I won't let you draw me into one of your convoluted little sex talks. I want to know if you have any idea what happened with our students. With your outlander skills, I thought perhaps you would have some insights I don't have."

"I'm as lost in the fog as you are. That horrible business this morning was like nothing I experienced before—"

There was a burst of magic that screamed across both mages' nerve endings, cutting short whatever the barbarian had intended to say. Medwind pressed her hands to her temples; Rakell shut her eyes tightly and clenched her teeth. The effect was the magical equivalent of fingernails dragging across a slateboard. It brought both mages to their feet, ready to flay the perpetrators.

When it ceased, Medwind said, "You know who did that, don't you."

"My Senses work just fine—unfortunately. Apparently Faia and Yaji are having a fight."

"With that much energy flying around, they're going to blow each other up."

The Mottemage spoke through gritted teeth. "Faia and Yaji, who are quickly becoming everyone's two favorite students, might blow each other up. What a comforting idea. That will be a nice educational experience for them, too. Oh, dare I hope to be so lucky?

Help me put up noise-shields so that I don't have to listen to them when they do it."

"You aren't seeing the seriousness of this," Medwind commented.

"I don't want to see the seriousness of two squabbling children. I have much larger problems worrying me right now, and I think those problems should take the precedence they deserve."

"Tell me that when Ariss is a melted puddle of slag in the middle of the bog," Medwind muttered. "And me roasted to a cinder with it, and nine healthy husbands out on the Hoos Plains that I haven't seen in ages—dead and gone and no one to give me a proper Hoos burial. You didn't see what was left of Bright. I did."

"Nonsense, Medwind. You're just terrified of the idea of dying in Ariss, Song."

"That's because you won't let me tell you what to do with my head if I die."

"It's going to be buried with your body, Song. That's the civilized thing to do."

"See!" Medwind said. "See! I have every right to worry about it, then. That's the wrong thing to do."

"I don't want to hear it."

Medwind hid her face in her hands and sighed. "I know. I know."

In the middle of deep sleep, in the middle of lonely night, the nightmare came for her.

Fear-pain-death. Fearpaindeath, closer and closer. Otherpain, ownpain, enveloping. Darkness/no eyes/no light/lost. Pain. Hot-cold-hot . . . no air, no air, I-cannot-breathe-Icannotbreathecannotbreathe . . .

:*Come here!*:

Pain. Skin pulling from bones—her skin, her bones. Liquid lead pouring down her throat.

:*No!*:

:*COME HERE!*:

Pain, pain, pain-pain-pain! Winter-cold, melting-hot, and hands all over her body, moving her arms, moving her legs, so that she walked through the blackness like a marionette in the market.

:*L-l-leave—me—alone!*:

:*I want you.*:

Icy, belly-freezing fear, and in the midst of the confusion, one thin tendril of rationality.

Shield!

Struggle to find the grounding line. Gods, where is it? Find-it-somewhere-down-here/I-know-it's-here.

:*You cannot fight me.*:

:*Will—fight—you.*: The line, oh thank-the-gods-thank-the-Lady, the line, here it is.

Energy. Just a little.

Through the feet, into the belly. Gods-it-is-so-hard-to-hold-it—so-slippery—

And the angry black weight of the hating thing fought against her grip of the energy like a demon.

But suddenly she could breathe.

And when she could breathe, she could think.

With the little energy she'd pulled in, Faia cast up shields, and the pain lessened. She fed more energy into them, and the confusion decreased, and as it decreased, she was able to locate and draw in more energy. She fed the shields until once again they glowed blue.

Even blind, she could "see" the blue of the shields—but once the shields were strongly in place and the evil, angry thing was confined outside of them, her sight came back. She became aware that she was slumped against the wall of her dorm nearest the door, and that her roommate, Yaji, was being dragged backwards toward that door, fighting silently against an invisible enemy.

Yaji was as surely in the thrall of that immense evil as she had been, but Yaji had neither the skill nor the strength to fight it.

Faia used every bit of her ability, and expanded the shield to include and enclose her hapless partner. The young apprentice promptly collapsed on the floor and began to scream. Faia dropped to her knees and, after a second's hesitation, wrapped her arms around her roommate.

"It's okay," she whispered. "You're safe now. Sh-h-h-h-h. Yaji, stop it. *Stop* it." She alternated between shaking the other girl and holding her, until finally Yaji quieted down to occasional skittish hiccups and a few stray sobs.

Yaji's glance ran from the bolted door to the tightly closed windows, and rested on Faia's face.

"What . . . what in the . . . hells was that?" she whispered.

"Something hungry," Faia answered. "It was trying to get me, too."

"I tried to stop it," Yaji said. "I couldn't."

"I *almost* could not. I do not know what it was, but it was strong."

Yaji wrapped her arms around her knees and rocked slowly from side to side. "I think I know why it came here, though. I broke my shield when we were fighting—didn't draw it in. I must have loosed an elemental when I did that . . . and . . . and it waited until we were asleep and our defenses were down before it came after us."

"I really do not think you did that, Yaji." Faia looked out the window into the darkness. "I do not see that thing being set loose just from you forgetting one of your hand-waves. It was probably . . ." she wrinkled her nose doubtfully, and paused, then shrugged, ". . . probably something that was already out there. I might have pulled it in when I set up such a . . . a *noisy* shield."

"Don't try to make me feel better, Faia. I was sloppy with my pentacle. That's just asking for trouble. You leave energy scattered around like I did, and it's like leaving food around for wild dogs." She shivered. "And what's really bad is that when the instructors find out, they'll drop me back a level. At least a level."

Faia sighed. "If it worries you that much, then we shall just make sure they do not find out."

"What?!"

"Why should they? Whatever it was, we ridded ourselves of it. We are both fine. We will clean up the energy in here, then see if we can track it back to wherever it came from. I do not see why the dear frelles need to know about it. Really, I do not."

Yaji looked relieved for almost a full minute. Then her brow wrinkled. "What if it comes back?"

Faia shivered. That did bear thinking about. She gave the possibility her complete attention. Finally, she sat down on the bed in front of Yaji. "I have an idea. You will clean up your shield energy. Then I shall set faeriefires to guard the room. Then we will sleep."

"I don't think I'll ever sleep again."

Faia shook her head slowly. "You will sleep."

Later, feeling secure within the faeriefire-guarded shields, and finally drowsy herself, Faia listened to the steady breathing on the other side of the room, and reflected that she could have made a pretty good prophet.

Faia woke long before first bell with a strong urge to stretch her legs and think, and to have another look at those giant otters in the lake. She went through her shields, but left them intact so Yaji could sleep, and headed out for the lake.

She returned to the giant rock where she had seen the otters. In the chill, damp pre-dawn fog, Faia found her rocky perch cold and slick. She shivered and pulled the warm wool *erda* close around her, and fished the rede-flute from her pocket. The giant otters were not on the rock. *In this fog*, she mused, *they could be right beside it, though, and I would never see them.* There was Seeing, of course. She didn't like it—not after her memories of the horrible Seeing in

Bright—but she really wanted to get a closer look at those big beasts.

She closed her eyes and reached out over the lake.

There was the usual slight background glow of birds, fish, insects, and small furbearers. No people. Nothing big and familiar. And as for giant otters— nothing that could be mistaken for one or several of those, either.

Oh, well, she thought, a little relieved, *I will just play the flute and hope they come to that.*

She relaxed, and drew in energy, and focused on playing something she hoped would attract otters. She took a deep breath, and put her lips to the flute.

At that moment a hand gripped her shoulder, and a shrill voice in her ear demanded, "What in the names of the seven ugly gods do you think you are doing out in this fog at this time of the morning?!"

Faia jumped and dropped the flute, which careened toward the water. She scrabbled after it, and caught it, and nearly tottered into the lake in the process.

Her breathing was fast and she was shaking as she turned to face the unwelcome intruder. "Yaji," she snarled, "do not ever sneak up on me that way again."

"This is the second morning you skulked out of the room. I want to know why. And I want to know what happened last night."

Faia raised an eyebrow.

Yaji smirked. "I wasn't really asleep by the time you left the room yesterday. I simply didn't choose to follow you then."

"The reason I am out here does not concern you."

"I think it does."

Faia glowered at her roommate. "It doesn't have anything to do with last night. I just needed to think." Faia was more and more certain that, no matter whether her relationship with Yaji had improved or not, she did not want to share the giant otters with her. The otters were Faia's secret—and before she thought about the dreadful attack of the previous night, or her miserable classes later in the day, she wanted to think about the otters. By herself. "Go away and leave me alone for a while," she added.

Yaji stood on the boulder in the mist. Her long black hair fell freely, and her delicate gown billowed slowly in the slight breeze. Tatters of fog blew between her and Faia, giving Yaji an ethereal, ghostly appearance. She looked, in fact, very like one of the fragile young love goddesses Faia's mother had told stories about when Faia was little. Even as a child, Faia never cared for fragile young love goddesses, and discovering that her roommate looked like one when standing in damp, sticky, miserable fog did nothing to improve her feelings towards Yaji.

"I don't want to go away. I want to know what you're doing." The other girl crossed her arms and lifted her delicate chin.

Faia faced a nearly irresistible urge to throw Yaji into the lake. Reason told her that if she did such a thing, at some time in the near future, she would very likely find something unpleasant, and probably slimy, in her bed. With regret, she restrained herself.

Instead, she decided that telling Yaji a disemboweled version of the truth would be the easiest way to get rid of her. More than anything at the moment, she wanted that. So she concocted a little lie.

"If you must know," Faia said, feigning resignation, "I am trying to catch an otter to make into a pet."

"No animals are allowed in the dorm."

"And what of the cats and the dogs hidden under every bed in the place?" Faia knew this would be a telling point.

Yaji wrinkled her nose. "There aren't any in my room—I don't want to be bothered. If you really want an animal, though, I suppose I wouldn't report you if you got a kitten."

"I do not want a kitten. I like otters."

The other girl looked appalled. "Otters smell like fish!"

Faia shrugged. "The whole city smells like fish. I did not think you would notice."

Yaji would probably have made a brilliant retort right then, but one of the giant otters popped its head out of the lake and spoiled everything.

Faia winced. So much for her secret.

At the sight of the colossal animal, however, Yaji reacted considerably more violently than Faia would have anticipated. Her eyes grew round and frightened, and she began making passes in the air with her fingers. Her reaction was not surprise, Faia realized, but terror.

"You didn't mean one of *those*, surely!" Yaji's harsh gasp was almost inaudible.

"Well, yes, I did. Actually." Faia thought Yaji's reaction was excessive, but also puzzling.

"Lady Mother, Faia," Yaji whispered, "that's not an otter. That's a Fendle."

Others were up before the first bell. Medwind and her Mottemage sat in the sunroom, staring out at the dim light of first dawn.

"Another one of our students went missing last night, and there are reports from Mage-Ariss of more hedge-wizards who are suddenly missing. There were four times when I felt the start of that mind torture again—but each time the victims were weaker, and more quickly hidden. There is something else, Rakell. Last night I also felt a failed attack. The disturbance struck out at one of our students, but that student suddenly shielded." Medwind Song sat cross-legged at her Mottemage's feet. "Lady Motte—I fear. And I know shame at my fear."

The Mottemage curled in her chair and stared out her window into the featureless fog. Her voice, when she finally spoke, was as insubstantial and featureless. "Our shields are worthless. Our watchers—seemingly blind. And our finest students, abducted in the dark of night, seem helpless against this evil, whatever it may be."

She stroked Flynn absently as he lay curled on her lap. Her eyes looked at something invisible and far away. "I, too, know fear, Medwind. And though I was never the warrior you are, still I have faced my share of evil. In these attacks, I feel the taint of something strong and old. Where it has been before these last few days, I don't know. But now it is free, and it is here."

"Why is it taking students?" Medwind shifted nervously.

"If I knew that, I would, perhaps, know what it was. At the moment, I could rest easier if I knew what it was doing with the students it takes."

Flynn stretched and shifted. Suddenly alert, he stared at Medwind and hopped onto her leg. He reached up and grabbed at her nose-ring with his stubby, furry fingers.

"Touch that and die, cat," Song growled.

Flynn pulled back and sat watching the tiny arc described by the jewelry. His tail twitched in irritation.

"Sooner or later, we're sure to find out something," Song told the master mage.

"I wish I were as sure." The graying head shook slowly.

"A Fendle?" Faia looked into the deep brown, winsome eyes of the giant otter, then glanced at her roommate.

Yaji nodded vehemently. "A Fendle. One of the myths of Ariss. Hundreds of years ago, the story goes, the city wasn't divided. Male and female magicians worked side by side as equal partners. Earth, wind, water, and fire were drawn upon by all. But some of the sajes, led by one wicked Master Saje, plotted for power, and by bribes and trickery in the councils and meeting rooms, they limited the realms of women's influence. When they had accomplished this, they began warping and twisting their magics. Without the women's voices of reason and demands that they work only for the good, these evil men began drawing the energy from pain and death to fuel their horrible spells. That perverted magic created a monster that overwhelmed its creators, and devoured them. And the other men either bowed to the monster and called it master or refused to accept responsibility for the evil their brothers had wrought.

"So one old Wisewoman of great power created the Fendles, who are, according to our legend, sensitive to magic—protective of good magic and repelled by evil. The story goes that they led the old Wisewoman and some of her colleagues to the growing monster, the source of Ariss' evil, and helped fight the battle that divided Ariss and eventually conquered the horror. The Wisewoman and her friends and the Fendles pursued that great evil to the gates of hell. The Wisewoman and the other mages were killed in a final skirmish, but the Fendles survived. They were given the charge of standing guard throughout eternity, to see that the monster never escaped. It was said that the Fendles would never be seen again, so long as the evil was contained.

"I always thought it was just a myth," Yaji added.

Faia studied the great beast that had begun nuzzling its head against her waist. She scratched it behind the ears, and thought. At last, she whispered, "Then if this is a Fendle, that means ..."

"It means that the gates of hell have broken open, and its denizens have been freed. Oh, gods." Yaji's eyes were round and frightened. She stared at the Fendle as if it were the chief devil of saje hell.

The Fendle chittered excitedly, and looked toward the deep wilds of the forest.

Yaji said, "I think we ought to get back to the dorm. We won't say anything about the Fendles ..."

Faia was shaking her head.

"I don't want to know why they're here," Yaji continued, her voice taking on a pleading note. "Faia, I just want to go back to my studies and forget I ever saw a Fendle. I want to forget about that incident last night. I want things to be normal again."

The Fendle nattered angrily and snapped its teeth in Yaji's direction. Then it took Faia's hand gently in its mouth and pulled her toward the forest.

"Yaji, you said the Fendles were the guardians of the gates of the hells. Have you thought that whatever it was that tried to catch us last night might be the evil thing this beast is pledged to fight?"

"Yes," Yaji said. Her voice, ending on a rising inflection, indicated that she had indeed considered the idea—and wished she hadn't.

Faia frowned, irritated. "If we do not find out why it is here, we might not escape next time." Faia looked into the beast's dark eyes. "You are trying to tell us something?"

The Fendle's response was an excited trill.

Faia pulled her hand from the Fendle's mouth and rested it on one side of the big beast's head. "I could talk to my dogs, and they could answer me. Will you let me try to talk to you?"

The Fendle purred.

I hope that means "yes," Faia thought.

She rested the other hand on the Fendle's round, wet, soft-furred skull and closed her eyes. She could see the bright lifeforce and feel the Fendle's Self. As she studied what she saw, she suffered a pang of unease. A dog's Self was completely open. No part of its mind was beyond her touch. The Fendle, like humans, had a barrier around part of itself beyond which she could not see. So the Fendle was complex, like humans; not simple, like a dog.

The part of the creature's mind that she could speak to urgently wished that she accompany it into the woods. There was something in there it wanted her to see.

"Yaji, I am going with the Fendle. You go back to

the school and tell the Mottemage and Medwind Song
about what has happened."

Yaji's eyes darted from the sweet-faced Fendle to
Faia. She shifted anxiously from foot to foot, and Faia
could almost see her figuring the distance from the
lake to the dorm through the thick fog, and remembering the thing that had tried to abduct her the night
before.

"I don't want to walk alone back to the campus. I'll
go with you," Yaji said. "When we've seen what that
animal wants us to see, we'll tell the Motte and Song
together."

Faia nodded. Secretly, she was relieved to have
another person along. She had no wolfshot, only one
little throwing knife, no sling. She did not even have
her brass-tipped staff anymore. If she were attacked,
at least Yaji should be more help in a fight than nothing. Maybe.

They set off through the fog, the Fendle leading
with its sinuous, rollicking gait. It would race just to
the point of disappearing into the fog, then turn and
look back. It was obviously impatient.

"I don't like this," Yaji said. She trailed a step
behind Faia. Her long skirts were hiked to her knees
and tucked into her belt, and her delicate shoes were
muddied and stained.

Faia did not mistake her complaint for one of displeasure over the state of her clothes, however. As the
trees closed over their heads and the fog thinned
slightly, Faia felt a malevolent presence. "I know. I
wish your myth made the Fendles a sign of good fortune." Faia was suddenly finding it necessary to shove
branches out of her way. The undergrowth became
denser by the step, the ground soggier, the walking
more precarious.

"Faia," Yaji whispered. "What happens if we get
lost?"

Faia shook her head. "I do not get lost. I call the
faeriefires, and they lead me where I need to go. The

only reason we are following the Fendle right now is because only it knows what it wants us to see."

Yaji looked slightly relieved. "If you're sure . . ."

"I am."

Yaji subsided into silence and concentrated on her walking.

The Fendle crunched and crashed through the undergrowth, and Faia and Yaji followed. The fog refused to thin any further.

Slowly, Faia became aware of a faint scent that had been tugging at the back of her mind, demanding recognition for the past minute. At the same time that she realized the smell was there and began trying to figure it out, Yaji's whisper sounded in her ear again.

"I smell something strange."

"I, too."

"What is it?"

I do not know—shut your mouth and let me think a minute, Faia thought. She said nothing, though— merely shrugged.

Initially the smell was faint, slightly sweet, somewhat unpleasant. As it increased, it became overlaid by a strongly metallic scent, and the sweetness became cloying, and . . .

Bright. It smells just like Bright. I could never forget that smell. . . .

And with the memory of the smell came the recognition of what she was probably walking into. The stench was almost overpowering. Faia shuddered. "Yaji, I do not think you should go any further," she said. "I think this will be bad—very bad."

Her protective instinct was a moment too late.

"Faia, look there," Yaji whispered. "What is—oh, gods, that looks almost like . . ."

Yaji screamed. Faia would have joined her, but she simply could not breathe.

Hands were what she recognized first. Hands, with bloodied fingernails, and fingers spread and splayed.

Not, she realized, hands that were attached to bodies. Just hands. Lots of them.

No, she thought. *No. I cannot look.* She pressed her face against the rough bark of the nearest tree, and squinted her eyes tightly shut. And with the last of her conscious control, she sent up a faeriefire beacon to blaze over the charnel grove.

Cleanup had been a nightmare. Medwind Song was sure she would never erase the images of the slaughtered young women from her mind. Peeling the shocked Faia away from her tree and dragging hysterical Yaji back to campus had been no pleasant tasks, either. But one ugly chore still remained.

She stood in front of the assembled students of Daane University with the Mottemage at her side and took a deep breath. "By now," she started, "most of you have heard rumors of what Faia Rissedote and Yaji Jennedote uncovered today. And I am certain you have started hearing tales of the appearance of Fendles, and wild stories of what that is supposed to mean. Rumors on campuses get exaggerated. And even though things were bad, I imagine what you have heard has become worse than the truth by this time. I am here now to separate the rumors you have heard from the facts.

"There were seven young women involved. Not ten, or thirty, or a hundred, as I am sure some of you have heard. Seven. Three were students from this campus. The other four are unknown, but we expect they are some of the hedge-wizards reported missing from other parts of Mage-Ariss in the last two days. Due to the condition of the bodies, it will be difficult to identify them. We were only able to recognize our three students because we knew we were looking for them."

She shuddered as she recalled the exact condition of the bodies, but she continued doggedly. After all, her students needed to know what they were up against.

"You may think it harsh of me not to sweeten the facts for you, but whatever it was that killed those women is still free. We have no reason to think it has quit hunting. That means any one of you may be its next target. You have to be on guard.

"The Fendles are here, out in the lake right now. I don't know whether this means the gates of hell have broken loose and its demons are free among us as the stories say—or whether their presence has any meaning at all. Old myths frequently have a grain of truth to them, but rarely more than that."

Rakell, she noted, nodded agreement at her last remark. "You must not assume that the end of the world has come because the Fendles have arrived," the director interjected.

"Nevertheless," Medwind resumed, "precautions have been been taken to prevent any recurrence of this disaster, and the Mottemage and the Instructory have set out regulations that you will all follow."

Medwind heard a few rebellious mutters from the back of the room.

"There will be no punishment handed out by the Instructory for failure to conform to these regulations," she said, pointedly staring at the protesters in the back. "We assume that you are intelligent enough to see that these rules are for your protection, and that those of you who choose not to follow them can face the consequences as they occur. I suggest that you go into the secondary cold-storage room to view the bodies of your classmates if you choose to follow this second path, however."

All signs of rebellion died as the import of Medwind's suggestion sank in. *Good. I was right to push for no punishment. Now they won't play any games with the rules, thinking that they're getting away with something by sneaking past us. They'll remember who the real enemy is—and who it isn't.*

Rakell stepped forward. Her gravelly voice picked up where Medwind's left off. "The first and most important rule is this—you will stay in pairs at all times until the killer is caught. Please realize that this means that you will bathe in pairs, you will study in pairs, you will toilet in pairs. From this moment, your roommate is the other half of your body. You will be inseparable. No one—absolutely *no one*—is to be left alone in a hallway for just a moment while you go back to get something you forgot. No one is to leave you alone while you entertain visitors. There are no exceptions.

"Second, you will maintain personal shields at all times.

"Third, you will avoid the lake.

"Fourth, you will not permit anyone who is not a student, instructor, or Councillor, access to the campus. If you see a stranger on campus, you will report that stranger to an instructor or to one of the Council Regents, who will be on guard here until the killer is caught.

"Fifth—" Rakell started. Medwind heard her voice catch and soften. "Fifth, you will please remember that the students we lost were among the strongest and most magically capable on campus. They were not able to protect themselves. Don't let yourselves get into any situations where you might need to try." The Mottemage's eyes pleaded with the gathered mass of her beloved students. "Please—be careful."

"It has to be the sajes," Yaji said.

She sat at one table waiting for class to start. Faia sat cross-legged on the bench beside her. Around them, a group of classmates debated the cause of the murders.

A lean, mahogany-skinned girl nodded. "They split the city so long ago. If it weren't for them and their power-hungry tactics, mages and sajes would still be working together."

Faia asked, "Why would they murder mage students, though? You say that they have their own half of the city. No mage bothers the working of the sajes."

"Mages wouldn't. Women have honor. You just don't understand men, hill girl." Yaji looked at Faia disdainfully. "No matter what they have, it's never enough. They always want more."

Faia snorted. "Do you actually know any men? Have you ever worked with one? Shared a house with one? Bedded one?"

The expressions on the faces around Faia told her she had just committed blasphemy.

"Gods, no!" one student snarled.

"Have you?" another asked.

"All three, and plenty of times," Faia said.

The ring of young women pulled back from her.

"Every conjugal contact a mage has with a man takes away a portion of her power," Yaji said. "By devoting energy to men, she sacrifices her strength for unimportant things."

"That should give you something to think about, then," Faia said, and laughed. "Imagine what I could do if I had never tumbled any of the shepherd boys in the village." She shook her head in scorn. "Who told you that? To me, your story sounds like an excuse made up by old women who did not wish to supply their students with alsinthe. I have more power than any of you, and I have had all the men I wanted, and as often. And, no matter what you think, men have honor too."

"Go out and tell that to the sajes who murdered our classmates," one girl yelled.

"You do not know that a saje did murder your classmates," Faia yelled back. "You have no proof."

"Saje-lover," one student muttered. Others took up the refrain.

Medwind Song entered her classroom to find a fight starting. As soon as the students noticed her, the snarls died down. She stood in front of the class, suspiciously sure of the cause of the disagreement, and plastered a false expression of curiosity on her face.

"What's been going on?" she asked.

There was a pregnant silence.

"We have been discussing the murders," Faia finally said, glossing over the dangerous mood that had sprung up in the room.

Becoming something of a politician, our Faia, Medwind thought. *That is something for the common good, in any case.* She glared at her students. "It is time for class now. Please keep your speculations for appropriate times." The tall barbarian brought a small, spiny training ball from her pack and set it in front of her students. "Today we're going to work on using attack mode through defense shields. This is a repeat lesson—you should be competent at it by now."

Usually, Medwind's announcement of combat lessons would have been met by groans and displeasure. It was an indication of the mood of the campus that no one even questioned a refresher course.

When the frelle tossed the ball at the first of her students, it was slowed by the shield and pushed back by the force the student mustered. That marked the first time in memory that Medwind had not managed to hit at least the first student with the ball.

Good, she thought. *Maybe I won't lose any more of my children.* She continued grimly, tossing the ball, watching it fly away, and wishing for something she could offer her students that would guarantee them their lives.

After class, she stopped Faia and Yaji before they could leave.

"I need you two to come with me. The instructors are meeting to determine our course of action, and we want to know anything the two of you can tell us." She stepped into the crowded room, and studied the mob. "The rest of you, go to your next classes, and stay in pairs. If you are done with your classes for the day, go straight to your rooms and shield your quarters carefully. Tomorrow, at second bell, we will be meeting in the downstairs corridors of your dorms. We will go to *antis* as a group."

The instructors acted like an older version of the classroom crowd. Faia waited until Yaji had given her version, then told the assembled women what she had felt and seen. She described the method by which she fought off the invisible attacker. She told about being led by the Fendles to the bodies in the woods. And finally, she made it clear that she could not point any fingers at the sajes. She was as fair as she knew how to be.

Again, everyone was certain the sajes were responsible.

Rakell stood in front of the group after they finished grilling the two roommates.

"There are a few pieces of information none of the rest of you know yet. You need to know now. First, we have now obtained identification from families of two of the other women Faia and Yaji discovered. They were, as we had suspected, some of the more competent and powerful of the hedge-wizards in Mage-Ariss. You of the Council already knew when these women disappeared. What you did not know is that each woman was murdered in the same way; first the hands were cut off and the stumps cauterized to stop the bleeding, then the skin was flayed and certain organs were removed, and then the throat was cut. The method indicates that pain and suffering were prolonged in every case for as long as possible without causing death. The abilities of the victims and the fact that this pattern was followed consistently followed convinces me that this was a ritual and suggests to me that the deaths were an attempt to raise power."

The Mottemage paused. "There is one other thing. I hesitate to mention it, because I fear it will be the beginning of a greater nightmare than we already face. Still, facts are facts. A ring was found at the site of the murders, under one of the bodies." The older woman wrapped her arms across her chest and closed her eyes. "It is a ring of the style commonly worn by lower-level sajes. The presence of this ring may give us a strong clue to the identity of our killer. It also may give us a motive, if a lower-level saje was using blood magic to increase his strength."

Under the outcry that followed the Mottemage's announcement, Yaji leaned over and yelled in Faia's ear, "I told you so."

Faia bit her lip. "Then I was wrong. I was just so certain men could not do something like this to women."

"Men are beasts," Yaji yelled.

"I never knew any who were," Faia muttered to herself.

The Council members asked nonmembers to leave, so that motions could be heard and a vote taken on the proper course of action.

Faia and Yaji and Medwind went outside and sat on the hard stone benches that lined the grassway between the Mottehaus and One Round Way.

Traffic thinned and the sky darkened while they waited, and the Tide Mother rose red and garish and ugly and cast its ruddy shadows over the whitestone of Ariss. Faia had a vision in which blood, and not the nearby planet, stained the city—and when the Councillors finally came out of their meeting and the Mottemage came over to join the trio, Faia was sure the omen had been a true one.

"It's to be war," the Mottemage whispered.

No more needed to be said.

Medwind rested on her padded floor mat, breathing in the heavy scent of powdered amber, stoneweed, and musk burning on the brazier. Her fingers rolled restlessly across the worn skin head of her drum. She closed her eyes and remembered the felt walls of her *b'dabba*, the same incense thrown into her cookfire, the sounds and scents of camp—horses, laughter, the sizzle and scent of goat cooking on a spit, children screeching and playing one of a hundred versions of tag. She hungered for the chill, dry air of her homeland, for her good Hoos warsteed between her knees and one of her brawny Hoos husbands at her side. This city with its bogs and fogs and paranoias, its stupid intrigues, its infuriating sequestration of women from men, got no better no matter how long she waited.

I'm next in line to head the University. When Rakell steps down, or, gods forbid, dies, I'll step into her place. I could make some changes then . . . maybe.

She angrily pounded out a war-riff. *Or I could go crazy trying. Ariss has been fending off "barbarian" ideas for centuries. Even Rakell, who has been my best friend for almost ten years, can't take my political suggestions seriously. Who am I to think that I could change all of Ariss—or even all of Daane?*

Now the idiots on Council want to wipe out every human being in Saje-Ariss without having any idea whether the sajes are really responsible or not. Just because of a ring that may not even be related to the murders. Medwind's drumming got faster and harder. *Not so. It's because they don't like men.*

The barbarian, who had at some personal risk created a secret entrance to her quarters in order to smuggle her lovers in and out, rolled her eyes at that. *That just proves they're idiots.*

No matter how sure the rest of the mages were of the sajes' guilt, Medwind wasn't convinced. And before she participated in annihilating half a city, she was going to have to be rock-solid certain.

Tomorrow, she thought, *I start doing a little tracking— my way. All this time in the city may have made me slow and stupid—but a stupid Hoos is brighter than a brilliant Arisser.*

I'll find the ones who killed my students. And only they will pay.

*   *   *

There would be war.

Faia struggled with this thought, and tried to see the justice in it. Mages were going to destroy the saje side of the city, and all the people in it—men, women, children, magical, mundane, guilty, and innocent.

Men were not the way these women claimed. Faia knew that. The mages' angry rhetoric simply did not make sense.

She lay on her bed and stared at the dorm windows. There was nothing rosy about them at the moment. The cheerful pink glass was occulted by shutters, barred against the blackness of midnight—darkness and fear were held at bay by the gleam of lamps and the glow of shields. Yaji's bed had been moved next to hers. There was supposed to be safety in numbers.

Safety from men. Men!

How can they be so afraid of men?

She rolled over on her side and looked at her roommate, who stared at the shadows flickering on the ceiling. "How can you hate men so much, Yaji? There are none in your life."

"I don't hate them. I just don't need them. Men are a sign of failure."

"Failure?"

"If I fail to win my place as a mage in one of the Universities, or in the Greater Council of Ariss, I'll be expected to have at least one child. I suppose I'll have to consort with a man then. Full mages are above those base needs, though—and I have no intention of being a failure."

"Do you not want a bondmate and children? And have you never had a brother, or boys who were friends?"

"I had a brother. His name was Abenyar. He lived at home with my mother until he showed signs of magical ability. When his talents manifested, he was transferred to the saje side of the city and barred from returning. I haven't seen him since he was eight. . . ."

He ceased to be my brother when he left to become a saje." Yaji's voice held a faint tinge of regret. "And no, I don't want children."

Her voice became bitter. "All my life, I heard from my mother how dreary it was raising babies, being kept from the life she could have had—according to her, *should* have had. Every time a townswoman came to her door, wanting a spell or an amulet, I watched my mother die a little. She let everyone know that she could have been *here*, designing new plants or new animals, working on better systems of research—developing cures for illness, or wards against growing old, or even finding the spell to counteract death—but instead, there she was, working birth control spells. Successful mages maintain their concentration—how could a mage ever work and still find the time to bond to a man or mother a brood of squalling brats?"

"Why did she leave the University, if she loved it so much?"

"She was seduced by some ignorant merchant boy, and she got pregnant. The University refused to continue her training. The Mottemage who was here then threw her out."

"So you do not like men because your mother does not like men. But have you thought that your brother is on the other side of the city? That if the mages destroy the city, they will be killing your brother, too?"

"Abenyar isn't my brother anymore," Yaji said, but her voice cracked when she said it.

Faia felt a moment of triumph. Yaji *did* care about her brother. Now all that was necessary was to make Yaji admit it. "You and your brother must not have gotten along," she said, trying very hard to sound solicitous. "That is very sad. A brother is a wonderful thing. My brothers and I had such fun—we used to ride the plow horses and chase the sheep and the goats, and we sat in the barn in a cave we hollowed out of the hay and told ghost stories. Denje used to

steal Mama's handpies and bring them out to us. We
sat in the dark, smelling of hay and animals, and ate
until our faces and hands were sticky with pie juice,
and told of the One-Eyed Woman's Lover, and Pie-
bur's Spirit, and the Horse Who Comes for the
Dying." Remembering her brothers and her childhood
in Bright, Faia's eyes filled with tears.

"Ben and I took Mother's airbox once," Yaji whispered. "Right after we both discovered we could work
magic. We flew it around the courtyard and over the
back wall into the main city. We got lost and ended
up with the airbox stuck on the top of a building and
Mother spent the whole day looking for us. It was
the most fun I ever had.

"The sajes came and took Ben away just a few days
after that," she added. "I cried for months. I never
saw him again."

"You cannot let them kill him," Faia said.

"What if he's one of the killers?"

"Do you think he is?"

"No."

"I do not, either. And I do not believe it is right
to kill good people who have done nothing wrong. If
the mages do what they want, they will kill many innocent people."

Yaji sighed. "Yes—you may be right. But what can
we do?"

"I have an idea. I will go to the saje side of the
city, and I will talk to some of the sajes. I can tell
when someone lies—not magically, but by signs my
mother taught me to look for—I will know after I
have talked to these sajes if they are involved."

"That's stupid. If they're involved, they'll just kill
you."

"If they are not involved, they deserve a chance."

"I don't think dying is a good way to test your
theory."

Faia grinned. "Neither do I. But if I am wrong,
I can fight. I will not die easily, I think."

Yaji laughed, startled. "There is that," she agreed. "But I want to come with you."

"Could you steal and ride a wingmount?"

Yaji wrinkled up her nose and shuddered. "I hate *horses*. Horses that fly were creatures created by women with evil minds."

"Ah. Then I think perhaps you should stay here."

"What if whatever it was comes to get me again? I can't fight it off by myself."

Faia sat up and rested her chin on her knees and wrapped her arms around her legs. "Yes, you are right. . . . I know! We shall set a trap. Any magical thing that attempts to enter the room will look for the weak part of the shield. So we will *make* a weak part in the shield which will funnel into a mirror drain—"

"A mirror drain?"

"Two little mirrors that face each other. A pentacle is drawn on one, and reflected into the other—the reflections go on forever, gettting smaller and smaller. We hill-folk use them to trap spirits."

"Do they work?"

"Usually only once per bogan—so if we get anything, do not touch the trap. I will clean it out when I get back. You won't be able to get the nasty back in if it gets out."

"Not a problem. I wouldn't dream of touching your spirit trap."

"Then get two mirrors and let us get started. It is getting late."

"You aren't going tonight."

"I'm going as soon as you get those mirrors and tell me how to find the place I want."

"You're crazy."

"No . . . but someone is. I just want to know who."

Chapter 6

WINGMOUNTS AND OTHER ODD PASSIONS

THE driving wind bit into her cheeks, and the cold, miserable fog soaked through Faia's *erda* as if it were not there. She struggled to keep the wingmount under control, wishing with all her heart that she had paid more attention to the commands Medwind Song had used to direct her beast that first day.

"You can't get lost." Yaji's voice echoed in her memory. "The city is built in a circle. Faulea University is the saje-training center. That's the place you want to find. It's across the circle from here—if it weren't so damned foggy, I could even show it to you. Even if you miss it, Faia, all you have to do is fly back around the circle until you see the towers here.

"Fly along a rim road, not one of the spoke roads. It will take you longer, but you won't fly over the city's hub that way, where the administrative mages and sajes have their posts—the border is guarded heaviest there, so if you avoid it, you'll have less chance of being spotted."

Faia had been unsure. "What do I look for? How do I recognize their university?"

That had been the smallest worry, apparently. "It's built like Daane—all of whitestone, and it will have a Greathall, rows of dorms, big blocks of classrooms, and the towers for the instructors and the senior magicians. Just watch for the towers ... but stay away from them. That's where the university's powerful sajes will be."

Faia had nodded. It had all seemed so sensible and so simple.

Stealing—no, "borrowing"—the wingmount, had been ridiculously easy. They were stabled in quarters separate from the horses, but still across the throughway on the other half of the campus. Traffic was light because of the fog, and there were no guards at the wingmount stables. The Council Regents policed the lake and the dorm doors and patrolled the grounds. Faia had simply slipped down knotted sheets out of her window, thanked the Lady for the fog, and ran like a dervish across the throughway, then crept to the stable.

It seemed odd. *The horses are guarded,* she noted. *Why not the wingmounts?*

The beast she stole had been reluctant to leave its nice, dry, warm stable, and getting it off the ground in the heavy fog had been frightening.

She recalled her first and only other experience with wingmounts in vivid detail. Mostly, she recalled landing. Suddenly, Faia tried hard not to think about landing.

But her question about the lack of guards on the wingmount stable was answered. *No one but idiots and the desperate ride a wingmount in full daylight. Who would expect someone to try flying one of the beastly things at night?*

She discovered she had more pressing problems, anyway. With the dull red gleam of the Tide Mother making pink gargoyles of the obstacles in the fog, and the dim flickers of light that appeared briefly through the city's windows and then disappeared again into the shrouded darkness, Faia wondered how she could ever hope to find the saje university—or even her way back. Anything that might have been a landmark was occluded by the pervasive mist.

She wished she could see clearly—and realized suddenly that she might actually be able to do that. She recalled thinking that clouds had felt very much like fog on her first flight. She had flown above the clouds. Perhaps she could fly above the fog.

She urged the wingmount upward. He seemed happy to comply. They rose steadily through the murk—

—And suddenly they were above it. The final wisps and tatters fell away, and an unsuspected world lay below them. It was a silent, storm-tossed ocean of pale pink, its eerie, twisting waves reflected against the starry black of the sky—an ocean that stretched away in all directions except for the thick black line of the cliffs that ran far to the east.

The hub of Ariss, situated on the peak of the mound on which the city was built, sat slightly above the fog-line, a tiny island full of danger. All else was buried—except, Faia noted with glee, for a dotting of towers that peeked their crenellated heads out of the mist.

The towers all look alike to me. But not all of those towers belong to the saje university. Some, Yaji said, are for other kinds of training schools. So which of those hold sajes?

Faia remembered the two sajes she'd seen standing on the bridge in Willowlake. She brought their images back to mind—two gaudily dressed men with long hair and long, gold-decorated beards. She damped down her energy as much as she could and called a tiny faeriefire, then gave it their image, and instructed it to take her to them.

The faeriefire shot off directly toward the right front

tower of the saje square, and she urged the wing-mount after it.

No sooner was the faeriefire darting toward its destination than she had second thoughts about her solution. The faeriefire would go, not just to the university the sajes occupied, but to at least one of those sajes. It would find them wherever they were and hover right in front of them until she arrived, or worse, until they followed it back to her—and they would be powerful instructors—with unknown tempers.

Faeriefires were willful things—some of her folk had said they were elder spirits; some, that they were disguised woodsprites; and some, that they were the very eyes of the Lady. They would help one who beseeched them properly—and they had never failed Faia. But she still feared they could abandon her if she annoyed them. Did she dare call the fire back?

Did she dare let it continue on its own?

No, she decided. She didn't.

She concentrated. *Someone at the same place, but a student. Someone I can trust. And the person that I need to speak to.* The faeriefire sped on, course unchanged. *Please,* she begged.

The faeriefire slowed. The wingmount overtook it, and then the green beacon led them down into the fog. Faia could see forms of trees, the bulky masses of buildings, then what seemed to be a greensward—a clearing—and then the ground came up, her mount backwinged wildly, and Faia lost her seat and fell, hitting the ground solidly.

For a long moment the pain was everywhere, and points of brilliant white light whirled around the insides of her eyes. Then the pain pulled itself in and settled companionably in her stomach and ribs. She gasped for air like a beached fish.

The wingmount snuffled at her gently.

"I am dead," she groaned.

The faeriefire darted around her head.

"Leave me alone."

The faeriefire began swooping back and forth between her and one pair of closed windows in the nearest building, a few yards away, from which flickering light emanated. The wingmount, concerned, gave her a nudge with his nose.

"A lot of good it does for you to worry now," she whispered, and forced herself to sit up. "That was a terrible landing."

She stood, groaned again, then walked slowly to the window, leading the wingmount. As tall as she was, she wasn't tall enough to see inside. The faeriefire had come to rest on the outside sill, however, so she knew (or hoped) she was in the right place.

There was nothing nearby she could move to stand on. There were no shrubs or close trees to climb. There was merely the building, the window, and the grass.

"Stand still, you," she told the wingmount. She steadied herself against the building and climbed onto the beast's back. Carefully, she stood on the tiny saddle.

There! Clear view!

A thin, redheaded young man in voluminous blue velvet robes stood facing the far left corner of the room. She could make out the jutting, hairless line of his jaw, and the patterning of freckles across the backs of his hands and the curve of his cheek.

He raised a black metal staff high over his head with his left hand, and with his right, reached into one of an assortment of small jars that sat on a stand at his side, and pulled out some powder. This he sprinkled into the brazier at his feet. Orange smoke puffed into the room. He repeated the process, this time gesturing with his staff at one of a dozen chalk scrawls that lined the walls. The smoke turned bright yellow.

She could hear him chanting, but the words were unintelligible. Another wave, another toss, and the smoke turned green. He began to sway from side to side, and the volume of his chanting increased. He picked up a stack of silver disks and tossed them into the air, where they hung motionless. He tossed the staff into the air and it came to rest mid-air with the coins. He waved his arms in a manner that began to remind Faia of an irate farmer chasing cows out of his corn, shouted another string of gibberish, and dumped a handful of bright blue powder into the brazier.

The smoke turned blue. The coins and the staff began to circle through the air. Then, ominously, the brazier sputtered and the airborne objects crashed to the floor. Thick black clouds poured from the little brass pot, and the unlucky saje, wheezing and coughing, grabbed a ceremonial broom from the wall and began beating at the source of the smoke.

Faia saw him bump his work table. Several jars smashed to the floor, their powdered contents scattered everywhere—including into the blaze in the brazier.

There was a loud WHUMP.

The wingmount shied. The faeriefire flickered and vanished.

Faia tumbled to the ground and landed like a rock. She lay in silent agony, unable to pull in enough air to breathe, much less make noise.

The windows above Faia flew open and acrid smoke poured into the pink-fogged night. The young saje leaned out the window and gagged and coughed.

Faia, temporarily helpless, stared up at him.

He noted first the winged horse, then the fallen girl on the ground beneath him. His eyes grew round.

"My gods—" he wheezed between fits of coughing. "What—are you?"

The Revered and Most Noble Mottemage, Frelle Rakell Ingasdotte, holder of the Lifetitle of Geste-Motte, Chair of the Mage-Ariss Committee for Life-Experiment, Head of Daane University, and fourth in

line of succession to lead Mage-Ariss, couldn't sleep
worth a damn.

Flynn had bounced on her face earlier, teasing her
out of bed by landing on her and then darting for the
tower window, until she finally walked over and
looked out. The view had been spectacular—her
tower surrounded by an ocean of pink fog waves; the
massive architecture of the central hub of Ariss lurching like a behemoth from the storm-tossed sea silhou-
etted against the lurid red-purple of the planet Tide
Mother; one of her prize wingmounts soaring off
towards Saje-Ariss with Daane's most promising new
student aboard. . . .

It had taken second and third looks before she
could believe that last.

She mixed a healthy dollop of cream with the fifth
of the steins of deep-burgundy Zheltariss, sloshed the
contents around until the drink was marbled-burgundy
with wide white stripes, then took a long, slow pull of
the concoction.

"There is always a reason, Flynn," she intoned.
"This shit doesn't happen but for a reason." She took
another drink. "I just want to *know the gods'
bedamned reason!*"

Flynn leapt onto the windowsill next to where she
stood and looked longingly at the small pitcher of
cream.

"Here," she snarled, and pushed the pitcher to him.
"Drink it. You would anyway when I wasn't looking."
She turned her face back to the window.

"I can't believe Faia is a traitor—but that was her
on Makketh, flying straight for Saje-Ariss. Even if she
hadn't conjured a faeriefire, I'd have recognized her
power signature." Rakell buried her head in her
hands, and sighed deeply. "None of this makes sense.
The killings started just before she got here . . . but
after she destroyed Bright. She claims the killer,
whatever is was, attacked her and Yaji, but miracu-
lously they survived when no others have. I felt the

shielding, but not the attack. Now she sneaks out in the night to the other side of the city. Why? She knows enough of our plans to destroy us if she is a traitor. How can she not be a traitor?

"Flynn, what kind of a monster is she?"

Flynn, head buried to the shoulders in the cream-pot, made no reply.

"You're just a cat anyway, hey, Flynn? You wouldn't know the good guys from the bad guys if they wore signs. Just as long as you get fed, you like 'em."

Flynn lifted his cream-coated face from the emptied pitcher and blinked at her owlishly. With great care, he began his bath.

The Mottemage managed a slight twist of a smile, then returned her attention to the window, scanning the sky for her prodigal student.

The redheaded saje shed his blue velvet robe with a quick shrug, and tossed a little rope ladder over the window. An instant later, he'd climbed down to kneel on the wet grass next to Faia, where he studied her with an expression of mixed curiosity and concern.

"Are you hurt?" he finally asked.

"I fell off a wingmount for the second time in one night. I am sure I have felt better before."

The redheaded saje grinned. "I'll bet you have. Who are you, anyway? What are you doing here? Women aren't allowed on the campus."

"So I have been told. I believe I would be even less permitted than most women. My name is Faia Rissedote. I am a mage-student from Daane University. I came here to talk to a trustworthy saje, and the faeriefire led me to you."

"Whoosh!" The man sat back on his haunches and glanced from Faia to the wingmount and back. "I guess that explains the fancy horse—mage-student, huh? I'm Kirgen Marsonne—I guess I'm trustworthy, depending on what you want. But we need to get you inside. Even in the fog, someone might notice you."

She nodded. "What about the wingmount?"

"Tie it to one of the trees in the center of the quad and hope no one pays any attention, don't you think?"

Faia propped herself up on one elbow and winced. "A moment or two and I will be able to do that."

Kirgen shook his head. "We may not have a moment or two. Someone could come along any time—we students keep odd hours. Look, you climb up the ladder into the room, I'll tie up the horse and be right back."

"Lead him; do not ride him," Faia warned.

"But I'm a good rider."

Faia looked up from her position on the grass and grinned ruefully. "So am I."

With Kirgen gone, she pulled herself to her feet, and started up the few rungs of the ladder. Her ribs ached dully until she inhaled, when they blazed with stabbing, white-hot pain; she suspected she would be living with that for a few days. Her back and left shoulder and left hip still screamed in agony from the second fall. She wondered how long it would take before she could breathe without regretting it.

Hand up. Leg up. Breathe. Groan. Hand up. Leg up. Breathe. Groan. She would have rested partway, but she heard the muffled sound of people talking, that grew louder with each passing instant, as if they were coming closer. She forced herself to hurry.

Finally at the top, she threw her least sore leg over the ledge and pushed herself into the room— but her left foot snagged on the corner of the window as her torso cleared the ledge. Her momentum carried her forward, and she clawed for a handhold that wasn't there. She couldn't stop herself. She went feet over head and thudded ignominiously back-first onto the pile of velvet on the floor, where she lay staring up at the last eddies of smoke that swirled around the ceiling.

"All-damn," she whispered.

Kirgen poked his head over the ledge. His bright blue eyes were looking down at her again. He was trying without much success to keep from laughing. "You didn't."

"I did."

"I'm surprised they let you out without a keeper."

"They do not, truth to tell. I stole out without their knowledge. But I am not like this at other times. I am merely having a bad night."

"If you say so," Kirgen said with a doubtful expression. He vaulted gracefully into the room and pulled the rope ladder in behind him. "Here, let me help you up."

He reached out his hand—his hand which wore a heavy gold ring with a deep blue stone. She noted the ring, but took his hand anyway, shivering a little, and got up, and suddenly she was looking down at him.

His eyes grew round. "Whoosh," he murmured again.

"You are surprised I am so tall, yes?"

"Oh, yah. Seeing you in the dark, I didn't realize you were so pretty, either." He winked, and Faia felt her cheeks redden. "But let me take your cloak, and you sit down and catch your breath." He indicated one of two rickety wooden chairs shoved against the wall to make room for the magic work. "You wanted to talk."

Faia took the offered chair carefully. The pain was not so bad, she found out, once she sat still. She studied the open, earnest face that seemed so much like her own, and wondered how she could tell Kirgen about the murders, the return of the Fendles, and the mages' plan for revenge. Words that had seemed so reasonable on back a wingmount flying through the air in the middle of the night seemed considerably less so in the man's warm, bright, messy room. She faltered, and changed from her intended approach.

"What were you working on?" she asked.

"Homework," he said, and sighed. "Fifth-level evocation of a helpful blue-smoke godling—a controller of fire and air. I haven't managed one yet. If I don't get it right by the end of the quarter, I'm going to be back in sixth year again next fall, messing around with pots full of powdered salepsis and vertinyger sal and doing the same damn thing."

"Ah." Faia closed her eyes and rubbed her temples with her fingertips. "I wish I had not asked." Evocation of godlings, odd concoctions of powdered plants and resins, symbols and drawings and muttered incantations—and all she knew was the drawing down of faeriefires, a couple of tricks with fruit and meat, and the tending of her sheep. It would be so wonderful to run away and hide in the hills and never return to strange, terrible Ariss. She shifted in the hard seat and adjusted her tunic. *So the indirect approach will not help me.*

She squared her shoulders and took a deep, rather painful breath. "Kirgen, to ask you about your homework—that is not why I came to speak to you, in any case."

"No. Of course not." Kirgen leaned forward in his seat, resting his elbows on his knees. "You're here for something important. What?"

Lady, I wish I could read his feelings just by sitting next to him. If I could control him the way I did my sheep, I could know whether or not the sajes had some great plan to take over Mage-Ariss. But the reading of minds, as some of the mages do, as even Yaji does sometimes—that is beyond me. I only came close to that during—well—

She remembered a private moment with Baward, once, looking into his eyes at the moment of their greatest passion, when she knew—really knew—all that he felt. She had, for those few instants, heard his thoughts. And she had discovered, much to her surprise, that Baward loved her.

Well— She bit her lip and looked speculatively at Kirgen Mar. He was attractive, and attracted, and it wouldn't require much of a push to shift him to a moment of amorous dalliance. *Actually, that might work. But it wouldn't be right. That would be using a gift the Lady created for personal pleasure to get information. No—I cannot do that.* She stared into the saje apprentice's wonderfully freckled face. *I shall have to do the best I can without resorting to that.*

Attack head-on, she thought.

"You must tell me which sajes tortured and murdered the mage students and hedge-wizards in Mage-Ariss."

Kirgen's mouth gaped, and his eyes went blank with bewilderment. "What—the . . . whuh . . . What!?" he sputtered. "Sajes—murdered . . . *students*? Tortured and murdered mage-students—and hedge-wizards?. *Huh!*" He stared away into space for a long time, shook his head slowly, and finally took a deep breath and looked directly into her eyes. "Are you *sure*?" he asked.

She kept her eyes fixed on his, and didn't blink or flinch. "No," she said bluntly, "but a saje's ring, very much like the one you wear, was found under one of the flayed and dismembered bodies."

His already fair skin went gray. "Flayed—and dismembered? And a saje-ring. . . . I can see where the mages would be upset. They sent you to find out, then?"

"You do not realize just how upset they are," Faia noted dryly. "I came without their knowledge, to find out the truth, and maybe offer the sajes a chance at survival. They might kill me if they find out I was here. They intend to destroy you."

"*Me!?*" Kirgen squeaked. "Destroy *me*! I didn't do anything!"

"No. Not just you. They intend the instant and total destruction of all Saje-Ariss."

There was a long silence.

"Oh. Oh. Oh . . . farkling gods," Kirgen whispered.

"Yes." Faia smiled grimly. "Exactly."

Medwind Song walked up the last turn of the tower steps in the Mottemage's private stairway, rubbing her eyes and swearing in barbarian tongues. Her head hurt from lack of sleep and even more from the angry, abrupt mindcall she'd gotten minutes before. She pulled Rakell's door open without knocking and stomped in. Flynn, ever the opportunist, rubbed against her ankles and darted down the tower steps toward his cat-door and the freedom of the cold, foggy night.

Medwind made no attempt to retrieve him. She kicked the door shut behind her and mumbled, "What did you want, Rak—Mottemage?"

Rakell went right to the point. "Your prize student, your hedge-wizard protégé, stole one of my wing-mounts and defected to Saje-Ariss."

Medwind blinked and shook her head. She mouthed her Motte's words silently, eyes narrowing in disbelief. "Yeah? In this fog? That's crazy." She looked out the window, at the surreal view from the Mottemage's tower window and her hands knotted into fists. When she turned back to face her superior, her mouth twisted into a grim, lopsided smile. "She probably wanted to find some boy for a tumble on the grass and didn't realize she could do that locally."

"I'm not making light of this."

"Oh, hell, Rakell—I'm not either! I know this is bad—or at least it looks bad. One, if she's trying to help somehow, she's likely to end up getting herself killed, and if she's on our side, we need her. Two, things not always being what they seem, she may be a saje-sympathizer and a traitor instead of a nice country bumpkin kid—though how that could be, I don't

know. Three, it may all be a clever act, and she may
be the *killer*."

"I've thought of all those things."

"I know you have, Rakell."

"*Mottemage*."

"*Rakell* . . . we've been friends for years. Tonight,
I don't want to stand on formality; I don't want to be
your second in command. I want to be your friend.
I know Faia a little better than you do—"

"—Neither one of us knows her much at all. No
one does."

"Yes. I know. But I've watched her. I've paid
close attention. She doesn't think the way you do, or
the way I do. She's from a completely different world
than either of us. And I don't think she would intentionally hurt anyone. Whatever she's doing, I'm sure
she has a logical explanation for it, and I'm willing to
bet that she is trying to help."

"Are you willing to bet your life? All of our lives?—
because that's what you'll be doing, Medwind."

Medwind sighed, leaned against the window casement, and stared into the dark at the pale froth of
pink fog below. "I believe in Faia. I don't really
know completely why, but I do. She has principles
and morals. She cares about people.

"She also doesn't understand the situation with
Saje-Ariss, she knows nothing of politics, and she is as
naive as a human being can possibly be. Deep in my
gut, I don't think she harbors any active malice—but
she could destroy us simply by trying to help." The
Mottemage walked over and rested her hand on her
protégé's shoulder. "Medwind, we have to find her."

Medwind pressed her cheek against the cold stone
casement and sighed. "You're right, of course."

"Mindsearch. Now, please, Medwind."

"As you wish."

Flynn lurked on the huge bridge-rock that stretched
into the center of the lake—the cat was almost

motionless, intent, thinking "invisible-harmless-not-cat" thoughts at the fish that swam ever closer, tempted by the twig he twitched in the water.

One big bluefish struck Flynn's lure, and with quicksilver grace Flynn stretched and caught and flipped it out of the water. He pounced, bit, cracked the spine, and began to eat, picking the heavy bones out daintily with his stubby, furry fingers. In his inscrutable way, he was grateful for the fingers, and for the delicate range of movements suddenly made available to him. He stopped briefly, spread his furry, claw-tipped hands and studied them. With a warm glow of self-admiration, he gave each finger a light wash before falling back to his feasting.

Two V's of water arrowed toward him, silent in the fog-shrouded dark. Two noses sniffed the warm scent of cat; four huge, round eyes watched him hungrily.

Flynn banqueted unaware.

Without warning, the ripples erupted into huge black shapes that lurched out of the still water to land on either side of the tomcat, trapping him on the rock promontory.

Flynn hissed and spat, yowled, swore, arched his back and raised his hackles, danced sideways—and frantically looked for, but never saw, an escape route. One of the man-sized beasts lunged in, huge jaws gaping, and retreated with five bloody slashes on its nose. The other, nearer the land, watched and waited.

Flynn turned in terrified circles, trapped on two sides by water and on two by the lake monsters. During one circuit, a huge paw ripped at him from behind, and his left hind leg became a mass of bleeding ribbons. He screamed in rage and pain. The monsters inched closer.

He crouched, shivering—damp, bleeding, terrified—and his furry fingers trembled across a long, thin object. It was a fishbone, remainder of his repast, which lay under his belly. He gripped it, tensed for a leap. From his right side, one monster charged. Hanging onto the bone, he launched himself straight at the face of the other beast, landing on its nose, driving his impromptu stiletto deep into one of the creature's eyes, raking his hind claws across its face.

It shrieked in agony and fumbled at the bone, while Flynn scrambled over the top of its head and raced three-legged down its back, across the rock promontory, and toward his tower home.

". . . so, you see, we aren't trying to take over Mage-Ariss. We sajes are trying to quantify the stuff of life. We are unlocking the mysteries of the spheres; we're researching the history of Ariss and the whole of Arhel; we're doing investigations into the nature of magic itself. We aren't warriors—we're scholars."

They had talked for hours, while Faia observed Kirgen with every wile, guile, and subtlety she possessed. There was no indication that any part of his training had centered on violence, no indication that he bore animosity toward women, no sign of great desire for power to control others—and the faeriefire had led her to the person she needed to speak to. Faia trusted the faeriefires—so she felt she could trust Kirgen to be enough like his fellows to show her what she needed to see.

Her smile at Kirgen was radiant. "I knew they were wrong about the sajes. I know men, and they do not. So." She embraced him in a spontaneous hug. "Now I can tell them that they must look elsewhere for that terrible killer, that the Sajes are not responsible. I will not let them destroy Saje-Ariss."

Kirgen pulled her closer and hugged her gently in return.

The warmth and the tender strength of his arms around her felt so good. He smelled musky and masculine, still slightly smoky from his earlier mishap; she pressed her face against the smooth skin of his neck and felt hunger wakening in her belly that had been dormant since Bright burned. "Ah, Kirgen," she whispered, and kissed him lightly at the base of his neck, once, and then again. She felt his startled shiver.

His arms tightened around her, and his breath quickened across the back of her neck.

She ignored the twinges of her ribs and bruises and scrapes. It had been too long since she had felt something like this. Slowly, she twined one hand through the coarse waves of his hair, and slowly, she left a line of little kisses from his shoulder up his neck and along his jaw. His heart pounded against her breasts.

She turned to look at him——his eyes were wide and intent, his pupils huge. His lips trembled as he tangled his fingers in her hair and pulled her into a careful, gentle kiss.

She closed her eyes and deepened the kiss. His rough stubble scoured her cheek; his lips caressed hers hungrily.

When she pulled away, he looked startled and disappointed. Faia shook her head and smiled, and began working as fast as she could at the lacings of his jerkin.

"Oh." His smiled uncertainly and stroked her hair and her back. "You're so beautiful."

She grinned impishly. " 'All women are goddesses/ Once the dark falls,' " she told him. "At least that is what Faljon says. Just be glad you will not have to see me in the sunlight. You might change your mind."

"Whoever Faljon is, he isn't very nice."

"But he is usually right. He has one about men and the sizes of their—"

"I don't want to hear it."

She laughed and stood and tugged his jerkin off over his head. "—the sizes of their feet. But I will not tell you." She traced the muscles of his chest with her fingers and stroked the light coating of red hair that narrowed to a downward-pointing thread at his navel.

He stood, too, and fumbled with the laces of her jerkin. "I shall do that," she whispered, and removed it in one quick tug. She hissed at the sudden pain that pinched at her ribs.

He stared. "What's the matter?"

"I was trying to forget I fell off my horse." She grinned ruefully and rubbed her ribs. "My wounds just reminded me."

"Poor thing," Kirgen said, and bent over and kissed the spot she rubbed. His kisses crept higher, and became light, feathery nibbles. With a soft moan, he pulled her against him.

"Are you sure you want this?" he whispered.

"I'm sure," she said.

Faia suffered a momentary twinge of anxiety. *No alsinthe, though,* she thought. *I have none in my room at the dorm, I have none with me . . . but I can go to the market tomorrow and get some. Tomorrow will still be in time.*

Besides, she reassured herself, *it will only be this once. . . .*

The Mottemage watched Medwind Song, waiting in the tense stillness for her answer.

The barbarian frelle sat, as she had sat for nearly an hour, in a chalkdrawn circle facing a black mirror with tall white candles lit on either side of her. Her unfocused eyes stared into the ebon glass. Her breathing was so slow it was almost imperceptible.

Then she jumped a little, startled, and stiffened into intense concentration. Abruptly, Medwind chuckled. The sound fell like an anvil into the ice-bound silence of the room, shattering it into sharp, invisible shards.

Rakell's voice cut, another icy blade. "Well? What are you laughing at?"

Medwind shook her head gently and smiled up at her mentor from her seat on the floor. "Believe it or not, Rakell, my little joke was the true answer all along. She's found herself both boy and bed."

The Mottemage howled, "What! That brainless

ninny! That idiot! What does she think she's
doing—"

Medwind waved a hand to cut her off. "Actually,
I can tell you what she's doing. She's having a good
time ... but she also seems to be concentrating on
his intent and his honesty. It appears that she's invok-
ing what little empathy she has on him to see if he
was involved in the murders."

Rakell quieted. She stood, staring thoughtfully at
the lean, dark woman on her floor, and her face
clouded with confusion. "Dig deeper. Did she have
a reason to suspect him?"

"It appears that she summoned a faeriefire to guide
her to a trustworthy saje. The whole plan of hers
seems rather juvenile and poorly thought out, but she
apparently felt our decision to annihilate the sajes was
unfair (*Which it was*, Medwind added to herself) and
she wanted proof that the sajes—or at least most of
the sajes—weren't involved. So she has questioned
this young man at length, and is satisfied that he is
innocent."

Rakell sighed. "And does she intend to sleep with
all the rest of the sajes to determine *their* innocence?"

"I believe that the bedding was unplanned, Motte."

The Mottemage hit her head with the palm of her
hand several times in quick succession. "Of course it
was!" she snarled. "How silly of me. Gods save me
from idealistic children! So she has proven his innocence to herself, and therefore she must fall in love
with him?"

Medwind stretched and pinched out her candles.
"She's a hill girl. They don't equate sex with love,"
she noted. "And, ethically, I have to admire Faia.
She's going about it the wrong way, but she's trying to
prevent what she sees as an injustice from happening."

"Not you, too, Frelle Medwind," the Mottemage
growled in warning. "Don't you start with that 'poor
innocents and sweet men' theme. I won't have it."

Medwind opened her mouth to protest, but the

Motte cut her off. "And don't think I don't know about your 'secret' activities, either. I know all about the trapdoor in your room and your midnight visitors. Your taste for virile young men hasn't been a problem to this point, Medwind. And I'm very forgiving of your barbarian upbringing, and your heathen distaste for celibacy—but don't let that cloud your thinking on this issue." Rakell paced. "The sajes are guilty— maybe not all of them, but some of them. And the bastards need to be destroyed." She stared past Medwind out the window, eyes narrowed with hatred. "They're going to regret killing my students—my children. They're going to regret it, Med."

Faia's unbound hair spread across Kirgen's chest like a silk blanket. She nestled against him on his narrow cot, watching the smile play across his face.

"What are you thinking?" she asked him.

"Oh . . . that this would be a very nice place to be a hundred years from now. I could be content never to move again."

Faia laughed with delight. "So true. But just think. You would miss your classes on the so-important evocation of a cheerful number seven fire-breathing god—"

"Helpful fifth-level blue-smoke godling."

"As you wish. And I would miss my wonderful classes on how to renew rotted apples."

Kirgen chuckled. "That sounds exciting."

"Especially since my mother taught me how to do that when I was a small child."

The first gray light of dawn filtered through the fog into the room, and Faia propped herself up on her elbows. Her smile vanished. "You were wonderful, and this has been wonderful, but I must leave now, Kirgen."

"I suppose you must. When will I see you again?"

"I do not know that you ever will. We can hope,

I suppose, but the situation in Mage-Ariss is very grave."

Kirgen slipped his jerkin back on, and handed Faia hers. "You're right." He sighed. "What should I tell the sajes? Should I tell them *anything*?"

Faia pulled on her own clothes. "You must—mmph!—do what you feel is right. I do not know"—her voice became muffled, then clear again as she worked her face free of the leather jerkin—"a good answer to give you. Maybe there is no good answer."

"Perhaps not. Faia—"

His voice broke, and Faia tensed. "What?"

"Thank you," he finished. "For not believing that all of us could be so evil."

Faia remembered Rorin and Baward and half a dozen other shepherd boys, and her brothers and her uncles, the dim and distant memory of her long-dead father, and the few men her mother accepted as lovers, and she smiled gently. "I *know* men. They do not."

"And now I know women," Kirgen noted. "They are not so frightening as I was led to believe."

There was a bloody, bone-chilling scream right outside the Mottemage's door, a long, high-pitched howl that froze both Rakell and Medwind in their places.

It quavered into silence, and Medwind whispered, "Merciful goddess, what now?"

Rakell ran to the door, summoning her shields around her as she went. "Back me up, Med," she yelled.

She flung open the door, hoping to catch whatever was out there off guard.

The steps were empty, except for wet, dirty, bleeding Flynn, who bolted into the room as if pursued by the nine dog-demons of Mejjora and ran under the lowest chair in the room.

From his hiding place, his blue eyes gleamed out balefully.

"Flynn?" the Mottemage croaked.

Medwind and Rakell traded glances, and Rakell stared back down the spiraling steps. As far as the curve, there was nothing, and even beyond, she sensed nothing, although the familiar power signatures of Daane instructors were nearing various doors. They'd been, she reasoned, wakened by the screams.

"It was apparently Flynn," she finally told Medwind, sounding disappointed that it wasn't one of the killer sajes—or worse.

She carefully closed and bolted the door, and turned to watch her head instructor.

Medwind was belly-down beside the chair, trying to coax the big tomcat out of hiding. She'd reached under and pulled back a scratched and bloodied hand, and had decided on the more politically sound approach of "Here, kitty, kitty, kitty."

"He looks badly hurt, Rakell," the barbarian said. "His left hind leg is mangled and I can't get him out so I can look at it. Here, kitty, kitty, kitty ..." she added.

The cat shuddered and hissed and spat. The Mottemage joined her friend on the floor.

"I'll take care of this, Medwind. Flynn," Rakell said in a cold, commanding voice. "Come here."

The hair on the back of Medwind's neck rose, and gooseflesh stood on her arms. *Compulsion spell*, she thought. *The Mottemage's magic is strong enough to compel an army forward. Just the backwash of it draws me.*

But the cat crouched and glared.

"Flynn," Rakell commanded again, "COME—HERE."

Medwind, her face pressed into the floor, her hands gripping furniture to keep herself from crawling to her superior, was not in a position to see the cat's response. But she heard him. He spat and hissed.

And Rakell's magical compulsion lifted. "Damn!" the Mottemage muttered. "Nothing *ever* makes a cat do what you want it to." She stood and stomped into the kitchen and came back a moment later with another small pitcher of cream and a slab of raw fish, which she placed in the middle of the rug, but where Flynn could see them.

Then she joined Medwind on the floor, gave her a self-deprecating little smile, and said, "Here, kitty, kitty, kitty . . ."

And now I know women. . . .

Kirgen's words echoed in Faia's memory as she clung to the back of the wingmount. *Could the sajes know as little of Ariss' women as the mages know of the men? Is this city nothing but a flock of old, lonely virgins plotting in their towers how best to hurt each other? How strange and how sad. Kirgen was no skilled lover, but I had thought at his age he would have been with a woman before.*

She urged the wingmount downward as she approached the Daane tower.

Can they not see how much they need each other? How much better their lives would be if only they would let themselves trust each other again.

That shall be my job in this city, she decided. *I will make them all see that men and women should be together, not apart.* She smiled, and drove the wingmount down into the billows of fog. The Tide Mother was setting as the sun rose over the horizon. The garish pink faded, replaced by white.

The wingmount recognized its home pastures and set its wings into a glide. When it whinnied, it was answered by a stable full of its brethren.

"Hush, beast," Faia said. "You'll get us both caught." But nothing moved around the wingmount stables, and she grinned. *Almost home free.*

"There she comes," Medwind told the Mottemage. "Right over the fog-hills, staying low. She has no idea she's been missed."

Rakell sat on the floor, her fingers stroking the now nearly healed wounds on Flynn's leg. She seemed totally lost in the concentration of healing, but she looked up briefly from the purring cat and said, "Bring her to me at once.

"Yes, Mottemage," the barbarian murmured, and left.

Yaji paced from one side of the dorm to the other, stepping over clothes and projects and musical instruments, twisting her hair, and praying to all the old gods whose names she could remember. From time to time she stopped and studied the primitive little glass mirror trap, with its pentacle scrawled on one surface. Nothing appeared to have changed, and she had not thought to ask Faia what the trap would be like if it were full. She bit her lip each time, twisted harder at her hair, and resumed her pacing.

Dawn crept through cracks in the shutters and shone off the pale rose glass beneath them.

And Yaji, tired and frightened, could only think that with sunlight came safety. She opened the windows and unbarred the shutters and shoved them open to admit the light.

Tattered fog, thinning even as she watched, swirled and blew in ragged wisps across the lawn. A flurry of whinnies came from the direction of the wingmount stables, and her heart leapt. *Let it be Faia, back safe,* she prayed.

Silky brown undulations caught her attention, and she stared through the remaining fog at the path that led from the student dorms to the lake. A line of Fendles hurried down it. Their movements seemed furtive, but Yaji decided after quick deliberation that was too much credit to give simple animals. "Probably raiding the trash piles behind the kitchen," she muttered. She continued watching them, but they did nothing more interesting than run single-file out along the long rock that went toward the center of the lake and dive into the water.

She turned her attention back toward the direction of the wingmount stables. *Come on, Faia. Hurry, or you're going to miss first bell, and then I'll have to miss breakfast.*

"Don't move."

Faia, cleaning the wingmount's tack before she returned it to the rack, froze.

Medwind Song, breathing hard, eyes dark-circled and angry, stepped in from the far doorway and came to stand beside her.

Faia's brain scrambled for reasons why she might plausibly be in the tackroom of the wingmount stables before first bell on a class morning, but nothing was forthcoming.

"Frelle Medwind ..." she began anyway, hoping inspiration would strike in midsentence.

Medwind cut her off. "What the hells kind of a stunt were you trying to pull by flying to Saje-Ariss and bedding a saje-apprentice?"

Well, I suppose that means I do not need to think of a plausible story, she decided. *Just as well. Mama never approved of lies. And Faljon says, "Liars are vipers/who bite their own tails."*

"I was trying to prevent a terrible mistake from happening," she told Medwind. "The sajes are not guilty—at least not all of them. We cannot destroy them all."

"Even if you are right—and just so you'll know, I think you are—you cannot solve a problem by creating new ones. Even you admit that some of the sajes could still be involved. By going to Saje-Ariss, how can you be sure you have not made things worse? You went to the enemy—don't interrupt, Faia. The saje-ring we found is still compelling evidence, so we must consider at least some of the sajes the enemy. And *which* sajes? *I* don't know, and neither do you."

"So . . . you went to the enemy, and you told the enemy of our plans."

"Kirgen is not the enemy."

"Probably not. But what if his best friend is?"

Faia clenched her fists. "I had to do something. We cannot slaughter guilty and innocent together!"

Medwind sighed. "This I know. Faia, you must tell no one, not even the Mottemage, but I find this kill-all approach as abhorrent as you do. I am working on the problem, trying to find the true story of the Old Woman and the Fendles, for this horror we are living through now is rooted, not in the present, but in the past; not with the mages and sajes of now, but with those from hundreds of years before. This two-faced city's past returns to haunt us. Not until we can unravel the mystery of the Fendles' return will we discover that which they hope to protect us from."

Faia smiled. "Good luck."

"Thanks. In the meantime, you are in deep muck," Medwind added. "The Mottemage intends to skin you and nail your hide to the wall for her cat, Flynn, to sharpen his claws on, I think."

Chapter 7

A GASP BEFORE THE ROAR

THE frightened thoughts of the follower scurried like rat feet across the leader's mind.

:She returns, Sahedre.:

Sahedre's angry response lashed out at the hapless follower. :Well for you, Takai. Had she vanished forever while you held the watch, I would have killed you slowly. That she escaped without your notice in the first order—for that, I think you must still die. But not yet. I give you a chance to redeem yourself.:

:What of my wounds?:

:You dallied while on watch—they are no honest battle wounds. Learn to live with them.:

:But—yes, Sahedre.:

Sahedre calmed, mollified. :You know now which of these children she is. You shall not touch any others for the nonce. I do not need the energy. So. We shall let peace return to the University. But at your first opportunity, bring the mage-girl to me. I grow weary of waiting. I wish to regain my life.:

:If I bring her to you—will you forgive me?:

Sahedre's mental chuckle was chilling. *:Perhaps. But you had best hurry. I'll not be so sweet for long.:*

In pairs, the students hurried along paths toward the Greathall. Faia could see them clearly from her vantage point beside the window in the Mottemage's tower. With her whole heart, she wished herself with them. But wishes were useless things.

"—You will not leave the campus again until this issue with the sajes has been settled." The Mottemage stomped back and forth in front of Faia, punching the air for emphasis. "You will not go off campus with Yaji, nor without her. You will not go to the market, nor to the alehouses, nor to the musicrooms."

Faia bit her lip. "Mottemage—"

"Listen! I am not through speaking with you yet. How dare you fly off at night?! Fly, by the gods— and on my Makketh, too! How dare you leave your roommate unprotected?! How dare you make such a major decision regarding our policy toward the sajes all alone?! How dare you bed the enemy?!" The Mottemage's face deepened to an unflattering red-purple hue. "Answer me, damn you!"

Faia shivered and hung her head. "Kirgen isn't the enemy, Motte. He had nothing to do with the murders."

"You didn't know that before you met with him last night. He could as easily have been, and have killed you. And we'd be scraping pieces of you into our cold-room today, labeled so we didn't bury part of you with part of someone else. That was a stupid stunt, Faia. Stupid!"

"I only wanted to help."

The Mottemage rounded on the girl furiously. "Some of the greatest disasters in history have been perpetrated by those who meant well. Delmuirie's Barrier, that cost the life of the idiot who erected it, that traps us from the world outside Arhel, is there because Delmuirie only wanted to help. The Singing Stones of the Fey Desert mesmerize and kill a few poor lost souls every year, but the sajes who built them there didn't mean for this to happen. They just wanted a desert beacon. They just wanted to help.

"Heavens preserve me from people who just want to help!"

"I am sorry," Faia whispered.

The Mottemage softened a little. "Girl, I understand that you aren't one of us yet. Nothing here is like home; you don't know how we do things; you don't agree with all the things we do. No one blames you for being different. But gods, devils, and bugs on the floor, child, don't go bounding off on some damned foolish save-the-world errand without checking with the Mage Council first. I'd like to see if we can get through this without anyone else being killed."

Faia jammed her hands in her pockets and stared at the floor. "I will not do it again, Motte."

The Mottemage brushed graying strands of auburn hair out of her eyes and sighed up at her student. "I know you won't. Your punishment still stands. This—" she clasped a soft, heavy gray bracelet around Faia's wrist, "will stay on until I take it off. It will scream the instant you step foot out of your permitted area. It will get louder with every step you take, and it won't stop until you get back where you belong. I don't like doing this, but I also don't feel that I can trust you.

"I'm not angry, Faia, but the times are too dangerous to be left in the hands of children. Now get out of my office. Yaji will be stuck in your dorm room pretending you two slept in until you show up. I'm sure she's starving by this time."

"So how much trouble are you in?" Yaji munched on a crunchy, sweet kafarol and sipped her steaming cup of tea.

Faia flicked one eyebrow upward. One corner of

her mouth curled into a sardonic smile. "How much trouble is it possible to be in?"

"That much, huh?"

"Yes. Probably even more. I am confined to the campus. No trips to the market, no trips anywhere."

Yaji laughed. "She thinks she can keep you on campus?"

"She thinks rightly." Faia waved her wrist with the bracelet at Yaji, and said, "I cannot remove it. I have tried. And while I wear it, it will make noise and alert everyone nearby if I try to sneak out."

"That's terrible."

"I am a prisoner here, now more than ever."

"I'm really sorry, Faia." Yaji studied her roommate with an expression of sympathy. "You've had a rotten time, haven't you?"

"Except for last night, yes, I have."

Yaji caught something in Faia's tone, and her smile became conspiratorial. "So what happened last night?"

Faia grinned and told her.

Yaji was wide-eyed. "Does the Mottemage know you slept with him?"

"We did not actually sleep."

Yaji reddened. "You know what I mean."

"Did I tell her we frolicked naked around his room and had wild, wonderful sex for most of the night? Of course not. After you told me that mages are not allowed to bed men or they get kicked out of training? I am not crazy."

She stopped and stared into space. "Or am I? Oh, gods, we have to get to the market. No—I cannot go. You have to go to the market for me."

"What for?"

"Alsinthe."

"Alsinthe, Faia?"

"It is an herb. Brewed into a tea and drunk within a day or two after mating, it prevents the accidental birth of a child."

The city-girl whistled softly. "Oh, Faia—what are you going to do?"

"Probably nothing. It was really the wrong time of the month, I think—but my mother told me never to take chances."

"This time, I'm afraid you'll have to." Yaji shook her head with regret.

"Why so?"

"You can't buy alsinthe in Ariss. It's called 'baby-not' here, and it's illegal. It's illegal to prevent the conception or the bearing of a child. Tampering with the gods' decrees, it's called."

"The gods have blessed little to do with that." Faia sighed. "That makes as much sense and anything else in this accursed city, though. I suppose I should have guessed."

"Faia, I'm sorry. What will you do?"

"What can I do? I shall hope for the best."

Kirgen sat in the outer office of Als Havburre, the Fourth Sub-Dean of Saje-Studies, Political, and kicked restlessly at a loose tile in the floor. He watched the shadows creep across the ranks of gray and yellow squares, one block at a time. He noticed the spider busily crafting a web in the dusty corner window. He sighed, loudly and intentionally, for the eighth time in a row, and watched the shave-headed clerk in the corner stiffen and flinch. He got up and paced back and forth near the clerk's desk, squeaking his boot sole each time he came up behind him, and was finally rewarded when the clerk's pen nib exploded from the pressure and splattered ink all over the clerk, his desk and his paper.

"Look, you," the clerk snarled, "I've already told you—he doesn't meet with students on Tidedaes or Terradaes. I'll make an appointment for you for next Watterdae—"

"And I already told you, this is an emergency."

The clerk looked bored. "So you say. Tell me what

the emergency is, and I'll tell him, and he'll decide whether it needs to be dealt with today or not."

"I'll tell him. Not you."

The clerk smiled around gritted teeth. "If you don't tell me, you won't see him."

"If you don't let me in to see him, I'll keep you company for the rest of the day."

They stared at each other across the desk, the clerk red-faced and scowling, Kirgen smiling with insane cheerfulness.

"Excrement," the clerk muttered bitterly. "I don't get paid enough to put up with this." He opened the door a crack, leaned in and yelled, "Sir, student to see you. I can't get rid of him, and he won't let me get my work done until he talks with you personally."

Kirgen heard a spectacular burst of swearing and some rapid-fire mumbling. Then the clerk said, "I know, sir. I tried to tell him, but he won't listen."

The clerk's face returned from behind the door wearing an evil smile. With a mocking bow, he said, "Go right in. I'm sure the Sub-Dean will be delighted to see you."

After Kirgen finished his story, the Sub-Dean stared at him in astonishment.

"You're Kirgen Marsonne? Fifth level? Specialty path in Fire Elementals, minor in Chemistry?"

"Yes, sir."

"Amazing that you've made it this far. Insanity usually shows up sooner." The Sub-Dean walked over to a little blackwood calendar that sat on one dusty shelf beside his desk and ticked the inner wheel through three cycles. "Let's see ... the Brotherhoods don't get going again for another two Majors," he muttered to himself, "so you can't be pledging one of those." He turned back to Kirgen and his eyes narrowed. "Or are you already a member?"

"Sir?"

"Member of a Brotherhood."

"Yes, sir." Kirgen drew the sigil of the Rat and Trap in the air, hoping the man might be a brother.

The Sub-Dean looked at him with distaste. "I never approved of the Brotherhoods. Elitist, I thought. And silly. So this is some Brotherhood prank?"

"No, sir. This is real, sir."

"Girl flies on her horse to your bedroom window in the middle of the night and tells you all of Mage-Ariss is about to blast all of Saje-Ariss to eternity and beyond for some supposed murder plot we're suspected of being involved in. That's ripe. Have any idea how utterly ludicrous you sound?"

Kirgen squirmed on the hard wooden stool and tried to look righteously indignant. "You can see the hoofprints outside my window if you like, sir."

Sub-Dean Havburre snorted. "I just bet I can. Look—we trade with Mage-Ariss. If there were any gory murders over there, I would have heard of them. And as for the return of mythical beasties from the hells, I certainly don't think news like that would hide around waiting for you to bring it to me. I'll tell you what, though, young saje Marsonne. I'll run your story through channels, and if I get so much as a squeak that indicates there might be truth to it, I won't have you suspended for a term for barging in here disrupting my workday. Satisfied?"

The Sub-Dean sat down at his desk and picked up a sheaf of papers. Kirgen felt that he had been excused.

He couldn't just leave. "Is there enough time to go through channels?" he asked. "What about the attack, sir? We're all in danger."

"From mages? Please, Marsonne, haven't you learned anything? Sajes do things with their magic—mages just make things. They make pretty little flying horses and trees with three kinds of fruit and heavier-bearing wheat. We command the elementals and raise storms and travel from place to place in the blink of an eye. You're worried they will attack us?"

"Yes, sir." Kirgen looked the Sub-Dean straight in the eye. "Yes, sir. I'm worried."

Frelle Delis stood in front of her Advanced Botanicals class and announced, "Today, instead of your regular studies, you will be participating in a war drill. The frelles have written out the ritual that we will be following to charge our weapons in the coming battles. As students of magic and future members of the mage community, charging the weapons will be your responsibility, since you do not have enough experience to use them."

The frelle scurried from student to student, handing out slips of drypress.

"This is the ritual. We'll be using blackstone as a practice focus. It is stable and fairly inert—if you make a mistake, it won't destroy everyone in the room. However, it could still damage us all, so please pay attention to your technique. We will work with more dangerous materials as the battle date draws nearer—in actual battle, you will be focusing your energy on the mages themselves. By that time, you will have no margin for error—so please, ladies, remember that your lives and ours will eventually rest on what you do here."

The work tables had been pushed back. Now Faia knew why. She had a sick feeling in her stomach as she watched the frelle place the blackstone focus in the center of the cleared space. *They cannot ask me to do this*, she thought, and knew that they not only could ask her to do it—but would.

Faia took the drypress leaflet, folded it without looking at it, and slipped it into her pouch. Then she found a seat well away from the center of the room, and took it.

Frelle Delis stopped and smiled brightly. "I want you to participate, too, Faia—not just watch. If you can't read the words, I'll be happy to help you."

"It is not the reading, Frelle Delis. I think I could do that now. It is the drill."

The frelle stared at Faia and the friendly expression in her eyes vanished. "What about the drill?"

"After what happened in Bright, I swore I would never use the Lady's Gifts again—but I came here because the mages convinced me I would not hurt people if I knew how to use the Gifts, and I might hurt them if I did not." Faia's hands curled into fists which she pressed with all her strength into her belly. The sick feeling would not leave. "The mages said they would teach me how not to kill. Now you want to teach me *to* kill." Faia stared at the ground, dejected. Tears blurred her eyes and down the back of her throat. "I cannot."

Delis paled. "No one is asking you to destroy guiltless villagers. We are not at war against innocent people. This is war against sajes—people who tortured and slaughtered *our* people. My students." Her voice cracked, and she paused to catch her breath. Faia saw the instructor's anguish. Delis spoke again, softly but with intensity. "The Magerie needs every one of us to add our strength against that evil—evil so terrible that the Fendles left the gates of the hells to help us fight. We need you. In your heart, even you must understand this. If we die in battle and you have not helped us, our deaths will be on your hands."

Faia wiped the tears from her cheeks and shook her head. She looked into Delis' eyes. "Your deaths will be on your own hands, Frelle Delis. You chose the path of war. If you are so afraid of dying in battle, perhaps it is because your heart tells you what you are doing is wrong."

Frelle Delis pressed her lips together so tightly they turned white. She turned her back to Faia without another word, and directed the rest of her students into the center of the classroom.

In a shaky voice, Delis told her students, "Form a circle about the focus, and begin by reading the chant."

She stood to one side of the circle and watched.

The students droned:

> "Hail, Kallee, darknight mother—
> We embrace your hungry glory
> And your sundering voice.
> Our cause is just;
> Lend us your sword."

"Again," Delis said. "With more feeling." She demonstrated, and her voice rang with emotion, echoing among the high vaulted ceilings of the stone room.

The student chanted again—and again. With each repetition, their faces changed. They became submerged in their instructor's anger—in their own fury at the death of their classmates—until the room crackled with energy. Delis was satisfied. "Better. Now you must learn the "Song of Mehtrys." This song will bring the power to the focus.

She sang:

> *"Atczhilloth, atczhilloth,*
> *Yetzhirah, breyiah."*

The students imitated the melody. When they went through it a few times on their own, Delis added the descant. The eerie harmonies and dissonances echoed off the high ceilings of the stone chamber and set Faia's teeth on edge. Delis split the group into two. The girls with very high voices she taught the second part. They practiced a bit longer.

When Delis finally had them channel the energy they raised into the blackstone, the stone burned with an ugly red blaze.

This is real magic, Faia realized. *There is power here—as strong and as real as the power I draw from the earth and the sky—but it does not come from earth or sky. This is magic they feed with their own anger and fear—and hatred. This magic could not be used for good. It could never be turned from its intended purpose. This is the evil they most fear—and it is born by their own hands.* She shivered, enveloped by the seething wizardry that her classmates had drawn down. The atmosphere in the room recalled to Faia a day when she stood on the side of the mountain, watching the sky blacken and the thunderclouds build—a day when she knew she had no shelter, and the sky was about to open up and devour her.

After the class, Yaji came over to where Faia sat. The aura of compressed rage built by the ritual still clung to the city-girl—Yaji stared at Faia blearily for a moment, as if she were a stranger. The two walked down the long corridors to their next class; they were almost there before Yaji finally shook off the last lingering effects of magic.

"Are you sick?" Faia asked.

"I'm fine now. That spell just took a lot out of me."

Faia nodded. "That was not good magic."

"Would you just leave it alone?!" Yaji snapped. "Gods on hot rocks, Faia—the war is wrong, the instructor is wrong, the magic is wrong! You can't always be right, Faia. Nobody is always right. You just can't get along with anyone, can you?"

Her roommate shrugged. "This war *is* wrong, and the instructor *is* wrong, and the magic *is* wrong. And I *am* right."

"That will be small comfort if the Council executes you for treason after this is all over."

"I would rather be right and die than be wrong and kill."

Faia's roommate sighed. "I admire your courage," Yaji said softly. "I think you're an idiot—but I truly do admire your courage."

After *nonce,* Yaji and Faia hurried back to their dorm. Once their door was locked and their shields were erected, Yaji sprawled on her bed with a sigh of relief. "I used to love to walk across campus at night," she told her roommate. "Now I feel as if I'm going to be sucked back into that horror that grabbed us every time I walk out of the room. And after dark is worst of all."

"I know. My nightmares will not go away. I dream of that voice dragging me into a pool of lightless fire—and of blazing eyes staring at me—and every time I wake, I expect to find it was not a dream at all." Faia sat cross-legged on her own bed and brushed her hair absently, staring at the shuttered and locked window. "I wish I could just go home. I wish I could just go anywhere. I am so scared. If I could get this bracelet off, I would run away."

In the two fivedays after the Council voted to destroy Saje-Ariss, Medwind Song scrambled to find some proof that she was right. The barbarian and the hill girl shared a high opinion of men, and a doubt that sajes were involved in the perfidy and horror of the campus's bizarre murders. Medwind suspected that the murders were tied into the Fendle prophecy instead, and had spent every waking minute in Mage-Ariss' libraries, looking for some substantiation for her theory.

It had been a long, frustrating search. Medwind Song traced one finger down the index of her last available sourcebook, a little-known illuminated tome titled *Magickal Historie of Ariss-Magera*, by one Lady Melipsera. It was so old the sheepskin vellum it was written on was yellowed and brittle, in spite of the library's careful preservation, and the hand-calligraphed and hand-illustrated pages were faded and difficult to read. Medwind guessed it had probably been written only fifty to seventy-five years after the original incident with the Wisewoman and her Fendles. It was the only copy that existed, and one of Medwind's other sources on the incident made a brief reference back to it. Medwind held great hopes that at last, she could get to the heart of the ancient mystery.

She sat in the dry cold of the book storage room in which the massive, gaudy tome was housed, wearing the white leather gloves the librarian provided and being careful to treat the pages with special reverence because the librarian was standing right beside her, watching her with eyes that would have made a starving raptor's look friendly.

Once she unraveled the archaic spelling, she found an entry on the Fendles. Melipsera had the annoying habit of addressing her readers directly, and she was flowery, but Medwind's eyes immediately picked out details in the *Magickal Historie* account that hadn't been anywhere else. She read,

Chapter 18—The Battle of The Ladie Sahedre Onosdotte and the Fendelles Againste the Sajes and the Forces of Eville

Ariss was not, in yeare River-Five-Lion-Nine, splitte in twain as it is todae."

Which would put the split a good twenty-five years later than conventional sources claim. Interesting, if she's right.

Nor Ariss-Magera nor Ariss-Sajera were begat at that time; the citie was simplie Ariss, and renouwned far and wide for its graces and majestie. But alle was not welle, and thee must remember that I withe mine owne eyes saw what came to passe of these straunge events.

For there was amonge the number in the Magerie one faire Mage, the Ladie Sahedre Onosdotte, who loved and was loved by alle. She taughte her especial and kindlie magickes and alle listened. But wicked Sajes amonge the scholars did take her magickes and perverte them, and did use them to make greate monstres and terrores, and they did kille babies and eate them in terrible rites, and they did seake to wrest Ariss from the handes of those who loved the greate citie. And this did wounde the Ladie Sahedre greatlie, and did breake her heart.

And withe her broken heart did she make magicke, and then did she weep greate tears. From these tears sprange fourthe the sweete Fendelles, faire creatures with sad eyes and greate pure hearts as broken from grief as the heart of their Mistresse.

"Oh, please," Medwind muttered. "Spare me the maudlin rantings of the ancients. One more 'greate, sweete, pure, faire' word and I'm going to throw up all over this book."

Which would be redundant, she decided. *It reads like good old Melipsera already did.*

But, regardless the questionable origin of the "sweete Fendelles" from the Lady Sahedre's tears, there were Fendles. And somebody, somewhere, had to know what they were for.

Medwind took a long, slow breath to strengthen her resolve and read on.

The Ladie Sahedre challenged the eville Sajes to sette bye their eville, and joine with the Mages in the pathes of goodeness. In answer, the Sajes did *mehevar* upon the children of the Mages of Arisse, pure and innocent, and they did use them in their terrible rites, and they did kille them and gain power therebye, and did make their actions known to the Ladie Sahedre, with muche laughter and mocking.

Then was battle enjoined of which thee shall never see the like (*one hopes,* Medwind thought,

considering the current situation), wherein the
Sajes and their eville beastiarie of monstrous
heroes, their wind-devilles and fire-devilles, their
smoke-demons and watter-wightes, did align
againste the poor, noble Sahedre, daughter of
alle that is goode, and her few smalle Fendelles.
And the goode Mages of Ariss were appalled by
the greateness and the wickedness exceeding of
the Saje armie, and by the valiant fighting of the
wise Sahedre and her loyal companiounes, and
did lende their armes and their heartes to the
battle. Then there was muche bloode and dying,
and great anguishe.

Alle this I saw withe mine owne eyes, that I mae
tell thee trulie, whilst I was but a childe. And
mine own mother did die in the battle against
the Sajes, and mine own father did fight on the
side of eville, so that now I knowe not whether
he lives, nor care I, for I am not his issue, and
he is no father of mine.

And the Ladie Sahedre and the brave Fendelles
foughte to the gates of the Helles, with all the
Mages, and at the laste, the Ladie Sahedre took
grievous woundes and did die, and the Fendelles
in their fury did rise up and did make greate
magickes and in their anger at the death of their
faire Mistresse did overcome the Sajes at laste,
and did force them back through the gates of
the Helles, and the Fendelles did magickallie
lock the gates and did chain themselves to them,
that they might better guard againste the evilles
inside for alle eternitie.

Thus came the citie to be divided, and the
Mages and the Sajes to forsake each the other.

And all of this historie I have from my mother's
mother, that thee mae know it is true.

"Not that your mother's mother might have any grudges to bear against the Sajes, Melipsera." Medwind pulled out her notepaper and quickly wrote the details the *Historie* account added—the name of the Wisewoman, the year, and the name of the ritual, the bit about child sacrifice.

Child sacrifice is pretty nasty business, she thought, *and that part of the account at least rings true. But the business of the Fendles working magic . . .*

She carefully closed the book, and nodded to the librarian that she was finished with it. She handed back the soft leather gloves, as well, and after brief thanks, left.

Creatures created by magic cannot work magic. Melipsera knew that. She wrote enough of the standard texts on magic—some of her work is still in use. Medwind grinned suddenly. *Thank the gods, only in revised and updated versions.*

Melipsera was my last hope. It took me a full fivedays just to find her accursed book, and she gave me almost nothing of any use.

She tapped her heels to her horse's flanks and got set to aim him home along Three Round Way, when the quadrangle of towers of the Faulea Lyceum caught her attention. The university was within sight but in the other direction, only about two miles away, and higher on the hub of Ariss. But it was separated from her by two thick, well-guarded walls, watched over by men who held the sajes interests at heart. However, in Faulea Lyceum there would also be a library with books—lots of books. All of them from the saje point of view.

And maybe, just maybe, the sajes will have something to say about the Wisewoman and her Fendles that the mages don't.

She steadied her big roan and sat rock-still in the middle of traffic, ignoring the shouts and curses of the other travelers. She scrutinized the tower, and then glanced down at the abhorrent red Daane uniform with loathing. There was no way in Arhel that a tenured frelle from the mage-training university could get into a saje university library.

A wicked smile crossed her face.

She'd bet anything, however, that a literate Hoos barbarian, bringing gifts and oozing awe and lust, could.

When she finally headed toward home, it was at a gallop that sent pedestrians diving for the curbs and that would have lost her her throughway access pass if she'd gotten caught.

While on the other side of the city, Medwind read of the doings of the Lady Sahedre and her Fendles, Faia sprawled on her stomach on the big rock, trailing her fingers into the lake and wiggling them at the fishes. The sun beat down on her back and warmed the soles of her bare feet that waved in the air. Her boots and her books lay in the grass on the shore, along with Yaji's.

Yaji finished sweeping the last bits of a fish skeleton she had found lying on the rock into the water, and with a shudder of revulsion, she turned to Faia. "I hate this place. We aren't supposed to be here. Besides, it smells and it gives me the shivers."

"Then go back to the dorm." Faia's gloomy voice echoed off of the water and bounced back in little whispers.

"Great. Let's go. We've done with classes and drills. We have the whole rest of the day to study or read or work on our own spells—or something."

Faia lay her head down on her arm and glanced over her shoulder at her roommate. "I'm not going back to that damned room. If you don't like it here, you go on back, but I am staying."

"You want me to get in trouble, too? Is that it? You know we have to stay together."

"I am only saying, you do what you want to do. This place is the only freedom I have right now. You can go anywhere. You can just find one of our classmates who can stay with me, and off you could go with someone else—out into the city or anywhere. This is the only place *I* can go that is not four damned stone walls and a roof."

"You're miserable," Yaji snapped. "You have just gotten more and more impossible—"

"—You try being stuck on this campus forever with a stupid screaming bracelet around your wrist and see how you like it."

Yaji stood up. "You've only been stuck here two fivedays, and it isn't like it's forever. Besides, we need to work on your reading, Faia. You're finally getting the knack of it. Why don't we go back to the dorm and go over Pictusa's *Meditative Magic?* You liked that one."

"I am not of a mind to study now."

"But you're doing so well."

Faia sighed. "Go away, Yaji. I want to be alone for a while."

"But—"

"Nothing has happened to anyone since we found the bodies and started keeping watch. The instructors are about to lift the curfew and their restrictions and set everything back as it was. You have heard everyone say that the Council is discussing termination of the drills and reversal of the war decision. No one has even seen the Fendles in the last few days. Whatever was killing the mage-students is gone now. So I shall be fine."

Yaji threw a vicious glance in Faia's direction and tromped off the rock. "May your afternoon be pleasant," she snapped. "I hope the fish eat you." She picked up her books and her shoes and flounced over the lawn in the direction of their dorm.

"And greetings of the season to you, too," Faia muttered.

Rakell relaxed in the yearling paddock of the wing-mount stable with several beautiful but wingless colts and fillies. She chided herself for taking time away from her ledgers and her students and her Council business and the war preparations—but she kept on sitting in the straw anyway, scratching their ears or feeding them slices of apple and staring off into space.

She was tired. *Old and tired*, she decided. *And depressed.*

She reflected that she should have felt better with every day that passed uneventfully, but an aching weight still pressed between her eyes and into her heart. Even yet, no one truly knew who was responsible for the deaths of her students or the other young women, and she was no nearer finding out than she had been when the terror first struck. The Mage Council perched on the precipice of all-out war, waiting only for a shove from a recognizable enemy to throw them into that bottomless chasm. The first-strike attack was ready. The defenses against saje retaliation were ready. Trade with Saje-Ariss had been cut to a trickle of non-essentials, and mage spies had all been prepared for a pull-out from Saje-Ariss to safety. But now the mages in the Council sat helpless, waiting and watching—because the enemy had vanished like mist in sunlight.

Old, tired, depressed—and a failure.

Because this, she could not help but realize, would be the landmark event in the record of her tenure as the Mottemage of Daane University—an academically adequate but uneventful rule, finished by a war that would blot out any meager educational accomplishments she might have taken with her into the history books.

I always had great hopes for the future, she thought. *I wanted to bring mage-studies at Daane to new heights. I wanted to be the mage who finally broke the cell-code, the one who learned to fix magically created characteristics so that they could be passed on from generation to generation. And I knew that when I*

*had this wonderful knowledge, my position in history
would be secure. I would pass the secrets of the universe on to my adoring protégés so that they would
never be lost, and I would be assured of a place in
the memory of my peers.*

"But I've failed, haven't I?" she asked one colt who
nuzzled at her pockets hopefully. "I can give you
wings, but I couldn't make your mama and daddy so
that they could give you wings. And your babies will
be as firmly nailed to the ground as you are right
now."

*It rankles. Nothing I've accomplished will survive
me. The one student who understood my work and
worked in my field is dead, my other protégés have
different interests, the rest of the students who could
use my techniques aren't far enough along to learn
them yet—especially not Faia, who could be the one
who learns to break the cell-code if she would just
acquire some control—*

"Stargazing by day?" The husky voice from above
was full of laughter.

Rakell jumped and stared up. Medwind Song
peered over the high stall gate at her, grinning
fiercely.

*And then there is Medwind Song. My barbarian
friend, my most promising protégé for years—and her
interests are not in new research, or even in applica-
tions, but in dusty books and arcane papers and the
"mysteries" of the dead-and-gone past. A heathen
viewpoint, if ever there was one.*

"I was getting ready to start the wing-work on this
batch, Med. You blew my concentration. And, heavens have mercy, you look like a nightmare."

Medwind laughed. "Thanks—and I've seen your
concentration before. That was stargazing."

Rakell ignored the jibe. "Why have you painted
yourself up like a tabby-cat and stuck that bone thing
through your nose again?"

"It's *esca* and a *sslis*, dear Mottemage, and I'm

riding over to the Faire to buy some things. I thought I'd get a better deal if I dressed up."

"You'd get a better deal if you looked like a normal human being."

Medwind laughed merrily. "You keep saying that, Rakell—but, you know, I think with a 'nize, tick Hoos akk-zent'—and my 'nize, tick Hoos svord' on my hip— I will make out fine."

"Have it your way and pay three prices. You still look like hell. And what are you bothering me for, anyway?"

"It was purely accidental. I came to get my old tack out of storage."

"Lot of trouble to go to for a shopping expedition, old friend." Rakell got up from her seat on the straw bale and brushed coarse, clinging straw-dust off her pants. She cocked her head at an angle and studied her friend from the corners of her eyes for a long moment. "I don't think so," she said at last.

"Honest—I came to get my old Hoos saddle and bridle."

"No. I wasn't referring to why you're here. I was referring to where you're going. All of a sudden, I don't think you're going to the market. What are you really up to?"

Medwind smiled at her mentor and shrugged. "Research. It's important."

"Ah. I see. And I suspect that I should not ask any more than that." The left corner of Rakell's mouth twitched with the smile she tried hard to suppress.

"That would be best, I think," the barbarian agreed.

"Don't get yourself killed, then."

White teeth flashed in a cocky grin. "I never do."

The heat was becoming oppressive. Kirgen shed his blue-velvet robe and wiped the sweat from his face. He noted the confectionery that sat next to the Raronde Building of Herbal Arts, and the short line of young men that stood in front of it buying sweet ices. If he hurried, he'd have time to get something cold and wet before his next class.

He changed directions—and was immediately intercepted by two full sajes whose gold-bound beards and gold-braided hair gleamed against the splendor of their velvets and silks. Each sage took one of his arms, and without a word, both executed a neat about-face that headed all three in the direction of the university's back gate.

Kirgen felt his heart drop into his belly. "Hey—" he started to protest.

"Don't make a scene," the first saje warned. "As it is, we've debated conjuring you into deep-freeze, and I only won the argument by a narrow margin."

Kirgen swallowed hard and nodded and hoped that the winner of the debate had been taking the side "against." Deep-freezing someone was exactly the sort of thing sajes did plot, and argue about, and bet upon, and that he was the subject of one such prank was entirely possible—but he hadn't done anything—lately—that would warrant the attention of full sajes, who usually picked deserving victims for their weirder experiments. Holding out the hope that he was involved in a simple case of mistaken identity, he whispered, "My name is Kirgen Marsonne. I think you have the wrong student."

"We know who you are, Marsonne," the first saje said, dousing that hope.

"Where are we going?" he asked in another whisper.

"Speak normally—whispering will look odd," the second saje advised. "We're going to meet with a few people who would like to hear your tale of the girl on the flying horse."

"Now? But I told the Sub-Dean about that a long time ago."

The two sajes stopped so abruptly that Kirgen stumbled. "How long ago?" the first asked.

"One or two fivedays ago," Kirgen said.

"Damn," the second muttered, and the first nodded. "How could he hold onto information like that?! Havburre is going to have a lot to answer for."

"Havburre doesn't know what in the hells is going on, and never did, but nobody caught on to that until he'd already made tenure. That's why he got shunted off to that dusty old office and the Fourth Sub-Dean spot."

"We ought to fry this kid for taking sensitive information like that to a Fourth Sub-Dean anyway."

Kirgen yelped. "Nobody else would see me! He wasn't going to, but I hung around and bothered his clerk until the fellow got angry and let me in. And Sub-Dean Havburre didn't believe me. It wasn't my fault."

"Well, Marsonne, if we have as much trouble on our hands as I think we do, you're going to find that mighty small consolation."

The sajes put their heads together and muttered at each other for a brief time. Then the first said, "Never mind the prelim group. We don't have a fivedays to debate this anymore. We'll have to take the second option."

"It's on your head," the second saje snapped. "I'll alert Faulea's Sajerie. You take care of the bellmaster—and him."

Little children fell silent and stood on the walkways with their sticks and strings dangling forgotten from their fingers. Their mothers caught sight of the object of their fascination, and with shrill cries, raced out to hurry them inside. Carpenters put down their hammers, bakers laid aside their dough, hawkers ceased their bellowing—and on Faulea Spoke Street, a stunned hush surrounded the apparition that moved proudly up the hill toward the university.

The apparition was not silent. Medwind Song's wrists jingled with tiny coin bracelets, her ears sported bell-laden hoop earrings, the up-curved toes of her best black boots rang with silver jangles. Even her horse's bridle, carved red saddle, and silver hock-rings were bell-bedecked. And, as she was a feast for the ears, so too was she a feast for the eyes. She had braided her hair over the Hoos red-feather war crest, so that the ruddy feathers seemed to sprout from her skull and trail in billowing waves down her back. Beaded and be-ribboned necklaces nestled over the red-black-and-silver brocade *staarne* that glittered in the sunlight; the ruby eye of her nose-*sslis* sparkled merrily; her sword and dagger and flatbow gleamed with utilitarian menace. Under the sacred cat-patterning of the *esca,* her face wore a haughty smile.

She was, she noted with real pleasure, still quite able to scare the hells out of a crowd.

A velvet-swathed saje, whose magnificence paled in her shadow, stepped from the walkway and bowed from the hips in the fashion that was Hoos-approved for the harmless and unwarlike.

"*Mekaals-ke-areve ho-ve k'ehjherm, bahaada,*" he said in frightfully bad Trade Hoos. "For what you (many) this place flee-like-a-scared-goat, sweetie?"

Medwind bit the inside of her cheek to keep from howling, and made the appropriate Hoos saddle-bow, which was not so low as the saje's bow—because a Hoos warrior preferred not to spill arrows or drop her bow or tangle her sword or dagger when bowing to new-found friends, in case the weapons might be needed to beat the stuffing out of the same new-found friends right away.

She spoke Arissonese, and intentionally mangled the accent. "I bring books, fine Hoos books, vis pictures, for jour book-hus. I vould like reading in jour book-hus," she said, and smiled. "We trade, jess?"

She could tell the saje found this idea appalling.

"Books? Oh, yes, I'm sure we can work something out. You want to use our library, though? You want to read?"

"Jah. I vish to read. Jah, jah. I read verra goot—

not speak so verra goot—I read verra goot. I vant look at all jour books. Right now."

The saje looked doubtful.

Medwind wanted to laugh so much her sides ached in sympathy. *I haven't had a chance to play full-out barbarian in ages. This is wonderful.* She let herself get into the part. "I bring trade books—gifts," she told him solemnly. "You vill like dem. I show jou."

The saje was backing up and shaking his head slowly. He continued to look doubtful. "I'm sure they're very nice books, but we don't grant library access to every stranger who asks, ah—what is your name?"

"My name iss Saba ... how to say? ... Riverwalker—I am *Huong* tribe of Hoos-people, jess?" She nudged her mount imperceptibly, so that the warsteed began to dance and shift beneath her, which made the bells ring, and caused all her weapons to clatter. Then she made a great show of calming the huge red beast. "I am great warrior-magician of my people—much loved."

The saje became edgy.

"Yes, honored Saba. Huong tribe. . . ." He looked down and muttered into his beard, just loud enough that Medwind could pick up his whisperings. "Huong tribe ... Huong tribe ... where have I heard of the— oh, hells!" He straightened and his eyes met hers, and Medwind saw a sudden respect—one might even say fear—in them. "*Huong* tribe. Ahh. Bearing *gifts.*" He came to a decision. "Right. You will follow me, and I will take you to the library—er, bookhouse—and give your gifts to the librarian, and he will let you read. We are honored, noble Saba," he added with another deep bow. "*Greatly* honored."

There are some advantages, Medwind noted, *in being from a tribe known far and wide for the fondness with which it looks on other peoples' heads—and for the skill it has developed in acquiring them without the consent of the owners.*

Led by the saje and followed by townfolk, she rode up the cobblestone street, a parading hero. At the great staircase that led to the double-doors of the massive whitestone library, she dismounted with a rattle and a clank, fixed one young saje-apprentice with an evil expression, and demanded, "You, boy, you vill hold horse for me, jess?"

The student looked at the saje who led the barbarian, and Medwind noted with glee the quick interchange of panicked glances. When the student looked back at her, his eyes were round and white-edged. "Yes," he agreed. "I'll hold horse—er, your horse—for you."

Medwind pounded him on the back. "Verra goot. You goot boy." She stroked her index finger along his jawline and smiled appreciatively. "You gotta goot head, boy. Verra goot."

The apprentice gave her a sickly grin, and behind her, the saje gasped and started coughing. Medwind's smile widened. "You vatcha horse now," she said again, and strode up the expanse of whitestone steps with the saje scurrying behind.

The chief librarian was a kindly old gentleman with beard and braids so long they swept the ground. The saje made another bow to Medwind, then to the librarian, and the old librarian smiled politely to Medwind and made slight obeisance with his head. Medwind bowed more deeply to the old librarian, and the saje introduced them. "Chief Librarian Nokar Feldosonne, this is the honorable Saba Riverwalker. Warrior Saba, this is the Revered and Ancient Nokar Feldosonne."

Medwind played her barbaric role to the hilt. "Greetings from the glorious realm of the Hoos Domain, Oh Ancient Nokar (bow). Bright blessings on jou and jour hus (bow) and on jour families for seven generations (bow)."

The grizzled man stared at Medwind, his quick, bright old eyes lingering on the details of her tribal costume and make-up. He muttered, "Holy Saint Futhyark." Then, in only slightly accented Huong Hoos, he said, "Welcome, Saba, warrior-magician, battle veteran of the Pelarmine Siege and the War of Stone Teeth, woman with nine husbands and three herds of goats. We are honored by the presence of so rich and mighty a woman. What are the stranger-names of your children, that I may give honor to them?"

The saje who had led her in gaped at the smooth rush of exotic syllables that poured from his superior's mouth. Medwind would have done the same if it would not have compromised her dignity.

"I have no children. It is my only grief," she answered in her native tongue. *Just my luck—an honest-to-gods Hoosophile scholar. Sharp old buzzard, too,* she thought. *Wonder if he's sharp enough to notice that my crest doesn't match my name. This could make things sticky.*

"I grieve with you," the old man continued in his fine Hoos. "I see that you wear no necklaces for the Booar War or the Char River War."

Yeeks. Haven't been home in a while—I missed those. "I have forsaken the battlefield for a time, noble Nokar," she ad-libbed, "and have sojourned far from my beloved *b'dabba* and my adoring husbands, seeking wisdom," Medwind said, "and now I come at last to your door, honorable keeper-of-books. And I bring gifts."

The old man's eyes gleamed. "Books? Hoos books?" He turned to the saje and shoo-ed him out. "Ha! She's got books for the library, Virven. Thanks for bringing her, but no need you staying around. I'll see you later."

Virven tugged on his beard and started to argue, then changed his mind and left with a relieved look in his eyes.

Medwind dug into the beaded and brocaded black-and-red pouch at her side and pulled out two waterproof bear-gut tubes. She removed the tops and laid two creamy white scrolls on the library desk. *"Philosophies of Angdoru.* Only a copy, but a good one," she said in Huong Hoos, handing him the first.

He looked at it and smiled. "Lovely. We completely lack Angdoru's work—and I came to admire him greatly when I traversed the Hoos Domain. And the other?"

"The original copy of a work done by a lesser writer. Still, though it is unworthy, it is something you may not have." She handed him the other scroll.

"Sayings of Medwind Song." His eyes met hers with a twinkle of delight, and in his impeccable Hoos, he burbled, "Do not sell yourself so short, Warrior-Mage Song. We have several translated and bound copies of this, but certainly not the original scroll. And if you agree to autograph this copy for me before you go, I'll let you dig through my library. If you tell me what the hells you're really after, I may even help you look."

Medwind laughed in spite of herself. "Dammit," she said, switching back to Arissonese, "how long did you know?"

"Dear scholar," the old man grinned, and also changed languages, "when a mighty and much-decorated warrior in full ceremonial dress arrives on my doorstep in strange times, wearing the headdress of the mighty Song family and claiming the name of the piddling Riverwalkers, I think to myself that the times get even stranger. And when this same warrior, of supposed lowly Riverwalker origin, happens to have the original manuscript of a fairly well-known treatise on magic by none other than the infamous *Medwind* Song, Hoos warrior-turned-barbarian scholar who just happens to teach next door in Mage-Ariss, my belief in coincidences snaps like a dried oak twig under the hoof of a warhorse."

"Well said, old man. Would that I knew so much about you."

The old man chuckled. "I'm just as glad you don't. You might take a fancy to my head, and I like it where it is. So. What are you looking for?"

Medwind rubbed her palms together and nodded. "Everything you have on war in Ariss in the year River-Five-Lion-Nine—I have reason to believe the city actually split that year, and not twenty years earlier, as I'd always supposed. Also Fendles, cross-referenced with Lady Sahedre Onosdotte, a ritual called *mehevar*, and maybe ancient child-sacrifice."

"Fascinating." The old man chuckled gleefully. "Just fascinating. The times get even stranger. If we find your information, dear Song, you must let me know what you need it for. Rumors bedevil my days, and whispers leech my brain nights, until I would gladly roast an ox or two for the first person who could give me a few decent facts."

It was Medwind's turn to chuckle. "For a roasted ox, I'll see what I can do."

The old man led her into the stacks, and Medwind cheerfully followed.

:*She waits at the rock, Sahedre.*:
:*I did not ask reports of you—only results. Can you lure her closer?*:
:*I think so, Great One. But if this works, the rock will be a good enough place. And if we succeed, she will surely follow.*:
:*Then we shall go to her.*:

The Mottemage's bracelet weighed around Faia's wrist like a millstone, tying her to a place and a way of life she became daily more sure she didn't want. With Yaji gone back to the dorm, the silence of the lake surrounded and enveloped her, and increased her loneliness and despair. She dipped her fingers in and out of the water and listened to the soft "plink, plink" of the droplets she scattered, and basked in the hard afternoon sunlight that beat down on her back. Her eyes were half-lidded against the glare; her breath went slow and lazy; her belly soaked up the heat of the sandstone through her thin leather jerkin.

I wish I had stayed in Saje-Ariss, she thought. *Or that I had taken the damned wingmount and started flying and just kept on going until I got someplace I liked.* She slapped the water, splashing a wave across the glass-smooth surface that sent ripples racing away in all directions. *I would have been fine if I'd done that.*

The soft "ploosh" of something heavy going into the water sounded from around the tree-covered point off to Faia's left. The splash was followed by six more.

Faia looked up. At first there was nothing, and then she could make out the smooth "V" of something swimming toward her. It became a line of somethings, one after the other—and she recognized the Fendles.

They haven't abandoned us, she thought, first delighted—then frightened as she realized, *If they haven't abandoned us, neither has the killer.* She sat up and watched them racing across the lake toward her.

The Fendles swam up to the rock, and jumped on it one by one, chittering with anxious, high-pitched squeals. She caught the terror in their eyes and in their movements, and flashes and fragments of their thoughts. Slowly she began to understand, and cold fear settled into her belly, heavy as lead. Something—something terrible—was coming.

Chapter 8

THE BELL

THE colt fluttered his new wings and craned his neck around to look at them. They were nearly transparent, without the smooth downy furring they would develop as the colt grew to adulthood, but already they showed faint promises of the smoke-edged coloring that was Rakell's trademark on the wingmounts.

Rakell grinned and chased the finished colt out of the altering room to pasture. Months of preliminary work had paid off. All the subtle changes in metabolism and all the delicate rearrangement of bone and ligament, muscle and nerve that had gone before—tedious, careful changes that lacked the visible results her students so loved—were behind her. Now the dramatic changes—the unfolding of the wing-buds and the opening of the extra chambers of the heart—were being completed right on schedule, and with magnificent results.

This fiddling with the wingmounts has become the best part of the day for me, she mused. *Teaching grows tiresome, and the administrative work is a nightmare—if I didn't get to do my experiments in the stables, I think I'd lose my mind.* For what seemed like the hundredth time, she considered stepping down and leaving Daane in the hands of Medwind Song—and for what seemed like the hundredth time, she had to face the prejudices of Mage-Ariss against the barbarian Hoos—and, for that matter, against any outsiders. The time still wasn't right; she began to wonder whether it ever would be.

Maybe I ought to tell Medwind that I don't think the Magerie will accept her as head of Daane. She shook her head in sudden disgust. *And then again, maybe I ought to get off my ass and fight for her place in the Magerie. Gods know she's capable, and bookish enough to suit any of the scholars. After this war business is behind us—*

Enough of politics. She turned her attention to the last two beasts—the two delicate fillies who waited in the holding corral. "Now, little ones," she asked with companionable cheer, "who's next?"

Flynn, lurking among the rafters on the top of the stone wall that divided the stalls, peered down at the Mottemage and yowled.

Rakell glanced up. "Hush, cat. I'm working."

Flynn yowled again, louder, hackles rising. He glared out the door and crouched and spit at something beyond Rakell's line of sight.

She sighed and got up from her comfortable straw bale, muttering, "Fine, beast. I'll look. But I won't chase off that raggedy-ass tom who's been poaching in your territory. You can fight your own battles, slug."

Or most of them, anyway, she thought, remembering Flynn's wounds of the fivedays before. *Wish I had an idea what did that to you. I'd fry it, whatever it was. . . .*

She looked out the door and across the pasture, straining to see what Flynn glared was glaring at. She noted the heavy traffic of the throughway, then the rolling greensward near the dorms, and the far edge of the lake. The near edge was hidden by the traffic.

Probably visible to you, up there near the rafters. But damned if I'll climb up there to see what bogey's offended you. I haven't the time . . . or the knees.

"Go catch mice, Flynn," she snapped. "I'd tell you to play with matches, but I'm sure you would."

Flynn's blue eyes scowled at her. He hissed out the door one more time.

"If it bothers you that much, go eat it. But leave me out of your cat fights. I have wingmounts to finish."

Flynn, instead of stalking off with wounded feelings as he usually did when he didn't get his way, hunkered down in an alert crouch, eyes fixed on the mysterious point outside the barn.

The Mottemage forced her attention away from her eccentric cat and back to the fillies. "Lump of sugar for the next baby," she said and held out a hand. Both fillies hurried forward, and she clipped the halter around the quicker of the two and led it from the holding corral into the altering pen.

She secured the harness, then settled on her straw bale and rested her fingers on either side of the young horse's nose. Eyes closed, she pressed her forehead against the velvet skin of the muzzle. Her mind projected slow tendrils of energy that poked and twined along pathways of the filly's cells, teasing new shapes out of tissues and bones, shifting masses to make some things lighter, some things sturdier, creating better pathways for oxygen, more efficient handling of fuel—finishing, as a sculptor would, the final buffs and polishes of a masterpiece.

Rakell was, in truth, a very long way away from her own body at that moment.

And above her, Flynn sat guard.

Kirgen chased along in a lopsided sprint, dragged by one arm behind the galloping middle-aged saje, who had introduced himself on the run as Paf, First Clerk of Faulea University.

"Where are we going?" Kirgen yelled as he ran.

"To Saje Blayknell's quarters."

"Who is he and why are we going there?"

"Can you transport?" the saje yelled back.

"No," Kirgen panted.

"Well, Bendle's been to the classrooms by now, so most of the Sajerie is already on its way to the Basin—and I can't transport either. But Blayknell can. He'll get us to the Basin. Besides, he's the one and only Bellmaster. Only he has authority to call a Conclave."

Kirgen mulled that over, his mind racing faster than his feet. There had been two Conclaves called in his lifetime. The first, when he was very small, had been when a malignant fire-demon escaped the pentacle that held it and started destroying the Sajerie, one saje at a time. Not even rumors of the cause of the second escaped the secrecy of the Conclave—students often asked about the Road-Five-Rat-Three Bell Night, but their questions were invariably met with such ferocious stares that they changed the subject. And now there was to be a third Conclave.

Paf and Kirgen hauled up, puffing and gasping, in front of the Bellmaster's tower. Paf eschewed the stairway, preferring the students own time-honored method of slinging rocks against one of the third-story windows for getting the man's attention. "Blayknell," he bellowed between gasps, "we have a situation down here! Hurry, man!"

A grizzled head popped out the window, mere fingers' breadths away from the last rock that went sailing upward. "Paf, that was too close," he yelled back as it whizzed past his ear. "I'll set firesprites after your balls if you ever do that again."

"No time for jokes. We need you to call a Conclave—and we need transport to the Basin."

The man paled and vanished from the window without another word, and re-materialized beside the saje and the apprentice the same instant in a tiny puff of blue smoke, startling them both. "Conclave?" he whispered. He shoved his face close enough that Kirgen could smell the potato-leek soup he'd had for lunch, and count the pores in his skin. "Why a Conclave?"

Paf gave a whispered, rapid-fire version of the Faia-on-a-wingmount story, and added the bits of information the Faulea sajes had gleaned from spies, the Council, and alterations in trade patterns. "They've been bloody close-mouthed over there in Mage-Ariss—but we have enough to go on in spite of that, I think. It all adds up to treachery, maybe war," he finished.

"Then you believe that girl's wild tale of murder and mage-revenge was true?"

Blayknell and Paf turned to Kirgen. Kirgen nodded, feeling flutters like crazed bats racing about in his gut. Somehow, he had not expected to be this involved once he told his story. He'd expected authorities to take over, to settle things, to let him go back to his classes and his life. In fact, he'd expected to be ignored—as he had been after talking with the Fourth Sub-Dean. That had been fine. This was terrifying. "Yes, sir," he answered, and tried not to choke on the words. "I don't think the murders had anything to do with us—but I believe the story."

"Truth be known, I do too," the old man agreed. "But, gods, man—a Conclave?" He rubbed his hands together nervously. "Must it be a Conclave?"

Paf said, "We agree the threat is real, and that it threatens us all. The likely solution will be to strike first, or if not that, to get our defenses up and cut off trade immediately. Therefore, all the sajes must be compelled to gather as soon as possible, from wherever they are. We've already lost a fivedays. We don't know how much time we have left."

Kirgen paled when he heard Paf's assessment of the situation. A first strike? A first strike would put Faia in danger—Faia who'd risked her life to help the sajes, and Faia with whom he'd made love (*for the first time,* he admitted to himself, *and the second*). . . .

Protect all the sajes, or protect Faia. We can't do both, damn-all. And I'm a saje. He whispered a hasty prayer to the God of Justice for the hill girl's protection, and turned his attention back to Paf and the Bellmaster.

The Bellmaster looked grave. "Very well," he said. "You will come with me, while I carry out my duties. No Bellmaster ever rings the Conclave bell alone." Blayknell grabbed Paf and Kirgen by a shoulder each, and the next instant, time and space lurched and twisted, and all three stood in the Belltower at the top of the Hub.

The delicate bone-white tower, one of the greatest marvels of the marvelous city of Ariss, had no stairs. It soared like a needle toward the heavens, gazing down at all of Ariss, higher than the highest sajetower, a delicate spire of magic and illusion. Its white-stone surface was glassy smooth and gleamed with the fine blue haze of barrier spells.

Inside, three ranks of bells lined the center of the tower, with seven bells to a rank—and each bell was different. There were small bells and large bells, bells of bronze and copper, blue-metal and brass, silver-clad and gilt, carved, painted, etched, runed, and inscribed. They were lovely enchanted bells—intent, waiting gracefully and with purpose . . . all save one. That one lurked apart in the ranks, bulky and misshapen, misbegotten, the demon spawn of the bellmaker's art. It was ominous, colorless, dark, and massive, as huge and cold and ugly as doom.

Kirgen felt hunger and anger emanating from the grotesque bell—and his skin crawled.

"That bell," the Bellmaster said, "is the Conclave bell." He pointed to the bell that warped Kirgen's stomach into knots. "When it was poured, three powerful saje criminals under a geas were impelled to throw themselves into the mold. They died—but their souls remain locked into the Conclave bell for as long as it survives. They gave the bell its power to demand compliance."

Blayknell shuddered. "Nevertheless, it's a nasty piece of work. Its name is Soul-Stealer. It killed a Bellmaster once. Likely as not, it will try to kill me."

He took a long ebonwood mallet out of a box full of mallets of different colors. Then he stood in front of the nightmare bell, and took a single deep breath, and swung.

The first peal went straight through Kirgen's bones. It grew; it stretched; it took on a life of its own. It resonated through the tower, becoming wilder and fiercer—and Blayknell sounded the bell again and then again, first slowly, then faster. Paf and Kirgen covered their ears and stared, while the Bellmaster picked up speed, beginning to beat the bell like a madman, like one possessed. The banshee wail—the riveting, howling, ghoul-born, ghastly voice of the bell—drove on and on, and Blayknell kept swinging, face white, sweat flying, breath coming in gasps. In the city below, other bells sounded back, answering in voices that were frail, pitiful imitations of the great demon bell that led the saje through his hellish dance.

The whites of Blayknell's eyes showed, and froth lined his lips—and still he rang the bell. Paf screamed in Kirgen's ear, "It's got him. Grab him, or he'll die, and we'll be stuck up here."

Kirgen and Paf lunged at the saje. Kirgen dived for the Bellmaster's knees and bowled him over; Paf sat on his mallet-arm. The devil-bell shrieked a final protest, and shivered slowly down to silence.

Below, the streets of Saje-Ariss were empty and hushed.

But the silence was not a welcome silence after the damned-soul screeching of the bell. It was the nervous, expectant silence of the prisoner who has seen the first head fall to the axeman, and who waits, praying he won't be noticed, and dreading the next head to fall may be his own.

Faia stroked the Fendles who cuddled up against her. "Hush," she whispered. "Easy, easy—I have shielded us. The thing you fear could not get through my shield before, and will not now. We are safe enough here."

The Fendles settled onto the warm rock and gazed adoringly into Faia's eyes, nuzzling against her like big dogs, letting her scratch their ears and rub their bellies.

The smallest of the Fendles was injured. Faia had not noticed before, but now she saw that the creature's left eye was opaque and draining. "Come here, darling," she coaxed, wiggling her fingers as she would have to call a cat. "Come here and let me look at your eye."

The Fendle reluctantly edged toward her, and Faia saw that something had pierced the eyeball. *How awful. It has surely lost the sight in that eye for good.* She winced in sympathy. But her mother had taught her the healing lays that pertained to animals, and she had learned a few things from the University as well—*beyond that be-damned reading and writing*—she thought with a frown. She kept her shields up, but re-centered and grounded, and pulled in all the energy she could hold. Then, with her fingers tingling, she held both hands above the creature's eye and commanded,

"Be as you were,
Whole, hale and healthy,
Full of life and youth and strength—
Mended, bless'ed
By the Lady,
By whose hand I give you grace."

At the last word, she touched the Fendle's eye—

—And felt as if she were being sucked dry. The Fendle chirped and squeaked in terror, and Faia's knees buckled as energy poured through her body and into the animal at an impossible, uncontrolled rate. For an instant, for less even than an instant, she thought she saw the face under her hand shift, becoming less a Fendle and more a terrified young woman—

—*Oh, Lady, help!*" she thought—

—And up on the Hub, a bell pealed—if the tortured scream that came from its throat could be called anything so benign as a peal—and the mage-girl's hands fell away, spell broken.

Faia's blood turned to ice. The Fendles leapt up and hissed, staring off in the direction of the Hub, at the Belltower. On the campus behind her, streams of students and instructors poured out of the buildings and milled around. Even inside of Faia's shield, the urgent clamor went on and on, making her dizzy, demanding that she hurry—somewhere—calling and commanding and insisting until she threw her hands to her ears and shrieked. The Fendles, caught inside her shield with her, milled and spun and hissed, their ears flat back against their skulls, their hackles raised.

Faia stared at the Belltower, noting tiny movements from shadows inside the bellroom—and then there was silence and the shadows vanished. The world held its collective breath and waited.

Minutes passed and nothing happened. The crowd that milled about on the greensward stopped rushing to and fro. Faia heard puzzled cries, and then people filed back into their buildings.

She calmed down. The bell had confused her and unnerved her. But nagging on the edge of her memory was something important she needed to remember, something *wrong*—

She couldn't bring it back, whatever it was. The Fendles kept distracting her. They were still frantic. They hissed and snapped at each other and circled around her feet, gazing up at her with soulful, plead-

ing eyes—*They want me to fix it . . . whatever it is,*
she realized. *They protect us, but they want me to
protect them—dear Lady, help me.*

"What can *I* do," she asked. The injured Fendle,
whose eye was still opaque, but no longer draining or
infected-looking, took her jerkin in its mouth and
started to pull her down off the rock toward the
woods, and, Faia noted, in the direction of the Belltower as well.

"I can't," she told it. "This bracelet won't let me
off the campus."

The Fendles looked at each other.

*I would swear they understand what I say. But
how could they?* She shivered. *The face . . . —that
was it! That was what I was trying to remember!—
the Fendle's face that was almost a girl . . . did I really
see that?*

The biggest and most grizzled of the Fendles shoved
past the other six and right up to Faia. It took the
bracelet delicately between its teeth and snapped—
and the bracelet fell to the ground.

Fear raced through Faia's veins.

*Oh, Kallee—I could not get that bracelet off, no
matter how hard I tried. And I really tried. And . . .*
she reflected soberly, *I may not control my magic well,
but I am strong. I am very strong.*

The big Fendle was looking with curious intensity
into her eyes.

*I did not understand how powerful they were . . .
though if I had thought about it, I suppose I would
have realized. They fought off the demons of hells,
did they not?*

She battled with fear. The Fendles were her
friends, the friends of all women.

:Yes,: something said in the back of her mind.
:Quite right. The friends of all women . . . :

Pictures—faint, blurry little pictures—began to form in
her head. The Fendle was sending the pictures, trying
to tell her something. She stroked its soft fur and let

herself gaze deeply into the limpid brown eyes, and murmured to it as she would have Huss, "Fendle . . . dear Fendle . . . show me what you see."

It had worked with the dogs, and it worked with the Fendle. She caught the pictures that skimmed the surface of its mind. She saw the murdered girls lying in the woods, and herself coming to find them, with Yaji behind her.

You know who killed them, do you not, Fendle? she thought. Aloud, she said, "It was not the sajes who killed them, was it? I talked with one of them—he was a good man. He could not do such a thing, and I do not think the rest of them would, either."

The Fendle hissed, and opened its mind further to Faia's gentle probing, and the pictures became clearer. The pictures were of the killings themselves, of the girls being dragged into the woods by men, being tortured horribly, then mutilated, and then killed. The backs of the men were to her as she watched through the Fendle's eyes, until the last of the murders were completed. Then one of the men who seemed to be the leader, a slender redhead in a deep blue robe, turned slightly as if he had heard a sound—

"Kirgen!" Faia gasped. Her stomach lurched. It couldn't be, but she could see him so clearly. She looked for the freckles on the backs of his hands and on his cheeks, and they were there. She looked closely for the ring—the lovely blue saje ring that had given her those brief second thoughts the first time she saw it—and the ring was there, too. The quick, casual way in which he brushed his hair back out of his eyes was the same, and the easy grace with which he moved.

Faia's cheeks dampened with tears. "Oh, Kirgen, why?" she asked.

:*Because, dear child,*: the Fendle answered, abruptly speaking directly into her mind, :*Kirgen is your enemy, the enemy of all womankind. He is a saje of enormous power. He led the blood magic to become*

*mighty, and he succeeded, becoming so potent that he
was able to lure you with his lies, appearing to you
as a simple student.:*

"Then why did he not kill me?"

*:Why should he? You believed his tale willingly,
and spread the story of his kindness and gentleness
and of the goodness of the sajes into the Magerie.
Through you, he would soon have had access to all
the mages—for if they believed you, they would have
trusted the sajes, would they not? Were they not e'en
now lowering their defenses and preparing to acquit
the sajes in their minds.:*

"So it was rumored. Yes," Faia whispered. "Yes,
they were."

*:You were his good tool, child. He knew just what
to tell you, and just how, that your suspicions would
be allayed. And you believed. Your trusting naivete
could have brought down all Ariss-Magera, were we
not here to guard you.:*

Something was wrong with that, Faia felt. Something about the picture, something about the whole
tale rang false—

*:Even when you hear their war-bell ring, you would
choose to believe the innocence of those blood-stained
sajes? You are a fool, little girl, though a sweet fool.:*

But Kirgen was so wonderful, Faia thought.

The Fendle barked sharply, in an almost-human
laugh.

*:The wicked often seem so. But child, war
approaches you, and will devour you and all your city
without our help. At this moment, your dear sajes
gather to plot the downfall of Ariss-Magera—and there
is none among the Magerie strong enough to lead the
mages against them. Except, dear child, for you. You
must become the new Wisewoman who shall lead the
Fendles to victory.:*

Faia pulled her hands away from the Fendle's head,
but never broke eye contact. "I cannot," she whis-

pered. "I have strength, but I cannot kill. I could not lead you."

:*This is defense of good people, girl. Not killing. Defense. You must save these women—and you are the only one who can, with my help. I can help you. You have the necessary power; I have experience. If you will open your mind to me, and let me, I will leave a part of myself inside of you in Soul-Touch. Then you will have my experiences to draw on. And you will not make any more foolish mistakes of this sort.*:

Faia felt the persuasion of the Fendle's sweet gaze, felt the soothing caress of the Fendle's thoughts in her mind drawing her down deeper into the Fendle's bottomless eyes. She felt tired, and silly, and ashamed that she had been tricked by such an evil schemer as Kirgen—*But he was so wonderful!* her own voice protested again in the back of her mind—and she trusted the Fendles, of course she did ... had they not fought the very devils of the hells for the women they served? ... and holding back on this one little thing was so nonsensical ... the Fendle was right, of course—she had to lead the Fendles, had to lead the mages, it wasn't killing, it was defense and how could she hope to lead the mages against the sajes if she didn't have the experience ... but, the Fendle let her understand, she had to accept the Fendle's gift ... she had to accept of her own free will ... she had to say the words ... just two little words. ...

"I accept," she told the Fendle in a slurred whisper.

There was a sharp, painful "snap" in her mind, and she felt sheer, claustrophobic terror as *something* shoved her out of the way. She tried to fight back, tried to push with her arms and legs against the invisible thing, tried to scream—

But instead, she heard her voice saying calmly to the Fendles, "I have her. She was too powerful to force, but she accepted willingly, the little idiot, and she had the magic to allow me to complete the transformation from inside her. We have succeeded, dear comrades."

And Faia, watching with terror through eyes she no longer controlled, saw the dear old, grizzled Fendle she had talked with fall over dead. She watched the soft, furry body shift and transform, becoming first the body of a handsome woman in her late fourth decade, and then with increasing speed an older and older woman, until within minutes it had become skin over bone, and that dried skin flaked off and powdered down to dust and blew away in the faint breeze. The remaining Fendles kicked the bones into the water, barking their terrible laughing barks.

"Wel-come b-b-back, S-s-s-sahedre," one Fendle hissed.

Yaji leaned out the window. Faia still sprawled on the boulder in the lake, looking very much like a mite on a pebble from her viewpoint in the dorm. *Still sulking out there, stubborn as a cat with the fishmonger's fish, damn her eyes—instead of up here in the dorm where she ought to be. And if one of the mages catches her out alone again, I'll get strung to the tetherpole right along with her. I got off lucky before, gods alone know why—I'll bet the Mottemage doesn't overlook me a second time.*

Faia kept right on laying there, sulking, when Yaji noticed a line moving toward her through the water. Faia wasn't paying much attention.

What—? Yaji had time to think, and then the first of the Fendles hopped up on the rock with Faia, followed by six more.

Yaji tensed and bit her lip. *I don't like those misbegotten wierdlings,* she thought, *even if they were the salvation of the city hundreds of years ago. I don't like them, and I wish Faia would just chase them off. Look at the way they're crowding around her. It isn't right.*

Yaji felt Faia's circle go up. *Gods, she's loud.* She

smiled wryly. *I couldn't even sense energy use before she moved in—unless it was on the scale of that firestorm she loosed. Since I've had it bouncing around me at her volumes, I've gotten pretty good at picking it out of the background noise.*

I'm surprised. As a roommate, old Faia hasn't been too bad.

I think, Yaji left the window and headed out the door, *that I will go pull her away from those Fendles, and keep her from getting into any more trouble. Heavens help us all if the Mottemage confines her to her room. She'll probably accidentally level Ariss.*

Yaji was trotting out the door toward the greensward when the bell sounded.

:*Hurry!*: it demanded. :*You're late. Go, go, go, hurry—you must, you must, you must—*:

Her direction changed, and her feet raced toward some unknown destination without her conscious volition. Yaji felt helpless, sucked once again into playing puppet while some other will pulled her strings—but the shield training Faia had drummed into her had stuck. Yaji ignored her running feet, concentrated on the energy of the earth beneath her and the air above her, and threw one of her roommate's protective magical spheres around herself.

Her feet quit running, and the compulsion to be elsewhere died down to an irritating urge. Yaji could think again.

She found herself surrounded by other students from her dorm and some of the junior frelles who hadn't yet earned space in the tower. They pushed and clawed and ran blankly into each other and her in their hurry to be *somewhere*—the unknown somewhere where the bell told them to be. She fought to get past them, to get to the lake, but she was hemmed in.

At last, the damned bell quit ringing. Yaji waited a moment, then dropped her shield.

The frelles were first among the unshielded or

poorly shielded to regain their composure. They began organizing the mage students and directing them back into their buildings, instructing them to wait in their rooms to hear whatever news the frelles could glean. Then they took off toward the Greathall, where, presumably, the Mottemage or Medwind Song would arrive soon to tell them what the ringing of the saje bell meant.

Yaji ducked behind shrubbery and waited for the crowd to clear, then jogged across the greensward to the lake.

She could see Faia—and the Fendles. And she began to have a nasty feeling about the whole situation. Faia sat on the rock with her head thrown back and her mouth hanging open, as one of the Fendles stared into her eyes. The tableau held for several minutes, then shifted abruptly as the staring Fendle fell over, apparently dead. With uncharacteristic caution, Yaji angled into the undergrowth at the edge of the woods instead of going straight for the rock. Then she moved in as close as she dared, keeping low.

Faia stood and laughed wickedly and said something to the other Fendles that Yaji couldn't hear, and then Yaji had to shove her fist into her mouth to stifle a scream. The dead Fendle became, briefly, the corpse of a human woman that decomposed before her eyes.

Oh, gods, she thought. *Oh, gods—*

She closed her eyes and held her hands over her mouth. Faia's laugh, unspeakably evil, echoed across the lake. Yaji shuddered and closed her eyes tighter, wishing the awful sights and sounds she'd been witness to into oblivion. Suddenly, behind her, the bushes crackled, and she heard a gentle snuffling. Yaji opened her eyes and froze, praying that whatever was behind her would fail to notice her. Then a wet nose pressed against her arm, and she leapt and spun to face—

—Two Fendles. Two grinning, needle-toothed Fendles, with deceptively sweet brown eyes, that hissed at her and pushed her backward through the underbrush toward Faia. Yaji tried to remember how to draw up the attacking firebolt that her instructors had demonstrated years ago as part of the personal defense course, and failed. She fell back again on Faia's psychic protection shield, which, she noted grimly, didn't make any appreciable difference in keeping the very physical Fendles at bay.

A hand settled lightly on her shoulder from behind her, and Yaji squealed and spun around. She found herself facing her roommate, who studied her the way Yaji herself had studied insects that found their way into her picnic drinks.

"Faia," she shrieked, "help me out. Something is wrong with these be-damned beasts! Get them away from me."

"Faia? I know no *Faia*, child," her roommate said in a cool, cultured, oddly ancient-sounding voice. "I am Lady Sahedre Onosdote, the champion of woman-kind. And you, my dear, have seen too much for my liking."

"F-F-Faia," Yaji stammered, "this isn't funny. Stop it."

"Yes, of course. How forgetful of me." Faia/Sahedre nodded thoughtfully, then smiled at Yaji. "To you, I appear as your friend, Faia, since I wear her body. Trust me, she has no use for it now. But you . . . you have seen me dispose of my own old and ruined body, and I greatly doubt you would be inclined to keep your silence."

"Yes, I—"

The stranger in Faia's body cut Yaji off. "No matter. You present yourself in time to solve a pressing problem of mine. There were seven Fendles. Now there are only six. Some especially bright person might notice this, do you not think so, little girl?"

"No, Faia," Yaji said. "No one will notice.

"Little liar." The woman laughed. "And you must

call me Sahedre. Faia is dead and gone and already forgotten. As you will be, if you do not help me."

One of the Fendles shoved its nose hard into the small of Yaji's back, and Yaji fell forward. Sahedre caught her roughly, and shoved her grinning face down into Yaji's.

"Pity the body with the magical talent wasn't yours. I'd have liked to wear your elegant little frame around, instead of this brawny peasant carcass. But after this is over, I'll save your body for one of my servants. It will do well enough." She looked at one of the Fendles. "Would you enjoy this as a gift, Mehandelia, for your hundreds of years of service?"

The Fendle chirruped sweetly.

"So," Sahedre smiled again. "We shall give you to Mehandelia. In the meantime . . ."

Sahedre whispered hissing syllables under her breath and stared into Yaji's eyes. Yaji tried desperately to look away or to shield herself, but she couldn't. She felt her bones melting with agonizing speed, and fire lanced through her muscles. Her face felt as if it were ripping in two. A blurry, dark brown mass grew between her eyes. Her fingers ached, and she stared down at them, horrified. Sharp black claws replaced her fingernails, and her fingers shortened and twisted and grew webbing. Brown fur grew out of the backs of her hands and her arms.

She screamed, "No! No!" and all that came out of her mouth were frightened chirps and squeaks. She fell to the ground and stood, four-legged and unable to stand back up on two legs. She glared up at the mage who now towered above her, and hissed furiously. *I'll kill her,* Yaji thought. *If ever I get the chance, I'll kill her.*

Sahedre ripped Yaji's clothes off, and nodded at her with insane brightness. "You make a lovely Fendle, dear," she said.

*   *   *

Nokar Feldosonne shoved another heavy tome in Medwind's direction. "In this one, Sahedre is the Vaydia, the human incarnation of Terrs."

"Terrs?" Medwind looked over the paragraphs he indicated.

The old man chuckled. "Terrs is the goddess of death and destruction. She rips through saje mythology like a scythe-wielding fiend through a nursery, and she supposedly comes to live among us from time to time in the form of the Vaydia, the beautiful torturer and killer."

"Nokar, this is the seventh saje version of the "Wisewoman-and-Fendles" myth I've read, and *none* of them have a damned thing in common—except that Sahedre and the Fendles are always portrayed as evil incarnate."

"The germ of truth at the heart of the lies." The librarian nodded sagely.

"You don't understand. The Wisewoman is a Mage-Ariss hero—supposedly she saved the world from the encroaching evil of the sajes. In your books, she is the evil the world was saved from."

"At risk of my head, I'll note that the mages would have a stake in portraying her as a hero instead of a villain. She being female, I mean."

"Lay off the headhunter jokes, old man. I haven't done *vha'atta* in about fifteen years, and I'd hate to start back with a sorry specimen like you."

The old man cackled gleefully.

Medwind nibbled on the tip of her braid and stared at nothing. "The mages have a vested interest in portraying their own as heroes; the sajes have the same vested interest." Her eyes flicked over the ancient saje. "Which you must admit."

The saje nodded silent agreement.

"After over four hundred years, it will be impossible to know who lied. But I have to know."

"Well, I agree that knowing who lied will be impossible, but I fail to see any urgency in unraveling the matter now. Old myths are fascinating, but hardly a life-and-death issue."

"What if—hypothetically, of course—I told you that the Fendles are back, and swimming in our lake at Daane?"

The old man's eyes narrowed, and his gold-bound braids swung like pendulums as he leaned forward and planted his hands on the garnetwood library table. "Hypothetically, of course, I'd be inclined to go see for myself. Barring that, I, too, would want to know the truth behind the myths."

From the opposite side of the table, Medwind leaned forward in imitation of his pose, and her eyes locked with his. "Then help me find it. Help me find the truth, and stop a war, because somehow, all of this is linked together."

He started to agree—and the Conclave bell began to ring.

He winced, and beckoned her with one crooked finger. "It may all be linked—and your myths and Fendles may be at the heart of this mystery. But the time for looking through books has just passed. I'll break all precedents and tell you that if you would stop a war, you'd best come with me—there's not been a mage in Conclave since the Split, but the time may have come to join forces."

Medwind hurried to his side, and felt his bony fingers dig into the muscles of her upper arm. The the world turned simultaneously upside-down and inside-out.

When her vision cleared and the urge to retch had passed, she found herself in the midst of a giant bowl carved out of stone, with a solid stone roof arching high overhead. She was surrounded by a constantly shifting stream of sajes of all descriptions who appeared in puffs of colored smoke and ran wildly for the steps carved in unbroken rings around the sides of the bowl.

"Hurry," Nokar yelled over the riot that surrounded

them. "We have to get out of the way so others can come in." He yanked with the fingers that were still embedded in her arm, and bemused, she followed.

They swarmed up the rows and rows of stairs, until their progress was blocked by sitting sajes above them. Immediately Nokar turned and sat, and Medwind did the same. Both gasped for breath. Beside them, sajes thumped down, and almost simultaneously, sajes took seats in front of them as well.

Watching the crowd pour in, an image struck the mage. *What bowl fills from the top to the bottom?* she thought abruptly. *A new riddle, and one none of the tribes could answer. I could garner a few trophies for that—though I'm sure the losers would scream foul. The idea of an arena such as this one would be rather foreign to my dear Hoos.*

The Basin filled, and the steady stream of newcomers dwindled to a trickle, then to a few startling pops that dumped embarrassed late arrivals onto the arena floor in front of the watchful eyes of the full house. Then the smoke settled, and the arena floor lay empty.

Nokar jabbed her in the ribs with one bony elbow. "Keep quiet and don't call attention to yourself," he whispered.

"Dressed like this?" she whispered back. "You've got to be kidding!"

"No problem. We have a couple of male Hoos warriors affiliated with one of the other Universities. The gender differences in Hoos dress aren't significant to the untrained eye. As long as no one realizes you're mage, not saje, things will go well enough." Nokar fell silent and scanned the crowd.

Medwind relaxed a bit and let her own eyes wander across the crowd that filled the Basin.

Heavens, she thought, *there are a lot of sajes. More of them than mages.* The realization made her uncomfortable. *Lots and lots more. What if they declare war on us? Not that the thought of odds slowed any of the Magerie down when all this started. The Mage Council seemed to think these men would be dirt beneath our heels.* The sheer masses of saje-qualified men seemed more overwhelming to Medwind tactics-and-strategy-trained mind every instant. *I think there would be less dirt beneath our heels than the Divine Councilmotte believes. And considerably more on our faces.*

Too, the sajes were represented by a broader spectrum of society than were the mages. Medwind spotted plenty of the highborn university types she'd always equated with sajes scattered throughout the crowd. She also saw a broad slice of the poor and the foreign, of smiths and bakers and brewers, of hedge-wizards and holy-wizards, of merchants and tinkers and drinkers of ale.

When the bell rings, if they can come, they do, she thought. *How odd. The Magerie loudly touts its egalitarianism, and throws out any who fail to maintain all of its nit-picky little standards. They'd be happy to be done with me if they thought they had the grounds. The Sajerie makes no lofty claims, yet opens itself to all.*

A great, brawny gold-haired fellow in an odious purple-orange-yellow-and-black-patterned robe claimed the center of the arena and raised his hands, commanding silence. He got it.

In that robe, he could probably command the attention of the fishes in the sea and get it, Medwind thought, distracted from her reverie and wickedly amused. She nicknamed him Flamboyus.

Flamboyus bellowed in a sonorous voice, "To the assembled, to the gathered, to the drawn—the compelled, the chivvied, the desired: Hail, welcome, well met."

The audience answered as one voice, "Hail, welcome, well met."

"The bell rings, terrors rise, and we come at the

moment of distress, for darkness falls in daylight," the leader continued.

"Darkness falls in daylight," the assembly agreed.

Wordy, wordy, wordy, Medwind thought. *And not very interesting. They could lose the liturgy and improve this production sixty–seventy percent.* But she droned out the responses with the rest of the patchwork crew.

"We call forth the Bellmaster, the Lord of Singing Metal, Leash-of-Ghosts. Oh, Walker Among Spirits Chained, Oh, Bravest Saje—tell us what we fear."

"Tell us what we fear," roared the assembled host.

Beside her, Nokar Feldosonne watched for movement like a hawk hunting mice. Nothing happened.

Everyone waited.

Time passed in silence. Individuals of the assembly shifted in their seats, or looked around the Basin, or sighed; all of them continued to wait. The expectant silence grew heavy with unborn doubts that hatched rapidly into bitter whispers.

". . . a trick, a jest . . ." Medwind heard.

". . . some fool prank to draw me away from my shop . . ."

". . . have his hide, if I find out who . . ."

". . . but how the hells could someone unwarranted ring the damned bell?" asked one.

". . . bet the bell ate him," another suggested.

"Now there's a cheerful thought, Eumonius. You always do see the bright side of things. . . ."

The whispers grew conversational, grew argumentative, grew to shouts, as the mob began to demand answers of Flamboyus, who was trapped at the center of all the attention. He raised his hands in a placating gesture and began to say something.

With a WHUMPH! he was enveloped in a dense cloud of black smoke that sent him coughing and sprawling into the first three rows of sajes. This had the effect of dumping a number of well-dressed scholars into the laps of a number of poorly dressed roustabout types, and vice versa. Fighting broke out, and was only quelled when the leader of the litany stood up and knocked together the heads of the two nearest brawlers.

Silence crept back into the Basin and reclaimed its seat.

Medwind leaned forward, fascinated. In a marvelous, bizarre day, this was ultimate theater—and now, with an entrance worthy of Hoos hellspawn, more players joined the play. She couldn't remember the last time she'd been this entertained.

The smoke cleared to reveal an old, battered, down-trodden saje; a portly, effete scholar; and a muscular young redhead who had Medwind licking her lips.

"Has the call for the Bellmaster been given yet?" the scholarly fellow asked the leader in a whisper that carried beautifully to the top rows due to spectacular acoustics.

"A bloody long while ago, thank you very much." Flamboyus was furious. "Where the hell were you?"

"The bell tried to steal the Bellmaster's soul, and we had the very devils' own time getting him out of the belltower."

A soft murmur ran around the Basin at this news.

"Damned bell ought to be broken and recast, with better sajes in the mix," Medwind heard.

"Yeah," another voice noted dryly. "Let's just cook some nice guys into the bell. Great plan. You volunteering?"

The first was silent a moment. Then he said, "Nice guys? Let me give you my recipe for Three-Infants-and-One-Virgin Fricassee."

Medwind snickered, as did Nokar. He whispered into her ear, "Same response we get any time someone suggests recasting the bell. Three convicted necromancers went into the bell brew the first time. Not very nice chaps, really, and they keep trying to kill the Bellmasters—but it was hard to find a good grade of convicted necromancer back then, I suppose. I doubt we'd do better now. And volunteers are nonexistent."

"*You* want to volunteer?" Medwind asked with a grin.

"Have I given you my recipe for Three-Infants-and-One-Virgin Fricassee?"

"Right."

Down in the arena, the gray-skinned, sweating Bellmaster, propped up by three strong men, cleared his throat and began to address the crowd. "Fellows of the Sajerie—we face possible doom and annihilation from Mage-Ariss. I present to this gathering Kirgen Marsonne, who obtained news of this one week ago from a mage-student who flew into Faulea University on a wingmount to tell him."

Faia. Medwind closed her eyes and shook her head. *Whether she meant to or not, she has managed to betray us, hasn't she?*

Chapter 9

THE PRICE OF HISTORY
AND LIES

KIRGEN, Faia's contact in the Sajerie, told the tale fairly—Medwind was grateful for that—and the sajes listened equitably. But what they were presented with was the suspicion (correct, Medwind knew) that the mages were plotting against them, and Kirgen's and the Bellmaster's real fear that the sajes were about to be wiped out for having done nothing wrong.

Kirgen finished his recounting of Faia and the wingmount's late-night ride. Medwind's "Flamboyus" stood quickly and announced, "We will now hear opening opinions. Hold applause and comments from the audience to a minimum. Hear what the speakers wish to say. Speakers, only one comment per person. Debate shall follow these initial statements."

Sajes moved into the arena one by one to give their opinions and offer courses of action.

The first speaker took his place at the center of the arena. He was portly and shopkeeperish, with a red face and beefy hands. His balding forehead shone

223

with the sweat of nervousness at facing such a crowd, but he never faltered. "Despite the separation of mage from saje for all these hundreds of years, I for one do not believe the mages to be unreasonable," he announced. "I recommend approaching the mages with a detailed report of what we have heard and asking to hear what they have to say. I wouldn't treat one of my employees any differently if they had been accused of stealing from the till."

There were a few calls of "Hear, hear!" but most of the audience kept its silence.

A lean, elegant man followed the shopkeeper into the cleared circle. "Certainly, Rosbul, you treat all your employees with great fairness—but I will note that your employees are not rising up to destroy you. Now is not the time for generosity toward the mages. Now is the time to annihilate those who would destroy us without warning or parley, and save our own skins and those of our families in the process."

"War is the only answer," a young, tense man offered when he took the circle. "A quick, incisive strike that will take out the mages but not destroy the surrounding population seems most humane."

The fourth saje also favored war. The next two sajes in a row preferred some form of negotiation; they were followed by a crew of angry men who wanted to see Mage-Ariss wiped off the map.

Medwind listened to the procession of sajes and kept count of their opinions. *It seems to be running about four to one against peace,* she thought, dismayed.

Nokar Feldosonne noted the direction the speeches were taking, too. He grabbed Medwind's arm and pulled her to her feet; the two of them raced down the side of the Basin through the packed rows of sajes. She crashed down stone steps until her knees ached; she jingled like a burgher's purse and clanked like an armored warhorse, clambering over gorgeously dressed sajes and burly, short-tempered merchants impartially. In her wake she left buzzing protest.

When they reached the line at the bottom and took their place at the end of it, Medwind whispered to Nokar, "What are you doing, old man?"

"You've heard the speakers," he whispered back. "By the mood of the assembly, I'd guess the Sajerie will vote for a pre-emptive first strike against Mage-Ariss if you don't tell them what you know."

"I only suspect, Nokar. I don't *know* anything!"

"Then sell the Conclave your suspicions. But you'd better peddle your wares convincingly, or you won't have a home to go to—if they let you live to go."

Medwind wrinkled her nose. "Thanks so much. If I survive this, I may do *vha'atta* to your head after all."

While they waited, Medwind couldn't help glancing around the soaring wall of sajes that rose above and around her. Some noticed her, grinned at the costume, then frowned as they realized the person in it was female, not male. Those who noticed nudged the sajes next to them and whispered. The nudges and whispers spread through the crowd.

When finally the line in front of her was gone and Medwind stepped into the circle, a lump formed in her throat and her heart raced. Eyes, thousands of hostile eyes, stared at her with expressions that ranged from fury to disbelief.

They'll kill me, she thought.

Flamboyus left his sideline seat again, this time approaching Nokar. "This is highly irregular," he remarked. "This woman has no voice in Conclave. Why is she here?"

"I'm waiving my right to speak, Burchardsonne. She will speak for me."

The burly man pondered for a moment. "Very well, Nokar, but on your head be it."

Nokar gave Medwind a sidelong look, and grinned ruefully. "So I've heard," he muttered. "So I've heard."

The old man rested one hand on the warrior's

shoulder. "I've given up my voice and my vote for you, Song—and for the chance of preventing bloodshed," he whispered. "You will only get one chance to say anything here. Don't waste it."

She nodded solemnly, and as she took her place at center stage, she looked up into the crowd, slowly turning until she had seen the full round of sajes that towered over her.

Now, what do I say? she wondered. *What can a warrior hope to say that will bring peace?*

She took a deep breath and began. "My name is Medwind Song, of the Huong Hoos, ten years tenured mage in Daane University." She swallowed hard. She'd faced warriors in battle, and would, at that moment, have preferred the black-and-white simplicity of battle to presenting a bad case to a room full of the enemy. "I will tell you now that what you have heard so far is true. The murders happened, the sajering was found among the bodies, war against the Sajerie was planned, the Fendles have returned—and one of my students did fly to Saje-Ariss without permission to warn you of our plan of attack, and your danger.

"What that student did not know, and what you have not therefore heard, was the depth of apparent evidence we have against the sajes. We found the ring, true, but we are as knowledgeable as you about the ease with which a trinket can be tossed among bodies to deceive and mislead. The ring would have cast suspicion, but not conviction. However, each of the bodies was slain in the ancient saje ritual style of *mehevar*—the same necromantic ritual that is historically noted as the cause of the First Ariss War and the split between Mage- and Saje-Ariss."

There was a sudden undercurrent of angry whispering that spread through the assembly like flames through dry grass. One man, ignoring the Conclave rules, shouted, "*Mehevar* was developed by mages! Don't blame that on the Sajerie."

Medwind, frustrated, snapped, "We have only our histories to go by, and those claim sajes as the sole developers and users of *mehevar*."

"And our histories categorically state *mehevar* was purely the creation and technique of mages!"

Medwind nodded and looked into the eyes of her "enemies." She licked dry lips. "There are, to put it mildly, discrepancies in the historical records of the Magerie and the Sajerie. Mage lore says the Fendles are good; saje lore, that the Fendles are evil. Saje lore says the mages were torturers; mage lore, that the sajes were torturers. In our books, the Wisewoman was a hero; in yours, she was a devil. Now the past, which was dead and gone, is alive and walking among us once more in the form of the Fendles—and in the ritual of *mehevar*. There is truth to be found here—truth that must be found, but we will not find it among the tomes of history in the libraries of the Magerie or the Sajerie. 'What is the truth?' is not an academic question for us anymore, to be debated in learned letters and presented in papers. Now, in the balance with truth hang life and death for all of Ariss.

"We have a little time—I will tell you that there have been no *mehevar* murders in Mage-Ariss within the past fivedays or so, and while the Magerie waits and watches, it will not strike Saje-Ariss without additional cause. The ringing of the Conclave bell will undoubtedly cause consternation among my colleagues, who already feel threatened—it would be best if we move quickly to find answers, before someone panics. With great trepidation, knowing as I do the danger in this route, I suggest that we use some of the time we have to reach back into the past, into the days when the Fendles first lived and the war began between the mages and the sajes. I suggest that we look at the true past, and see the truth."

She glanced around the arena with pleading eyes, and prepared to make room for the next speaker.

"It is all very well, Medwind Song," one saje hissed, "to speak of looking into the past and seeing what really happened, but the histories are the only record. There is no other way."

She moved back into the center of the arena and crossed her arms over her chest in defiance. "Not so," she argued. "There is a way to visit the living past. It is a Hoos magic, and it is deadly—of the mighty Hoos Timeriders who go out, only half return . . . and of those who return, more than half come home without their minds. None who venture into the Timeriver walk out unchanged."

Another saje in the arena laughed, "Myths of barbarian magic! Ha! If there were a way to view the past, we of the University would have found it. Not a rowdy mob of horse-bound goat-herding tent-dwellers!"

Another saje responded to the insulter—"What you know about barbarian magic would sit on the point of a dagger and still leave ample room for what you know about everything else, Fondar. Be quiet and let the woman speak."

Titters echoed through the Basin.

Medwind swallowed hard and looked around her at the sajes. These were not some faceless enemy; they were people. That they didn't like her, or didn't trust her did not matter—but she had to make them believe her. The murderer of the mage-students might still be one of them; that was not impossible—any more than it was impossible that the murderer might be one of the mages. But Medwind's mind would admit no possibility that all of the sajes had conspired against Mage-Ariss. There were too many reasonable men among them.

She knew suddenly how Faia had felt, thinking of half the city unfairly condemned to death. *If I die, I'll die having done the right thing*, she thought.

"It is possible to see the past, unfolding before the Timerider's eyes as fresh as if it were happening that instant—and I know how to find the Timeriver," she admitted, "but I have never ridden it. Worse, the facts we need lie more than four hundred years behind us, and to follow the Timeriver so far upstream, while it branches and rebranches and meanders among the endless empty spaces of what-might-have-been must mean near-certain death. I cannot promise that I will find my way back. But if the Sajerie will anchor and tether me, I will go."

"Why not, if you can see the past, just look to see who killed your students?" one saje asked.

"The question is reasonable, and if there were no Fendles swimming in the lake at Daane, it is what I would suggest. Gods know, the trip would be safer. But the Fendles *are* here, and they are creatures of history—beasts whose significance has been lost or distorted through the years until no one knows any more what their presence means. They participated in the Mage-Saje War—and they are here at the beginning of what is about to become a second Mage-Saje War. Why? What do they mean? This is the price of history and lies, that we bury our pasts to hide the dirtiness of our foundations from ourselves, then forget whether our houses have been built on rock or sand. Now we must pay the price to find the answer."

From the upper reaches of the circle, one of the Sajerie's Hoos members called out, "I have driven the drum for the Timeriders of the Stone Teeth Hoos—to my knowledge, no one has ever gone back more than twice a lifespan and returned. But I will drive the drum for Song."

Burchardsonne, Medwind's "Flamboyus," took the floor from Medwind. "I feel it would be in our interests to know the truth, and quickly. As Speaker of the Conclave, I declare the floor closed to further statements. We will explore this Hoos Timeriver, and, once we have found what we can from that avenue, we will open the floor to debate."

Medwind, Nokar Feldosonne, and the Stone Teeth Hoos drummer met in the center with Burchardsonne.

"Show us what we must do to travel the Timeriver," the Conclave speaker said.

Into silence so deep it had weight, Medwind began to outline the forms of the magic of Timeriding.

Sahedre closed her eyes for an instant and scanned the lifeglows that emanated from the university grounds. Then, abruptly, she gathered her Fendles around her and ran flat out to the wingmount stables. Woman and beasts crept through the opened barn doors and paused inside, still and listening.

Faia, watching through Sahedre's eyes, was lost for a moment in the sudden darkness of the massive, cobblestone stable. When she could see, she made out long, dim rows of stone stalls leading off to her left and right. The homey scent of dried hay and sweetfeed mingled with the stronger smells of horse and manure. Flies droned; nesting swallows flitted in and out feeding their nestlings; and two fat old cats dozed in the rafters above Faia's head—otherwise the stables seemed empty. The wingmounts were out to pasture. The sounds of the city were present, but muffled, distant, and strangely unimportant. The atmosphere of the place was of peace and drowsy contentment.

:*She is here!*: Sahedre's exultant burst of thoughtspeech startled Faia out of her mental repose.

:*She, who?*: Faia wondered.

Sahedre picked up the errant query.

:*Your Mottemage*,: she answered. :*Your idiot Mottemage is deep in a trance, playing with her quaint little winged horses. She knows nothing, nothing, of the ringing of the Conclave bell, nothing of my presence—! Oh, this is too rich!*:

Sahedre trotted noiselessly down the right passage and looked over a gate near the end.

The Mottemage was, as Sahedre reported, deep in trance. The filly on which she worked curled at her feet, its gauzy new wings growing and unfurling like the petals of an exotic flower.

Sahedre laughed and pushed open the gate and strode into the stall. Faia felt power surging around her as the Wisewoman drew in energy for an attack. At her feet, the Fendles bared their teeth and shivered with excitement, ready to leap.

:*Mottemage!*: Faia mindscreamed. *Mottemage! Watch out!*:

:*She will never hear you*,: the Wisewoman remarked, and chuckled. :*Not in time, in any case.*:

The Timerope was built with the name of the mythical Wisewoman and the ghost-image of a body of a Fendle; with the gathered anger that always, always the innocent died and the guilty lived; with the chanted words of the woman who had seen too many wars; with the barely breathed prayers of men who hoped for peace. It shimmered, cold glowing yellow, ethereal, encasing the barbarian Song at one end, coiling deep into the heart of the earth at the other. It was almost a sentient thing, that knew the name of its destination and the reason for its journey. With Medwind or without her, it would try the passage to the past, and fight its way back home. Beside the Timerope flowed the deep and murky currents of past, present, and future; the infinite river of mind.

The Timeriver was summoned into Medwind's sight as the drum pulsed, as the voices chanted in hushed monotony, as the past was coaxed into solid form by reverence and longing and need. It shimmered into being in the dark, hot, cavernous Basin. The River was not water, was not cold. It was warm and wet, thick as blood, dark as nightmares—it streamed past Medwind as she stepped into it and swirled around her in time to the pounding of her pulse, which was the beating of the drum, which was heavy and strong in her ears.

She slipped completely into the stream, still able to

feel the hands of her human anchors touching her, surrounded by the glowing light of the Timerope that webbed around her like a net. As the hands of the anchors fell away, she headed upstream, against the current.

She looked back almost at once, to see the glowing tree-trunk-wide streamer of her lifeline behind her, leading back to her anchors, back to safety. And already she could see the bifurcations in the downstream flow that were the principal danger of her trip home. Frightened, she promised herself she would not look back again.

The pulsebeat, heartthrob, drumsurge drove her— she swam against the tar-black, sticky-thick current that protested her nonconformist passage.

Images flashed by, fast—so fast—yet with total and unforgiving clarity, and voices cried out in nonsense sounds and were silenced with such speed that only the impression of emotion remained to haunt the spying voyager. Laughter clanged with brittle notes, crying left a residue of lingering pain, fear shivered through the torpid fluids of time in malingering currents—the dead arose with shocked expressions on their faces and squalling infants leapt back into their mothers' wombs; grievous wounds undid themselves, curses unraveled and blessings reversed. She spotted, flashing past, the Fendles, undoing the flaying of one student after another in the deep woods where the bodies had been found. Her mind registered dull shock at this turn.

The drum beat faster, and Medwind Song began to understand the agonized madness of returning Timeriders. The voices, howling gibberish, never grew fainter—only faster. And the backward-leaping images never grew indistinct. Her mind would not disengage from the dramas and traumas enacted in reverse in front of her eyes. She was forced to see and understand the actions that raged around her: the removal of a knife here would spare the life of a child, the giving of a gift there would stop a war. Yet, knowing everything, when her hands reached out to touch and repair, they touched nothing and passed through, and her heart contracted in anguish.

Behind her, she knew without looking that the Timeriver was a maze, growing more convoluted with every pulse of the throbbing cadence, and that the Timerope that linked her to home and sanity grew thinner and stretched tighter with every drumbeat. . . .

—that quickened—

—and quickened—

—that drove her pulse and her body faster and faster through the sweet-sticky, deadly congealing waters of time—

—through every personal agony that stemmed from the splitting of Ariss—

—back to the point where the one special pain she sought began.

With an agonizing wrench, Time reversed, and for Medwind the Timeriver seemed to disappear. She stood in the center of a classroom—a university classroom—one that looked exactly like—

She started, and shook her head. She had never felt before the ancientness of her surroundings in Daane. *This is the Basic Sciences lecture hall in Daane—centuries ago!* she realized. She was surrounded by students, all oddly dressed, with quaint hairstyles—and again she felt the schism between her present and the past. Male and female students sat side by side on the hard stone benches, old-style pens and lecture pads spread out on the trestle tables in front of them. At the front of the class, a darkly handsome woman in her early forties sat on the top of her desk, lecturing passionately.

"The individual human life," she was saying, "is insignificant in the face of history. The actions of only a talented few people will actually matter in the larger view of time. The rest will live and die unnoted by the people of the present or the future, unremarked—wasted.

"You are not destined to take a place among the ordinary masses. You are special, with talents and visions that set you apart from and make you better than them. It is your destiny to change the world, to harness the stars to do your bidding, to command the very firmament—and it is your destiny as well to be surrounded by human cattle, who will add nothing to life . . . and take much from it.

"But all of you, as senior magicians, can make use even of the most useless of humans. Through *mehevar*, you can turn wasted lifeforce into greater power for yourselves, and make real for the whole the wonderful visions you are able to imagine for the future. From admitted unpleasantness, you will bring forth great good."

"From *mehevar*?! There is nothing good about *mehevar*! You would justify anything, you bitch!" Medwind screamed.

"Lady Sahedre," one student asked, unaware of Medwind's outburst, "what is *mehevar*?"

The instructor nodded. "Very good, Perchon. *Mehevar* is the science of drawing strength from death."

"It's necromancy, you dung-heap, you filth!" Medwind interrupted again.

The Lady Sahedre lectured right through Medwind's furious response. "These are the essential points of *mehevar*:

"First—the more vital the lifeforce, the more strength one will obtain from it. Therefore, a mage would give you more power than a mundane, and a child more even than a mage. Infants and young children before puberty are your best choices.

"Second—the more potential lives connected to the *mehevar* subject, the more power you will obtain. Fertile subjects will be more useful than those who, for whatever reason, are infertile.

"Third—the less this life-potential has been drained away by actual births, the more you will benefit. Therefore, the virgin is a preferable subject to the mother or father—"

"How dare you tell them to murder children?! How dare you call the unfulfilled promise of a child 'wasted lifeforce'?! How dare you—"

The Timerope contracted with a convulsive shiver, and Medwind swirled for only an instant through the murky waters of Time. She briefly glimpsed the terrifying onrush of maze walls, black and forbidding, before she was ripped out of the Timestream again and thrown into a wooded glade.

She found herself standing to one side of twelve dark-robed strangers who stood with knives poised above a young child. Voices rose and fell in a deep, lilting chant. The beautiful child watched with drugged, frightened eyes and struggled faintly against the coarse hemp that bound her to the rock. She pleaded for the magicians to let her go. Medwind realized what was about to happen, and lunged at the nearest of the knifewielders, screaming, "No! Stop it, stop it!"

She passed through the scene of the impending sacrifice. Nothing in the tableau changed. She couldn't alter anything. Helpless, she shuddered and pressed her eyes closed, unable to watch.

The child cried out for her mother, and there was a lingering, high-pitched scream that wavered and cut off abruptly as the Timerope contracted again and threw Medwind into a scene further along in time.

She was in a darkened room. The windowless walls were paneled in black wood, and the darkness was broken only by a few feeble candles that flickered hopelessly in wall sconces. In the room stood the same dark-haired instructor, the Lady Sahedre Onosdotte, and six male and six female magicians, all young, all still clad in black robes. Medwind recognized the twelve students from the classroom and again from the scene of the sacrifice.

"Your sacrifice was *my* child, you bastards! My child, who I hid and kept safe from all of this; *my* child, who knew nothing of magic. I protected her. I watched over her. I wanted none of this for her."

A frail, parchment-skinned young man protested, "It was your own requirement, Lady Sahedre, that no mage or saje breed or bear children. You said that parenting dulled the magical faculties, and tore loyalties into too many directions—that one who had a child would be too weak and prone to mercy. . . . How could we have known you had not followed your own rules?"

"I made the rules for those who studied under me! They had nothing to do with me! Your feeble attempts at logic will gain no favor."

"We knew not that you had a child, Lady." (*It's news to me, too,* Medwind thought.) "Elsewise," the girl continued, "we would have found another. The magic was strong—"

Tears ran down Sahedre's cheeks. "Tell me not of your magic, nor of my beloved Beliseth's death. . . ." Her hand tightened around the staff she held.

Medwind could see the power building. *Here it comes,* she thought.

"Tell me not how you successfully commanded the winds with the tracings of my daughter's soul. Tell me not that she died well, or conversely that she died badly."

Sahedre's voice dropped, and took on a scratchy, hissing note. "Instead, let me tell you somewhat. All of you are henceforth dead to the world of humans, cursed for all time to walk as animals, voiceless, loveless, and joyless, for the joy and the love of my life you have stolen from me. You will pay for Beliseth's death, and all of Ariss with you, until my child is restored to me—"

"Your child is dead, Lady. None can bring her back."

"Then for her the whole of the world shall die, too—for if she lives not, then I wish none to live. And because you killed her, you shall die both first and last!"

Sahedre swung her staff at the twelve students, and they were enveloped in a blazing red haze. Through it, Medwind could see them crumpling and folding, like candles melting on a hot day. Their screams and pleading became rough barking and chirping. The haze pinkened and faded and died—and twelve Fendles stood at Sahedre's feet.

"This is your first death, your little death. Now you shall serve me, to bring my justice to Ariss, and if you fail to serve me well enough in in your death-in-life, you shall serve me one last time—replenishing me with your sufferings in death-in-*mehevar*."

The Timerope convulsed, and tossed Medwind from the the dark room to a meeting of women, where Sahedre claimed her child had been absconded and murdered by male magicians trying to claim power, and then yanked her into a grotto where massed forces of enraged women, led by Sahedre and the Fendles, readied their attack on unsuspecting men. From there, scene after bloody scene followed, with wives killing husbands and husbands killing wives—with children slaying sleeping parents—with pitched battles in the streets—with runnels of blood seeping from the death-throes of the city into the surrounding countryside—

And from there to a meeting between several of Sahedre's "insignificant little nobodies," their identities lost long ago in the annals of history, as they discovered the truth about Sahedre and her Fendles. By this time, only six Fendles survived—and, of course, their creator, the Lady Sahedre, daughter of Onos.

Medwind watched scenes of their capture and the subsequent tribunal with exhaustion. The Fendles were consigned to the hell of Timehold, and Sahedre, in a fitting twist, was first transformed into another Fendle, then imprisoned with them.

The Timerope pulled her into the depths of the Timewaters one final time, and sent her careening headfirst into the swirling maze of possibilities, following the fragile line of overstretched, glowing thread that was all that could guide her back to her life.

Sahedre released a tremendous bolt of energy into the Mottemage's back, but the energy grounded in the filly on which the Mottemage had been working. The little animal took the brunt of the blast, twitched once and fell dead. The older woman toppled into the hay, while six of the seven Fendles launched themselves at her, teeth bared.

"Stop," Sahedre said, and the Fendles froze in place, still hissing and snarling.

The Mottemage rolled onto her back, stunned and held down by Sahedre's spell. She stared at the woman who towered over her, and whispered, "Why? Why, Faia?"

"Not Faia," Sahedre corrected. "I would that you knew the shaper of your death. Mistake me not for the ignorant child whose body I wear. I am Sahedre Onosdotte, four centuries ago a mage in these very halls. You would know of me as the Wisewoman. I have returned from hell and beyond to reclaim my place and my power, and as I do not think you would willing give me my rightful honor, I must kill you." She smiled slowly as she looked down on her captive. "Such a pity, too. You do pretty work."

Faia sensed a weakness in Sahedre's control of the hill girl's body. The Wisewoman's attention was fixed firmly on the Mottemage. Faia stretched as best she was able, reaching to reoccupy her own form, and drew what energy she could reach to herself. She released the energy in a formed bolt—a levinbolt— that she shot straight into the *persona* of Sahedre with a mental scream of rage. She simultaneously struggled to overthrow the Wisewoman—to force Sahedre out of her mind and her body.

Faia had access to almost no power at all, but Sahedre had been lulled into confidence by Faia's long quiet. The sudden mental howling and the internal warfare cost her the control of the spell that bound the Mottemage. The Mottemage leapt to her feet and shielded herself, and readied an attack against the ancient Wisewoman. Then she paused, an expression of doubt on her face.

Faia read the doubt, and realized her superior knew she was fighting Sahedre Onosdotte, but saw only the body of another student—Faia's body.

:Kill us!: Faia pleaded, directing her terrified mind-shouts at the Mottemage. :This is all my fault, and I cannot stop her! Kill us, Mottemage!:

"Gods," the Mottemage whispered, "Faia's still alive in there."

Sahedre took advantage of Faia's sudden distraction. She shielded herself, hurled up a mental wall around Faia, then faced down the Mottemage. "Yes, but not for much longer, I think. She annoys me. But later I will deal with her. Now you will die."

"My shield is a good as yours."

"Irrelevant," the Wisewoman whispered. She smiled at the Fendles. "Attack," she told them.

All but the smallest of the Fendles—which hid in a corner and mewled—were on the old woman in an instant, their teeth and claws rending and tearing. Sahedre battered at the Mottemage's shield at the same time. Faia suspected the Mottemage would not long survive the combination of mundane and magical attacks.

Then a tiny, pale shape launched itself from the rafters, and with a yowl of rage, charged the Fendles. Flynn, barn nail in stubby-fingered paw, declared war on the big beasts. The cat leapt on the back of one Fendle and sank his teeth into its ear and stabbed his nail into its eye. The giant beast screamed and slashed at him with its claws; he leapt off and darted and lunged, avoiding its attack with near-impossible grace.

To Yaji, huddled in the corner, the arrival of the screeching cat was a catalyst. If a tiny cat could attack creatures many times its size, how could she cower and hide? She leapt on the Fendle Flynn had blinded, and sank her teeth into its throat. She snapped her head back and forth, hanging on in spite of everything the other beast could do, and did not let go until her enemy was limp and lifeless. Then she sought out another Fendle to attack.

To the Mottemage, the arrival of unexpected reinforcements was a lifesaver. Relieved for an instant of the harrying, she released a successful levinbolt against Sahedre.

Faia felt the levinbolt's searing pain, and her eyes blurred briefly. She struggled to wrest her body from Sahedre's control, but the weakness from the Mottemage's attack affected her as much as it did the usurper. As she regained strength, so did Sahedre.

Flynn, meanwhile, buried his nail to the hilt in the eye of a third Fendle, and the beast writhed in the hay, trying to dislodge the foreign body. Sahedre gestured at him and snarled, "Stop, cat!"

The cat glanced at her with contempt and followed up his attack of the downed Fendle. The Fendle's nose spurted blood, and it hissed and struck at the cat. Flynn leapt gracefully out of the way, and his Fendle ally darted in to close with the injured beast.

Forgot bedamned cats were immune to mind-control, Sahedre thought. *Fendles will have to fight their own battles.* She noticed the little Fendle, Yaji, attacking her other fighters, though, and pointed at her.

:You—stop.:

Yaji froze in mid-leap and toppled into the hay. She lay unblinking while the fight stormed around and over her.

Rakell hurled another barrage of energy at Sahedre. Faia felt Sahedre's shield buckle again, and cheered.

Then one Fendle ripped through the tendon's at the back of the Mottemage's leg, and the older woman collapsed onto the blood-drenched straw.

Flynn, hissing and spitting from the back of the Fendle that had downed the Mottemage, failed to notice his third victim suddenly right itself and lurch at him from behind a mound of straw. He dodged as soon as he saw it coming, but he wasn't fast enough. His shoulder and side came away bloody. He screeched and dug his claws into that Fendle's remaining eye. The Fendle pinned him, and with one swipe of its claws, raked him open from throat to tail. Flynn twitched and flopped in the straw at the Mottemage's side, then lay still.

"Flynn!" Rakell croaked. The cat's destruction cost her what concentration she had left. The surviving Fendles felt the breach of her shields and were instantly at her throat.

Sahedre got in one good blow, and then a second. Rakell's struggles to keep off the attacking Fendles grew weaker.

:*The Fendles are human!:* Faia mindscreamed at the Mottemage. :*If you change them back to their true forms, they die!:*

The Mottemage looked surprised, and with the energy that remained to her, she struck at the Fendle nearest her. With an electrifying scream, it metamorphosed into human shape. The woman, returned to her own body, aged and died as horribly as had the human body Sahedre once wore. The Mottemage reached for another, and the mob of Fendles backed off.

The Mottemage propped herself up in the straw and glared at Sahedre. Weakened and bleeding, she still erected a tenable shield around herself—and loosed one oddly formed, startlingly accurate levinbolt that took Sahedre by surprise.

The Wisewoman toppled—and as quickly as she fell, the surviving Fendles turned traitor and attacked their ancient master, teeth bared, lead by Yaji, whose stop-spell had vanished with Sahedre's power.

Sahedre screamed and struggled ineffectually. Then she yelled, "I die! Oh, I die!" The melee ceased.

From under the layer of furry, biting bodies came the weak voice of the hill girl. "Mottemage, help me! Sahedre is gone!"

Faia lay on her back in the red-stained straw, body battered and bleeding, throat torn open, wide-eyed and helpless-looking. The Fendles backed away, and the Mottemage lowered her shields and bent down to touch her student.

Faia, still pinioned inside Sahedre's cage, tried to mindscream :It is a trap!: but Sahedre, prepared this time, skillfully muffled the thoughtcall.

Then the supine Wisewoman laughed and gestured into the air. The lines her finger traced were duplicated in blood on the Mottemage's face, then down the older woman's neck and chest. Flesh puckered and peeled; arteries spurted and soaked the straw and the dirt-packed floor.

:No, damn you, no!: Faia mindscreamed at the Wisewoman—to no avail.

Faia struggled for control of her body—tried to shut out the Mottemage's screams—tried not to see her collapse. When Sahedre began her butchery on the suddenly defenseless and dying woman, Faia broke free of the Wisewoman's control with one last mind-shout to the universe at large.

:Help her, someone!:

Then, unable to face her own powerlessness, and unwilling to watch the Mottemage's assured death, she released her grip on her senses, and pulled into the dark, safe loneliness of her mind.

The dark, sleek furry form of a single Fendle streaked out of the stables, across the road, across the greensward, and straight into the lake. It dove and shot like an underwater bolt for the far shore, then swam along that shore to the cove furthest from humanity. There it huddled in the water under the overhanging trees and cried.

I'll never go back, Yaji wailed. *I'll never be able to go back! I'll have to hide here for the rest of my life. What is going to happen to me?*

Chapter 10

WAR OF WIZARDRY
AND SOUL

MEDWIND struggled through the roaring current, swimming furiously after the pale yellow line of the contracting Timerope. She became trapped in an eddy and was thrown toward the dark mouth of an alternate stream. The Timerope bent, and she could see that it would break off if she fell past the point of the "island" of darkness that marked the bifurcation of the streams. She fought valiantly and corrected her course, only to be pulled toward yet another wrong turn.

I'm too too far from home. Most of the four hundred years of tangled, branching Timeriver is still ahead of me. My arms feel like lead, my breath won't come, and my brain insists I'm going to drown in this awful stuff. This— she realized with despair *—this is why half of the Timeriders never come back.*

She yearned for a chance to stop and catch her breath, but the legends and the reports of surviving Timeriders agreed that there was no way to pull out of the stream without breaking the rope.

All around her, the conversations of people long dead screamed and babbled. She found them even more disconcerting now that they were running in the proper direction. She dove through folk and events, trying not to see them, trying only to concentrate on the position of the riverbanks and the myriad tangles and crossings of the everbranching streams.

She fought on.

Somewhere, seemingly hours along, she began to develop a horror of getting the thick ooze of the Time-river into her nose and mouth. She struggled to keep her head high, and her swimming worsened by another degree.

She had one hope. The closer she got to her destination, the thicker—and stronger—the Timerope got. It had been the thickness of a massive old oak when she left the Basin—only the thickness of a strand of finespun wool yarn by the time she'd reached Sahedre's past. Now, as she contended with the deafening roar and spuming Timeflows of a savage stretch of rapids, she noted the Timerope had attained the same girth as both of her thighs.

Bits and pieces of the history in which she swam began to look familiar. She placed herself about a hundred years in her past. *Three-fourths of the way back*, she told herself, elated.

Hope gave her strength, and she swam on.

The waters grew more placid, with fewer branchings. She had not realized how peaceful and uneventful the period preceding her life had been. She allowed herself to float in the river, attentive but relaxed, and let the Timerope drag her along.

The rope's girth continued to widen, and with a jolt she began to recognize events from her own early years in Ariss. She saw herself with Rakell, not yet the Mottemage, as her friend tutored her patiently, obviously hoping to change Medwind from a plains warrior to a cultured city-woman. She saw Rakell's succession to Mage-Ariss' fourth highest office, the

Mottemagery of the University of Daane, and her own subsequent rise in stature in the Magerie.

The waters roughened, and multitudes of branches spread out in front of her again.

A sudden burst of images overtook her. There was Faia, and the leveling of Bright, and there, her runaway spell that freed the Fendles from captivity. There were the Fendles, murdering her students— she could see it plainly now—and planting the ring among the bodies. Faia on a rock, suddenly surrounded by Fendles—the water grew rougher, and Medwind struggled to stay above it and still see and hear what was happening—Faia, and one Fendle that became Sahedre for an instant, then died and crumbled to dust.

And Sahedre's voice coming from Faia's mouth. Sahedre gloating that she had overthrown Faia in the battle for control over Faia's body. Sahedre changing Yaji to a Fendle. Sahedre with the Fendles at her heel, in the stables, and Rakell and her damned cat Flynn and the Fendle Yaji fighting against the whole motley mob of them—fighting—

—and dying—

—and dead.

The massive Timerope convulsed and shriveled away to nothing, spewing Medwind out of the Time-river and up into the waiting hands of her anchors.

Once out of the warm stream of Time, she shivered spasmodically. Then she sobbed and screamed to be let back into the River.

It was a bad moment for the sajes. Kirgen released his hold on the Timerope and stared with the rest of the sajes at the quivering, death-pale Timerider who lay helpless on the floor of the Basin. Medwind Song's breath came in ragged gasps, and her limbs twitched and jerked. She was obviously afraid of something, obviously grief-stricken by something—and obviously *changed*. Her face and body seemed younger, harder, more muscular. There was a feeling of depth and ancient knowledge to her that hadn't been there before. But those were subtle changes. The shocking alteration was one of appearance. Her hair, which when she left had been blue-black as ebonwood in starlight, was burned pure glowing silver by the river of Time. And her eyes, once the rich bottomless blue of autumn skies, were now the cerulean-white of ice . . . or moonstones. She had gone into Time a woman. She returned a raving, dying goddess.

Kirgen shuddered. Goddesses were not cheerful company.

"She's in shock," the Hoos drummer bellowed, seeming unsurprised by the changes in her. He shoved a mug full of hot green fennar at Medwind. "She has to get this down or she'll die." He held her head with one hand and forced the cup to her lips.

She pushed it away weakly, and tried to kick him. The sajes surrounded and held her, and again the drummer forced her to drink.

She finished the cup. Her muscles relaxed—slowly. Her color improved and her voice lost its unintelligible tremor. Kirgen could finally make out what she said.

"Let me go back. Rakell is in there," Medwind was repeating over and over. "She's dead. Rakell is in there, and she's dead, and I never got to say goodbye."

"Who's Rakell?" one of the sajes asked.

Slowly the question penetrated her exhaustion. "The Mottemage—" she answered. "My best friend— my only friend—Sahedre and the Fendles just slaughtered her—" The barbarian went into another spasm of grief.

There was a moment of silence as the significance of this struck the Sajerie. The murder of the Mottemage could be the trigger that set off Mage-Ariss.

But it took time, and several more mugs of hot green fennar, to get the whole story out of Medwind Song, and more time after that for her to gain enough strength to propose a plan, and longer still to ready a rescue party to attack Sahedre and the Fendles. By then, events had moved onward.

Sahedre lay in the straw, bleeding and still, for only a few minutes. Then, with difficulty, she sat up and looked around her. The pain that ate at her body was formidable, and she was tired—agonizingly tired—but considering how well things were going, she would live with that. Three of the Fendles lay dead on the floor. Two were missing—the one the Mottemage had returned to human form who had immediately thereafter crumbled into dust ... and Faia's little friend Yaji, who had apparently escaped. A problem, that, but only a small one. One Fendle remained in the stables, watchful and cowering. The dead winged filly, the disemboweled cat, and the flayed Mottemage completed the picture.

Sahedre felt the power from the Mottemage's *mehevar* coursing through her. *Almost enough,* she thought. *Almost—but not quite.*

Her wounds throbbed, and still bled profusely. She could, she thought, heal them—but that would make her story of a saje attack less impressive. She ached worse inside than outside—gnawed at by a curious, dull lethargy—she shook it off. No time for that.

She eyed the surviving Fendle with distaste. "Took a liking to my throat, did you, Malner? Wished me dead, then thought perhaps that I would forget your indiscretion? Thought I would remember how much I needed you? I knew you hated me, but you would have done well to have hidden it a bit longer."

She shrugged once. "You *were* correct. I do still need you." She smiled. "Come here, then."

The Fendle stayed crouched in its corner.

Sahedre fingers drew a sign in the air. "I said— *come here.*"

This time, a pawn that moved knowingly to its own sacrifice, the Fendle slowly advanced.

"Better. I never found out who actually wielded the knife against my Beliseth. Never. I suspected you, Malner, but none of your soon-to-be-Fendle associates would confess, nor would you tell me. The rest are gone. You alone remain to pay the price I had intended to extract from all. Very well—now is the time that I require payment."

The Fendle's eyes were white-rimmed, and it struggled ineffectually to back away from the Wisewoman.

"A death for a death, Malner. You for Beliseth—and I have still gotten the worse of the bargain. No matter. Your death will also give Ariss-Magera into my hands to dispatch against Ariss-Sajera. Two cities for a life—that is better payment." She looked down into the panicked brown eyes. "Would I could take the whole of the world," she whispered, "or have my Beliseth back."

While the Fendle struggled to escape, Sahedre began the ritual of *mehevar*. The Wisewoman laughed as she listened to the beast's screams.

The frelles huddled in the Greathall in terror. The mindscreams were upon them again, the terror of a soul being ripped and rent from its body and consigned to nothingness.

The Mottemage did not come, and did not come—and the ghoulish daylit echoes of carnage continued and continued until the frelles, huddled together to comfort each other, screamed in sympathetic anguish with the dying soul.

In the silence that followed there was no peace.

"The second slaughter in as many minutes," Frelle Jann whispered. "That was the meaning of the Saje bell. The attack has started. The sajes have come. If we just wait here, they'll find us and kill us."

Young Frelle Tardana muttered, "The Mottemage or Medwind Song should have been here by now. Where are they?"

One of the assistants said, "I saw the Mottemage down at the wingmount stables."

Jann snapped her fingers. "Of course. The most recent batch of mounts was ready for finishing today. She'll still be there—in a trance, most likely, for then she would not have heard the bell or the death-screams." The redheaded frelle stared at the ground for an instant, muttered something to herself, and nodded.

She glanced around the room at the assembled University staff. "Tardana, you organize the rest of the frelles, and get all the students back here to the Greathall. Begin to build the power for our strike. Mersa, contact the Hub and let the others on the Council know the sajes have attacked. Litthea, you know Song as well as anyone. Find her. She is the one who devised the majority of our strategy against Saje-Ariss. We need her here now.

"I will go down to the stables and rouse the Mottemage from her work. We shall all meet back here."

Sahedre sensed the presence long before she actually heard the footsteps in the corridor. _Someone is coming,_ she thought. _Good. Appearance now is everything._ She smeared the fresh-killed Fendle's blood over her to add drama to the appearance of her own wounds, lay back in the straw, and arranged herself in an artful sprawl.

"Mottemage?" a high voice called from just inside the stable. The voice echoed down the stone corridors. "Motte? It's Frelle Jann. The saje attack has started. We need you."

Perfect, Sahedre thought.

"She must still be in trance," the Wisewoman heard the frelle mumble.

Sahedre heard footsteps, and the creak as the gate swung open, then a sudden gasp and an instant of silence—followed by a perfectly gratifying scream.

The Wisewoman let the scream carry for several

seconds. *That should bring a few others. A bit longer, mayhaps a bit louder, dear—*

Enough, she decided. *Time now to bait the hook.* Sahedre groaned, weakly.

The frelle heard, and flinched. "One lives? Who?"

Sahedre groaned again, slightly louder.

She located Sahedre among the bloody bodies. "Gods, oh, gods, wake up, you—whoever—" Frelle Jann's voice stopped cold, and when she spoke again, her tone was murderous. "*You!* Open your eyes! Tell me, what part did you have in this, you bitch?"

Sahedre fought the impulse to open her eyes in surprise. *What!? Me?* she wondered. *How can she already suspect me?* She groaned again, and slit her eyes open slightly, and croaked, "Sajes . . ."

"No doubt," the other voice said bitterly. "And just as in Bright, none live but you to tell the tale." The frelle kicked the wounded woman viciously in the thigh. Sahedre held her response to a faint moan. "You have amazing luck," Jann snarled. "Death rides on your shoulder like a pet bird, striking all but you."

Ah, how easy to forget—you see not me, but Faia. Well, Sahedre thought, *you have amazing luck, too, little frelle, to kick me and survive. Not for long, though. You will pay when your usefulness is past.*

Several frelles and students ran into the stables. "Frelle Jann," one called, "who screamed?"

Sahedre heard them running down the corridor, then into the altering stall. There was another brief, charming round of screaming, and some equally delightful crying. *The dear late Mottemage was apparently quite popular with her subordinates. So much the better.*

Frelle Jann said, "Faia still survives, but she seems badly wounded. She may not live."

Do not sound so hopeful, dear.

"Has she spoken?"

"She said, 'Sajes.' Nothing else."

"So all is as you said. But the sajes have killed the immortal Fendles. They're stronger than we thought."

"Apparently so."

"Where are they, then?"

Sahedre whispered from her bed of straw, "Preparing to—attack the Hub. I—heard them—when they thought me dead. They wanted to be rid—of the leaders."

"*Medwind!*" one voice blurted out. "Is she dead as well?"

"Who can say?" Jann muttered. "Perhaps Litthea has found her by now."

"What will we do with the bodies of the Mottemage and the Fendles and—"

Frelle Jann cut them off. "We will leave them, and bury them when we can. Grief and sentiment are for times of peace. This is war."

Sahedre watched through slitted eyes as two students carried in a makeshift litter crafted of horseblankets and shovel-poles.

"What is that for?" Jann snapped.

"Faia. We're taking her to the Greathall. The healers will be there."

"Don't bother—she's done for," the frelle told them. "Leave her here to die in peace."

Little snake! Sahedre thought. *You shall suffer for that, Frelle Jann.*

"She's still breathing, and she knows what happened," one of the students said. "There's some hope."

"I said *leave her!*" Jann snarled.

The other student walked over to the frelle and whispered, so low that Sahedre could barely hear her, "It would look bad for you, Frelle, to leave her here when all know how you hate her. Though I'm sure you are right and she is beyond saving, think of your reputation. Better the hero than the villain at a time like this—especially with the Mottemage dead and her unpopular choice as successor missing—and you the favorite of the Council."

Sahedre did not miss the calculating look that sped across Jann's face and vanished in a heartbeat. She did not miss, either, the alteration in Jann's tone as the frelle said, "You are right, Derla—I was drowned in grief because of Rakell's death. I don't have any hope for Faia, but bring her to the Greathall. We have to try."

Once inside the Greathall, a stout young Healer with dimples and several chins was summoned from the chanting circles of mages and brought to Sahedre's side. One of the students gave her a rapid-fire report of the occurrence in the stables. The young woman nodded grimly and knelt on the floor beside Sahedre.

"I don't know if you can hear me," she said softly, "but my name is Brynne. Frelle Brynne, First Instructor of the Healing Arts at Daane. I'm going to take a look at you, and I need you to hold very still."

"Deep cuts, bruises, some rough wounds on the throat—" the Healer mumbled, as her fingers poked and prodded over Sahedre. "Oh! A spell, too. Very powerful and tenacious—"

Sahedre suppressed a smile. *A powerful spell, indeed. I have some aches and some scratches—*" But she groaned once, for effect. "Sajes," she whispered. "Sajes everywhere. . . . I can't stop them. . . ." She thought she would thrash a bit on the litter, then decided not to. She was surprised that it took such effort even to whisper. She lapsed into silence.

"We're going to get them. Believe that, child." Brynne's voice was hard stone and cold fury. She murmured a soft, lulling incantation.

"What are you doing?" Frelle Jann asked.

"Diagnostic test. I can sense the burrowings of a massive spell, but I can't quite make out—" The Healer gasped. "A settling spell. Gods on hot rocks— why would the sajes put that on her?"

Frelle Jann asked, "They put a—what—what did they do? I don't recognize the spell you named, Brynne."

"Settling spell. She's been overcome by lethargy—she wouldn't even have realized that she was spelled. She would have simply lain in one place until she starved, convinced that at any moment she would get up and go on with her life.

"I'm going to do some things that hurt, Faia," the Healer added, "but the spell is working on you right now. It will soon destroy you unless it can be stopped."

Nonsense, Sahedre thought. *I'm laying here because this is all part of the plan—*

The Healer said a few more words in a gentle sing-song. For a moment, nothing happened. Then incredible pain blazed through Sahedre's body. She screamed. Incoherent with anguish, she writhed on the litter.

Freed from the spell, she came up off the litter in a fury. "Jann!" she screamed. "I'm going to—"

A strong hand settled on her shoulder and forced her back to the floor. "You are going to lay back down again, Faia. A weaker woman would have died of your wounds, and you are still bleeding," the Healer said. "Whatever you had to say to Frelle Jann will wait a few moments more."

She tsk-tsk'd over Sahedre's wounds, washed her off, made her drink several unbelievably foul elixirs, then said with typical medical cheer, "Bad, but not as bad as all that. Big, strong, healthy girl like you—took a bit more than they thought you would, I'd say. All that blood off of you and you look like you might just make it."

She touched Sahedre's throat with puzzlement. "These are animal bites, though, not knife wounds—and they are bad ones. They damn-near took out the artery." She closed her eyes and pressed her fingers against the ripped flesh, and Sahedre's throat burned.

The Wisewoman cried out.

"There, now—hurts like the hells, doesn't it? But that's healed it. You'll have a nasty scar, but you'll not be in danger of breathing through your neck. So—what bit you?"

Damn, damn, and damn-all! Bloody Fendle bites— or—wait. This could solve the Yaji problem nicely. It could, indeed work very well. "A Fendle." There were gasps from around the Greathall. "The sajes did something to them," she told Frelle Brynne and Frelle Jann and the rest of the assembled women of Daane. "I don't know how, but they knew of the Fendles— and they had some magic that turned them against us."

"I imagine they found out about the Fendles when you stole the Mottemage's wingmount and flew to Saje-Ariss to tell them, Faia," Jann snarled. "I imagine that's why you survived, too, don't you think?"

I forgot about this peasant-idiot's trip. It would be her body I needed! Hells, this makes things difficult.

She ignored Frelle Jann and continued. "Yaji and I ran to the stables when we heard the Mottemage scream. The Fendles came with us. All of us—the Mottemage and her cat, the Fendles, and Yaji and I, fought side by side until one of the sajes did something and the Fendles turned on us. The sajes spelled us, and we all fell together—they did *mehevar* on the Mottemage, and then on one Fendle. They spirited Yaji off to Ariss-Sajera, and left me for dead, I suppose, and the Fendle that lay beside me as well. That Fendle *was* dying, but as its spirit left its body, it came into me."

Frelle Jann's expression hardened, and her eyes narrowed. She studied Sahedre with intense scrutiny. "Just what do you know of *mehevar*, Faia?" the instructor asked sharply.

Ah—Faia would not know a thing of it, would she? She scrambled for an answer. "The sajes called their ritual by that name—the Fendles told me more of it."

"I thought the Fendles were turned against you?"

"The Fendle, I meant to say. The one that gave me its spirit when it died. I'm sure the ones that escaped are still dangerous."

"Leave the girl alone, Jann," Frelle Brynne snapped. "She has fought demons today, and nearly died trying to save our Mottemage." The Healer gave Faia a gentle pat on the shoulder and a worried frown. "Escaped?"

"They must have. There were seven, remember. There weren't that many dead in the stables."

Frelle Jann nodded. "Quite true. There weren't that many. How very clever of you to notice—considering how badly injured you were at the time."

The Wisewoman glared at Jann. The others were so willing to believe—Sahedre could feel their carefully tended and nurtured rage and hatred toward the sajes swelling in the room, fed by the rituals they were performing—aimed, conveniently, at her preferred target. Only Jann, whose hatred was aimed at her, kept seeing the flaws in her alibi. She needed Jann out of the way. She needed the cooperation of the rest of her intended victims.

Enough, then, Sahedre thought. *I feel stronger by the moment, and Faia's strength and the power of the* mehevarin *course through me. I need not tolerate Jann any longer. The time for my revenge is finally come, and she shall not keep me from it a moment longer.*

She pulled in the necessary earth and air energy, and spread a delicate, unobtrusive shield around herself and the mages in the Greathall. She filled the space inside the shield with her own hatred of the sajes, augmenting the already thick atmosphere of paranoia in the hall. Gently, then, she spoke to Jann.

"We are fighting the sajes," she said, and reinforced her statement with a magical aura of sincerity. "We must not fight each other." Underneath her words was the command, :Obey me.:

Jann was a strong mage, but she did not have Sahedre's four hundred years of pent-up fury and hunger behind her. When Sahedre looked into her eyes, her will overwhelmed the young frelle, and everything the Wisewoman asked seemed suddenly reasonable—and Jann nodded politely, and said, "Yes, of course. How shortsighted of me."

Sahedre then faced the assembled women of Daane University.

They moved through their rituals, spiraling the force of their wrath into a maelstrom that pulsated and surged, waiting only release and direction.

Their anger makes them mine, she gloated—and reached out a hand, and pulled their unwholesome fire into her belly, and made it hers.

"*:The sajes must die,:*" she whispered into their minds. *:This is all you want—it is all I want. Give yourselves to me, and I will give you the power to bring them down.:*

They were already so close to the edge, so open to this voice that promised them what they wanted. To a woman, the mages opened themselves and welcomed in the voice that promised victory and revenge—and to a woman, they toppled headlong into Sahedre's abyss.

:Now,: she said, *:I tell you first that I am Lady Sahedre Onosdotte, the ancient Wisewoman of Ariss-Magera, and master of you all. I have returned to lead you against the sajes—we shall leave nothing of them but wisps of smoke in the rubble of their city.:*

She felt the surge of excitement in her followers—her slaves—and she exulted. The destruction of Ariss rested in the palm of her hand. She commanded the energies of the mages, and expanded the shield further, to cover the whole campus of Daane and to bring any stragglers into her sphere of influence. She would need to spread the shield further soon—she would have to bring every soul in Ariss-Magera under her command, so that she could channel the life energy of half the city into her attack against the other half. To do that, she would have to replenish her strength with *mehevar* frequently just to keep all her fronts covered. She needed to detail someone to bring her young children—in the meantime, adults would have to do.

Frelle Jann, she decided, would be a good first subject.

Meanwhile, she thought, *I need to get the attack on Ariss-Sajera underway.*

:*The battle begins now,*: she announced. :*Ariss-Sajera will be reduced to dust, and everyone in it. You will first destroy the sajes' University, then the Saje-Hub. When every saje has been obliterated, you will then annihilate every living thing in the rest of the city. You will not stop until the city of Ariss-Sajera is empty and dead—or all of you are.*:

She waved an arm and shouted, "Send forth the storms and the fires! Send forth the wind and the water! Focus it, send it—send all of it! Now!"

Sahedre's vassals reached up their hands and willed forth doom on Saje-Ariss. And lightning cracked from newborn stormclouds that billowed out of the Greathall in an ugly stream of night-dark poison, and winds screamed and twisted in the skies above Daane, before they raced in funnels toward their destination.

Yes! the Wisewoman thought, and laughed with joy. *Yes! I have waited lifetimes for this—and it is all I had hoped for, and more.* She beckoned to Frelle Jann. "We need more magic, dear girl," she said, and drew the frelle to her. She caressed the young woman's cheek with her knife.

"More magic . . . and you are going to give it to me."

Medwind, still too weak to stand, gave Nokar Feldosonne a mind-picture of his destination. He passed the picture on to the rest of the transport-specialists. Everyone gripped weapons, made last-minute checks of ammunition, and one by one, signaled their readiness.

Medwind nodded at Nokar; Nokar knelt beside her cot and rested one hand on her shoulder. He began the backward count.

"Three—two—one—NOW!"

Medwind once again felt everything twist and wrench and spin inside her and around her. This time, the wrongness didn't stop. She became aware of the others in the rescue party, trapped in the same non-place. She could feel their frustration and their growing fear. A smooth, gleaming, impassable wall arrested their progress.

:Go back!: Nokar commanded. *:Retreat! Retreat!:*

Medwind felt no panic in the old man's mind—only calm intelligence and quick recognition of the obstacle that blocked him.

Hell of a commander—for a librarian, she thought with admiration, as the world buckled further in on itself and shifted again.

Then space untwisted, and Medwind groaned and sprawled on the Basin floor. Around her, other members of the stymied rescue party did the same. Sajes throughout the towering seats gave startled cries.

Through the swirling cloud of multicolored smoke, Nokar's voice could be heard, explaining to the sajes in the auditorium, "They've shielded the University. We can't get through."

Without warning, the Basin rocked from side to side, and tiny bits of masonry from the top of the dome crumbled down to dust the sajes below. The low rumble of an earthquake mixed with the howl of tornadoes and the green glow of mage-light that arced and spit through the cracks in the ceiling.

"We're under attack! Disperse!" Burchardsonne shouted. "The south field—quickly!"

With a "whoosh" the Basin cleared.

Medwind found herself slumped neck-deep in the swamp to the south of Ariss, Nokar's hand locked on her braid, surrounded by the thousands who'd simultaneously fled the Basin. A sluggish breeze dissipated the saje-smoke.

One man behind her cried out once in anguish, then cursed dully and without emotion. She turned to see why and looked away quickly. A young man, one of Mage-Ariss' would-be rescuers, had materialized partly in the swollen base of a primordial swamp-cypress that grew nearby. He was dying even as she glimpsed him, and she was utterly helpless to save him. The sight of his face—of his agony and his resignation—would stay with her, she thought, for the rest of her life. She noted that other sajes averted their eyes from him, and from the few others who suffered the same fate.

Nokar pulled her to a sitting position and leaned her against a tree. He said bitterly, "We always knew that we would lose a dozen or so sajes with the emergency evacuation of the Basin. No one could ever come up with another big, nearly clear space that would take everyone at once and wouldn't endanger innocents. So we knew we would be taking our chances.

"It doesn't seem right that Chak was one of the ones we lost, though. He was a scholar," the old man added. "Loved books, loved learning—I'll miss him."

"The senseless deaths were what *I* hated most about war," Medwind admitted. "My inability to love killing was the embarrassment of the Huong Hoos, to be honest. So I left. There was no room in my tribe for a life-loving warrior."

"You'll never fit into somebody else's world, Song. You have your own ideas—you won't let someone else think for you. The only place you will be accepted be the place you make for yourself." Nokar studied her intently. "You'll get to your own place someday."

"If I live that long."

The old man's mouth twisted in a humorless smile. "Yah. There is that."

The evacuations' survivors were finally assembled around Burchardsonne, Nokar, Medwind, and the remains of the hand-picked rescue team. To the north, the refugee sajes could see the green blaze of Faulea University—burning—and hear the raging winds that battered the helpless city.

"We can't get into Daane to stop this," one young sage said. "So what do we do now?"

Burchardsonne looked grim. "We have few alternatives. First, we can blast back randomly. Anything we aim at that mage-shield will likely bounce off and scatter away from the target. We'll probably hit nothing but innocents."

"We should try it anyway."

Burchardsonne looked from face to tired face. "Should we? We know who the enemy is. Should we destroy people who aren't the enemy, simply because they are unlucky enough to live near her?" He shook his head. "I don't think so. Second, we can do nothing. That will give over the city to Sahedre Onosdotte—and I don't want to see what she will do with it.

"We have a third option only if one of you can make it work. I want some idea of how we can break through that barrier."

There was a long silence.

"Thoughtspeech," Medwind offered. "Break through to those on the campus near her, tell them the true story about Rakell's—" Her voice broke, and she had to catch her breath before continuing. "—About Rakell's death—and let them raise rebellion against Sahedre from inside the shield."

"Surely she's thought of that, and blocked against it."

"It won't kill any innocents if we look and find out."

Burchardsonne sighed. "True enough. But who's going to try it?"

Medwind looked up at him from her place at the base of the tree. "None of you would know who to talk to—none of you would know what to say to keep from getting your minds blasted by someone who thought you were trying to attack. It will have to be me."

Nokar Feldosonne shook his head vehemently. "You are as near death as you need to get, Medwind." He crossed his arms and furrowed his brows. "Something this taxing, right after your ride through the Timeriver, is likely to kill you."

"Maybe—but that doesn't mean I'm wrong."

The old librarian bit his lip. "No, it doesn't."

"This is war, Nokar, Burchardsonne. Don't be afraid to lose a few players if it will win you the battle. I always figured I was meant to die in combat anyway. Not as some old woman sleeping on my mats." She managed a weak smile.

The old librarian didn't return it. "You are right, and I can't change that. So go." He looked into her eyes, and she read pain there—and concern—and maybe something else. "But come back."

The barbarian nodded. "I'll try." She closed her eyes and forced the natural swamp-images of seeping water and swimming snakes and biting insects out of her thoughts. She breathed slowly, narrowed her focus to a tightly controlled whisper, and sent her mental murmur questing toward Daane.

:Listen,: she said. :Help is on the way. Can you hear me?:

Her question, to her astonishment, slipped through Sahedre's shield like a dagger through silk. Sahedre had blocked physical and magical approaches . . . but not mental. Medwind probed across the campus, immediately found the familiar mind of her fellow instructor, Litthea, and slid inside.

Instantly, wrongness enveloped her. Where she should have been met by the identifiable forethoughts of her friend and colleague, she was instead overwhelmed by a foreign, hypnotic urge to "kill the sajes." She felt compressed fragments of her friend

Litthea's self as if from a great distance—but Litthea
was trapped, seduced by the evil that commanded her
in her own body. The mind and wishes of Sahedre
overrode everything, and Litthea had no choice but to
obey. Medwind fought free from the gluey trap of
Sahedre's magic, and rushed out of Litthea's mind.
Sahedre's virulent personality vanished. Medwind's
lean frame, miles distant, shook with relief.

Close, she thought, repressing panic. *If Sahedre
had felt me, she could have had me. Who is left that
I can talk to?* she wondered. *Whose mind is still safe?*

Her delicate psychic probe skimmed from colleague
to student, from student to friend, all across the campus. She darted down, a hummingbird seeking nectar,
and flitted back in revulsion each time. Every mind—
every single mind in the university—was poisoned by
Sahedre's control.

How can she force them all— Medwind started to
wonder.

And the telltale horror of the start of another sacrifice for *mehevar* invaded her skull.

That's how. Gods! Will it never end? In answer
to her own question, she thought, *No, it won't. She'll
kill forever, because that's where she gets her strength.
As long as Sahedre lives, people will die to feed her.*

Medwind's mind rang with the pain and the fear of
the victim—Frelle Jann, she realized, noting familiari-
ties of shading and character in the tattered and dying
soul that screamed for mercy. The barbarian fled back
to her distant body, too weak to witness the torture
and annihilation of another colleague without embrac-
ing madness.

As she fled, she felt a lone mind, frightened and
surrounded by darkness, weakly and futilely protesting
the killing.

*One survives in Daane who has free will? Who is
it? And where is she hiding?*

But she was already headed back to her body, and
too weak to reverse long enough to identify the

protester. She found herself, still leaning against the tree, propped up by a saje on either side, weak and sweat-slicked and shaking. It was more effort than she could imagine, just to speak. "Sahedre had—all of th-th-them in mind-thrall," she whispered. "I b-b-briefly touched one mind that had managed to hide from her—but I didn't have—time to r-r-reach into it." The chill of the breeze on her wet skin, the coldness of the swamp water on the parts of her that were submerged, and the hard shiver of fever-wrack gripped her. Her limbs shook and her teeth rattled.

The librarian knelt beside her and gripped her hand. He rested his wrist lightly on her forehead, then laid his fingertips on her neck to measure the pulsing beat of her blood. His eyes darkened with worry. "We need to get her out of this swamp," he told Burchardsonne. "Fast—or she's going to die."

Medwind smiled up at Nokar. In Hoos, she told him, "Just leave me. Old man, I'd m-m-make you one of my—husbands if I h-h-had the chance. I like you. But I'm n-n-not g-going—to survive this. You get rid of Sahedre. Then make sure—I get a—good Hoos f-f-funeral—with l-l-lots of horses and all. And honor f-for my head."

"Sheepshit," Nokar snapped back in Hoos. "Don't give *me* your noble-warrior-dying-bravely act. You're going to survive—we need your help to get rid of Sahedre." He did a sudden double-take. "You'd really take me as one of your husbands?"

Medwind managed a faint grin. "Yah, old man. Even make you—a H-H-Hoos warrior if you—survived the w-w-wedding night."

"You'll live now just for that, by the gods. I claim Hoos honor on your word. Your husband, huh? *There's* a hell of a way for an old man to go down in glory."

In Arissonese, he told Burchardsonne, "I'm taking Song to Demphrey's healer's station out on Tenth Round in the Ka district. Find Demphrey and send him along. If you come up with anything that will win us this war, contact me there. Otherwise, I'll find you when I can."

Medwind heard this with fading interest. She felt the old man's fingers once again on her shoulder, but noticed only the first part of the wrenching of the universe before darkness overtook her.

For an instant, Faia had felt someone else, someone not tainted by the bloodlust in Sahedre's soul, who went questing through the darkness she occupied. She reached out, cried out briefly for release—

And then the light of that other soul vanished, and she was left again in empty blackness.

There is something on my face. Crawling. It itched and tickled, but she didn't have the strength to brush it off. She opened her eyes, and found herself eyeball to eyeball with an enormous roach.

Medwind Song, rising to consciousness out of what seemed an eternity of fire and pain and darkness, did not find this a good omen.

"A-a-agh!" she groaned. The roach scuttled off.

It was replaced in the narrow circle of her vision by the flowing beard and locks and wrinkled visage of Nokar Feldosonne. This seemed an equally bad omen, for it indicated that the horrors she began to recall were not phantasms brought on by too much booze, but real events.

"I liked the cockroach better," she croaked.

"Nice to know I'm appreciated. Healer Demphrey says you might live. He says you need rest."

"How is the war going?" She didn't really need to ask. She could hear the howling of the wind, the lash of torrential rains, the steady thunder of explosion as fireball after fireball battered the saje city.

"We're losing badly."

"Then Healer Demphrey can—well, no, he probably can't. It usually isn't anatomically possible. But he can keep his advice to himself." Medwind managed to pull herself up on one elbow. The world spun wildly, but she ignored it. "Look, Nokar, I have to go back. There is someone in Daane that I might reach. I think I know where to look."

Nokar brushed stray hairs off Medwind's forehead. "It's no good, Song. You've been under Demphrey's drugs and spellings for almost four hours. In that time, Burchardsonne has sent dozens of Mindspeakers into Daane. Most fell into Sahedre's clutches and died. The few who made it back report that there is no one under her shield who is not in her thrall. And in that time, she's done half a dozen *mehevarin*, and expanded the shield to encompass about a third of Mage-Ariss."

"What happens when the shield is attacked directly?"

"The damage bounces back directly onto the senders. Burchardsonne lost two units that way. He won't try a third."

Medwind lay back on the slab she occupied and stared up at the reed thatch poking between the wide-spaced ceiling beams. "I see."

"We've lost this one, Medwind." Nokar sighed. "And this one is for the whole of Arhel, I'm afraid. Sahedre is unstoppable."

"I see." Medwind closed her eyes. "I'm going to sleep a while, old man. Don't wake me up if the world ends. I'd rather not know."

She felt dry lips brush her cheek. "I'm glad you're going to rest."

When goats have kittens, Medwind thought. She gave a very good imitation of a woman drifting off to sleep. When she heard Nokar sigh again and walk away, she summoned what little energy she could and sent her mind searching back along the path she'd traveled earlier.

The spark of light was returning. There had been others, casting back and forth at a distance, but this one was coming straight to Faia. She could feel it as if it were the full blaze of the sun breaking through a pinhole in her prison.

She stretched out and greeted it.

:*Who are you?*: she whispered.

:*Medwind Song. And you—are* Faia! *Of course. She must have forgotten about you.*:

:*She did not need to forget about me. She has me trapped and helpless—I cannot harm her, and she cannot put me to work, so why should she waste any of her precious energy to control me? But you—what are you doing here?*:

Medwind sent the tiniest flutter of a laugh into Faia's mind. :*I came to see if you would try to rescue us.*:

:*Hah! I would be astounded if I could rescue me. Not much hope of that, I am afraid.*:

Medwind's next comment was long in coming, and thoughtful in tone. :*It would be the same thing. Let me tell you what I've found out about her, and you see if there's anything you can use.*:

Faia listened patiently, only interrupting once to remark—:*This fiend had a* daughter? *Easier to imagine a blood-spider suckling its young than her a mother.*:

:*Nevertheless, the death of her daughter Beliseth was the start of this whole disaster.*: Medwind's thoughtvoice wearied. :*I must go. I am too weak to stay any longer. Faia, there is nothing else that we can do from the outside. And you are the only one left on the inside. If our world is to survive, it will only be because of you.*:

Then she was gone, taking the light and hope of her presence with her.

Faia, in her blind cage, was vaguely aware of Sahedre surrounding her. If she concentrated, she could hear the other woman's now-unguarded thoughts. *Maybe Medwind Song was right. Maybe Sahedre has forgotten about me,* she thought. An idea occurred to her. She wondered if she could steal through Sahedre's memories for a look at the child, Beliseth, without alerting her mother.

Stealthily, she extended a thin fiber of thought into the other woman's mind. She kept away from Sahedre's noisy, angry awareness, and concentrated on the darkened backways of her past. Beliseth was not hard to find. All Sahedre's past thoughts were wrapped around her. Every waking moment was overlaid by pictures of a sweet-faced green-eyed child with soft blue-black curls that tumbled half-way down her back. In the clearest memories, she was about eight, growing early into beauty. Faia could sense her mother's enchantment and adoration of the child. Younger images of Beliseth were fuzzed slightly by time, but even as a young child, and before, as a toddler, there was never anything but love in the memories Sahedre held of her daughter. Faia rummaged carefully, and found Beliseth again as an infant, round and pink and dimpled, and even deeper, located Sahedre as she concentrated on the movement in her belly, the first delightful quickenings of life.

Faia backed out, and held her breath. An idea occurred to her, breathtaking in its simplicity—and in its cruelty. *Could I do that, even to Sahedre?* she wondered.

She stretched a little, peeked out through the eyes Sahedre controlled, saw what was left of the bodies of instructors and other women's small children in piles around the Greathall—all victims of Sahedre's *mehevar* and her pursuit of the destruction of Ariss.

I could be that cruel, she decided grimly. *This time, to this woman, I could be that cruel.*

She drew in passing surges of the power Sahedre had forgotten to guard, stored it, hid it, squirreled it away. She waited until Sahedre's energy began to lag, until the madwoman began to cast about for another sacrifice to increase her strength. Then, with feigned amazement, Faia screamed a sudden mindshout that tore across the Wisewoman's consciousness—:*I am pregnant?! I am PREGNANT! And she is a girl!*:

She dumped her carefully tended images of Beliseth as an infant and Sahedre's memories of pregnancy back at her.

Sahedre's concentration shattered. She paused everything and sent her awareness careening into Faia's belly, into her womb—and the shout came back, *I am pregnant! Oh, I am! Oh, Beliseth, I shall have you back! I shall!*

—And Faia's mind scrambled for her body, flowed back into the cells that were her soul's home. She *reached*—deep into the center of the earth, and up into the sky—and *pulled*. She drew the earth's pure energy inward and expanded, forcing the dark and sullied presence of Sahedre smaller and smaller and tighter and tighter, until the other woman had no place left to hide.

Sahedre snapped out of her distraction, and still full of *mehevar* and hatred, resisted. She pressed against the hill girl's spirit, attacked Faia's determination to destroy her, shot insinuations of weakness and unworthiness into Faia's heart.

But Faia's magic was not drawn from the malice of others, or from their deaths. Faia drew her strength from the near-infinite energy of earth and sky, and her confidence from the assurance, finally, that she was doing right.

Sahedre lost ground. She lost control of legs and arms, of eyes, of tongue—and her shield crumbled, and her mind-thralls broke free from their chains—

Ariss rang with the Wisewoman's furious mind-screech, as her soul was forced completely out of Faia's body—

—Into nonexistence.

There was silence.

And standing alone in her own body, in the sudden startling light after the tenebrous gloom of Sahedre's soul, Faia was beset by niggling worries.

What did she mean, "I am pregnant?"

Chapter 11

AFTER

In the dark, cold water of the lake, Yaji's flesh and bones suddenly burned in agony and her breathing became short and labored. She shrieked and chittered, and floundered to shore. Dragging herself up the muddy bank, she collapsed. Her black claws retracted and the fur on her short, twisted limbs thinned. The limbs themselves began to stretch.

Human, she thought. *I'm becoming human again.*

She watched the wonderful transformation through pain-blurred eyes.

When it was done, she lay drowsy and content for a few minutes. Then her situation made itself apparent to her.

She sat up. "I'm naked," she remarked in a conversational voice to the overhanging woods and the lapping waters of the lake. "I'm naked. I, Yaji Jennedote, have been lying in mud. I am on the far side of the lake, with nothing between me and the University but more mud and woods with thickets and brambles and snakes and gods-only-know-what else in them. And I can't swim!"

"The war is over, Medwind!" Nokar's voice in the room was jubilant.

Medwind Song, lying on the table, did not move.

"Medwind?" His voice dropped a whisper. "Medwind?"

He ran out of the room and grabbed the Healer. "She isn't breathing! Demphrey, godsdammit, she isn't *breathing!*"

Demphrey said softly, "The war is over, man. It's over."

"*Demphrey*," he shrieked, "*she isn't breathing!*"

The words penetrated the Healer's relief, and he snapped into action. They raced back into the room. "Force air into her lungs," Demphrey told Nokar. "Put your mouth on hers, hold her nose closed, and breathe for her."

He watched the old man while his own fingers felt urgently for a pulse. "Yes, that's right. Keep breathing for her." He probed along her neck and at her wrist a moment longer. "Nokar, I can't feel her pulse. I'm going to have to jolt her heart with a lightning sprite. When I tell you to back off, do it, or you and she are both going to end up dead."

Burly, ugly Demphrey rested his hands on Medwind's chest—left hand on the right side above her breast, right hand on her ribs under her left arm. "This trick is as old as any we have—sometimes, though," he confided to the librarian, "it works."

Nokar kept breathing into Medwind's lungs. With every breath, he thought, *Live, damn you. Live, Song. Not to marry me. Not because I love you. Just live.*

Demphrey readied his firesprite, which hovered above his left hand. "Into the left hand, through the heart, out of the right hand and wait above the bed," he told it. The sprite, blinding blue-white, flickered its comprehension.

"Ready," he said. "Get clear, Nokar! Now!"

The woman's body jolted on the bed, and the fire-sprite erupted into view again.

Demphrey felt for the pulse. "Keep breathing her, Nokar," he said. After a moment, he shook his head. "Still no pulse. I'm giving the sprite more energy. We'll try again."

He's hands made passes in the air, and the sprite glowed brighter. He then repeated the procedure he tried before. Medwind jolted again as the sprite passed through her, but again there was no pulse.

"I'll try a third time and make the sprite still a bit stronger. If she's too far gone for that, we'll have to quit."

On the third try, there was a faint puff of smoke, and the smell of burnt flesh. Nokar watched with weary eyes as the Healer felt despondently for the pulse.

Demphrey stood a moment, and his eyes widened in surprise. "Damn-all," he whispered. "It worked." Suddenly he was all blurring arms and legs. "Breathe her, breathe her, dammit, or we're going to lose her," he snapped at the old man. He grabbed a box full of dosing tubes and jammed the needle of one into the visibly pulsing artery in Medwind's neck.

"What—you doing?" Nokar asked between breaths.

"Giving her heart a solution of sweet-syrup for energy, and when this is in, some herbals that will strengthen the heartbeat. If you feel her start to breathe on her own, back off."

They worked, old man and young healer, for what seemed forever. When they were able to stand back and watch, Medwind Song lay on the table, breathing shallowly on her own, eyes closed in unconsciousness.

"Now what?" Nokar asked.

"Now we wait."

There was no time to think, no time to return for her things. She had her pack and her dagger and the bloodied and torn clothes on her back. Her *erda* and her hat, her other clothes, her rede-flute, her books— all were back in the dorm. She did not dare return for them. The angry voices of the frelles were coming closer—and they were screaming "Kill her, kill her!"

They meant Sahedre, but they would not believe that Sahedre was dead, that Faia was innocent. They wanted blood.

Faia wanted no more of killing—not in self-defense, not for any reason. Her soul felt sullied and darkened by Sahedre's actions, by her own stupidity—and the dead who lay in the Greathall, dead because of her ignorance, accused her with their white and staring eyes.

Guilty or innocent, she also had no wish to die.

She ran.

Out through the back of the Greathall, across the yard toward the thronging street beside the University, into the traffic, and across. She ran as far around the wingmount stables as she could. Behind her, voices shouted and pursued. She felt energy being drawn for an attack. She shielded and ran on.

She escaped the campus grounds, still running. People with dazed expressions stared at her as she shot past. One of her pursuers shouted that she was a murderer, and the numbers who pursued increased.

She darted down an alley, twisted into another, narrower alley, and darted down yet a third, that curled around itself and stopped in a blank-faced stone wall. Faia crouched down behind some merchant's empty crates.

Trapped! I wish I were invisible, she thought.

Memory asserted itself. Her nerve endings still remembered the way Sahedre had controlled magic. Her body recalled the steps between calling up energy and making it do what one wanted.

Faia spun a mist around herself—she willed herself to appear to be just another packing crate as the first of her hunters charged into her alley.

"She's in here. I know she is," bellowed one. "I swear I saw her run this way."

"Check the crates," a second woman yelled.

The first woman peered from crate to crate, working her way toward Faia.

A lanky, dirty, half-starved kitten stood up from a pile of refuse, stretched gloriously, ignored the people yelling in the alley, and with great deliberation strolled over to Faia, looked into her eyes, climbed up in her lap, curled up again, and promptly went back to sleep.

The first woman stared right at Faia as she called back to the other woman, "This big crate has a cat in it. Think she might have turned herself into a cat?"

"Not a chance," the other woman called back. "Unless the thing is hill-lion sized. Law of conservation of mass, remember?"

"Forgot. She isn't here, then."

"I didn't think so. Well, let's keep looking. She has to be somewhere."

Faia sat in the alley with the cat on her lap until dark. The merchant stepped out into the alley once, dumped fresh scraps and wasted food onto the top of the refuse pile, and hurried back inside.

Faia and the cat picked through the trash. The hill girl found a sizable quantity of spoiled meat and some rotted apples. She altered both into something she dared eat, then shared her repast with the kitten. When they were finished, she picked the little beast up and put it in her pack. It didn't protest, so she slung cat and pack over her shoulder and trudged into the night.

"I have to get back to Daane."

Those were the first words out of Medwind's mouth when she finally regained consciousness.

Nokar stared at her. "You must be joking. They're still rioting over there—and with you showing up now, they are likely to kill you."

The barbarian grinned at him through smeared and

streaked *esca*. She lay on the hard pallet, pale and weak—her once-glorious Hoos garb stained, muddied, and tattered, the feather crest in her hair bedraggled, every breath still a struggle—and she actually grinned. Nokar felt the hairs on the back of his neck prickle to attention.

"No," he said.

Her grin broadened. "You need a little adventure, old man."

"No," he said again.

"Think of it as part of your wedding test—your *kikassa mekku*."

"You want me to take you over there—"

"Just a quick hop. I have a few things I need to pick up. I need to get my shrine, my skulls, my Hoos things—it won't take long."

"There is nothing in this world that you cannot live without."

Her grin vanished, and for just a moment, Nokar saw the anguish behind her frail good humor. "There is the other thing, too. Rakell is dead. I owe her *vha'atta*."

"You are crazy. They won't understand—they'll kill us both if we get caught."

"Then we better not get caught. She was my best friend, old man. There are things that honor owes best friends and good warriors."

Nokar nodded. This was Hoos thinking, not Arissonese thinking—and there were plenty of times when he preferred the Hoos. "Very well. As part of my *kikassa mekku* then."

"If we don't go soon, it will be too late."

His bony hand rested on her shoulder, and the nighttime city of Ariss twisted and re-formed around them.

Nokar took those things that Medwind indicated from her quarters in the tower—the jewelry, the brightly painted human skulls in their oilskin containers,

the ceremonial garb, the weapons. When she was
sure she had the things she needed, he shifted everything into otherspace, and left it there. "We'll get it
all when we've finished," he told her. "It will wait at
least that long."

"The stables, then," she whispered.

He took her again through the twists of space and
time, and they materialized in the corridor, outside of
the room where the Mottemage was murdered.

Medwind went in first. "Wait," she told him, and
stumbled alone into the stable. The Mottemage's
mangled body had not been moved. It lay exactly as
Medwind had seen in her Timeride, Flynn next to her
in death as he had been in life. The dead Fendles
were gone—Medwind suspected that they had
returned to their human form when Sahedre's magic
died, and vanished into dust as had the others she had
seen.

Morning was coming, and soon, the University
would rouse from its exhausted sleep and drag forth
to count the cost of its bitter war. The mages would
dispose of the other bodies, and they would eventually
remember and come for Rakell's. Before then, Medwind had to be done and gone.

The barbarian crouched beside her friend's body
and took pouches of red and blue and gold powder
from the leather bag that always hung at her side.
She dipped the knife's goat-bristle-tipped handle into
one pouch, and traced the ancient patterns of *vha'atta*
across Rakell's flayed cheeks and forehead. Tears ran
down Medwind's face and salted the corners of her
mouth.

"Honored friend," she said in her own tongue, "not
Hoos, not Huong, but sister still, I grieve your passing.
Warrior, you who fought and died with grace and fairness, you have earned the flowered plains of Yarwalla,
but I beg you, do not yet take up your place—your
place among—the fighters and—the poets—"

Medwind stopped, unable to continue. "Gods,

Rakell—why did you have—to—die?" She wrapped her arms around herself and rocked back and forth, silent, tears streaming.

The ringing of first bell, from somewhere far off—not echoed by the bells at Daane—brought Medwind back to the task at hand. She gulped, and continued.

"—But I beg you, do not yet take your place among the fighters and the poets, for I still—need you—greatly." She finished, gently stroking the designs on the Mottemage's face.

The remaining flesh began to hiss and smoke and boil off under the powders. Medwind nodded. "Good," she whispered. "I got here in time."

Medwind sang the ancient ritual song—

> "I call you back from Yarwalla/
> I claim for you vha'atta/
> Because you are strong/
> And have gone on/
> But I am weak/
> And remain.

After the song, she sat a moment. "You would never let me explain to you, dear friend," she whispered. "You would not walk the Hoos Path, so I could not tell you more. I hope this is what you would have wanted."

She unfolded an oilskin bag exactly like the ones that housed her painted skulls, and waited.

When she walked out of the stable to greet Nokar, she carried another.

Faia stole scraps of food from windowsills and trash heaps, ate what little she could stomach, fed the rest to the scrawny kitten, slept in alleys in the daytime hidden behind middens or under boxes, moved at night. North she crept, always north. It took her three days to get out of the city, and then Faia only managed her escape by hiding in a trashwagon overnight, under a load of the city's ubiquitous refuse of fishheads and offal, and being drawn past the searching city guards, who apparently did not consider anyone desperate enough to hide out in that.

The kitten was in ecstasy over the mountains of dead fish—not a point in his favor, she thought. Faia spent a great deal of time fighting off nausea, and doubted that she would ever be able to eat fish again.

The trashman dumped his load into the oily, reeking waters of the bog and drove off without looking back.

The cat shrieked in rage at his sudden soaking.

Faia stoically stood and slogged her way to the road. She had no idea where she was going—only that she was.

Midday heat beat down on the dirt road. Faia, from her resting place under the shade of a massive and gnarled bitterroot, stared down the hill at a spume of dust that roiled up from the stretch of road she'd just traveled. She scratched the kitten behind the ears and murmured, "Let's see if we want company or not." She sent a carefully shielded exploratory tendril toward the dustcloud—and a slow smile spread across her face.

"Friends," she murmured. "How about that?"

Through the dust she began to make out a cart, drawn by two sorry, swaybacked horses.

When it got close enough, she stepped into the middle of the road and waved and yelled, "Medwind Song! Well met on this hot and dusty day."

Medwind Song, in informal Hoos dress, lay on a nest of cloth and pillows and blankets in the back of a cart packed high with provisions and possessions and crates of books that was driven by a saje as ancient as time's father. Her glorious warhorse, coated in road dust, trotted behind; her gear and her muddied and tattered war dress were draped across the great beast's back.

Faia looked down into her instructor's nest at her.

"I am happy to see—you look unwell, Frelle Medwind!" Faia noted. "What happened to you? And what happened to your hair?"

Medwind Song gave her one-time student a tired smile. "It's a long tale. Maybe I'll tell it to you someday. But for now, my husband, Nokar Feldosonne, and I are heading north," Medwind told Faia.

The hill girl was bewildered. "You are to be the next Mottemage. You cannot leave Ariss."

Medwind sighed. "Trust me, I can and I am, and everyone in Mage-Ariss is breathing a sigh of relief. I was given the choice of staying and being tried for treason—for going into Sage-Ariss during a time of war and consorting with the enemy—or leaving Ariss for good. If they had any idea what else I had done, they would have executed me on the spot. Leaving that cloistered, noisy, fish-stinking hell was not the hardest decision I ever made."

Faia laughed dryly. "Nor I."

"No, I imagine not. When I publicly returned to the university, Yaji and I explained to the Magerie what had happened to you—and to all of us—and no one is actively trying to find you to kill you anymore. Still, I don't think you ought to plan any little visits to Daane in this lifetime."

"My heart breaks," Faia told the mage. "How is Yaji?"

"Much nicer," Medwind noted. "Time spent as a Fendle seems to have done her a world of good. I'd almost recommend the treatment for a number of other students I can think of."

"I am sure she is glad to be done with me."

Medwind gave Faia an inscrutable look, then shook her head. "Actually, you were the second friend she ever had. But she got her first friend, her brother, back."

Faia was startled.

Medwind noted her widened eyes and her quick intake of breath. "Things in Ariss are changing because of the war. The mages and sajes have realized, at last, how much their feud cost everyone. And even though they will try to pin the blame on Sahedre and you, they can see that their own ignorance of each other was at the heart of the matter this time. Mage-Ariss and Saje-Ariss aren't one, yet—but even as we left, the first of the walls were coming down."

The hill girl whistled in amazement.

"So—where are you headed?" Nokar asked.

"I know not. I cannot return to Willowlake—though I would love to see Aldar again someday. I dare not try to find Kirgen—I do not even know if he still lives. There is no more Bright. I thought to head north, where it is warmer, so that I will not have such a hard winter while I am great with child."

"Then you really are pregnant?" Medwind asked. "I thought that scream of yours a clever trick you came up with to fool Sahedre."

"You heard?"

"I heard, all right—it nearly became the last thing I ever heard—"

"—And lucky for you it wasn't," Nokar interrupted, "because if I'd had to search through the Hundred Hells to find you—"

"I thought the sajes had seven hells," Faia whispered.

"The sajes can't make up their minds," Medwind answered.

"—I might have been tempted to leave you there," Nokar concluded. "And there *are* a hundred hells. Those idiots who claim another number ignore the perfect symbology of the number one hundred, which—"

"—Isn't where you would have found me, anyway, idiot. I would have been in the eternally green foothills of Yarwalla, with goats and husbands and children, wearing the necklaces of a thousand victories and reading the lays of Yarwalla's greatest eternal poets."

"Not so! You would have been circling around the

Wheel, resting before you chose another life," Faia said.

Medwind snorted and changed the subject. "You were saying you're pregnant."

"Oh. I thought the tale a ruse as well. I did not discover until after I escaped the city that the tale was truth—then only when no food in the world would stay with me."

"An experience I've never had," Medwind said.

Nokar laughed. "But we're doing our best."

Faia looked at the mage, then at the old saje, then at the mage. "Would you like some alsinthe?" she asked. "I found some growing along the road once it was too late to do me any good."

Medwind chuckled. "I'll take my chances. It can't be that bad." At Faia's scowl, she laughed and hurried on. "Come with us. We'd be grateful for the company, and a fellow mage could be quite helpful. We thought to set up shop near the Omwimmee Trade Border."

The old man chuckled. "Medwind thinks she'd like a life as a stay-at-home magic merchant."

Faia gave them both a calculating look, then grinned.

"I'll come. If I can bring my cat."

"Then get the cat and come on."

They were well down the road when the kitten uncurled itself from its perch on a bale of cailtecloth, and began to stalk the *sslis* in Medwind's nose.

Medwind noted something odd about Faia's kitten. "Where did you get this beast?" she asked, her voice abruptly sharp.

Faia was startled. "The kitten? He found me hiding in an alley, and came along for the company. I imagine he is one of the offspring the Mottemage's cat left behind him."

"He has hands."

"Oh, yes. He uses them quite well, too."

Medwind was silent for a long, disbelieving minute. "By damn, she did it after all, and she never found out," she whispered. "She made a trait that would carry itself on. Not with something useful, like wing-mounts. Not with everbearing redfruits. Not even with self-feeding philos plants. But with *Flynn*! Medwind's voice got louder, and merrier. "Ye gods and spawn of madness, she's gifted the world with a plague of handed cats."

"I think she would be pleased," Faia said, smiling.

"Think? I'd bet anything—and that will be the first thing I tell her." Medwind laughed—her first real bellylaugh in days. "Give the joke that keeps on giving—that always was her philosophy. And Flynn being the randy tomcat that he was, the city must be full of them. I'm happier than ever to be well out of the City of Fogs and Bogs."

GLOSSARY OF ODD OR FOREIGN TERMS

Animals

Blue hovie—(Arissonese) One species of a multitude of small, jewel-colored sauroids which have four wings and two legs. They are rumored to be survivors of "the time before Folk." Blue hovies are inhabitants of the southern reaches of Arhel and, like the other suspected "survivals," are plainly entirely unrelated to the rest of Arhel's fauna.

Dew-fly—(Arissonese) Radially symmetrical insectoid with a top-mounted whirling flight-propeller. Thought to be native to Arhel.

Kellink—(Wen Tribes) Lion-sized six-legged sauroid native to the northern jungles. A vicious pack-hunter whose saliva is poisonous to humans and other mammals.

Morka egg—(Kareen) Highlander tradition relates the existence of large, flightless sauroids long ago that were delicious to eat and that laid piles of eggs large as a man's head. If such creatures ever existed, no sign of them remains.

Naenrid—(Arissonese) Magical constructs that take the form of winged monkeys or winged foxes with human hands. They are used as assistants or "fetches" by sajes (and rarely by mages) and tend to be mischievous and difficult to control.

People

Bellmaster—(Saje term) Man responsible for the care and sounding of the magical bells housed in the Saje-Ariss belltower.

Darklingsprites—(Arissonese) Tiny, ethereal humanoid constructs of unethical mages and sajes. Their creation requires the use of pain, and the resulting creatures have evil dispositions and a tendency to mayhem. They can be useful to their creators, however, so there are always a few in existence.

Delmuirie, Edrouss—Credited as the creator of the Delmuirie Barrier, he is in some circles reviled, in some worshipped, and in some said never to have existed at all. It is guessed that if he lived at all, it was at least eight hundred and perhaps a thousand years before the incidents chronicled here.

Faljon—(Kareen) Ancient Kareen (hill-folk) philosopher, perhaps apocryphal.

Flatter-men, Flatters—(Kareen) Hill-folk terminology for any people who do not inhabit the Booar Mountains.

Hoos—Any of three separate and distinct tribes and their countless clans who occupy the Hoos Domains in the southeast corner of Arhel. The three tribes are the Chak Hoos, who are essentially agrarian; the Huong Hoos, who are nomadic herdsmen; and the Stone Teeth Hoos, who are hunters. Love of war is the only common ground between the three tribes.

Makcjeks—(Hoos pejorative) The Arissonese, and by extension, any city-dwellers. Literally "stone-maggots." An even less complimentary term used for outlanders in general and often as a synonym is *shesrud*, the literal meaning of which is "dung-worm."

Things

B'dabba—(Huong Hoos) Large goat-felt tent, dyed in complex, gaudy colors and patterns that reflect the status of the occupants. The permanent, portable home of the Huong Hoos.

Cat-patterning—(Huong Hoos) Face-paint pattern of the Song Clan. Black or gray *esca* mirrors the facial markings of a tabby cat. Ceremonial.

Delmuirie's Barrier—Magical shield that surrounds and protects the continent of Arhel and a small area of adjoining sea; impenetrable from either direction. Arhelers have tales of other people and places outside of Arhel, but these are considered fantasies.

Erda—(Kareen) Large square highlander overgarment of waxed felt or oilskin with one hole in the center for the head and an oversized flap that doubles as a hood. The *erda* can also be used as a tarp with the corners tied or staked; as a blanket; and as a carrysack. It is an extraordinarily ugly garment. No highlander willingly goes anywhere without one.

Helke—(Kareen) Frequently pejorative. Literally, an ancient and barren animal, usually a cow.

Keurn-cloths—(Kareen) Fertility cloths woven of fine wool with added items considered to have high sympathetic magic for pregnancy. Worn under skirts or pants by women wanting children. Perryfowl feathers are considered a good base for keurn-cloths because perryfowl lay dozens of eggs in a single clutch and clutch four or five times each warm season.

Kordaus—(Kareen) Cord strung with thirty-three beads, each of a different material. Each bead has a meaning. The kordaus is used for "scrying," that is, telling the future. The reader closes the eyes and runs the cord through the fingers three times, each time stopping when a bead catches on the fingers. The combined meanings of the three beads are the prediction. Reliability of the kordaus depends on the reader.

Sslis—(Huong Hoos) Nose ornament worn to denote sexual preference. The Huong have thirteen main ornaments that can be displayed in any combination. Because sex is a religious rite of the Huong Hoos and all forms are encouraged equally, the *sslis* does not segregate, but merely helps in identifying like-minded partners.

Staarne—(Huong Hoos) Elegant, flowing tunic designed for comfort and to hide the exact position of the vital organs while fighting. Covers the body to mid-thigh. Tunic and long sleeves are loose and billowy, wrapped at wrist and waist for convenience. Brightly patterned in ancestral clan designs. Exact cut also varies by clan.

Three-and-One—(Arissonese) Strategy board game played by two, three, or four players, using a large round board and one hundred and eleven small flat stones, each of two contrasting colors per player. The object of the game is to form the largest connected series of three stones of one color surrounding one stone of its complementary color. Game is the subject of tournaments, wide-scale betting, and occasional fistfights.

Tide Mother—The multicolored gas-giant around which the moon Trilling revolves. Arhel is a continent on Trilling.

Ideas

Antis—(Arissonese) The first meal of the day.

Bondmate—(Kareen) Publicly pledged sexual partner. There is no standard duration for the length of the bond union—the primary purpose of public bonding in the tiny villages of the highlands is to keep track of the genealogies of children, to prevent accidental inbreeding.

"Buy kellinks from Ranmeers"—(Arissonese) Pejorative. Ranmeers are a disreputable tribe from the far northern reaches above the Wen Tribes Treaty Line who have, from time to time, tried to sell immature kellinks to the unwary as work-beasts. Only the incredibly ignorant or stupid would buy one, however. (See, also—*ANIMALS, Kellink*)

D'leffik—(Huong Hoos) Pejorative adjective. Means "goat-molesting." The noun is *d'leffja*.

Getlingself—(Arissonese) The magical self, the self in touch with the unknown and unseen. The getling-self usually awakens at puberty. The same phenomenon is known to the Kareen as getting one's *Lady's Gifts*. (See also—GODS, *Lady*).

Kikassa mekku—(Hoos) A series of challenges which a Hoos warrior must undertake to win each husband or wife who is not a war-trophy. Tasks are set by the prospective spouse and are usually dangerous—it is considered dishonorable to give a Hoos warrior easy *kikassa mekku*.

Mehevar—(Arissonese) Ritual torture and murder by unethical magicians for the purpose of stripping the victim of the *getlingself* and transferring that magical potential to the murderer.

Midden—(Arissonese) Meal in the middle of the day.

My'etje—(Huong Hoos) Slang. Literal meaning is "baby goat." A term of endearment.

Stranger-names—(Huong Hoos). Public-use names of children who have not yet reached adulthood and been accepted as full members of the Hoos society. Stranger-names, unlike soul-names, have no magical significance, and cannot be used against the children by the ill-meaning. Stranger-names are dropped at adulthood—it is considered cowardly for a warrior to maintain a powerless name for camouflage or protection.

Vha'atta—(Huong Hoos) Secret ritual that involves the decapitation of enemy warriors of great renown and ancestors, for the purpose of magical preservation; and the keeping of painted skulls around the house. This ritual has given the Huong Hoos their reputation as headhunters, which they cherish.

Foods

"baby-not"—(Arissonese) Black-market herb. See—
Alsinthe.

Alsinthe—(Kareen) Sweet-tasting herb mixed with
foods or drunk as a tea that prevents conception. No
apparent side effects except the occasional allergy.

Akka-bread—(Kareen) Nearly impermeable highlander
bread that becomes edible when soaked in tea or
water. Almost copper in color, strong-tasting. Travels
well.

Erd glabon—(Arissonese) Costly gourmet dish popular in Ariss high society. Winchell's Silver hovie, or
the rarer and slightly larger Droman's hovie, mari-
nated in premium Zheltariss, browned on a spit, and
served in a golden sauce on a bed of wild herbs and
grains.

Fennar—(Southern Arhel) An appallingly foul-tasting,
thick green mildly alcoholic beverage served hot. Has
medicinal value as vasoconstrictor and antihypotensive.
Useful in treatment of shock. Made of fermented
fennarell, an herb.

Gath cheese—(Kareen) Ripe, odoriferous orangy-
yellow cheese popular in the highlands.

Handpies—(Kareen) Circles of golden-brown whole-
grain crust filled with various fruits.

Raisin-and-grain sweetballs—(Kareen) Highlander
travel-fare made of fruits and nuts held together by
bitter black molasses. Strong-tasting, not popular outside of the Booar Mountains.

Tare-ale—(Arhelan) A rich, bitter brown-to-black ale with a heavy head brewed from the native grain *tare'-hrodar*. First origins of the ale are uncertain, but attributed to the First Folk.

Zheltariss—(Arissonese) Thick, deep burgundy liqueur with a sweet, fruity taste. Popular when mixed in equal parts with heavy cream.

Gods

There are thousands of gods in Arhel. However, a few generalizations may be made.

The **Kareen**, for the most part, give thanks to the **Lady** and the **Lord**, two nebulously defined and all-encompassing deities who embody the earth and air, day and night, and male and female parts to every facet of life.

The **Hoos** have elaborate pantheons of sexually voracious, warlike gods of all thirteen Hoos sexual orientations. These gods tend to be viewed as capricious and dangerous, and prone to weird humor. The Hoos try to emulate their gods in all the important ways—when they aren't ignoring them entirely.

The **Arissonese** are not a unified people, but are made of up city natives and travelers from everywhere else. Thus Ariss has a cosmopolitan view of religion, where it doesn't interfere with taxes. For example, birth control is illegal in Ariss because there is a child-tax, and a high birthrate provides a solid tax base. So religions that stress birth control or abstinence are frowned on (except in the case of the Magerie and Sajerie, which are such ancient institutions that the rules of the city are formed around them, leaving them untouched.) One further generalization—Arissonese gods usually like to get money gifts.

And a final note. The **seven ugly gods** who rule the lowest and most horrible hell ascribed by any saje in Saje-Ariss are Makog, Dramfing, Shelfud, Grum, Torling, Keknok, and Wilmer. Just thought you'd like to know.

There Are Elves Out There

An excerpt from

Mercedes Lackey
Larry Dixon

The main bay was eerily quiet. There were no screams of grinders, no buzz of technical talk or rapping of wrenches. There was no whine of test engines on dynos coming through the walls. Instead, there was a dull-bladed tension amid all the machinery, generated by the humans and the Sidhe gathered there.

Tannim laid the envelope on the rear deck of the only fully-operated GTP car that Fairgrove had built to date, the one that Donal had spent his waking hours building, and Conal had spent track-testing. He'd designed it for beauty and power in equal measure, and had given its key to Conal, its elected driver, in the same brother's-gift ceremony used to present an elvensteed. Conal now sat on its sculpted door, and absently traced a slender finger along an air intake, glowering at the envelope.

Tannim finished his magical tests, and asked for a knife. An even dozen were offered, but Dottie's Leatherman was accepted. Keighvin stood a little apart from the group, hand on his short knife. His eyes glittered with suppressed anger, and he appeared less human than usual, Tannim noticed. Something was bound to break soon.

Tannim folded out the knifeblade, slit the envelope open, and then unfolded the Leatherman's pliers. With them he withdrew six Polaroids of Tania and two others, unconscious, each bound at the wrists and neck. Their silver chains were held by some-*things* from the Realm of the Unseleighe—inside a limo. And, out of focus through the limo's windows, was a stretch of flat tarmac, and large buildings—

Tannim dropped the Leatherman, his fingers gone numb. It clattered twice before wedging into the cockpit's fresh-air vent. Keighvin took one startled step forward, then halted as the magical alarms at Fairgrove's perimeter flared around them all. Tannim's hand went into a jacket pocket, and he threw down the letter from the P.I. He saw Conal pick up the photographs, blanch, then snatch the letter up.

Tannim had already turned by then, and was sprinting for the office door, and the parking lot beyond.

Behind him, he could hear startled questions directed at him, but all he could answer before disappearing into the offices was "Airport!" His bad leg was slowing him down, and screamed at him like a sharp rock grinding into his bones. There was some kind of attack beginning, but he had no time for that.

Have to get to the airport, have to save Tania

from Vidal Dhu, the bastard, the son of a bitch, the—

Tannim rounded a corner and banged his left knee into a file cabinet. He went down hard, hands instinctively clutching at his over-damaged leg. His eyes swam with a private galaxy of red stars, and he struggled while his eyes refocused.

Son of a bitch son of a bitch son of a bitch. . . .

Behind him he heard the sounds of a war-party, and above it all, the banshee wail of a high-performance engine. He pulled himself up, holding the bleeding knee, and limp-ran towards the parking lot, to the Mustang, and Thunder Road.

Vidal Dhu stood in full armor before the gates of Fairgrove, laughing, lashing out with levin-bolts to set off its alarms. It was easy for Vidal to imagine what must be going on inside—easy to picture that smug, orphaned witling Keighvin Silverhair barking orders to weak mortals, marshaling them to fight. Let him rally them, Vidal thought—it will do him no good. None at all. He may have won before, but ultimately, the mortals will have damned him.

It has been so many centuries, Silverhair. I swore I'd kill your entire lineage, and I shall. I shall!

Vidal prepared to open the gate to Underhill. Through that gate all the Court would watch as Keighvin was destroyed—Aurilia's plan be hanged! Vidal's blood sang with triumph—he had driven Silverhair into a winless position at last! And when he accepted the Challenge, before the whole Court, none of his human-world tricks would benefit him—theirs would be a purely magical combat, one Sidhe to another.

To the death.

* * *

Keighvin Silverhair recognized the scent of the magic at Fairgrove's gates—he had smelled it for centuries. It reeked of obsession and fear, hatred and lust. It was born of pain inflicted without consideration of repercussions. It was the magic of one who had stalked innocents and stolen their last breaths.

He recognized, too, the rhythm that was being beaten against the walls of Fairgrove.

So be it, murderer. I will suffer your stench no more.

"They will expect us to dither and delay; the sooner we act, the more likely it is that we will catch them unprepared. They do not know how well we work together."

Around him, the humans and Sidhe of his home sprang into action, taking up arms with such speed he'd have thought them possessed. Conal had thrown down the letter after reading it, and barked, "Hangar 2A at Savannah Regional; they've got children as hostages!" The doors of the bay began rolling open, and outside, elvensteeds stamped and reared, eyes glowing, anxious for battle. Conal looked to him, then, for orders.

Keighvin met his eyes for one long moment, and said, "Go, Conal. I shall deal with our attacker for the last time. If naught else, the barrier at the gates can act as a trap to hold him until we can deal with him as he deserves." He did not add what he was thinking—that he only hoped it would hold Vidal. The Unseleighe was a strong mage; he might escape even a trap laid with death metal, if he were clever enough. Then, with the swiftness of a falcon, he was astride his elvensteed Rosaleen Dhu, headed for the perimeter of Fairgrove.

He was out there, all right, and had begun laying a spell outside the fences, like a snare. Perhaps in his sickening arrogance he'd forgotten that Keighvin could see such things. Perhaps in his insanity, he no longer cared.

Rosaleen tore across the grounds as fast as a stroke of lightning, and cleared the fence in a soaring leap. She landed a few yards from the laughing, mad Vidal Dhu, on the roadside, with him between Keighvin and the gates. He stopped lashing his mocking bolts at the gates of Fairgrove and turned to face Keighvin.

"So, you've come to face me alone, at last? No walls or mortals to hide behind, as usual, coward? So sad that you've chosen *now* to change, within minutes of your death, traitor."

"Vidal Dhu," Keighvin said, trying to sound unimpressed despite the heat of his blood, "if you wish to duel me, I shall accept. But before I accept, you must release the children you hold."

The Unseleighe laughed bitterly. "It's your concern for these mortals that raised you that have *made* you a traitor, boy. Those children do not matter." Vidal lifted his lip in a sneer as Keighvin struggled to maintain his composure. "Oh, I will do more than duel you, Silverhair. I wish to Challenge you before the Court, and kill you as they watch."

That was what Keighvin had noted—it was the initial layout of a Gate to the High Court Underhill. Vidal was serious about this Challenge—already the Court would be assembling to judge the battle. Keighvin sat atop Rosaleen, who snorted and stamped, enraged by the other's tauntings. Vidal's pitted face twisted in a maniacal smirk.

"How long must I wait for you to show courage, witling?"

Keighvin's mind swam for a moment, before he remembered the full protocols of a formal Challenge. It had been so long since he'd even seen one. . . .

Once accepted, the Gate activates, and all the Court watches as the two battle with blade and magic. Only one leaves the field; the Court is bound to slay anyone who runs. So it had always been. Vidal would not Challenge unless he were confident of winning, and Keighvin was still tired from the last battle—which Vidal had not even been at. . . .

But Vidal must die. That much Keighvin knew.

From Born to Run *by Mercedes Lackey & Larry Dixon.*

✳   ✳   ✳

Watch for more from the SERRAted Edge:

Wheels of Fire by Mercedes Lackey & Mark Shepherd (October 1992)

When the Bough Breaks by Mercedes Lackey & Holly Lisle (February 1993)

MAGIC AND COMPUTERS DON'T MIX!

RICK COOK

Or ... do they? That's what Walter "Wiz" Zumwalt is wondering. Just a short time ago, he was a master hacker in a Silicon Valley office, a very ordinary fellow in a very mundane world. But magic spells, it seems, are a lot like computer programs: they're both formulas, recipes for getting things done. Unfortunately, just like those computer programs, they can be full of bugs. Now, thanks to a *particularly* buggy spell, Wiz has been transported to a world of magic—and incredible peril. The wizard who summoned him is dead, Wiz has fallen for a red-headed witch who despises him, and no one—not the elves, not the dwarves, not even the dragons—can figure out why he's here, or what to do with him. Worse: the sorcerers of the deadly Black League, rulers of an entire continent, want Wiz dead—and he doesn't even know why! Wiz had better figure out the rules of this strange new world—and fast—or he's not going to live to see Silicon Valley again.

Here's a refreshing tale from an exciting new writer. It's also a rarity: a well-drawn fantasy told with all the rigorous logic of hard science fiction.

69803-6 • 320 pages • $4.99

Available at bookstores everywhere, or you can send the cover price to Baen Books, Dept. BA, P.O. Box 1403, Riverdale, NY 10471.